MIS CON DUCT

Penelope Douglas

piatkus

PIATKUS

First published in the US in 2015 by New American Library
A division of Penguin Random House LLC.
First published in Great Britain in 2015 by Piatkus

1 3 5 7 9 10 8 6 4 2

All characters and events in this publication, other than those clearly in the public domain, are fictitious and any resemblance to real persons, living or dead, is purely coincidental.

A CIP catalogue record for this book
is available from the British Library.

ISBN 978-0-349-41021-0

Printed and bound by CPI Group (UK) Ltd, Croydon, CR0 4YY

Papers used by Piatkus are from well-managed forests
and other responsible sources.

MIX
Paper from
responsible sources
FSC® C104740

Piatkus
An imprint of
Little, Brown Book Group
Carmelite House
50 Victoria Embankment
London EC4Y 0DZ

An Hachette UK Company
www.hachette.co.uk

www.piatkus.co.uk

For our teachers . . .

PLAYLIST

"Home" by Three Days Grace

"Dangerous" by Shaman's Harvest

"Always" by Saliva

"Hazy Shade of Winter" by the Bangles

"Because I Got High" by Afroman

"Only Girl" by Rihanna

"You Know You Like It" by DJ Snake & AlunaGeorge

"Room to Breathe" by You Me at Six

"Untraveled Road" by Thousand Foot Krutch

"Drown" by Theory of a Deadman

"When the Saints Go Marching In" by Louis Armstrong

"To the Hills" by Laurel

"Failure" by Breaking Benjamin

"Paralyzed" by In Flames

"Glycerine" by Bush

"No Woman, No Cry" by Bob Marley and the Wailers

Dear Reader,

All of my books come with Pinterest boards to enhance your reading experience. Please enjoy Misconduct's *board at www.pinterest.com/penelopedouglas/misconduct-2015/ as you read.*

You will also find discussion questions at the end of this book.

Love is a game that two can play and both win.

—Eva Gabor

ONE

EASTON

While most Mardi Gras balls were lively, with performers from their parades that day in attendance to entertain the guests, this particular party overflowed with a very different vibe.

I looked around me at the rich and powerful who made up the guest list, sizing everyone up, their connections and names more of a résumé than their educations or careers.

And while everyone around me appeared relaxed—due to the heavy flow of champagne, I was sure—it was just a mask on top of their masks.

They weren't calm. They were working. Deals were being made and relationships bought, and the politicians were always on the job.

But still . . . there was a charge in the air. It was Mardi Gras in New Orleans, after all.

It was the time of year when many locals escaped the city, with the tsunami of tourists clogging the streets and the traffic turning what was normally a fifteen-minute drive into three hours as constant parades blocked your route.

The city and its surrounding areas hosted between forty and fifty parades every Mardi Gras season, and each parade had a krewe—a not-for-profit organization that donated money to build the floats, some costing as much as eighty thousand dollars, while the krewe members enjoyed the privilege of donning masks as they tossed beads and other trinkets into a bedlam of outstretched hands and screaming crowds.

This particular krewe was exclusive, almost aristocratic with its money and political connections. Lawyers, CEOs, judges, you name it . . . Anyone who was anyone in this city was here tonight. Hence why my brother accepted an invitation.

Jack knew that New Orleans society was like a candy-covered chocolate. You had to break through the shell to get to the good stuff.

Deals and relationships weren't made at conference tables or offices. They were settled over glasses of Chivas at a cigar bar or around ten pounds of crawfish at a filthy seafood dive in the Quarter with calliope music from the *Natchez* steamboat drifting in through the open French doors. People didn't trust signatures so much as they trusted your ability to bullshit while you were drunk.

All reasons I loved this city.

It held the history of weathered storms—of blood, sweat, music, agony, and death by people who expected to fall but knew how to get back up.

I offered the waiter a modest smile as I plucked another glass of champagne off his tray and turned back around, regarding the imitation Degas hanging before me.

Oil on canvas would burn quickly. Very quickly, I mused, inching closer as the chill from the champagne flute seeped through my manicured fingers.

God, I was bored. When I started fantasizing about inanimate objects going up in flames, it was time to call it a night.

But then I felt my phone vibrate against my thigh, and I straightened, pulling away from the painting again.

"Jack," I whispered under my breath as I set down my glass on a high, round table and clawed my dress up my leg to get at my phone strapped around my thigh. I hated carrying purses, and since my brother was here with me and had the credit cards, all I needed was a place to secure my cell.

Swiping the screen, I clicked on the text notification.

If you say anything rude, my future is ruined.

I shot my head up, a smile spreading across my face as I scanned the ballroom. I spotted my brother standing in a circle of people but facing me with a warning eyebrow raised and a smirk on his face.

Moi? I texted back, looking at him like I was affronted.

He read the text and shook his head, grinning. I know your vibes, Easton.

I rolled my eyes at him, amusement tilting my lips up into a smile.

Jack most certainly did know my vibes.

But he should've known better. I would never let my brother down. I might have inherited our father's quick temper and our mother's inability not to say things that shouldn't be said, but I was loyal. When my brother called, I came. When he needed me, I didn't ask questions. For him, I would tolerate just about anything.

I shall endure, I replied, my usual sarcasm evident as I met his mischievous hazel eyes.

Jack was three years older and about to finish his third year of law school at Tulane. Time and again, he dragged me to benefits, luncheons, and galas as he schmoozed his way through the New Orleans elite, making his connections and building relationships. All so he could secure the right job offers when he graduated a little more than a year from now.

I hated wasting time on things that didn't interest me, but Jack didn't have a girlfriend to bore with these functions, so I often stepped in as the dutiful "plus one."

Find something to play with, he teased. And don't get dirty.

I cocked an eyebrow across the room at him, hoping he saw the dare in my expression. Even through my black metal half mask.

If you say so . . . I taunted with my eyes.

I'd hung in there with Jack as he had made the rounds when we arrived, conversing and networking, until they started talking mistrials and mitigating circumstances. That was when I made my escape, choosing to wander and ponder in silence rather than be forced to smile and nod as if I had any interest in what they were talking about.

But now, glancing around the crowd and trying to take Jack's suggestion to find something—or someone—to occupy my time, I had to admit I wouldn't even know where to start.

My brother could work the room like a fine instrument—laughing and shaking hands just like a good ole boy—but I muddled around the edges.

In but not quite *in*.

There was a time when those roles were reversed.

And there was a time when I cared.

Leaning down, I inched up the sheer red layers of my gown to tuck my phone away in a concealed carry strap secured around my leg. Not that I was concealing a weapon, but it served a purpose nonetheless.

I let the hems of my gown fall back down to my feet, loving the weightlessness of the fabric as it brushed across my legs. Since it was February, it was still fairly cold outside, but I had been unable to resist the indulgence of the flowing, lightweight fluidity of the fabric though it was probably meant for spring.

For a girl who'd spent most of her upbringing in sneakers and tennis skirts, the gown earned me looks from men meant for the woman I sometimes had trouble believing I'd become.

Falling to the tops of my feet, the gown hugged my torso in a crisscross pattern on the front and back, but flared out only slightly below the waist in an A-line fit. It was bright red, and looked perfect with my black metal half mask, which curved over the top of my left eye, down the right side of my nose, and covered half of my right cheek in a lace pattern.

My only other accessory was a pair of diamond stud earrings given to me by my parents when I'd won the US Open junior tournament ten years ago.

Bending over, I slipped my heel off, the only part of the outfit I hated.

I arched my foot and then pointed my toes, rolling my ankle. Everything ached from the pressure of being packed together, and I didn't understand how other women lived in these every day.

Balancing myself on one leg, I grabbed my champagne glass and slid the other foot back into the shoe, but it stumbled out of my hand and fell to the ground.

Sighing, I leaned down to snatch up the heel.

But I stopped midbend, jerking back when someone grabbed my wrist and snatched the glass out of my hand.

"Careful," a low, deep voice warned.

I blinked, my eyes shooting between the hand on my wrist and the floor, where I had spilled half of my drink when I'd bent over.

I moved to straighten, but then I paused, seeing a man set the glass down and immediately kneel in front of me on one knee, avoiding the spot on the carpeting where my drink had spilled.

"Allow me," he suggested.

Ignoring the flutter in my chest, I watched as he took my ankle and slid my foot effortlessly back into my heel, his sure hands setting me right again.

The heat of his fingers spread up my leg, and I narrowed my eyes, a little annoyed that my heart was beating so fast.

He wasn't wearing a mask like most of the other guests. According to my father's general wisdom, it probably meant that he didn't play games or feel the need to be a part of the crowd. He wanted everyone to know who he was. Fearless, bold, a rule breaker . . .

But my inner cynic would say he'd probably just forgotten his mask at home.

He glanced up at me, a pert tilt to his lips and his hooded eyes taking me in with interest. I knew right away that he was older.

Significantly.

Probably midthirties, judging by the faint lines around his eyes.

And although that wasn't old, it was almost outside of my generation at twenty-three.

I liked that, too. If his hands were sure, maybe his tongue would be, too. Conversation-wise, I meant.

His black hair was cut close to the scalp on the sides and in the back, with the longer hair on top styled neatly. He was clean-shaven, and his tailored wool tux was a black deep enough to make everyone else's here look faded. His shoes outshined his Rolex, and thank goodness for that. Men with bling were high maintenance.

And he was handsome. The narrow jaw and high cheekbones accentuated his sharp black eyebrows over stone blue eyes.

He was more than handsome. He was seductive.

I felt a small smile tug at the corners of my lips.

"Thank you," I said softly, moving my foot back to the floor.

His fingers grazed an inch higher on my calf before letting me go, and I had to fight the chills that spread over my skin.

He was bold, too.

I held his eyes—the color of a cloud heavy with unfallen rain—as he rose, standing tall and not making any move to back off.

"Losing shoes, spilling drinks . . . Are you normally such a hot mess?" he teased, the confident mischief in his eyes turning everything below my waist warm.

I raised my eyebrows, shooting him a cocky smirk. "Feeling up strange women, condescending remarks . . . Are you normally so rude?" I asked.

His eyes held a smile, but I didn't wait for him to answer.

I plucked my champagne flute off the table and glided around him, back to the painting.

If he was the kind of man I'd hoped he was, he'd follow. He was attractive, and I was intrigued, but that didn't mean he didn't have to work for it.

I tilted the glass to my mouth, taking in the chilled bitterness of the bubbles on my tongue as I felt him watching me.

"You don't appear to be having a very good time," he observed, stepping up to my side.

His subtle cologne drifted through my nostrils, and my eyelids fluttered for a moment.

"On the contrary . . ." I gestured to the imitation Degas with my champagne. "I was just contemplating how some gasoline and a match would improve this painting."

He laughed under his breath, and I loved how his eyes shimmered in the dim light of the ballroom. "That bad, huh?"

I nodded, sighing. "That bad."

Standing next to him, I felt the full measure of his size. I was no shorty at five seven, but even in heels, I still came only to his shoulder. His chest was wide but lean, and I loved that I could make out the muscles in his upper arms when he crossed them over it. Even through his tux.

He looked down at me with the stern expression of a superior. "Do you often have pyrotechnic fantasies?" he asked, looking amused.

I turned back to the painting, absently staring at it as I thought about his question.

Pyrotechnic fantasies? No.

I had lots of fantasies, pyrotechnic and not, but how obvious would I be to tell him that? It was a cheap response to a leading question. I wouldn't be so obvious.

"I don't want to start fires," I assured him, staring at the Degas with the flute against my lips. "I just like standing in the middle of burning rooms."

Tipping back the glass, I finished off the champagne and turned to set it down, but he took the base of the flute, stopping me.

"How long would you stay?" he inquired, his eyes thoughtful as he took the glass from my hand and set it down on the table. "Before you tried to escape, that is."

"Longer than anyone else."

He looked at me quizzically.

"How about you?" I questioned. "Would you join the mayhem in the mad rush for the exit?"

He turned back to the painting, smirking. "No," he answered. "I'd already be outside, of course."

I narrowed my eyes, confused.

He grinned at me and leaned in to whisper, "I set the fire, after all."

My jaw ached with a smile I refused to bestow on him. I didn't like surprises, but he was interesting, and he looked me in the eye when he spoke to me.

Of course, I wasn't as interested in his answers as I was in his ability to keep the conversation going. I could indulge in small talk, but this was more fun.

I let my eyes drift away from him.

"I'm sorry you don't like the artwork," he said, regarding the piece on the wall.

My thigh quivered with the vibration from my phone, but I ignored it.

I cleared my throat. "Degas is a wonderful artist," I went on. "I like him. He aimed to depict movement rather than stationary figures in many of his works."

"Except this one." He nodded to the piece of the lonely woman sitting in a bar.

"Yes, except this one," I agreed, gesturing to *L'absinthe*. "He also tried to show humans in isolation. This one was called ugly and disgusting by critics when it was unveiled."

"But you love it," he deduced.

I turned, slowly moving along the wall, knowing he'd follow.

"Yes, even when he is copied by bad artists," I joked. "But luckily no one here will know the difference."

I heard his quiet laugh at my audacity, and he was probably wondering whether or not to be insulted. Either way, he struck me as the type of man who didn't really care. My respect probably wasn't what he was after.

I felt his eyes wash over my back, following the lines of my body down to my hips. Other than my arms, my back was the only part of my body left bare by the fabric and crisscross work.

Turning through the open French doors, I walked onto the wide, candlelit balcony. The music inside slowly became a faint echo behind us.

"You don't really care about Degas, do you?" I asked, turning my head only enough to see him out of the corner of my eye as I walked to the railing.

"I couldn't give a fuck less about Degas," he stated without shame. "What's your name?"

"You don't really care about that, either."

But then his hand grabbed mine, pulling me to a stop. I turned halfway, looking up at him.

"I don't ask questions I don't want the answers to." It sounded like a warning.

I curled my fingers, feeling my heart skip a beat.

While I'd gotten the impression this man had a playful side, I now understood he had other faces, too.

"Easton," I acquiesced.

Turning back around, I pressed my hips against the railing and gripped the banister, feeling him behind me.

I breathed in, the scent of magnolias from the ballroom filling my nose along with a tinge of the ever-present flavor indigenous only to the Quarter. Aged wood, stale liquor, old paper, and rain all combined to create a fragrance that was almost more delicious than food on a quiet morning walk down Bourbon in the fog.

"Wouldn't you like to know my name?" he asked.

"I don't ask questions I don't want the answers to," I replied quietly.

I felt his smile even though I couldn't see it.

I stared out over the Quarter, nearly losing my breath at the sight.

A sea of people covered Bourbon Street like a flood, with barely enough room to turn around or maneuver through the masses. It was a sight I'd rarely seen in the five years I'd lived here, preferring to avoid the French Quarter during Mardi Gras in favor of the local hangouts on Frenchmen Street.

But it still had to be appreciated for the awe-inspiring sight it was.

The streetlamps glowed in the late-evening air, but they served only as a decoration. The neon lights of the bars, jazz clubs, and restaurants—not to mention the throngs of beads flying through the air from the balconies and down to waiting hands—cast a colorful display full of light, music, excitement, and hunger.

Anything went during Mardi Gras. *Eat what you want. Drink your fill. Say anything, and*—I blinked, feeling him move to my side—*satiate all of your appetites*.

Mardi Gras was a free pass. One night when rules were taboo and you did whatever you wanted, because you'd wake up tomorrow—Ash Wednesday—ready to purge your sins and cleanse your soul for the next six weeks of Lent.

I envied their carefree revelry, wishing for the courage to let go, stop looking over my shoulder, and laugh at things I wouldn't remember in the morning.

"Such chaos," I commented, observing the crowds stretching as far as the eye could see down in the street. "I've never had a desire to be in the midst of all that."

I turned my head, meeting his eyes as I swept my long, dark brown hair over my shoulder.

"But I like watching all the commotion from up here," I told him.

He narrowed his eyes. "That's no good," he scolded with a hint of a smile. "Everyone needs to experience the madness of the crowds down there at least once."

"As you sidestep the puddles of vomit, right?" I shot back.

He shook his head, amused. Leaning his hands on the railing and cocking his head at me, he asked, "So what do you do?"

"I finish my master's degree in a couple of months," I replied. "At Loyola."

A moment of apprehension crossed his eyes, and I cocked my head. Maybe he had thought I was older than I was.

"Does that bother you?" I asked.

"Why would it bother me?" he challenged.

I tilted the corner of my mouth in a smile at his game. "You didn't follow me out here for the exercise," I pointed out, both of us knowing damn well where the night between two consenting adults could lead. "I'm still in college, for a couple of months anyway. We might not have anything in common."

"I wouldn't worry," he replied, sounding cocky. "You've held my interest this far."

My eyes flared, and I looked away, tempted to either laugh or chastise him in anger.

"So what do you do, then?" I inquired, not really caring.

He stood up straight and slid his hands into his pockets as he turned to me. "Guess," he commanded.

I peered up at him, also turning my body to face his.

Guess.

Okay . . .

Letting my eyes fall down his neck and chest, I took in the black three-piece tux with the silk necktie fitted around the collar of his white shirt.

Every hair was in place, and his statuesque face gleamed alabaster in the candlelight.

His shoes were shiny and unmarred, and the face of his Rolex, with its black alligator-skin strap, reflected the colorful glow of the Christmas lights across the street, which probably remained up all year.

It was virtually impossible to tell exactly what he did for a living, but I could venture a guess.

Stepping up, I reached out with soft hands and slowly opened his jacket at the waist, seeing his arms fall to his sides as he probably wondered what the hell I was doing.

Looking up at him, I tried to keep my breathing steady, but the heat in his eyes as he looked down at me made it difficult.

I inched forward, my body nearly touching his, and then I licked my lips and let my eyes drop to his waist.

"Well," I played, "I was going to say junior partner, but that's a Ferragamo belt."

His chest moved with his suddenly shallow breaths. "And?"

I looked up, meeting his mischievous eyes again. "And usually it's BOSS or Versace for this set." I nodded toward the ballroom, indicating the gentlemen inside. "But if you can spend four hundred dollars for a belt," I clarified to him, "I'm going to say *senior* partner instead."

He snorted but made no move to take my hands away.

"You're a lawyer," I finally stated.

He squinted his eyes, regarding me. "You seem to know a lot about men's belts," he observed, "and how to spot money."

I almost rolled my eyes. He either thought I was a debutante, used to expensive things, or a woman on the prowl for a rich man.

I was neither.

"Don't worry," I assured him, leaning back against the railing. "If you're lucky enough to get anything out of me, it will come free."

His body tensed, and he tilted his chin up, looking at me like he wasn't quite sure what to do with me. I dropped my eyes, grinding my fingers into my palms and trying to calm my nerves.

Why did I say that?

We weren't in a bar, where it would be assumed that if we got along we might go home together. He was flirting, and I was flirting, but I shouldn't have been so forward.

Even if it was what I wanted.

I may not do relationships, but that didn't mean I didn't like to lose myself in someone for a night. And it had been too long.

He stepped up, and my breath caught when he positioned himself in front of me, planting his hands on the railing at my sides.

Leaning down into my space, he spoke softly. "For such a young woman, you have quite a mouth on you."

And then his eyes fell to my lips, and my knees nearly buckled.

"I can stop if you want," I taunted in a quiet voice.

But he grinned. "Now, what fun would that be?" he shot back, still staring at my mouth.

I inhaled, bringing the scent of him into my lungs as my brain turned fuzzy with the aromas of spice and sandalwood.

"Tell me," he started, "if I'm a lawyer, how do you know that?"

"Well." I straightened. "Your nails are clean, so you don't work in labor," I pointed out, nudging my way out of his hold and walking past him to the stone vase filled with flowers. "Your clothes are designer and tailored, so you make money." I looked him up and down, taking in his appearance. "And it's New Orleans. You can't walk two feet without bumping into a lawyer or a law student."

I drew the flower petals between my fingers, feeling their silky softness as I sensed him approach my side.

"Keep going," he insisted. "What brought me here tonight, then?"

My jaw tingled with a smile. He liked to play.

That was odd, actually. I wasn't used to men who knew how to keep my attention.

"You were forced," I answered, thinking about the man I wanted him to be. Not one of those stuffy men inside, smoking cigars and patting themselves on the back. I wanted him to be different.

I went on. "You don't really know any of these people, and they don't know you, do they?" I ventured. "You felt obligated to attend tonight due to family pressure or maybe by your boss's request."

He watched me, a hint of something I couldn't place in his eyes.

"You're just waiting," I continued, "trying to determine when you can politely abandon the uptight political conversations, bad food, and roomful of people you can't stand."

He leaned against the railing again, regarding me as he listened.

"You're restless," I stated. "There are other things you wish you could be doing right now, but you're not sure you should or you're not sure they're things you can have." I raised my eyes, meeting his.

He stared back in silence, and I desperately wanted to know what he was thinking.

Of course, I'd been describing myself this whole time, but his gaze was locked on me, never breaking eye contact.

I moved closer to him, the February chill finally catching up with me.

"What will I do when I leave tonight?" he asked.

"You won't leave alone," I determined. "A man like you probably didn't *arrive* alone."

He cocked an eyebrow, challenging me, but he didn't deny it.

I stared at him, waiting for his admission. Was he here with someone? Was he bold enough to come on to me with another woman around?

He wasn't wearing a wedding ring, but that didn't mean he wasn't attached.

"And you?" He reached out and took a lock of my hair between his fingers. "Who are you here with?"

I thought about my brother, who'd probably been calling me, since I'd felt my phone vibrate twice.

"Never mind," he refuted. "I don't want to know yet."

"Why?"

"Because . . ." He looked up, focusing over my head out in the distance. "You distract me, and I like it. I'm having fun."

Yeah, I was, too. For the first time all night.

Attendees laughed and danced inside, while the two of us, alone in the cold night with only a few other people lounging around the large balcony, carried on with our stolen moment.

"I should really get back, though," I suggested, pulling away.

My brother was no doubt looking for me.

But he reached out and grabbed my hand, narrowing his eyes. "Not yet," he urged, looking behind me toward the ballroom.

I stopped, not making a move to take away my hand.

He stood in front of me, his chest nearly touching mine.

"You're right," he whispered, his breath falling over me. "I don't really like a lot of those people, and they don't really know me." His voice turned hoarse. "But I like you. I'm not ready to say good night yet."

I swallowed, hearing the soft trickle of a slow jazz tune drifting out from the ballroom.

"Dance with me," he commanded.

He didn't wait for a response.

Sliding a hand around my waist, he guided me in, and I sucked in a sharp breath, my body meeting his for the first time.

Raising my arms, I put my right hand on his shoulder and my left hand in his as I let him lead me in a small circle, remaining in our own small, private space. Chills broke out down my arms, but I didn't think he noticed.

I let my eyes fall closed for a moment, not understanding what made him feel so good. My hands tingled and my legs felt weak.

There was rarely ever a time when I felt drawn to a man. I'd felt attraction and passion, and I'd enjoyed sex, but I'd never opened myself up to someone long enough to connect.

Now I found myself not wanting this evening to end any way other than in his arms.

That's where I wanted this to go. I didn't need his name, what he did for a living, or his family history. I just wanted to be close to someone and feel good, and maybe that would be enough to satisfy me for the next few months until I needed someone again.

Shaking my head slightly, I tried to clear my thoughts.

Enough, Easton. He was good-looking and interesting, but I didn't see anything in him that I hadn't seen in any other man.

He wasn't special.

Looking up, I asked, "You're not enjoying the party, so what would you rather be doing right now?"

He shot me a small, sexy smile. "I like what I'm doing right now."

I rolled my eyes, covering up how much I also liked him holding me close. "I mean, if not this?"

He twisted his lips, looking me over like he was thinking. "I'd be working, I guess," he answered. "I work a lot."

So he'd rather be doing work than schmoozing and drinking at a Mardi Gras ball? I dipped my head, breaking out in a laugh.

"What?" He pinched his eyebrows together.

I met his eyes, seeing the confusion. "You prefer work," I stated. "I can relate to that."

He nodded. "My work challenges me, but it's also predictable. I like that," he admitted. "I don't like surprises."

I instantly slowed, nearly stopping our dance.

I said the same thing all the time. I never liked surprises.

"Everything else outside of work is unpredictable," I added for him. "It's hard to control."

He cocked his head and brought his hand up to my face, running his thumb along my cheek.

"Yeah," he mused, leaning in while his hand circled the back of my neck possessively. "But there are times," he said softly, "when I like to lose control."

I closed my eyes. *Jesus.*

"What's your last name?" he asked.

I opened my eyes, blinking. *My last name?* I had kind of liked keeping specifics off the table. I didn't even know his first name yet.

"Easton?" he pressed.

I narrowed my eyes. "Why do you want to know that?"

He stepped forward, charging me slowly and pushing me backward. I had to keep backing up so as not to fall. "Because I intend on getting to know you," he said. It sounded like a threat.

"Why?"

"Because I like talking to you," he shot back, his voice thick with a laugh he was holding in.

I hit the wall behind me and stopped, glancing over at the people sitting at the table across the balcony.

He closed the remaining distance between us and dipped down until his face was a couple of inches from mine.

I locked my hands behind my back, instinctively tapping the wall with my fingers and counting in my head. *One, two, three—*

"Do you like *me*?" He cut me off, a playful tilt to his lips.

I couldn't keep the smile off my face. I turned my head, but I knew he saw it anyway.

"I don't know," I answered casually. "You might be too much of a gentleman."

The corners of his lips curled, looking sinister, and he threaded his hand around the back of my neck and through my hair, gripping my waist with the other and pressing his body to mine.

"Which means I'm still a man, only with more skill," he whispered against my lips, making my breath shake. "And there's only one place I won't be careful with you."

A whimper escaped, and I felt his hand tighten in my hair. He stared at my mouth, looking like he was ready to eat.

"I think you like me," he whispered, and I could almost taste his hot breath. "I think you even want to know my name."

He inched in, and I braced myself, so ready for it, but then suddenly he stopped and looked up.

"Tyler, there you—" A woman's voice stopped midsentence.

I twisted my head to see a beautiful blonde, maybe seven years older than me with a slightly surprised but not angry look on her face.

Tyler.

That was his name.

And I shifted, forcing his hands to drop away from me.

Tyler straightened and looked at the woman.

"They're about to start," she told him, clutching her small purse in both hands in front of her. "Come inside."

He nodded. "Yes, thank you, Tessa."

She cast me a quick look before spinning around and walking back inside the ballroom.

Well, she must not be his wife.

Not that I thought he had one anyway, with no wedding ring, but she'd called him Tyler, which meant she was familiar with him.

I smoothed my dress down and touched my mask, making sure everything was in place.

"She's a date," he pointed out. "Not a girlfriend."

I shook my head, finally looking up at him. "No need to explain," I said lightly.

I was glad he wasn't married, but if he wanted to misbehave while he had a date in the next room, that was on him. I wasn't going to feel embarrassed.

But I was disappointed.

I looked around, avoiding his gaze, and hugged myself, rubbing my arms. The cold had turned bitter, and it sank into my bones now.

I hadn't wanted the night to end, but it was over now.

I'd liked it when I didn't know his name. I'd liked it when I was waiting to find out.

He leaned in. "I—"

But then he stopped, looking up with a scowl on his face, as a voice came over the microphone from inside.

"Give me your last name," he demanded quickly, pinning me with a hard stare.

"Now, what fun would that be?" I replied with his same sarcastic remark.

But he didn't see it as funny.

He shifted, tipping his head up and listening to the man on the microphone and looking hurried.

Why did he look so nervous?

"Shit," he cursed, and then leaned in to me, planting his hands on the wall behind my head.

"If you leave," he warned, "there will be nothing holding me back when we run into each other again."

A shiver ran through my chest, and my thighs tensed.

But I hid it well.

"In your dreams," I shot back. "I don't like lawyers."

He grinned, straightening and looking down at me. "I'm not a lawyer."

And with a smug look, he walked past me, back into the ballroom.

I let out a breath, my shoulders falling slightly. *Damn it.*

I was both sick with disappointment and filled with unspent lust. What an asshole he was for leading me on when he had someone inside.

I'd acted like I'd known he hadn't come alone, but I hadn't really believed it. Perhaps he thought he'd get my number, take her home tonight, and call me tomorrow.

But that wasn't going to happen.

Sex happened where and when I wanted it. I didn't wait for men who put me on a menu.

I felt my phone vibrate again, and I ignored it, knowing Jack was probably pissed I'd disappeared for so long.

Stepping into the lively ballroom, with glasses clinking and people laughing, I ignored the speaker on stage when I peered over the crowd and spotted my brother by the tall double doors.

He had on his coat and held mine in his hand, and he looked aggravated. I moved swiftly over to him, turning around so he could put my wrap on me.

"Where were you?" he complained.

"Playing," I mumbled, not even trying to hide the teasing in my voice.

The speaker onstage droned on, slurring his words, and the audience laughed at his jokes, everyone else drunk enough to find them funny.

"Well, I want to get out of here before the NOPD parade comes down Bourbon," Jack reminded me, and then turned to fiddle with his phone.

I'd forgotten about the parade.

At midnight on Mardi Gras, the New Orleans Police Department—in their fleet of horses, dogs, ATVs, cars, trucks, and officers—walked the entire length of Bourbon, clearing the streets, an act that signaled the end of Mardi Gras and the beginning of Lent.

Partygoers filtered down the side streets only to return as soon as the police had passed by. We had gotten a hotel room on Decatur for the night to avoid traffic back to school in Uptown, but we needed to hurry if we were to get through the crowd before the police blocked our route.

"Come on," he urged, making his way out the doors while I began to follow.

"So, ladies and gentlemen!" the loud voice boomed behind me. "Please help me welcome a man who I hope will soon be announcing his candidacy for the United States Senate next year!" Everyone started clapping as he shouted, "Mr. Tyler Marek!"

I spun around, my eyes rounding as I saw the man who had just pinned me against a wall outside step onto the stage.

Holy shit.

"Damn, I didn't know he was here," my brother said, coming up to my side.

"You know him?" I asked, glancing at my brother before turning back to the stage.

"You've never heard of Tyler Marek?" he scolded. "He owns the third largest construction company in the world, Easton. Rumor has it, he's running for the Senate next year. I wish I could've met him."

A politician?

Jesus. I'd stepped into that one.

I should've been embarrassed. These people were clearly his friends—or associates—and the ball was, at least in some small part, in his honor. I'd insulted the food, the attendees, and while everyone seemed to know exactly who he was, I'd had no idea.

I tightened my wrap around my body, seeing him give the crowd a playful look I was already familiar with.

And just then, I stilled, seeing his eyes catch mine, and heat rose in my cheeks at the slow, self-satisfied smirk spreading across his face.

He started to speak, but I no longer cared to listen.

If you leave, there will be nothing holding me back when we run into each other again.

I arched an eyebrow at him and then leaned over to the empty round table next to the exit and blew out the small candle sitting there. Smoke drifted up, filling the air with its pungent scent.

And without a backward glance, I left the ballroom, my brother following behind.

TWO

EASTON

Six months later

My brother was my best friend. Not many girls my age could say that, but it was true.

Most siblings fought at one time or another. Competition and grudges form, and you run the risk of treating each other like shit because you can. Family is family after all, and they'll forgive and forget.

But Jack and I never had that problem.

When we were young, we trained together and played together, and as adults, nothing had changed. He had never not wanted to be around me, and I often joked that he liked me more than I did.

And he would agree, always hinting that I was too hard on myself, but he was the same way.

It was a learned behavior in our home, and we didn't do anything half-assed. Although at the time I'd resented our parents pushing us as hard as they did, I supposed it nurtured qualities that would help us in any field we pursued in our futures.

"Come on." My brother heaved at my side, pulling to a stop and shaking his head at me. "Enough," he ordered.

I halted, sucking in air as sweat soaked my back and neck.

"Two more laps," I pushed. "You could've made it two more laps."

He gulped air and walked over to the edge of the path covered by the canopy of old oaks lining the trail in Audubon Park.

"It's August, Easton," he bit out as he put his hands on his hips and bowed his head, trying to catch his breath. "And we live in a semitropical climate. It's too hot for this."

Grabbing the T-shirt out of the back of his mesh shorts, he wiped the sweat off his forehead and face.

I followed, pushing the strands of hair that had fallen out of my ponytail back over the top of my head. "Well, now you don't get your smoothie," I grumbled, bringing up the bribe I'd offered to get him out here on a Sunday morning.

"Screw the smoothie," he shot back. "I should've stayed in bed. School is already kicking my ass, and I need the rest."

He dropped his T-shirt to the ground and gestured toward me. "Go on," he urged. "Lie down."

I walked over in front of him, knowing better than to argue. He'd had enough and wanted to get the workout over with.

I dropped to my ass and lay down with my knees bent, while he stepped on top of my toes, safe inside my sneakers, to hold me in place.

Crossing my arms over my chest and clutching my shoulders, I tightened my stomach muscles and pulled up and then shot back down until my shoulder blades hit the grass. I pulled up again, repeating the crunches over and over as my brother stood above me texting.

He was always working—texting, e-mailing, organizing—and it always had to do with school or something related to his future.

He was driven, committed, and controlled, and we were exactly alike.

According to studies, firstborn children were reliable, conscientious, and cautious, and my brother was certainly all of those. As a middle child, I was supposed to be a peacemaker and a people-pleaser with lots of friends.

I wasn't any of those things.

The only quality I shared with other middle children was a sense of rebelliousness. However, I hardly thought that had anything to do with my birth placement and, instead, had everything to do with my youth.

While many middle children often felt as if they didn't have an identity or anything special about them that set them apart, I, on the other hand, had had more attention than I'd deserved and had gotten tired of being under a spotlight. Tired of being special, gifted, and prized.

I wanted more—or less. However you looked at it.

I pulled up and fell back, never releasing the muscles in my abs. "I'm proud of you, you know?" I breathed out, looking up at him. "This is your year."

"Yeah." He smirked, his eyes still on his phone as he joked, "What do you know?"

Jack had just started his final year at Tulane Law School. Not only was he busy with classes, moot court, and the pro bono requirement for his degree, but he was also looking for an internship to get a head start in the field. He'd worked hard and deserved every inch he'd gained, never expecting anything handed to him.

"I know you're up at four a.m. every morning to study before class." I winced as my abs started to burn. "You refuse to date, because it'll interfere with your studies, and you take those insipid law journals everywhere with you: the streetcar, the coffee shop, and even to the bathroom—"

"Hey—"

"You're the hardest worker." I continued, ignoring his embarrassed protest. "And you're in the ninety-eighth percentile. You didn't get there by luck." I smiled sweetly, getting cocky. "I may get a sunburn basking in the glow of your success."

He rolled his eyes and stepped off my toes, dropping to the ground himself. We both turned to get on our hands and toes, immediately dropping and rising for push-ups.

We worked out together at least once a week, although it was usually more than that. Between finishing my degree and graduating last May and Jack's demanding schedule, we had no set days or times, but we made it a point to keep each other motivated.

My brother had never really been an athlete, but he'd grown up helping me train, so exercise was as much a part of his life as it was mine.

"I love you, you know?" He stared at the ground beneath him as he dropped down and pushed back up. "I should say it more."

I stopped and turned, sitting on my ass as I peered over at him.

He did the same, resting his forearms on his knees and looking solemn.

"It was hard growing up with you, Easton," he told me, staring off in front of him, looking somber. "All the attention, the way our parents prioritized our lives around you . . ." He trailed off, stopping short, and I knew what he wasn't saying.

Our parents had loved all three of their children—him, me, and our younger sister, Avery—but he knew and I knew, even though it was never talked about at the time, that I came first. My rising tennis career took precedence over everything.

Jack and Avery couldn't take any extracurricular activities if it interfered with my training schedule, and they'd had to sit through countless matches, invisible because our parents' eyes were always on me. Only me.

My brother shouldn't have been my best friend. He should've resented me.

He popped up off the ground and reached out, offering me a hand. I took it and let him pull me up, my body vibrating with fatigue.

"You never let it go to your head, though," he allowed. "You always acted like Avery and I were just as important."

"Of course you were," I stated without hesitation as I dusted off my shorts.

"Yeah, well, our parents didn't always think so." He sighed. "Thanks for letting me have this," he said, referring to our choice to move to New Orleans five years ago, so he could attend Tulane, "and thanks for letting me feel like a big brother for a change."

I laughed, raising my fists and jabbing at him. "Yeah, you're capable of it sometimes," I teased in a light voice.

"Sometimes?" He held up his palms so I could slap at them. "I'm three years older than you, Pork Chop."

"Only physically." I shrugged. "According to studies, men trail women in maturity by eleven years."

He jabbed back, and I blocked, pushing his thick arm off to the side and seeing him stumble.

"You and your statistics," he complained. "Where did you read that?"

"The Internet."

"Ah, the infinite abyss of reliable information." He threw a few more slow punches, and I bobbed and ducked as we danced in a circle.

"Why don't you try getting out of your apartment and testing those theories out on your own?" he challenged.

I hooded my eyes, annoyed. "I get out of my apartment."

"Sure." He nodded. "For work. Or with me. Or when you're on the prowl."

I inhaled an angry breath, jabbing him harder and finally catching him in the chest.

He grunted. "Ouch."

And then shit got real.

He straightened, steeling his body and moving in, punching faster and making me duck, swerve, and sweat.

On the prowl? He knew he shouldn't have made a dig at me.

Everything else could be Jack's business. We didn't make decisions without the other's input, and when our world had fallen apart five years ago, I'd let him hold my hand from time to time to make him feel useful, but my sex life was the one thing I kept private.

Most of the time I stayed so busy that I didn't miss men. And I certainly had no interest in inviting one into my life for anything long-term.

It wasn't that I hadn't tried, but I didn't like messy and unpredictable, and relationships made me feel caged.

But once in a while I started to miss being touched. I missed being close to someone and being wanted. Even if just for a night.

So I'd go out and get it out of my system and then come home, my feathers smooth again. Sometimes it was a "friend" who didn't have any more of an interest in a relationship than I did, but occasionally, when I wanted to push the envelope for extra excitement, it was someone new.

Someone unknown.

"I mean, at the very least," my brother complained, "try taking an actual self-defense class instead of testing out moves on me that you learned from YouTube."

I grabbed his hand and bent his arm at the wrist, making him hunch over with the pain. His face twisted, and I stepped up to him, gloating.

"You don't like being my tackling dummy?" I taunted, adding pressure to his wrist.

He twisted his lips in annoyance, and before I knew what had happened, he'd grabbed my leg out from under me and pushed me down onto the ground. I crashed to my ass, pain spreading up to my hips and down my thighs.

He shot down, coming to bend over me and pin my neck to the ground with his hand.

I squirmed and tried to pry out of his grip, but it wasn't working. I could feel my face tighten and rush with blood. I probably looked like a tomato.

He lightened his grip and narrowed his concerned eyes on me, speaking sadly. "You're lonely, Easton."

I blinked, the sound of my breathing flooding my ears and echoing in my head. I felt like I wanted the ground beneath me to open and swallow me up whole.

Why would my brother say that?

I was alone, not lonely, and it wasn't like he had room to talk.

And my life was good. My apartment was gorgeous, I'd graduated at the top of my class at Loyola, and I had just landed a great position as a history teacher at an elite private school here in the city.

I was going to be a part of the future, doing work that meant something.

And I was only twenty-three.

I'd been focused, and I was still very young. It wasn't like there was any rush. It wasn't like I was going to be alone forever.

He released me and sat back, pushing his sandy blond hair back on his forehead. "I just worry about you," he explained. "I still think you should talk to someone."

I sat up on my elbows and gave him a pointed look, staying calm despite the anger crawling its way into my chest. "I'm fine," I maintained.

"Really?" he challenged. "And how many times did you go back to check that you locked your front door this morning?"

I rolled my eyes, looking away. I should never have told him. My little compulsions made my brother nervous.

Okay, so sometimes I liked to make sure everything was in its place. Sometimes locking my front door four times instead of just once made me feel safer.

And sometimes I liked to count things.

But the truth was I simply liked to be aware of my environment and the people around me.

And I managed my habit well enough that people didn't notice. My brother probably never would have if I hadn't told him.

"I'm not the center of attention anymore," I reminded him. "Stop trying to keep me there, okay? I'm fine." I pushed myself up and got to my feet, dusting off my butt as he also stood.

"My bathroom door handle broke," I told him, inserting my earbuds in my ears before he had a chance to say anything else. "So I need to hit the hardware store."

"Well, do you want me to look at it?" He slipped back into his gray T-shirt as I veered around him back toward St. Charles Avenue.

I shook my head, joking as I walked away, "You wouldn't know what you were doing any more than I would."

"You got something against just hiring a repairman?" he shouted after me as I walked.

I turned, dishing his attitude right back at him. "You got something against tutorials on YouTube?" I shot out, and continued with my life motto, which he knew all too well. "Always go to bed smarter—"

"—than you were when you woke up," he finished in a mocking voice.

I smiled and turned on "Hazy Shade of Winter" by the Bangles before jogging out of the park.

I spent the hour after I returned home crouched down next to my bathroom door as I pored over the instructions on how to install my new doorknob.

Luckily I'd bought a general tool set when I'd moved into my apartment two months ago, after graduation, but the clerk at the store had suckered me into a cordless power drill, which I was enjoying way too much.

Knowledge made us stronger, and I liked being able to do things for myself. Every new challenge was a mental checkoff of something I wouldn't need to learn later.

My brother, however, didn't share my need for autonomy.

When I'd moved in, he'd bought me a coffeepot as a housewarming gift. I'd bought a fire extinguisher and a thirty-eight-piece handyman set.

He'd gifted me with a wine rack stocked with pinot noir, and I'd added two more dead bolts to the front door.

Our senses of self-sufficiency were different, but then they had to be. Our experiences were very different growing up.

I smiled to myself, embarrassment warming my cheeks as I drilled in the screws. I was glad Jack wasn't here to see how this was possibly the most fun I'd had all week.

I may have gotten overzealous and split the wood in the door when tightening the screws, too.

And I may even have crawled around my entire apartment tightening any screw I could find before I decided to put my new toy away for the day.

He'd have me committed. Or at least send me on a forced spa day.

After eating a sandwich for lunch, I showered and combed my closet for an outfit for tonight.

The new academic year started tomorrow, and my students' parents had been invited for an open house this evening at Braddock Autenberry, my new school.

Or my *only* school, as this was my first teaching position.

Having gotten my keys to the school a couple weeks ago, I had prepared the room, and it was all set for tomorrow. Tonight I could try to relax and tend to the parents making their rounds to the different rooms before school started in the morning.

Reaching into my closet, I picked out my red pencil skirt, which fell just above the knee in the front but was cut to drape just below the knees in the back, stitched with a slight ruffle there for flare.

Laying it on the bed, I dug back into the closet for my fitted black blouse. It had long, cuffed sleeves and buttoned up to the neck.

To finish off the outfit, my heels were plain black with a pointed toe. I twisted my lips at the sight of them, setting them on the floor next to my bed.

I hated heels, but tonight was "make a good first impression," kind of occasion, so I'd suck it up. I'd filter in sneakers and flats throughout the school year, though.

The outfit was conservative but stylish, and after I did my light makeup and my hair in loose curls, pulling back the sides and fixing a clip to the back of my head, I dressed with care, making sure not to wrinkle anything.

This was a brand-new start, and I wanted to make sure everything was perfect.

Once I'd fastened my watch to my wrist and put in the diamond studs from my parents, I smoothed my hand down my shirt and skirt, brushing off lint that wasn't really there.

Perfect.

I checked the windows, the stove, and both doors, making sure everything was secure—twice—before I left.

When I arrived at the school, in the heart of Uptown, I still had a couple more hours before the open house began. I checked my mailbox in the teachers' lounge, made some extra copies of my parent letter, and double-checked my laptop and projector to make sure my PowerPoint presentation was set to run.

We were supposed to have a mini speech ready to go when parents arrived, but I'd gauged—hopefully correctly—that parents would filter in and out, visiting classrooms in no set order, so I'd just designed a presentation with pictures and captions to play in the background. They could watch it or not.

Student textbooks were on the desk for their perusal, and copies of my syllabus and calendar with my contact information sat on a table by the door.

Other teachers at our staff development days this past week had talked about bringing cookies and chocolate-covered strawberries to offer parents when they visited their rooms, but after the school nurse scared the shit out of us with the EpiPen training on Wednesday, I'd decided not to take any chances with allergies. Bottled water, it was.

I let Bob Marley's "No Woman, No Cry" play lightly in the background from my iPod dock as I walked around, double- and triple-checking everything to make sure the room was ready to go, for not only tonight but for tomorrow, as well.

"Are you Easton Bradbury?" a voice chirped behind me.

I turned, seeing a redhead in a navy blue A-line dress hovering at my classroom door.

"I'm Kristen Meyer," she continued, placing her hand on her chest. "I teach Technology and Earth Science. I'm right across the hall."

I put a smile on my face and walked over, noticing that she looked only a few years older than me.

"Hi." I shook her hand. "I'm Easton. Sorry we didn't meet this week."

Our staff meetings were mostly departmentalized, and since I was US and World History, she and I had probably been in the same room for only a few hours during our staff meetings before we'd split off into groups.

Her red lips spread in a beautiful smile. "This is your first year?"

I nodded, sighing. "Yes," I admitted. "I've done observations and a practicum, but other than that, I'm"—I exhaled a nervous breath—"new."

"You'll get that crash course tomorrow." She waved her hand, walking past me into the room and looking around. "Don't worry, though. The first year's the easiest."

I pinched my eyebrows together, not believing that for a second. "I've heard the exact opposite, actually."

She twirled around, looking completely at ease with herself. "Oh, that's what they tell you to give you something to look forward to," she joked. "Your first year you're just trying to keep your head above water, you know? Learn the ropes, get paperwork done on time, spend countless hours preparing one thing only to find out the lesson bombed . . . " She laughed.

"What they don't tell you," she continued, leaning against a student desk, "is that college prepared you for nothing. Your first year, you're learning to teach. Every year after that you're trying to be successful at it. That's the hard part."

"Great," I said sarcastically, laughing and putting my hands on my hips. "I *thought* I learned to teach in college."

"You didn't," she deadpanned. "Tomorrow is baptism by fire. Get ready."

I looked away, straightening my back. It was my brain cracking the whip, so I wouldn't scowl.

Deep down I knew she was probably right, but I still didn't like being knocked off my horse when I'd spent months preparing.

I'd done the work, taking all the classes I needed and even extra ones. I'd read up on the latest research and strategies, and I'd opted not to lesson plan with the other history teachers in favor of planning on my own—which I was allowed to do as long as I covered the curriculum and standards.

My lesson plans were done for the whole school year, but now I was worried about whether I'd done a lot of work for nothing.

What if I had no idea what I was getting myself into?

"Don't worry," Kristen spoke up. "It's not the students that are the problem." She lowered her voice and leaned in. "The parents are very invested in where their tuition money goes."

"What do you mean?"

She straightened, crossing her arms over her chest and speaking quietly. "Public school parents tend not to be involved enough. Private school parents, maybe too much. They can get invasive," she warned. "And they bring lawyers to parent-teacher conferences sometimes, so be prepared."

And then she patted me on the back, like I'd needed comforting, and walked out.

They can get invasive?

I cocked an eyebrow and stepped up to the large side-by-side windows lining the wall to rearrange the plants on the sill. Peering out the windows, I noticed that the sun had set and parents and students were stepping out of expensive cars, making their way into the school.

The manicured ladies meddled with their children's hair, while the fathers conducted business on their phones.

I spun around, heading for my classroom door to prop it open.

I knew how to handle invasive.

Over the next couple of hours, parents and students filtered in and out of the room, following their class schedule to meet every teacher and learn their class route. Since my students would be mostly freshmen, I had a great turnout. Most parents wanted their sons and daughters to have the lay of the land before their first day of high school, and judging by the sign-in sheet I'd asked parents to fill out, I'd met almost two-thirds of my kids and their families. The ones I hadn't met, I would try to call or e-mail this week to introduce myself and "open the lines of communication."

I moved around the room, introducing myself and chatting with families here and there but mostly just watching. I'd adorned the walls with some maps and posters, while a few artifacts and tools used by historians and archeologists sat on tables and shelves. They moved from one area to another, taking in the clues I'd left as to what we'd study this year.

Even though I had about a hundred eighty days with the students, this was the night that was the most important. Seeing how your future student interacted with their parents offered a good indication of what to expect during the school year.

Which parent did they seem to fear more? (That's the one you would call when there was trouble.) How did they speak to their parents? (Then you'd know how they'd speak to you.)

A couple parents and kids still flitted around the room, but as it was almost end time, everyone was starting to leave.

"Hi." I walked up to a young man who'd been slouched in one of the desks for a while, sitting alone. "What's your name?"

The kid wore earbuds and played on his phone, but he shot his eyes up at me, looking annoyed.

I wanted to sit down and spark up a conversation, but I could already feel the apprehension. This one was defiant.

Catching sight of the name tag the PTA had stuck to the left of his chest when he'd showed up tonight, I held out my hand.

"Christian?" I smiled. "Nice to meet you. I'm E—" But I stopped and corrected myself. "Ms. Bradbury," I amended. "Which class will you be joining us for?"

But then his phone beeped, and he sighed, pulling out his earbuds. "Do you have a charger?" he asked, looking impatient.

I dropped my hand and tilted my chin down, eyeing him. Thank goodness I didn't believe in first impressions; otherwise I might have been irritated at his lack of manners.

He waited for me to answer, staring at me with blue-gray eyes beneath black hair, stylishly mussed, and I waited as well, crossing my arms over my chest.

He rolled his eyes and gave in, finally looking at the piece of paper lying on the desk. "I'll be joining you for US History," he answered, his flippant tone putting me on edge.

I nodded and took the paper, creased with half a dozen folds. "And where are your parents?" I inquired.

"My mother's in Egypt."

I noticed that he was in my first-period class and handed the paper back to him. "And your father?" I prodded.

He sat up, stuffing the paper into the back pocket of his khakis. "At a city planner's meeting. He's meeting me here."

I watched him stand up and smooth a hand down his black shirt and khaki and black necktie. He was nearly as tall as me.

I straightened and cleared my throat. "A city planner's meeting?" I questioned. "On a Sunday night?"

His white teeth shone in a condescending smile. "Good catch," he commended. "I asked him the same question. He ignored me."

I arched an eyebrow, immediately discerning that he and his father didn't get along. What were they going to be like in the same room together?

He affixed the earbuds back into his ears, getting ready to tune me out. "If I give you any grief, it's best just to call my mother in Africa rather than deal with my father," he told me. "Just a tip."

I shot up my eyebrows, breaking out in a small grin. He was a little pill.

But then so was I. I could understand where this one was coming from. We might just get along after all.

Turning around, I walked to my desk and slipped my phone out of the drawer. Dislodging the battery, I walked over and handed it to him.

"Charge it back up tonight and we'll exchange tomorrow morning, okay?"

He pinched his eyebrows together and slowly reached out his hand, taking the battery. Luckily we both had the latest generation of the same phone.

"According to the student handbook," he started, swapping out his nearly dead battery with mine, "we're not allowed cell phones in the classroom."

"In my class, you are," I shot back, standing my ground. "You'll find out more about that tomorrow."

He handed me the dead battery and nodded. I relaxed, relieved that he seemed to soften a little.

"Christian."

We both looked up, turning our heads toward the door, when the sharp tone startled us both.

Standing in the doorway, filling the space in a deep-black three-piece suit, white shirt, and gold tie was Christian. All grown up.

The stone-blue eyes narrowed on us under eyebrows that didn't curve but slanted.

Oh, shit.

I stood there, stunned still and not breathing as my fists instantly clenched.

I may have just met the son, but I already knew the father.

I looked away, blinking long and hard. *No, no, no . . .*

My pulse raced, and my forehead and neck broke out in a cold sweat.

I didn't know if he recognized me, but I couldn't bring myself to move toward him. What the hell was I supposed to do?

It was Tyler Marek.

The same man who'd danced with me, flirted with me, and told me there was one place where he wouldn't be careful with me was my student's parent?

Spinning around, I returned to the front of the room, choosing to ignore him.

I circled my desk and bent down to the open drawer so I could replace the battery in my phone. I didn't need to bend, but I could feel his eyes following me, and I needed a moment to panic in private.

I closed my eyes, inhaling deeply.

He hadn't seemed like the type to have a kid when I'd met him before. Had I been wrong? Was he married?

I hadn't seen a ring on his finger last February at the Mardi Gras ball, but that didn't mean anything nowadays. Men took them off as easily as they put them on.

What would happen if he recognized me? Thank God I hadn't slept with him.

I drew in a long breath as I replaced the case on my phone and closed my bag.

Licking my dry lips, I swallowed the lump in my throat and forced myself to stand the hell up and deal with it.

Straightening my back, I smoothed a hand down my blouse and shirt.

I gathered some of the surveys that parents had filled out and straightened them, setting them in the tray in the corner of my desk.

The other parents and students had already drifted out of the room, and I tensed, seeing his long legs coming to stand in front of my desk.

Tyler Marek.

I'd thought about him. More than I wanted to admit.

However, I'd resisted the urge to Google him for more information, not wanting to indulge my pointless curiosity.

I'd never expected to see him again, much less here.

"I've met you before, haven't I?" he asked, sounding almost sure.

I looked up, chills spreading down my arms at his sharp gaze. He held my eyes, calm and attentive as he waited for his answer.

I swallowed and steeled my shaky smile. "I don't believe we've met, sir." I held out my hand, hoping whatever memory lapse he was having would be permanent.

Of course, I'd been wearing a mask that night—a pathetic mask but still a mask—so his image of that girl in the red dress might be obscured. Hopefully it would stay that way.

Not that a dance and flirting were scandalous, but it would certainly be awkward.

He shook my hand, and I remembered how those same hands had held my waist, the back of my neck . . .

He squinted, studying me, and I wanted to sink into a hole, away from his scrutiny, because at any moment he'd remember.

"You seem familiar," he pushed, not convinced.

"I'm Ms. Bradbury." I changed the subject, walking around the desk. "Your son and I have already met. I'll be teaching him US History first period this year."

And with hopefully only one parent-teacher conference, and then you and I will never have to run into each other again.

It wasn't that I was embarrassed or scared. I could handle some discomfort.

But this guy had turned me on.

I'd looked back on our interaction often over the past few months. On quiet nights when I'd wanted someone's hands on me and the only person keeping me company was myself, I'd remembered that dance, his mouth close to mine and his eyes looking down at me.

I'd slept with other people since then, but strangely, he was always where my mind wandered back to when it wanted a fantasy.

And now with him close . . .

He continued to study me, an eyebrow arched, and I was suddenly nervous. He looked formidable. Not at all as playful as he'd looked that night.

"Christian," he called to his son. "Come here."

His son barely looked up from his phone or the video game he played as he walked past us.

"I've been here," he said, anger twisting his voice. "I need something to drink."

"There's bottled water by the door," I instructed, but he just kept walking, leaving the room without another word.

His father's jaw hardened, and I could tell he was angry.

"Excuse my son," he apologized. "His mother is away for a year, and he's a little out of sorts."

His mother. Not *my wife*, then.

The air-conditioning poured down from overhead, caressing my face, and I felt it waft lightly against my blouse, cooling the light layer of sweat.

Tyler and I were alone in the room, and I inhaled through my nose, smelling his intoxicating scent, which I could almost taste on my tongue.

I walked around him, toward the papers by the door. "Well, I know you have other classrooms to visit and not much time," I told him, "so here is a letter explaining my background and plans for the year." I picked up a single-sided letter off the desk and also a two-page detailed calendar, walking over and handing both to him.

"And there's also a syllabus with a rundown of dates when tests occur and when papers and projects are due," I continued as his eyes left mine to peruse the documents.

His eyebrows nose-dived as he studied them.

"All of this information is also on my website," I told him. "This is just a hard copy in case you prefer it."

I crossed my arms over my chest and tried to keep my voice light. "Do you have any questions for me?"

I probably sounded like I was trying to rush him out of here, but the longer he stayed, the greater the chance that he would remember me.

"Yes," he said quietly, still flipping through the papers. "I do have a question."

I stiffened, trying to remember to breathe.

"How long have you been a teacher?" he asked.

"This will be my first year," I said in all confidence.

He raised his eyebrows, the edges of his mouth curling. "I hope you're good."

I cocked my head, peering at him. "Excuse me?" I asked, trying not to sound offended at the innuendo.

"My son can be a handful," he clarified. "He doesn't misbehave, but he's willful. I hope you know what you're doing."

I nodded slightly and turned to go back to my desk.

Doesn't misbehave?

From what I'd already seen, he was very much a handful. I just hoped I didn't need to call his father or deal with him for anything.

Back behind my desk, I looked up and saw that he was still by the door, looking at me like he was trying to figure something out.

"Was there something else?" I tried to sound polite.

He shook his head as if he was still thinking. "I'm just . . . almost sure I know you."

"Easton?" Kristen poked her head inside my door, interrupting. "Some of us are going—oh, I'm sorry." She stopped, seeing the parent still in the room.

My eyes fluttered closed, and my stomach flipped.

Shit.

"Sorry to interrupt," she chirped. "Stop by my room when you're done, okay?"

And then she let the door close, leaving us alone.

I darted my gaze over to Mr. Marek, and he turned his eyes away from the door and pinned me with a sharp stare.

And then, like the raging sun over a cube of ice, his hard gaze melted, turning into one of knowing as realization hit, his eyes softened, and his mouth curled with amusement.

Fuck.

"Your name is Easton?" He stepped toward me slowly, every step shooting through my veins and making my blood rush.

"That's an unusual name for a woman," he went on, inching closer. "In fact, I've met only one other with the name."

I let the air drift out of my lungs, and I raised my eyes, meeting his.

But his eyes fell away from my face and moved down my body as if he was trying to connect who I was now with what he remembered from six months ago.

He finally met my gaze again and leaned in, looking expectant. "You haven't asked my name yet," he toyed.

The hair on my neck stood on end.

"Would you like to know?" he pressed, playing with me.

As the parent of a student, introductions were in order.

But he was having fun with me right now, and while I wanted a good relationship with my students' parents, I needed to sever the hand to save the arm.

I didn't know what would happen if he saw me as anything other than Christian's teacher, and that's the only way he should see me.

"Mr. Marek." I spoke calmly but firmly. "If you have no further questions, I'm sure your son is waiting for you. Again," I added. "Perhaps you should make sure he's okay."

The hint of the smile in his eyes immediately disappeared, and I watched him straighten and his expression harden.

He was insulted. Good.

I glanced to the door and back to him. "Have a good evening."

THREE

TYLER

"You're smiling," my brother, Jay, observed, sitting opposite me in the back of the Range Rover.

I ignored him as I watched the pedestrians race by, mostly joggers and some students carrying backpacks, as Patrick, my driver, took us home.

I wasn't smiling.

I was insulted, amused, and intrigued, picturing her beautiful and flushed face in my head.

Her blouse, buttoned up to the neck, her tight red skirt and those heels accentuating her shapely calves, and her proper little attitude were so different from what I remembered from last Mardi Gras.

But they definitely weren't a disappointment, either.

She'd been tough and sexy, almost untouchable, last winter, and she'd fascinated the hell out of me. She'd had a mouth on her that had amused me and had gotten me hard, and then she'd stunned me when she'd just up and left, not the slightest bit interested in making it easy for me.

But unfortunately, I hadn't been able to find her after the Mardi Gras ball.

She hadn't been on the guest list, which meant she'd come with someone, and I hadn't wanted to go poking around and start people talking, so I'd let it go.

But now here she was, my kid's teacher, dangerous and forbidden, which only increased her allure, and she'd been just as hot tonight as she'd been on that balcony all those months ago—the difference being now I couldn't fucking touch her.

I loosened my tie, my neck sweating even though the AC was on full blast, and I looked over at my son, sitting in the seat next to me with his head buried in his phone.

It was going to be a long fucking year.

"Well, get ready for a kick in the nuts." My brother leaned back in his seat, tapping his phone with its stylus. "Mason Blackwell just got a two-million-dollar donation from the Earhart Fellowship. They're officially backing him for representing their high moral fiber."

Mason Blackwell. My only real opponent for the Senate.

"High moral fiber," I repeated under my breath. "While I eat babies and bathe in blood, right?"

Jay chuckled, finally looking up. "They don't say that," he assured. "Not exactly anyway. They really don't say anything. You're a mystery," he chirped, his eyes condescending.

We'd had this conversation, but the issue was never settled for him. He just kept digging, hoping to wear me down, but there was no fucking way I was letting the press into my personal life. It was his responsibility to spin the media and keep the focus on what was important.

"This is your job," I reminded him, hardening my eyes so he knew I meant business.

But he shook his head at me and leaned forward. "Tyler." He'd lowered his voice to a whisper for my son's sake. "I can feed the papers whatever you want, but in front of the cameras you'd better start coming up with some answers. It's the twenty-first century, and people—voters," he clarified, "want to know everything."

"Things that aren't any of their business," I shot back in a low voice, hearing Christian's game noises continue undisturbed.

I had nothing violent or illegal to hide, but they were starting to prod about my kid—wondering where I've been in his life, and they were getting nosy about my past relationships. Shit that wasn't anyone's business.

But Jay wanted me to be an open book.

He pulled away, crashing back into his seat. "Kim Kardashian Instagrams her ass," he gritted out. "This is the world we live in, God help us, and I promise you, a little pic of what you had for breakfast would go viral more than any of your speeches or commercials. Get social. Twitter, Facebook—"

"You've got people handling that shi—" I halted, glancing at my son and then back to Jay. "Stuff," I corrected, not wanting to swear in front of Christian.

It had been a hard habit to break, and since Christian had always—always—lived with his mother, my language had never been something I worried about in private. Now I just had to remember that being around my son was like being at a public function or in front of the cameras.

Your true self isn't always the person people should see.

I had a team of employees to handle my website and social media, so I wouldn't have to. It was one of the first things I'd put in place last winter when I'd decided to start preparing to run for the Senate. I hadn't officially announced my candidacy, and the campaign wouldn't start for another six months, but we were already laying the groundwork and preparing.

My brother nodded. "Yeah, we have people handling your social media, but it would be nice if you added some personality here and there. Share fatherhood stories, funny anecdotes, selfies . . . whatever."

He waved me off. "People are addicted to that stuff. They'll eat it up."

I closed my eyes and leaned my head into my fingers, rubbing circles on my left temple. It was still more than a year until elections, and if I won, I'd be in for even more invasion into my privacy.

"I mean, look at him," my brother snapped, and I opened my eyes to see him gesturing to my kid.

I turned my head and watched my son, phone turned sideways, held between both hands as his thumbs shot out like bullets, tapping the screen.

That was practically all he did twenty-four/seven, and I couldn't remember the last time I'd seen his eyes. Every time I tried to spark up a conversation and ask what he was doing, he acted as if he'd barely heard me.

Jay was right. He was consumed. They all were.

"Do you have to be on that thing all the time?" I prodded, unable to hide the aggravation in my voice.

I knew he heard me, because I saw the minute eye roll he barely tried to hide.

"Christian," I snipped, reaching over and grabbing the phone out of his hands in an attempt to get his attention.

Or maybe just a reaction.

His jaw clenched, and he let out a sigh, barely tolerating me.

He'd been ignoring me ever since his mother and stepfather had left the country on their research trip a week ago and he'd moved in with me.

"Okay," he challenged, dropping his hands to his lap and looking at me with disdain. "What do you want to talk about?"

I cocked an eyebrow, taken aback a little. I'd expected him to argue—or maybe ignore me as usual—but had I wanted to talk?

I'd been trying to talk to him, connect with him, for years, but now I realized that I didn't know what I was going to say.

And he knew it. He knew I didn't know what the hell I was doing.

He breathed out a laugh and gave me a condescending look. "Gimme a break," he grumbled. "We barely resemble estranged brothers, much less father and son. Don't start something we both know you won't finish."

Then he reached out for his phone, but I hardened my expression and pulled my hand away.

"I need my phone back," he shot out, tension crossing his face. "Ms. Bradbury, or whatever her name is, lent me her battery, and I have to bring it back tomorrow."

"Too bad," I barked, stuffing his phone in my pocket and turning my burning eyes to my brother. "You know, that's really the problem here. Role models like teachers who enable children to continue to disconnect from the world."

"Well, you would know," Christian bit out at my side. "You disconnect all the time, and you don't need technology to do it."

I tipped my chin down, tightening my jaw. *Jesus Christ.*

If I weren't so fucking pissed, I might've laughed.

I remembered getting in my father's face time and again when I was younger. Christian looked exactly like me, but even if he didn't, there would be no doubt he was my kid. I'd been just as defiant at that age.

"Your energies belong elsewhere," Jay pointed out, trying to reel my focus back in, "and your time is sparse," he reminded me.

My energies belong elsewhere. My time is sparse.

Meaning my brother didn't think fighting a losing battle with my kid was a good use of my time.

I looked over at Christian, watching him stare at nothing out his window and finding my chest tightening.

My shit relationship with my kid was my own fault. It had been no surprise when he'd fought his mother and me about staying here for the year instead of going with her to Africa.

He needed time. Of course, it was time I didn't have, but even when I did try, he shut me out.

I knew I wouldn't win any fatherhood awards, but I had supported him his entire life and I'd always treated him well. I'd taken care of his wants and needs, and maybe I'd never pushed hard enough and maybe I'd never put him as a top priority, but I'd had no idea it was going to be this hard to bond with him later on. I didn't exactly get along with my father all the time, either, but I respected him.

Christian couldn't respect me any less than he already did.

And it was getting harder and harder to ignore the voice in my head that said it was too late.

The car turned up Prytania Street, dipping along one of many of the broken, potholed roads of New Orleans.

I turned my eyes out the window as well, the conversation in the car having gone silent.

I took in the evening bustle of the city, with its array of boutiques, shops, and intimate restaurants. Out of every neighborhood in the city—the Quarter, the Marigny, the Central Business District, the Warehouse District, Midtown, Uptown—it was the Garden District that captivated me the most.

Nestled between St. Charles Avenue and Magazine Street, Prytania had some of the best architecture in a neighborhood adorned with vibrant colors, flowers, and foliage, and the best restaurants located in buildings that probably wouldn't pass any health-code inspections. The wealthy and pristine blended effortlessly with the chipped and aged, and that was called character. You couldn't buy it, and you couldn't describe it.

But it was the same thing that made a house a home.

The nineteenth-century mansions loomed on both sides, protected behind their wrought-iron gates and massive live oaks lining the street. Gas flames flickered in lanterns hanging outside front doors, and cyclists cruised past with either backpacks strapped to their backs—probably students—or instruments secured to their bodies—street performers.

Lightning flashed outside, energizing the life on the streets, and then thunder cracked, reminding me that it was hurricane season. We'd be getting a lot of rain in the coming weeks.

We drove up the long street, entering the quieter and even more picturesque section, and then slowed to turn into my driveway, taking us deeper into the veil of trees, behind which sat my home.

The old Victorian, surrounded by a generous plot of land, was three stories tall and featured a pool and a guesthouse on the grounds. Even though it had been in desperate need of renovations when I'd bought it ten years ago, I hadn't doubted my purchase for a moment. The beauty of the home was in the quiet, isolated feel of its position even though I was in the heart of the city.

Bars, restaurants, and shops sat only a short distance away, but inside the house, you wouldn't know it.

The home was surrounded by an acre of land with the lushest grass and foliage I'd ever seen, as well as a few old oaks that created a canopy around the edges, hiding the house and allowing me the privacy I enjoyed.

And even though my son and I were barely on speaking terms, I knew he loved it here as well.

His mother and her husband lived in the more sedate Uptown area, not far from here in distance—only a matter of blocks—but worlds apart in terms of liveliness and culture.

After pulling into the carport, my driver got out to open our doors, but Christian swung his door open first and bolted out, obviously still angry that he'd lost his phone.

I hadn't planned on keeping it, but since he'd chosen to be disrespectful, I might, after all.

His mother had said that I needed to earn his love, and that may be true—he had no reason to like me, and I knew that—but I wouldn't coddle him, either. He'd show his elders respect, because it was good manners. If I tried to get his love first, he might never take me seriously.

Or he might not, either way. I really had no idea what I was doing.

I watched Christian barrel into the house by the side door, and I waved off Patrick when he tried to open my door. Picking up the papers I'd collected when I'd visited all of Christian's teachers, I handed them to my brother.

"His syllabi," I explained. "Find them online and download them to my phone, and then enter the important dates on my calendar as well as all of the teachers' contact information," I told him.

He nodded once. "Consider it done," he said, flipping through the papers.

My brother was my campaign manager, having left his position at my company to handle my political interests full-time last spring. He also tried to do anything that made my life easier.

"Is this her?" he asked, stopping on one set of papers. "Easton Bradbury?"

Her? And then I remembered that Christian had mentioned her name about the phone battery.

Jay slipped the papers into his briefcase and started typing quickly on his phone.

"What are you doing?" I asked.

"Googling her," he said matter-of-factly.

I breathed out a quiet laugh I was sure he didn't hear. Thank goodness for my brother and his tech savviness. He researched everything and everyone, and I was better for it. But I didn't require his interference when it came to my son.

I moved to get out but stopped when he spoke up.

"Twenty-three years old, summa cum laude from Loyola University—"

"I don't care." I cut him off, stepping out of the car.

But the truth was, I kind of did care. I liked my memory of her and hadn't enjoyed a woman nearly as much since our night together, and we'd only talked. Her mystery made the attraction more fun, and I didn't want that ruined.

Easton was a woman I'd wanted in my bed, but Ms. Bradbury was off-limits.

The lines were there, clear as day, and not to be breached. For the sake of my son and my career.

"How's my week looking?" I changed the subject as I entered the large kitchen through the side door.

"You're booked solid Monday through Wednesday between the office and meetings." He slammed the door behind him and followed me through the kitchen and down the hallway, past the living room and media room.

"But Thursday and Friday are calm," he went on, "and I confirmed your dinner this weekend with Miss McAuliffe. If you're still up for it," he added.

"Of course I am." I pulled off my tie, entering my den and slipping off my jacket.

Tessa McAuliffe was uncomplicated and low-maintenance. She was beautiful, discreet, and good in bed, and while my brother had encouraged me to form a steady relationship with her—or anyone—to help my campaign, I simply wouldn't be pushed into changing my life for a vote.

Getting into the Senate was important to me, but while I enjoyed Tessa's company for what it was, I didn't love her and didn't have the time to try.

And surprisingly, she never gave the impression she wasn't okay with that.

She was a producer and anchor for a local morning show, and from day one, there were never any misconceptions about what was expected from either of us. On occasion we met for dinner and then ended the evening in a hotel room. That was it.

Afterward, I'd call on her again when I felt the need. Or she'd call me. It never went beyond that.

I briefly contemplated seeking a serious relationship when I'd first started campaigning. Most voters wanted to see candidates representing good family values in their own homes—spouse and children—but I had been focused on work, and I refused to force my private life.

My son, my unmarried status, my thoughts about what it would be like to possibly have more children someday—once I'd proven I could parent the child I already had, of course—were private matters and no one else's business. Why the hell did it matter when it came to my ability to serve?

"The kid ate dinner, right?" I asked him, rounding my desk and turning on my computer.

He unbuttoned his jacket and tossed his briefcase onto one of the two chairs on the other side of my desk.

"Yeah." He nodded. "I had Patrick take him to Lebanon Café before the open house."

Patrick was a fan of falafels and Christian seemed to love anything with hummus. It was the second time in the past week they'd eaten dinner together. I reminded myself to make sure I was home for supper tomorrow night, though. With the fucking impromptu meeting with my father earlier, I'd had Patrick drop Christian off at the open house, telling him I had a city planner's meeting instead of that I was being grilled by my father.

At thirty-five, I still answered to him, and while as a son I hated it, I could appreciate it as a father. My dad had been a good parent. I only wished the apple hadn't fallen so far from the tree.

"All right, let's get to work."

I poured myself a drink at the small bar against the wall, and Jay and I spent the next two hours condensing a list of meetings to be set up with the who's who of political influence in the city. Unfortunately, campaigns fed off donations, and I'd insisted early on using my own money, because I hated asking anyone for anything.

After events and meetings were added to the calendar, I let Jay go home, and I stayed up refining my speech for the Knights of Columbus on Wednesday.

I rubbed the fine stubble on my jaw, wondering if Christian would like to come with me to one of these events. I couldn't imagine he'd find it interesting, but it might be a way for him to see what I did and to spend time together.

I shook my head, standing up and switching off my lamp.

I wanted too many things.

That was the problem. Too many goals and not enough time.

I'd been an arrogant and irresponsible twenty-year-old when Christian was born. I'd wanted what I'd wanted, and I'd blown off consequences, even after he was born. Now I knew the price of my actions, and it was a matter of having to choose. I knew I couldn't have everything I wanted, but I still didn't like making choices.

Leaving the room, I headed upstairs for my bedroom, but stopped, seeing the glow of a lamp coming out of Christian's cracked door down the hall.

Walking down to his room, I pushed the door open and saw him passed out on his stomach, fully clothed on top of the covers.

I went over and gazed down at him, feeling the same tightening in my chest that I'd felt in the car.

He looked so peaceful, his chest rising and falling in calm, even breaths with his head turned to one side. The two ever-present creases between his eyes were gone, and his black hair had gotten rumpled, now covering his forehead and sitting close to his eyes. I remembered seeing him once as a baby, looking almost exactly the same.

But back then he'd smiled all the time. Now he was always angry.

I sat down on the edge of his bed, pulling a spare blanket up over him.

Staring down, I felt my shoulders relax as I rested my elbows on my knees. "I know this is awkward," I told him, whispering. "It's different for both of us, but I want you here."

He shifted, twisting his head away toward the wall, still sleeping. I reached out to touch him but stopped short and got up instead, leaving the room.

I shook my head as I tore off my clothes and made my way to my bedroom.

Why was it so much easier to be with him when he didn't know I was there?

I headed a multimillion-dollar corporation. I'd traveled in every hemisphere and climbed a volcano when I was eighteen. I had some of the most intimidating people eating out of the palm of my fucking hand, so why was I afraid of my own kid? I stepped into my bedroom, tossing my shirt and tie onto a chair and slipping off the rest of my clothes.

All of the hardwood surfaces in the room—from the floors to the furniture—shined with the soft glow of the bedside table lamp, and I walked across the ornate area rug, running my hand through my hair and trying to figure out what to do with him.

His mother, despite her animosity toward me, was a good parent, and Christian got along with her. She was strict and provided routine, and that's what I needed to do for Christian.

And that not only included him but me as well. I needed to be home for meals. Or at least more meals. And I needed to be consistent. Checking his homework, attending his sports games, and staying on top of where he was and what he was doing.

I'd asked for this, after all. I'd fought him and his mother to keep him in the country this year.

I climbed into the shower, rolling my neck under the hot spray of the dual showerheads and letting it relax the tense muscles in my shoulders and back.

Easton.

I should Google her. She was a fucking mystery, and she was teaching my kid.

I grabbed the bar of soap and ran it over my chest and arms, thinking about how she'd behaved six months ago compared to tonight. Different but very much the same. In control, sexy, but with a distance I couldn't put my finger on. It was almost as if she were a reflection in a mirror. There but not really real.

Almost as if she were still wearing that mask.

I should've kissed her that night. I should've looked down into those blue eyes and watched her lose control when I shut her up and made her melt like I wanted to.

What I wouldn't give to strip off those prim clothes I'd seen tonight, pin her to the bed, and . . .

I sucked in a breath, slamming my hand into the marble wall to support myself.

Shit.

I swallowed, gasping for breath as I smoothed my wet hand over the top of my head.

Looking down, I saw the stretched skin of my cock, begging for release as it pulsed and throbbed.

Slamming the knob to the left, I breathed hard under the sudden rush of cold water, clenching my teeth in frustration.

Easton Bradbury was off-limits.

And don't forget it.

FOUR

EASTON

"Okay, so . . . " I started, slowly stalking between the rows of desks and smiling at the printout of a Facebook post in my hand. "The question posed in the Facebook group yesterday that received the most responses was 'Why did men ever stop wearing tights? I would've rocked that,'" I read to the class.

The freshman boys broke out in snorts while the girls giggled, remembering the lengthy conversation some of them had carried on last night.

Marcus Matthews popped up and jumped onto his chair, holding his hands up in the air and smiling as he soaked in the praise and taking credit for his question last night.

I shook my head, amused. "Sit down," I ordered, shooting my pointed finger from him to the chair. "Now."

He laughed, but quickly jumped down and took his seat, the rest of the class still voicing their amusement behind him.

During the three weeks since school had started, we'd moved quickly through the curriculum and had been studying the independence of America, the founding fathers, and the Revolutionary War, hence the men-in-tights question.

Out of all the activities I'd planned to engage them, the social media requirements were the most successful. The parents had all received a lengthy letter after the first day, explaining the rhyme and reason to social media in the classroom. The students—per school rule—were already required to have laptops, which made it even more convenient to jump online anytime we wanted without the need for a computer lab. And it fit in perfectly with my goal of educating students to live in the digital world.

Social media was a necessary evil.

There were certainly dangers, and there had been a lot of apprehension from parents at first, but once I'd called and e-mailed to smooth over any resistance, all was well. They eventually understood my position, and most parents found great enjoyment in seeing the class's interactions online, given that they weren't able to see the students' engagement in the classroom.

Parents and students were invited to join our private Facebook group, where I posted assignments, discussion questions, and pictures of what happened in class or videos of presentations. Over the days and weeks, participation grew exponentially as parents were able to take a bigger role in their children's education and see not only their children's work but others' as well.

Not that students should be compared, but I found it a great motivator when parents saw the work of students who held the bar higher.

We also had Twitter accounts and a Twitter board in the classroom, as well as private Pinterest boards, where students and parents could brainstorm and collectively gather research.

Only a few parents were still uncooperative—I glanced at Christian Marek, seeing him slouch at his desk—so I did my best to make accommodations.

But I knew those students still felt left out. I had considered the possibility of abandoning the entire method, because I didn't want anyone hurt, but once I saw the participation and benefit, I refused. I'd simply have to get through to the parents.

I allowed myself a small smile, grinning at Marcus's pride in himself. But the silence off to the back where Christian sat was almost more deafening than the students' excitement.

He stared at his laptop screen, looking half angry and half bored. I couldn't figure him out. I knew he had friends. I'd seen him eating with other kids at lunch and playing on the field, laughing and joking.

But in the classroom—or my classroom, anyway—it was like he wasn't even here. He performed well on take-home assignments, but he never participated in discussions and he did poorly on quizzes and tests. Anything that took place in the classroom was unsuccessful.

I'd tried talking to him, but I wasn't getting anywhere, and I was going to have to come to terms with the options I was left with to help him.

Like calling his father, which I should've already done but hadn't found the guts.

I turned back to the class, refocusing my attention. "Congratulations, Mr. Matthews." I nodded, teasing Marcus. "While your question was meant to be funny—no doubt—it did spark some interesting comments about the history of attire."

I rounded the front of the classroom and leaned back on my desk. "Since fashion is a very popular topic, we also delved into the history of women's fashion, and that led to a debate on feminism," I reminded them. "Now, of course, fashion wasn't a topic I was supposed to teach you this year." I smiled. "But you were critically thinking and you saw how topics like these are interrelated. You were discussing, comparing, and contrasting . . ." I sighed, eyeing them with amusement before I continued. "And it certainly wasn't boring to read your responses, so good job."

The class cheered, and Marcus shouted out, "So do we get Song of the Week?" He lifted his eyebrows in expectation.

"When your team has earned fifty points," I reiterated the rule.

I rewarded them individually, but I also had a team incentive, which allowed their group to pick one song to play in class once they'd reached fifty points, if all work was turned in and they demonstrated good citizenship online and in the classroom.

I walked to the Smart Board—today's version of a chalkboard—and picked up a stylus, tapping the board to activate it. The projector fed the image from my computer, and all of the students' numbers appeared on the board, ready to receive their responses.

"Don't forget"—I glanced up as I replaced the stylus—"group five is sending current-events tweets before seven p.m. this evening. Once reviewed, I will retweet them for you," I told them, seeing Christian talking to the girl next to him out of the corner of my eye.

"You are to pick one, read and reflect, and turn in your one-page, typed assignment—twelve-point font, Times New Roman, not Courier New," I specified, knowing their trick of using a bigger font, "and have that to me by Friday. Any questions?"

Mumbles in the negative sounded from around the room, and I nodded. "Okay, grab your responders. Pop quiz."

"I have a question." I heard someone speak up. "When are we going to use the textbooks?"

I looked up, seeing Christian's eyes on me as the other students switched on their remotelike devices, which I used to record their multiple-choice answers instead of paper and pencil.

I stood up straight, inquiring, "Would you prefer to use the textbooks?"

But Marcus blurted out a response instead. "No," he answered, turning his head to Christian. "Dude, shut up."

Christian cocked an eyebrow, keeping cool as he ignored his classmate. "The textbooks are provided by the school. They have the curriculum we're supposed to learn, right?" he asked almost as an accusation.

"Yes," I confirmed.

"So why aren't we using them?" he pressed.

I inhaled a long, slow breath, careful to keep my expression even.

Kids will challenge us, test boundaries, and throw us curveballs, I was told. Keep your cool, treat every kid like they're your own, and never let them see you falter. Christian certainly challenged me on all those levels.

Not only was he not performing up to his potential in class, but he also challenged me on occasion. Whether it be tardiness, flippant behavior, or distracting other students, he seemed to have a penchant for disobedience.

And as much as he tried to hinder me from doing my job, the person I was outside of the classroom couldn't help but admire him a little.

I knew from experience that misbehavior came from a need for control when you lacked it in other venues. And while I sympathized with him—and whatever he wasn't getting at home or elsewhere—he clearly thought he could get away with it here.

"That's a good question," I told him, walking around my desk. "Why do you think we don't use the textbooks?"

He laughed to himself and then pinned me with a look. "What I think is that you give me more questions when I just want answers."

I stiffened, my smile falling as students in the room either tried to cover their laughs with their hands or stared between Christian and me wide-eyed and waiting for whatever would happen next.

Christian had a self-satisfied look on his face, and my blood heated with the challenge.

I swallowed and spoke calmly. "Everyone open up to page fifty-six."

"Ugh." Marcus groaned. "Nice job," he shot over his shoulder, not looking at Christian.

Everyone dug their books out of the compartments under their desks, and the sounds of pages flipping and students grumbling filled the classroom.

I picked up my teacher's manual and cleared my throat.

"Okay, this chapter covers the contributions of Patrick Henry, Benjamin Franklin, and Betsy Ross," I went on. "I'd like you to read—"

"But we already learned about them!" Jordan Burrows, the girl sitting next to Christian, called out.

I pinched my eyebrows together, cocking my head and feigning ignorance. "Did we?"

Another student jumped in. "We did the book study in groups two weeks ago and the virtual museums," he reminded me.

"Oh." I played along. "Okay, pardon me," I said, moving on. "Turn to page sixty-eight. This chapter covers the presidencies of George Washington through Thomas Jefferson—"

"We already learned that, too." Kat Robichaux laughed from my right. "You uploaded our campaign posters to Pinterest."

I looked up at Christian, who hopefully was getting the idea.

We had been learning everything in the textbook, even though we hadn't learned it from there. Students absorbed more when they sought knowledge themselves and put it to practice by creating a product instead of merely reading from a single text.

"Ah," I replied. "I remember now."

Christian shifted in his seat, knowing full well the point had been made.

"So," I went on, "on page seventy-nine, there are twenty questions to help us prepare for our unit test tomorrow. We can spend the rest of class answering them silently on paper, or we can take ten minutes with the responders and then move on to start researching slave ships online."

"Responders," the students cut in without hesitation.

"We could take a vote," I chirped, not really trying to be fair but to drive the point home for someone in particular.

"Responders!" the students repeated, this time louder.

The class picked up their remotelike devices. For the next ten minutes, I displayed multiple-choice questions on the board, giving them about a minute to answer on their devices, and then, once their responses had been recorded in the program, I displayed the bar graph showing how many students answered a certain way.

Afterward, we jumped on our laptops while I continued to project on the Smart Board as we dived into the next unit with some questions and research online before the end of class.

As the students walked out, moving on to their next class, I watched Christian inching slowly along and peering out the window as he made his way out the door.

"Christian," I called as he passed by my desk.

He stopped and looked at me like he usually did. With boredom.

"Your questions are important," I assured him. "And very welcome in this class. But I do expect you to use manners."

He remained silent, his eyes staring off to the side. I knew he wasn't a bad kid, and he was certainly smart, but the curtain over his eyes lifted very rarely. When it did, I saw the kid inside. When the curtain was drawn, he was unapproachable.

"Where is your phone?" I asked. "You need it for class, and you haven't had it."

He'd also failed to return my battery.

Not a big deal, since we used the same brand of phone, and I was getting by with his, but the students were allowed to use their phones in class—kept in the corner of their desks on silent and facedown—to access their calculators, random number generators for our activities, and other apps I'd found useful for engagement.

I'd found the more you allowed them their technology, the less they tried to sneak it. And since all of these students carried phones, I didn't worry about anyone feeling left out.

"If there's a problem, I can speak to your father," I offered, knowing Christian probably wouldn't choose to be without his phone himself.

But Christian broke out in a smirk, meeting my eyes. "You will speak to him." He jerked his chin toward the window. "Sooner than you think."

And he turned, walking out and letting the heavy wooden door slam shut behind him.

What had that meant?

I twisted my head toward the window, and stood up to head over to the window to see what he'd been referring to.

But I stopped, hearing the intercom beep.

"Ms. Bradbury?" Principal Shaw's voice called.

"Yes?" I answered.

"Would you please come to my office?" he asked, the fake nicety in his voice turning me off. "And bring your lesson plans, as well."

I raised my eyebrows, my legs going a little weak.

"Uh," I breathed out. "Of course."

It didn't matter if you were fourteen or twenty-three, a student, a teacher, or a parent—you still got nauseous when the principal called you down.

And he wanted my lesson plans? Why? They were online. He could see them anytime he wanted to.

I groaned, slipping off my jacket and tossing it over my chair—which left me in my slim-fitting black pants and long-sleeved gray blouse. I grabbed the hard-copy plans we were instructed to keep on our desk in case of an impromptu observation.

Thankfully, I had second period free, so I wouldn't have students for close to another hour.

I walked down the hall and through the front office, past the students either waiting for the nurse or waiting to be disciplined. My heels fell silent as soon as they hit the carpet in the hallway.

I tucked the binder under my arm and knocked twice on Mr. Shaw's door.

"Come in," he called.

I took in a deep breath, turned the knob, and entered, nodding at Mr. Shaw with a small smile as he stood up from behind his desk.

Turning to close the door, I immediately halted, spotting Tyler Marek standing in the back of the office.

I looked away, closed the door, and turned back to my superior, tensing against my racing heart.

What the hell did he want?

"Ms. Bradbury." Mr. Shaw held out his hand, gesturing to Christian's father. "This is Tyler Marek, Christian's—"

"Yes, we've met." I cut him off in a stiff voice, stepping forward to stand behind one of the two chairs Shaw had in front of his desk.

Marek stayed behind, hovering like a dark shadow in the corner, and I knew what I was supposed to do. Shake hands, greet him, smile . . . No, no, and no.

Shaw looked uncomfortable, and it was my fault, but I had a feeling I wouldn't like what was going to happen.

He regained his composure and cleared his throat, gesturing. "Please sit down," he suggested, looking to both of us.

I rounded the chair and took a seat, but Christian's father continued to stand instead of taking the seat next to me.

"Mr. Marek has some concerns regarding Christian," Shaw told me, "and his performance in your class. Can you enlighten me as to what problems you're having?"

I blinked, sensing Marek stepping forward and approaching my back.

Suddenly I felt as if all of our roles were reversed. Shaw was the concerned, neutral parent, Marek was the displeased teacher, and I was the student being put under the microscope. How dare he treat me as if I didn't know my job?

"Sir, I . . ." I tried to rein in my temper before I said something I'd regret. "Sir, this is the first I've heard that Mr. Marek has concerns. I'd like to know what they are as well."

I couldn't hide the discomfort from my voice. I was far from friendly, but at least I hadn't sounded curt.

Christian was having problems, but it was still early in the year, and I was still trying to create a relationship with him. I'd sent home—even mailed on one occasion—reminders about the social media groups and highlighted copies of the syllabus with important dates. I may not have called, but it wasn't as if I hadn't done anything.

Shaw looked up, offering Marek an uncomfortable smile. "Mr. Marek, your support of this school has gone above and beyond, and we are so grateful to have your son here. Please, tell me your concerns and how we can help."

I let my eyes drop as I waited, his presence making my back tingle with awareness.

He stepped up to my side and lowered himself into the seat next to me, unbuttoning his suit jacket and relaxing into the chair, looking confident.

"On the first day of school," he started, looking only at Shaw, "my son came home and informed me that he had to have his phone in Ms. Bradbury's class. Now, I purchased an expensive laptop, like many of the parents in this school, because we knew what tools were needed for a school of this caliber. Those expectations are very reasonable," he pointed out, and I braced myself, knowing where this was going.

"However," he continued, "my son is fourteen, and I'm not comfortable with him on social media. I've gone into this Facebook group the students frequent, and I don't particularly like where some of these discussions venture. Christian is expected to maintain three different social media accounts, and he's conversing with people I don't know," he stated. "Not only is his safety and those who influence him of greater concern now, but also the amount of distraction he contends with. He'll be doing his math homework, and his phone will be going off due to notifications for Ms. Bradbury's groups."

I bit my tongue, both figuratively and literally, not because his concerns weren't valid, but because this had all been addressed if he'd cared to take interest weeks ago.

I cleared my throat, turning to look at him. "Mr. Marek—"

"Call me Tyler," he instructed, and I shot up my eyes, seeing the devious amusement behind his gaze.

I shook my head, annoyed that he kept working that into our conversations.

"Mr. Marek," I continued, standing my ground, "on the first day of school, I sent home a document explaining all of this, because I foresaw these concerns."

His eyebrow shot up. I was calling him out as an absentee parent, and he knew it.

I kept going, straightening my back and feeling Shaw watching me. "I requested that parents sign it and return it—"

"Mr. Shaw," someone called behind me from the door, and I stopped, grinding my teeth in annoyance.

"Sorry to interrupt," she said, "but there's an issue that needs your quick attention in the front office."

It was Mrs. Vincent, the secretary. She must not have knocked.

Mr. Shaw gave us an apologetic smile and rose from his desk. "Please excuse me for a moment."

I let out a quiet breath, frustrated, but thankfully no one noticed. Shaw walked around his desk and across the room, leaving me alone with Marek.

Wonderful.

The door clicked shut behind me, and I couldn't ignore the feeling of Marek's large frame next to me—his stiffness and silence telling me he was just as annoyed as I was. I hoped he wouldn't talk, but the sound of the air-conditioning circulating throughout the room only accentuated the deafening silence.

And if he did say anything that rubbed me the wrong way, I

couldn't predict how I would react. I had little control of my mouth with my superior in the room, let alone with him gone.

I held my hands in my lap. Marek stayed motionless.

I looked off, out the window. He inhaled a long breath through his nose.

I checked the cleanliness of my nails, feigning boredom, while heat spread over my face and down my neck as I tried to convince myself that it wasn't his eyes raking down my body.

"You do realize," he shot out, startling me out of my thoughts, "that you don't have a union to protect you, right?"

I clenched the binder in my lap and stared ahead, his thinly veiled threat and tensed voice not getting by me.

Yes, I was aware. Most private school teachers were hired and fired at will, and administrators liked to have that freedom. Hence, no benefit of unions to protect us like the public school teachers enjoyed.

"And even so you still can't stop yourself from mouthing off," he commented.

Mouthing off?

"Is that what this is about?" I turned, struggling to keep my voice even. "You're playing a game with me?"

He narrowed his eyes, his black eyebrows pinching together.

"This is about my son," he clarified.

"And this is my job," I threw back. "I know what I'm doing, and I care very much about your son." And then I quickly added, "About all of my students, of course."

What was his problem anyway? My class curriculum didn't carry unreasonable expectations. All of these students had phones. Hell, I'd seen their five-year-old siblings with phones in the parking lot.

I'd thoroughly reviewed my intentions with the administrators and the parents, and any naysayers had quickly come around. Not only was Marek ignorant, but he was late to the game.

He'd been well informed, but this was the first time I'd seen hide or hair of him since the open house.

"You're incredible," I mumbled.

I saw his face turn toward me out of the corner of my eye. "I would watch my step if I were you," he threatened.

I twisted my head away, closing my eyes and inhaling a deep breath.

In his head, we weren't equals. He'd put on a good front last Mardi Gras when he'd thought I was nothing more than a good time, but now I was useless to him. His inferior.

He was arrogant and ignorant and not even the slightest bit interested in treating me with the respect I'd earned, given my education and hard work.

I liked control, and I loved being in charge, but had I told my doctor how to do his job when he'd ordered me off my ankle for six weeks when I was seventeen? No. I'd deferred to those who knew what they were talking about, and if I had any questions, I'd asked.

Politely.

I gnawed at my lips, trying to keep my big mouth shut. This had always been a problem for me. It had caused me trouble in my tennis career, because I couldn't maintain perspective and distance myself from criticism when I thought I'd been wronged.

Kill 'em with kindness, my father had encouraged. "Do I not destroy my enemies when I make them my friends?" Abraham Lincoln had said.

But even though I understood the wisdom of those words, I'd never been able to rein it in. If I had something to say, I lost all control and gave in to a rant.

My chest rose and fell quickly, and I gritted my teeth.

"Oh, for Christ's sake." He laughed. "Spit it out, then. Go ahead. I know you want to."

I shot up, out of my chair, and glared down at him. "You went over my head," I growled, not hesitating. "You're not interested in communicating with me as Christian's teacher. If you were, I would've heard from you by now. You wanted to humiliate me in front of my superior."

He cocked his head, watching me as his jaw flexed.

"If you had a concern," I went on, "then you should've come to me, and if that failed, then gone to Shaw. You didn't sign any of the documents I sent home, and you haven't accepted any invitations into the social media groups, proving that you have no interest in Christian's education. This is a farce and a waste of my time."

"And have you contacted me?" he retorted as he rose from his seat, standing within an inch of me and looking down. "When I didn't sign the papers or join the groups, or when he failed the last unit test"—he bared his teeth—"did you e-mail or call me to discuss my son's education?"

"It's not my responsibility to chase you down!" I fought.

"Yeah, it kind of is," he retorted. "Parent communication is part of your job, so let's talk about why you're communicating regularly with Christian's friends' parents but not with me."

"Are you serious?" I nearly laughed, dropping the binder on the chair. "We're not playing some childish 'who's going to call first?' game. This isn't high school!"

"Then stop acting like a brat," he ordered, his minty breath falling across my face. "You know nothing about my interest in my son."

"Interest in your son?" This time my lips spread wide in a smile as I looked up at him. "Don't make me laugh. Does he even know your name?"

His eyes flared and then turned dark.

My throat tightened, and I couldn't swallow. *Shit*. I'd gone too far.

I was close enough to hear the heavy breaths from his nose, and I wasn't sure what he would do if I tried to back away. Not that I felt threatened—physically anyway—but I suddenly felt like I needed space.

His body was flush with mine, and his scent made my eyelids flutter.

His eyes narrowed on me and then fell to my mouth. *Oh, God.*

"Okay, sorry about that." Shaw burst into the office, and Marek and I pulled apart, turning away from each other while the principal twisted around to close the door.

Shit.

I smoothed my hand down my blouse and leaned over, picking up the binder of lesson plans.

We hadn't done anything, but it felt like we had.

Shaw walked around us, and I glanced at Marek to see him glaring ahead, his arms crossed over his chest.

"While Mrs. Vincent practically runs this school," Shaw went on, amusement in his voice, "some things require my signature. So where were we?"

"Edward," Marek interrupted, buttoning his Armani jacket and offering a tight smile. "Unfortunately I have a meeting to get to," he told him. "Ms. Bradbury and I have talked, and she's agreed to adjust her lesson plans to make accommodations for Christian."

Excuse me?

I started to twist my head to shoot him a look, but I stopped, correcting myself. Instead, I clamped my teeth together and lifted my chin, refusing to look at him.

I would *not* be adjusting my lesson plans.

"Oh, wonderful." Shaw smiled, looking relieved. "Thank you, Ms. Bradbury, for compromising. I love it when things work out so easily."

I decided it was best to let the issue lie. What Shaw didn't know wouldn't hurt him, and Marek would most likely zone out of his parenting responsibilities for another few weeks before I would have to deal with him again.

"Ms. Bradbury." Marek turned, holding out a hand for me to shake.

I met his eyes, noticing how one was not quite as wide as the other, giving his expression a sinister look as it pierced me.

Two things could be assumed about Marek: He expected to get everything he wanted, and he thought he just had.

Idiot.

The chilled pint glass was a welcome relief in my hand as I took a sip of the Abita Amber, the local favorite brew. It was mid-September, and the evenings still hadn't cooled down enough to be pleasant. If not for the humidity, the city might feel more comfortable instead of like a stuffy, packed elevator with no room to move.

I fingered through the container on my table, counting all of the sugar packets as I sat at Port of Call, waiting for my brother to join me for dinner.

Seven Equals, six Sweet'N Lows, five regular sugars, and seven Splendas. *What a mess.*

I twisted around, grabbing another container off the table behind me, and picked out what I needed. The little packages crackled as I pulled them out and fit one more Equal, two more Sweet'N Lows, three regular sugars, and one more Splenda into the uneven container on my table.

Leaving the rest in the borrowed container, I replaced it on the table behind me and then recounted all of the packets. Eight, eight, eight, and eight.

Perfect.

I took a deep breath and set the container back along the edge of the table with the condiments and napkins, and . . .

And I stopped, looking up to catch my brother standing at the table with a drink in his hand, watching me.

Shit.

I rolled my eyes and waited for him to sit down.

We hadn't seen each other in four days. I'd offered to help with student council after school this week, and he'd been buried in research and papers.

His white oxford was wrinkled and open at the collar, but he still drew women's eyes as he approached the table. He leaned back in his chair, giving me the eye that said he was thinking and he had things he wasn't sure he should say or how to say them.

"Out with it," I relented, shaking my head and looking at the tabletop.

"I don't know what to say."

I shot my eyes up, tucking in my chair. "Then stop looking at me like I'm Howard Hughes," I ordered. "It's a nondestructive disorder that's very common. It soothes me."

"Nondestructive," he repeated, taking a drink. "Was it five or six times that you went back into your apartment to make sure your stove was off today?"

I shifted, straightening my shoulders as the server came by, setting down waters on our table.

"Well, how am I supposed to remember if I shut it off after cooking the heroin?" I joked, and my brother broke out in a laugh.

I knew he thought my obsessive-compulsive bullshit was baggage that I needed help getting past, but the truth was, it was something I felt I needed.

Ever since I was sixteen anyway.

When someone you trusted steals your sense of security and holds your life in the palm of his hand for two whole years, your mind finds ways to compensate for the loss of control.

I felt safer when things were in order. When I had dominion over even the most trivial of matters.

My entire family—my parents and sister, now gone, and my brother—had paid a hefty price for letting someone we thought we could trust into our lives all those years ago.

In comparison, my little compulsive disorder was of no concern to me.

If I didn't count the sugar packets or make sure the stove was off four times this morning or brush my teeth for a count of one hundred twenty seconds, something bad would happen. I didn't know what, and I knew it was ridiculous, but I still felt safer carrying on with my day.

Normally, during work, when I was busy, it didn't concern me as much, but when I was idle—like now—I tended to fiddle, arrange, and count.

It was a false sense of security, but it was something.

Control over anything, even if it couldn't be everything, calmed me.

"So how's school?" he asked.

I leaned my elbows on the table and took a sip of beer. "It's pretty good. I like the kids."

The kids were actually the easy part. Keeping their attention was hard and energy-consuming, but keeping up with all of the side duties was more frustrating and a huge time suck.

"You look tired," he commented.

"So do you," I shot back, smiling. "Don't worry. I'm fine, Jack. I'm on my feet all day, and by end time I've hit the wall, but it's a good kind of exhausted."

"Like tennis?"

I paused, thinking about that one.

"Kind of," I answered. "Only better, I guess. I used to feel like I went out there on the court and gave my all. I used every muscle and every ounce of perseverance to fight through the struggle."

"And now?" he pressed.

"And now I do the same thing, but I know why," I answered. "There's a reason for all of it."

He watched me, a thoughtful look crossing his face. He seemed to buy what I told him, and why shouldn't he? It was true.

Tennis had been my life. It was fun at times and nearly unbearable at others, and while I hadn't known what the purpose of working and competing were, I went to bed with the satisfaction that I'd pushed my body to the limit and fought hard.

But I also never felt compelled to do it.

"Avery would be proud," Jack said in a low voice, giving me a small smile.

I looked away, sadness twisting my stomach.

Would she? Would my sister be proud that I was living her dream?

FIVE

TYLER

"So did you deal with it?" Jay asked about Christian's teacher as he trailed behind me with his face buried in a press packet for next Monday's television interview.

I pushed through my office doors, seeing Corinne, my assistant, pouring water into glasses around the conference table off to the left in preparation for our meeting this morning.

"Of course," I mumbled, rounding my desk and unbuttoning my jacket.

"Well, you canceled a TV spot for that meeting. You can't do that again," he warned.

I cocked an eyebrow and ignored him, looking over his shoulder to Corinne and mouthing, *Coffee*.

She nodded and left the room.

I let out a breath and focused on the computer screen, checking my messages. "I didn't ask for the TV spot to begin with," I reminded him. "I'm not even running for senator yet. Officially, anyway," I added. "Don't you think we're jumping the gun?"

"Tyler, that's what I need to talk to you about." His tone sounded annoyed. "You won't win anything until you step up the schmoozing. The reason campaigns have funds is because they run off donations."

I shook my head, glancing over my schedule for the day. "I don't like donations." I felt like I had to repeat that on a daily basis for him.

"Yes, I understand that. Believe me," he said, sounding even more annoyed, "I'm well aware of your feelings on the subject."

I didn't need help funding my campaign. I'd built the fifth-largest media company in the South, with interests in television, Internet, and communication. Then I'd sold it and started all over from the ground up, building one of the top-ten-largest construction companies in the world.

It wasn't that I'd disliked the media world. I'd hated it.

I'd thought that media would be a great place to network and be visible for my political aspirations, but making something that you couldn't touch felt empty.

I realized I didn't need to wait to get into office to make positive change. I could start now.

So once I'd felt satisfied that I'd taken the company as far as I could on my own, I'd handed it over, and now I built fleets of things I could touch. Towers, homes, skyscrapers, ships, and even the equipment that built these things. I produced something, and better yet, it was something people needed. Something that gave people jobs.

I owned the sixty-story building that housed my office, more real estate than I knew what to do with, and I certainly didn't need handouts from people who wanted to have a politician in their pocket.

I had accomplished my successes on my own, and I'd get the Senate on my own.

But my brother had different ideas.

"Tyler, let me explain something." He dropped his binder on the chair and planted his hands on my desk, leaning down. "When you're not vying for donations, you're also not vying for support. When Blackwell got a two-million-dollar donation, he also got their endorsement . . ." He explained it as if I were a child.

"He got the votes of everyone in that organization," he went on. "And their friends. And *their* friends," he added. "Donations aren't just about money. They're about other people putting their confidence in you. They'll publicly endorse you, because they have a stake in your success when you have their cash."

"Exactly." I nodded, the chip still weighing on my shoulder. "I'm not here to play chess with these people and be their pawn."

I twisted around, picking up an article I'd cut out from the table next to the window. "Look at this," I shot out, holding up the clipping. "Senator McCoy here cut funding for after-school programs to reroute the money from the state to the city parks in Denver," I explained. "However, the city parks don't show that money in their quarterly budget. So where'd the money go?"

The question was rhetorical, so I didn't wait for an answer. I dropped the clipping and grabbed the new printout I'd gotten off the Internet last night.

"And then this guy," I started, taunting my brother. "Representative Kelley wants to cut funding to women's clinics, because 'why do women need a separate doctor from men?'" I quoted him from the article and then looked to my brother, scowling. "This genius thinks both genders have the same reproductive system, and yet he gets to vote on legislation that determines medical treatment for women."

I started laughing, seeing my brother close his eyes and shake his head.

"This is why I'm running, Jay," I stated. "Not so I can be a contender in a popularity contest of who's got the most fucking friends."

"Oh, fuck you, Tyler." He groaned, running his hand through his hair and standing up. "I'm going for a drink, and tomorrow I am rebuilding you from the ground up."

And then he turned, making his way out of my office.

A drink?

I looked down at my watch. "It's eleven o'clock in the morning!" I argued.

"It's New Orleans," he deadpanned, as if that explained everything.

"And another thing . . ." He spun around, walking backward for the door. "Start being seen with a woman in public."

At that point I pursed my lips, pretty sick of all of his orders. "I thought you said me being single appealed to the 'single woman vote,'" I gritted out.

"Yeah, single. Not celibate," he retorted. "You look gay."

And then he turned around again, disappearing out the door.

I rubbed my hand down my face, feeling the back of my neck break out in a sweat.

Jesus Christ. Why was this so complicated?

Why was *everything* so complicated?

I didn't want the Senate handed to me on a silver platter—I'd planned to work, and I was proud of my platform—but these fucking games . . . who I dated, what I wore, orchestrating fake photo ops with my kid, who happened to hate me, just so we appeared to have a close family . . . All of it was bullshit.

I knew CEOs who wrote off prostitutes on their taxes, politicians whose kids were on drugs, and civil projects funded by gangsters. All of these people put on masks to offer a clean, well-put-together appearance that was nothing but a complete lie.

I wanted the job, but I didn't like pretending I was something I wasn't, and I didn't want to lose my freedom.

There was nothing wrong with me. I shouldn't have to change.

I picked up the coffee Corinne had set on my desk and walked over to the wall of windows, staring out at the city.

My city.

The mighty Mississippi sat like the breath of life not far in the distance, busy with its fleets of cargo ships and tugboats as it calmly flowed past the convention center, St. Louis Cathedral, and the French Market.

I sipped the black coffee, strong and bitter the way I liked it, and noticed the storm clouds in the distance, rolling in from south of the river.

My city.

Life existed in every inch of it. Between the flowers and moss that popped out of the concrete sidewalk slabs, the chipped paint decorating the shops on Magazine Street, and the musicians strumming their guitars in the Quarter, there was so much I never wanted to change.

And so much I did.

That's why I wanted to be in a position to give back and effect change in this city.

But I didn't want to play by Jay's rules. There were sides of me that I certainly didn't want in the spotlight but that I didn't want to hide either.

Like the part of me that had wanted to keep fighting her yesterday.

I narrowed my eyes, staring off out the windows.

I hadn't meant to come off as such a dick, but she'd made me nervous. She wasn't exactly approachable—not anymore, anyway—and her disdain was thick from the moment she'd walked into the room and seen me.

She acted like she hated me, and I wasn't sure why I cared.

After Christian had been bugging me time and again about the damn phone, I'd finally had enough and decided, on a whim, to go in and deal with it. I'd intended to make an appointment, but then Shaw—who I'd gathered at the open house was a major kiss-ass—insisted on handling it now to appease me.

I'd waited, and when she'd walked into the room, her long brown hair spilling around her, I could barely handle it.

All I could remember was that same rich hair cascading down the smooth skin of her back as I followed her out to the balcony that night.

God, she was beautiful.

I didn't care that we were fighting this morning, or that she looked furious with me. She was passionate, and if we'd been in my office instead, that meeting would've ended differently.

I glanced over at my black leather couch, imagining what she would look like on it.

She wouldn't be easy.

In fact, I had a strange feeling it would be like high school, and I'd feel like I'd scored if I just got my hand up her shirt.

But that was wishful thinking. I couldn't touch her.

Not that she wouldn't try to resist me anyway—the dynamics of our relationship had changed—but there was no way I could risk hurting my son or thwarting my ambitions.

Tyler Marek Seduces Son's High School Teacher.

Yeah, the headlines would sink me, and Jay would have a meltdown.

Brynne, Christian's mother, would cut me off from my son, and Christian would never forgive me. Our relationship was already teetering on the edge, and he only needed an excuse.

So why didn't knowing any of that make her less desirable?

I opened the oven, grabbing the pot holder and taking the plate out of the warmer. Mrs. Giroux, the housekeeper, had been great about picking up cooking as one of her duties since Christian had come to live here. She had meals waiting for us daily, but even though I tried not to, I did miss dinner once in a while.

Christian and I had eaten together probably five times in the last three weeks. On occasion it was my fault. Something popped up, or I'd been running late, but more times than not Christian avoided me.

He spent time with friends, choosing to eat at their house, or he'd scarf down his dinner before I got home. He was about as distant as his teacher.

I made my way down the marble hallway, carrying my plate, napkin, and a bottle of beer, past the columns to my office, but I stopped, hearing laughter coming from the media room.

"No, dude!" someone shouted while another kid laughed. "Look at these pictures! We should print those."

I narrowed my eyes, turning to the right and inching toward the room.

"Shit. Vince just tweeted," I heard Christian say. "Aw, that's sick! I wonder if this house is still around. Get on Google Earth."

My mouth tilted in a smile, hearing his excitement. Google Earth? Well, at least it wasn't porn.

I set the food down on the small table next to the double wooden doors leading to the room and pushed a door open, peering inside.

"Hey," I said, seeing my son and two friends sprawled out on the carpeted floor instead of using the recliners in the room. They all had their laptops in front of them and looked completely engaged in whatever they were doing.

Christian's eyes flashed to me, but then he focused back down on his laptop, brushing me off. "Hey," he mumbled, having lost his smile.

The other two were munching and working, and I stepped into the room, loosening my tie and taking off my jacket.

"Did you eat?" I asked, making my way to the center of the room.

Christian didn't look at me, only gestured to the pizza boxes on the floor before resuming his work on the computer.

I sighed, rubbing my jaw in frustration.

Christian was an only child, his mother having chosen not to have any more with her husband. As I'd worked and built my legacy over the past decade, I'd always assumed I'd have more kids eventually.

When I found the right woman.

It was the natural progression and how we marked our lives,

after all. Go to college, begin a career, marry, and have children. I hadn't wanted to be a father at twenty, but I wanted to be one now.

But how successful would I be if the kid I already had never stopped hating me?

"What are you guys up to?" I pushed, walking around behind Christian and taking a look at his screen.

"Just schoolwork," he answered, scrolling through pictures.

"Pirate's Alley?" I slowly inched in, recognizing the colors of the buildings and the Old Absinthe House sign in the photo.

"Have you ever been there, Christian?" I asked, looking down at the top of his head. One of his legs bent in toward his body, and the other lay straight out on the side of the laptop.

"Yeah." His voice sounded clipped as he reached for his friend's phone and started tweeting.

I studied the screen, seeing that he was on the Internet. I didn't know much about Pinterest, but it seemed to be a popular site. It looked like he was doing schoolwork, though.

"So what's the assignment?" I demanded, my own tone turning harder.

"Ms. Bradbury posted a scavenger hunt for extra credit today," he bit out. "We're mapping points of interest during the eighteen hundreds. Whoever is first, wins, okay?"

I could see the muscles in his jaw flex in anger, reminding me that my son was growing into a man with a fight of his own.

"She assigned this today?" I asked, trying to stay calm even though I knew the answer.

After I'd told her specifically that my son would not be allowed on social media for homework.

He had his phone after his schoolwork and on weekends, but clearly he was still able to get online and borrow friends' phones.

Christian shook his head and tossed his friend's phone back at him.

"No, right there." His friend leaned over and pointed out a pic on the screen, referencing the map on his phone. “This one’s on the corner of Ursuline.”

And I was forgotten.

But I’d barely noticed anyway, my jaw hardening at the mention of Ms. Bradbury and her foolish determination to continue to piss me off.

I yanked at my tie as I walked out of the room, and ignored the food I’d left on the table.

SIX

EASTON

I leaped to the right, landing on my left foot as I held the racket with both hands and slammed the tennis ball back across the court. Popping back upright, I raced to the center again, oxygen rushing in and out of my lungs as I bounced on my feet.

The next shot fired out of the ball machine low and high, and I lurched my arm back, taking the racket over my head and swinging hard, sending the ball straight for the ground and out of bounds on the other side of the net.

Shit.

I ran my sandpaper tongue over my lips, desperate for water from all of the exertion as I ran frontward, backward, and left to right, trying to keep up with the speed, trajectory, and spin I'd programmed into the machine.

I'd clearly overestimated the shape I was in.

Sure, I exercised. I ran and used my own small equipment to do strength training at my apartment, but tennis required muscles I rarely used anymore.

Every six months or so, I'd start to miss the game, the new challenge that every serve would offer, and I'd use my membership to access the pristine private courts at the gym.

I never played anyone, though. I hadn't played with a partner since the first round of Wimbledon, July second, five years ago, shortly before I moved to New Orleans with my brother. That was the day I'd gotten a code violation, a default on match point, and so, with no hope of winning, I'd walked off the court before the game was officially over and never returned to competitive tennis again.

My brother had tried comforting me, telling me that I couldn't expect to get my head in the game after what we'd been through earlier that summer. It had been a hard time.

Hell, it had been a hard two years prior to that, but it was still a moment I wished I could go back and change. My last match on a professional court had been my worst, and it was the only thing in my life I was ashamed of.

I'd behaved like a brat, and despite everything I'd accomplished up until that point, that's how people remembered the old Easton Bradbury.

But I would make damn sure that this Easton Bradbury never made that same mistake.

It was strange how something that felt like second nature at one time now felt so foreign. I used to do this every day. I'd wake up at five o'clock in the morning, eat a light breakfast or drink a protein shake, put on my gear, and hit the court for five hours.

In between I'd do my home study and eat, and then I'd go back out for either more practice or another workout.

At night I'd ice sore joints and muscles and read before bed.

I didn't go to school, I didn't go to parties, and I didn't have friends. That's probably why Jack was my BFF.

I grunted, feeling the ache in my grip as I squeezed the racket and backhanded the next tennis ball, sending it over the damn baseline.

"Damn it," I mumbled, pulling to a stop as I put my hands on my hips and dropped my head. "Shit."

I dug the remote out of the waistband of my tennis skirt and pointed it at the ball machine, powering it down just as a ball came flying toward me.

I ducked and then twisted my head in the other direction, hearing a car honk behind me.

Jack sat in his Jeep Wrangler laughing at me as "Untraveled Road" by Thousand Foot Krutch blared from his car.

I rolled my eyes and walked for the gate, handing the remote to the attendant and grabbing my gym bag. I tossed my towel into a bin before swerving around the fence and down the sidewalk.

"You only caught the end of that," I protested, climbing into the passenger seat. "I was hitting balls like crazy."

He smiled to himself, shifting into gear and pulling away from the curb. "You know you could play with me, right?"

I snorted. "No offense, but I want to be challenged, Jack."

His chest shook with laughter. "Brat."

I smiled and dug my phone out of my duffel before stuffing the bag onto the floor between my legs.

Jack had actually been a great sparring partner when I was younger. He'd even competed before it became obvious at an early age that it just wasn't a passion for him.

When my parents noticed that I was more interested and a lot more pliable, they let him off the hook and nurtured me. I never understood why it was so important for one of us to be competing at a high level in a sport, but I basically just wrote it off as a desire for them to be in the limelight and live vicariously, both of them amateur athletes in their day.

"You only come out here sporadically, and you always want to be alone," Jack commented, turning onto St. Charles and traveling past Tulane, heading toward the Garden District. "It's like you're forcing yourself to do something you don't want to do. As if you still feel obligated to play."

Spills of gold fell across my lap from the sunlight peeking through the trees overhead, and I checked my e-mail as I tried to ignore Jack's constant invasiveness.

He'd been like this since that summer five years ago, but I thought once I'd graduated college, he'd refocus more on himself.

"Easton?" my brother pressed.

My eyelids fluttered in annoyance, and I scrolled through messages, forgetting my brother as soon as I saw one from Tyler Marek.

I swallowed the thickness in my throat, my eyes moving over his name and trying to ignore the strange hunger that filled my stomach at the enticing thought of an interaction with him.

"Easton?" Jack pushed again, his voice sounding annoyed.

"Jack, just put a cork in it," I barked, clicking on the e-mail and reading Marek's message.

Dear Ms. Bradbury,

I was under the impression that we'd handled this.

While I understand you are a trained professional, there are certain things I will allow and certain things I will not. My expectations for my son's education follow the state standards, and I suggest you find a way to do your job—like all the other teachers in that school—that does not increase the burden on families more than the tuition we already pay. In the future, I expect the following:

1. My son is NOT permitted on social media for homework. I encourage an atmosphere free of distractions, so I demand work where this is not required. No argument.

2. I will be notified BEFORE anything less than an A for an assignment is entered into his final grades.

3. The rubrics for the presentation grades don't make sense. The presentations happen in school and are not something I can see, assess, or help him with. Performance assignments should not be graded.

4. Observing more experienced professionals in your field may yield a better understanding of student learning. If you'd like, I'd be happy to suggest to Principal Shaw that you shadow more adept teachers.

I trust that we will not have any other problems and you'll prepare accordingly. My son will NOT be bringing his phone to class in the future. If you have any concerns, please contact my office anytime for an appointment.

Sincerely,
Tyler Marek

Silvery shots of pain ran through my jaw, and I realized I was clenching my teeth and not breathing.

I closed my eyes, drawing in a long, hot breath.

Son of a bitch.

I dropped my head back. "Ugh!" I growled, slamming my fists down on my thighs.

"Whoa," I heard Jack say to my left. "What's wrong?"

I shook my head, seething. "A burden on families," I bit out, barely unlocking my teeth. "This asshole is a millionaire, and social networking is free! What the hell is he talking about?" I shouted at my brother. "Son of a . . . !"

"What the hell happened, Easton?" he demanded again, this time louder as he swerved and then righted the steering wheel. A streetcar passed us on the left, its bell dinging.

I ignored him and looked down, scrolling through my phone.

I'd programmed in parents' home and work numbers the first week, so I clicked on Marek's and found his cell phone number.

It was a Saturday, so I was guessing he wasn't at work. I refused to e-mail back. I wanted this dealt with now.

"Easton, what are you doing?" I could see my brother working the wheel nervously and glancing at me.

I shook my head, laughing to myself. "Shadow more adept teachers," I mocked, repeating his e-mail in a fake masculine voice as I looked to my brother with the phone ringing in my ear.

"I have to take time out of my hectic day to notify him personally every time his little prince gets a B?" I continued, complaining. "And why? So he can threaten me into not entering the grade?"

"Did a parent e-mail you?" he asked, slowly putting the pieces together.

I nodded. "Yeah. He expects and demands that I make changes, because he has a hang-up about my methods. Arrogant, entitled—" I stopped myself before my temper got away from me.

When there was no answer, I pulled the phone away from my ear and ended the call, clicking on his work number next. For men like him, the office never really closed. Perhaps he had a receptionist who could make an appointment.

The phone rang twice, and then I heard a click as someone answered.

"Good morning. Tyler Marek's office," a woman's pleasant voice chirped. "How can I help you?"

My heart pounded in my ears, and I could feel the pulse in my neck throb. I held back, almost wishing he wasn't in his office after all.

I needed time to calm down.

But I swallowed and pushed forward anyway. "Yes, hello," I rushed out.

"Easton, keep your cool," I heard my brother warn from my side.

I bit my lip to keep the anger out of my voice. "I'm Easton Bradbury calling for Mr. Marek," I told her. "I'm sure he's not in today, but—"

"Just a moment, please," she interrupted, and disappeared.

I sucked in a breath, realizing that he was in after all.

"Marek?" my brother asked. "Tyler Marek?"

I glanced at him, arching an eyebrow in annoyance.

"Easton, get off the call," Jack ordered.

His arm shot out, trying to grab the phone, but I slapped his hand away.

"Watch the road!" I barked, pointing at the street ahead.

"Easton, I'm serious," he growled. "Tyler Marek has a workforce of more than ten thousand people. He may be a senator, for crying out loud. It isn't your place to argue with him."

I shot him a look. *My place?*

My brother was worried about his career, but I didn't care who Marek was. He was still a man.

Nothing but a man.

"Ms. Bradbury."

I turned my head away from my brother, suddenly hearing Marek's voice in my ear.

Thick anticipation filled my chest, and I dropped my eyes, disappointed that I was actually excited.

"Mr. Marek," I replied curtly, remembering why I had called. "I received your e-mail, and I'd love to . . ." I trailed off, wiping the sweat off my hairline. "I'd love to schedule a meeting to sit down and work out a plan for Christian."

"We've already met," he pointed out, his voice clipped. "And it was not a productive use of my time, Ms. Bradbury."

I tried reasoning. "Mr. Marek, we both want what's best for your son. If we work together—"

"Ms. Bradbury." He cut me off, and I could hear people talking in the background. "Apparently I wasn't clear enough in my e-mail, so let me save us both some time. My son has no problems with any other teacher, so it goes without saying that *you're* the problem." His stern voice cut me, and I felt like shrinking. "You suffer from an overindulged sense of entitlement, and you forget that your job is on a yearly contract."

My eyes widened, taking in his threat that my job this year could belong to someone else next year. I fisted the hem of the skirt at my thigh.

"Now, I'm a busy man," he continued, sounding condescending, "and I don't have time for silly young women who don't know their place."

My skin stung from where my fingernail dug in. His son didn't have problems with me. Perhaps I graded harder than other teachers, and I might have had unorthodox methods, but most of the students enjoyed my class, including Christian. When he participated. If he ever challenged me, it was because his father wouldn't allow him the freedom to have the tools to participate like all the other students.

"Now, can I get on with my day and consider this issue settled?" he sniped.

Heat spread over my skin, and I bared my teeth. "You can go to hell," I shot back, raging. "No wonder he can't stand you."

"Easton!" Jack burst out next to me.

But it was too late.

My eyes widened, and my hand tingled, nearly losing my grip on the phone.

What the hell did I just say?

I opened my mouth, unsure of what to say. *I didn't just say that to a parent.*

I did *not* say that to a parent.

There was only silence on the other end of the line, and I squeezed my eyes shut, trying to find the words.

"Mr. Marek," I inched out in a softer voice. "I'm sorry. I—"

But then I heard a *click*, and the line went dead.

"Shit!" I cried, bringing the phone away from my ear and seeing CALL ENDED on the screen.

"He hung up." I looked at my brother. "I'm screwed."

Jack shook his head at me, his lips tight, clearly furious with me. He swerved to the left and downshifted, taking a sharp turn onto Poydras.

"Where are you going?" I asked, thoughts of Marek calling Shaw right now running through my head.

Insulting a parent wasn't good.

"To his office," he answered, his tone unusually defiant. "You're going to go apologize before he has a chance to file a complaint."

To his office?

"I . . . I," I stammered. "No!" I yelled. "No. Absolutely not! I can't talk to him right now."

But my brother didn't say anything. He just kept driving.

I put my hand to my forehead, panicking. "I can't believe I just said that. What was I thinking?"

"You weren't thinking," he retorted. "And you're going to go beg for forgiveness."

I shook my head. "Jack, it's completely inappropriate," I pleaded with him. "Please. I'm not dressed right."

But he ignored me again, speeding into the Central Business District and closer to Marek's office.

I looked down at my navy blue and white pin-striped tennis skirt with pleated ruffles on the back. It barely hit halfway down my thighs.

My peach-colored shirt was long-sleeved, but it was skintight, serving the purpose of absorbing my sweat but definitely not my humiliation.

I closed my eyes, groaning. I couldn't be less armed for a meeting with him.

Jack dropped me off in front of the building while he went to park in a garage. I stood out on the front sidewalk and tipped my head all the way back, scowling up at his building.

Big silver letters were posted on the front, spelling MAREK, the candy-apple-red glow behind the name reminding me of the dress I was wearing when I'd first met him.

The whole building was his?

I closed my eyes and took a deep breath, forcing the muscles in my face to relax.

Heading inside, I approached one of the check-in stations. I peered to the right and saw security running people through metal detectors.

Placing my palms down on the cool black granite counter, I forced a small smile. "Hello, I . . ." I hesitated, my nerves firing. "I needed to speak with Tyler Marek. If he's in," I added.

"What's your name, miss?" the young man asked, picking up his phone.

"Easton," I breathed out, willing my heart to slow down. "Easton Bradbury."

He waited, then finally spoke into the phone. "Hello. I have Easton Bradbury to see Mr. Marek."

"I don't have an appointment," I pointed out, whispering to him.

He offered a placating smile and waited for what the other person had to say.

He nodded. "Thank you," he told them.

Hanging up the phone, he typed something into the computer quickly, and before I knew it, he handed me a badge with a bar code and pointed me toward the elevators.

"He'll see you," he said, nodding. "It's the sixtieth floor."

"Which office?" I asked.

But he just laughed and continued to shuffle papers without looking at me.

I let out a sigh and made my way through security, letting them scan my card and push me through.

I took the elevator up, making several stops on the way for others to get off.

We stopped at three odd-numbered floors and three even-numbered floors, and I pursed my lips, knowing that didn't mean anything, but it still made me uncomfortable.

If we had stopped at *two* odd-numbered floors instead, the odds would've added up to an even number, and everything would've been fine.

I rolled my eyes, shaking my head. *God, I am sick.*

The only person left in the elevator, I watched the blue digital numbers reach sixty.

I straightened, steeling myself as the doors opened.

And I understood why the clerk had laughed at me when I'd asked *which office*. The sixtieth floor *was* Marek's office, apparently.

Ahead stood two tall wooden doors and desks belonging to two assistants on either side of the doors, one man and one woman.

The woman looked up from her computer and nodded toward the doors. "Go in, Ms. Bradbury."

I ran my hand down my clothes, smoothing them over before reaching up and tightening my ponytail.

But I'd already lost hope of salvaging my pride. Why hadn't I at least convinced Jack to take me home for a change of clothes?

Grabbing hold of a vertical bar serving as a door handle, I pulled one of the big doors open and stepped in, immediately spotting Marek ahead of me, standing behind his desk.

"Ms. Bradbury." He glanced up, one hand in his pocket as the other pushed keys on his computer. "Come in."

His eyes left mine and dropped down my body, taking in my

appearance, I would assume. Despite the air-conditioning chilling the room, I felt my thighs warm and heat pool in my stomach.

I squared my shoulders and approached his desk, trying to ignore the sudden powerless feeling.

Out of habit, I counted my steps in my head. *One, two, three, fo—*

But then I stopped in my tracks, catching something out of the corner of my eye.

I looked to my right, and my eyebrows shot up, seeing an oval conference table on the other side of a glass partition, filled with people. A lot of people.

Shit.

I swallowed, turning for the doors again. "I'll wait."

There was no way I was speaking to him with other people in the room.

"You wanted to see me," he snapped. "Speak."

I turned. "But you're busy."

"I'm always busy," he retorted. "Get on with it."

I groaned inwardly, understanding why he was so open to seeing me now.

A weight settled in my stomach, but I hid it as well as I could as I stepped toward his desk again.

I kept my voice low and gave him a fake close-lipped smile. "You're enjoying seeing my dignity as a muddy puddle on the floor, aren't you?"

The corner of his mouth lifted, and he locked eyes with me again. "I think that's understandable after your behavior, don't you?"

I averted my eyes, licking my lips.

I hated his gloating, but I couldn't say he was wrong. I'd earned this dose of humility. No matter how vile his e-mail was, I should never have lowered myself to his level. The animosity would only hurt Christian.

"Mr. Marek." I took a deep breath, bracing myself. "I had no right to say what I said," I told him. "And I was very wrong. I know nothing about you or your son, and I lashed out."

"Like a brat," he added, staring at me with condescension.

Yes, like a brat.

I dropped my eyes, remembering how I'd never gotten angry as a child. When I started to become a woman, though, I raced to fury, throwing my racket when I'd fault or yelling when I was frustrated.

I'd been under stress at the time, I'd been caged, and I'd hated the loss of control. Now I had control, and I resented anything that threatened it.

Marek kept pushing into my space—the meeting the other day and then the e-mail today—but I knew my job.

I knew what I was doing. Why didn't he see that?

I raised my eyes, staring back up at him. "I truly apologize."

"Are you really sorry?" He grabbed a gray file folder and a pen as he rounded the desk. "Or are you more afraid you'll lose your job?"

I narrowed my eyes. "You're insinuating I'm apologizing out of fear?"

He cocked his head, telling me with his amused eyes that's exactly what he was thinking.

"Mr. Marek," I said in a firm voice, standing tall. "I don't do things I don't want to do. I don't need to beg for anything or bow down to anyone. If I apologize, it's because I know I did something wrong," I affirmed. "It was a cruel thing to say, and you didn't deserve it."

A hint of a smile peeked out, but he hid it almost immediately. He let out a sigh, his eyes softening, and he turned around, making his way for the head of the conference table.

"Ms. Bradbury is Christian's history teacher," he pointed out to everyone at the table, looking back at me and grinning as he tossed the folder onto the table. "She doesn't think much of me."

I snorted, but I didn't think anyone heard it.

The man seated to his left laughed. "You're not alone, honey." He tipped his chin at me.

Marek grabbed a piece of paper, balled it up, and threw it at him, only making the man laugh more.

The two seemed close, and I faltered at seeing Marek playful.

"I'm Jay, his brother." The man rose from his chair and held out his hand.

I hesitated for only a moment before walking to the other half of the room and up the step to the table.

The office was massive, but it was partitioned by what had to be a ten-foot-long pane of glass separating—but not closing off—the room into two parts: Marek's office and a private conference area, probably for his convenience.

After all, why go down to another floor and meet with your personnel when you could make them all come up to you?

I shook Jay's hand, at once liking his easy smile and humor. I couldn't help but glance over, seeing Marek watching me.

His navy blue suit went well with the steel-gray walls, and I liked how some of his black hair had fallen out of place over his temple.

Everyone at the table—men and women—were dressed in business attire, and they looked like they'd been here a while. Papers, laptops, and phones were spread over the table in no discernible order, and I had to push away the pinpricks under my skin, urging me to organize their shit.

Plates with croissants and bagels were scattered about, while half-filled glasses of water sweated with condensation, their ice cubes having long since melted.

I wondered how long they'd been here. On a Saturday, no less.

"You don't have to worry, Easton. We're fine," I heard Marek say, and I shot my eyes back over to him. "Apology accepted, but my e-mail does still stand."

I rubbed my thumbs across my fingers, trying to remember what he was referring to.

He'd called me Easton.

"I'm against a fourteen-year-old on social media, and I can't imagine I'm the only parent uncomfortable with it." His tone was firm but gentler than it had been on the phone. "Adjustments will have to be made."

Ah, back to this.

I kept my face even, about to suggest again that we sit down and talk through this, because I wasn't giving up, but someone else spoke up first.

"Social media?" a man to my right asked. "Jesus, Facebook has taken over my kids' lives. It's all they do," he blurted out, chiming in on the conversation and looking around to his colleagues. "You know, my sixteen-year-old actually wants a mount in the shower with waterproof casing for his phone. I'm surprised he hasn't glued it to his hand."

I hooded my eyes, focusing on a spot on the table and hearing laughter sound off around me as everyone started backing Marek up.

"It's an epidemic," a woman agreed. "And dangerous. Do you know how many sexual predators find their victims online?"

Do you know how many victims of sexual predators drink water? Ban water!

Grunts of approval chimed in, and I could feel myself losing the moment of relief I'd felt when he'd accepted my apology.

My fists tightened, and I knew I needed to leave. Now.

"Exactly," someone else replied. "The more we put ourselves out there, the more disconnected we are from real life. I'm sick of seeing people's faces buried in their phones."

"Complete time suckage." Jay shook his head, speaking up. "And kids have no attention spans anymore because of it."

I no longer liked Jay.

I glanced at Marek, who watched me with a hint of a smile on his face as the wall against me grew higher and higher.

"And there are so many stories where kids are getting bullied," another gentleman droned, "or put in danger because of it. I mean, has being able to Instagram what you had for lunch really made our lives better?"

Everyone started laughing, and every muscle in my body tensed like steel.

"Kids don't need social media," someone maintained. "Not until they're old enough . . ."

Yada, yada, yada . . . I stopped listening. Everyone continued sharing their own two cents, but I just stood there looking at him.

He held my eyes, his mouth opening slightly as he raised the glass to his lips and took a small drink of water. He leaned back in his chair, relaxed and confident, because he knew he'd gotten what he wanted.

He still didn't see me as a capable woman. He still didn't respect me.

And when his eyes started falling down my body, raking over my waist and down to my bare thighs, I knew that he wanted something else.

The only thing he thought I was good for.

I inhaled a sharp breath and held up my hands, cutting everyone off in the middle of their rants. "You're absolutely right," I told them, my voice hard. "You're all absolutely right."

I offered a tight smile and looked around the table, everyone having gone quiet.

"Social media is a double-edged sword, bringing both advantages and"—I looked at Marek—"definite concerns. I agree with you," I placated.

Marek cocked his head, looking at me with interest as everyone gave me their full attention.

"However," I stated matter-of-factly, "it is here to stay. Whether you like it or not," I added.

I lifted my chin and let my eyes wander around the table as I began to circle. "We live in a data-driven world, and it is not something that will change."

I walked slowly around the table, speaking to everyone and feeling Marek's eyes on me.

"Let me break this down for you," I told them, crossing my arms over my chest and speaking slowly. "Every time we get a text or a tweet or a Facebook notification," I explained, "we get a shot of adrenaline. The constant influx of information has become an addiction—like a drug—and when our phones beep or light up, we get a small rush."

I met their eyes.

"And like all drugs, it isn't long before we need our next fix." And I gestured to their phones on the table as I spoke. "Which is exactly why you all brought your phones into this meeting with you right now instead of leaving them in your own offices," I speculated. "Sooner rather than later, you know you're going to feel that desperation, which will prompt you to check for a new e-mail or message. You're addicted to the information, same as your children."

"But in school?" a woman burst out. "Why should they have phones in school or be allowed to play around on social media for homework?"

"Because you let them have it at home," I shot back, trying to keep my tone gentle. "Do you expect the craving for it to end when they step onto school grounds?"

She twisted her lips and sat back in her chair.

"How does a teacher compete with the kind of hold social media has over his or her students' attention?" I asked them. "Because even if they're forced to be without their phones, they're thinking about their phones. They're hiding them. They're texting under their desks. They're sneaking to the bathroom to use them . . ." I trailed off, hopefully proving that the battle was real.

"I have two choices," I continued. "I can either fight it and treat it as a nuisance, or . . ." I calmed down, looking at Marek. "I can embrace it as a tool. Not only is their technology ensuring one hundred percent participation in my class," I pointed out, "but it is also teaching them community and digital citizenship."

I lowered my chin, pinning him with a hard look. "They do not merely attend a class, Mr. Marek," I explained, seeing his eyes narrow on me. "They interact with one another on multiple forums, seeing through social barriers and expressing themselves in the tolerant community that I oversee. They're learning, they're engaged, and they're treating one another well."

I moved around to his other side, standing more confidently than I had since the open house.

"Now, I understand you're a smart man," I went on, "and you couldn't have gotten where you are without being determined and intelligent. But I also think that you do whatever you want and say whatever you like without fear of accountability. I always have a very good reason for everything I do. Do you?

"Don't tell me how to do my job," I advised, "and I won't be so arrogant as to tell you how to do yours."

And before anyone had a chance to speak, I twisted on my heel and walked out.

SEVEN

EASTON

"What will you do with the textbooks?" I asked the librarian as I unloaded the old history books I'd been storing in my classroom.

She grabbed the stack and started pulling them off her counter, one by one, to load onto a cart.

"I think they'll be donated," she answered. "Although I hear you don't even use the new fancy ones we paid good money for."

I smiled, bending down to my rolling chair to pick up another four books to hand to her.

"Not that I don't appreciate them," I teased, and she shot me a wink.

If anyone had a problem with me not teaching from the textbook, it certainly wasn't her. She had been teaching in Orleans Parish for more than thirty years and had been in all types of schools, from the advantaged to the destitute. She knew how to make do with what you had and had told me the first week that the best teachers were facilitators. The more the kids did for themselves, the more they learned.

"Hey," someone chirped.

I twisted my head, seeing Kristen Meyer pushing her rolling chair toward the checkout desk as well.

"What's up?" She heaved a sigh, sounding out of breath.

"Just getting rid of the old history texts," I told her. "You?"

"Ugh." She unloaded a stack of what looked like typical library books on geology. "Is it winter break yet?" she whined.

I let out a laugh. It wasn't even October yet.

"All right, I've still got a few things to do before I head home for the day. Thanks," I told the librarian, and then looked to Kristen as I leaned down to start pushing my chair back. "Have a good night," I singsonged.

"Wait," she shot out. "I'll come with you."

She hurried, dumping the rest of the books on the counter and pushing her chair, following me out.

I exited through the double doors, moving out of the way and holding one open for her.

The school was quiet—all of the students and many of the teachers having already left for the day—and I breathed in, smelling the rain that I knew was coming. The sky had been dark this morning, heavy with thick clouds, and the current weather filled me with trepidation as the wind in the trees carried the warning of a storm that would, without a doubt, be angry.

A hurricane was in the Caribbean, heading for the Gulf, but as of right now, it wasn't set to hit New Orleans. I hoped we were only looking at a tropical storm, but either way, the school was closing for the next two days in anticipation of flooding.

"So," Kristen drawled as we pushed our chairs on their wheels down the hallway. "I heard something that can't possibly be true."

I kept pushing my chair, our heels echoing in unison down the hall.

"I heard that you"—she spoke slowly—"showed up at Tyler Marek's office this weekend and told him off." I could feel her eyes on me as I looked straight ahead. "And that you were wearing a miniskirt, no less," she added.

"I wasn't wearing a miniskirt," I grumbled. "How the hell did you hear that?"

She squealed, her mouth opening in a gasp. "So it's true?"

I turned away and continued down the hall, squeezing the chair in my fingers.

He'd talked to Shaw, after all?

Shit.

"It's okay," she soothed. "It's just that Myron Cates is one of Marek's vice presidents," she told me. "His wife and I became good friends when I taught her son last year, and she said her husband came home Saturday from work having witnessed a bold young woman serving Tyler Marek his ass on a platter."

She nodded and smiled as if it were an accomplishment.

I looked up at the ceiling, sighing. *Great.* Another parent I'd made a dynamite impression on.

"Are you . . ." she inched out, "like, seeing him?"

I shot her a look. "Excuse me?"

"Marek?" she suggested. "He's certainly handsome. And successful. And . . ." She eyed me, looking thoughtful, "and you're seeing him outside of school hours."

I shook my head. "This conversation is over."

I was not *seeing* him outside of school hours. This was how the simplest things could get twisted around and sooner or later the story doesn't even resemble the truth. Myron Cates's wife and Kristen Meyer were going to have me giving Marek a lap dance on a Mardi Gras float next thing I knew.

"Okay, good," she chirped. "If you're not seeing anyone, then come out with me tonight."

It was Monday, but the students had gotten a surprise two-day vacation due to the storm, so there was no school until Thursday.

"I have plans," I lied.

Even I knew I should've gone out and given it a shot. Kristen was a little annoying, but nice.

I just wasn't a particularly social person, and it had been a long day already.

Maybe another time.

But the next thing I knew, she plopped down on her chair and pushed with her feet, sending herself rolling down the hallway backward and smiling at me.

"Come on," she urged. "Live a little."

I couldn't help but laugh, seeing her sliding down the floor like a carefree child.

"Life moves pretty fast," she stated. "If you don't stop and look around once in a while, you could miss it."

I rolled my eyes. "Okay, Ferris," I joked, recognizing her *Ferris Bueller's Day Off* reference. "I know how to have fun."

She snickered, blowing out a breath. "I don't even think you know how to smile," she taunted.

I gasped in feigned outrage.

Plopping my ass down in my chair, I slipped off my heels and turned like her, pushing off with my foot, one after the other, and scurrying after her.

"I know how to have fun," I boasted, clutching my heels to my chest.

The hem of my navy blue dress rested at my knees, and I pedaled my feet, laughing as I caught up to her.

She picked up the pace, and I stood up, tossing my heels into the seat of the chair as I grabbed the sides of the chair and raced it.

"You can't do that!" she screamed, wide-eyed.

I flew past her, rounding the corner to our classrooms.

"There are no rules!" I shouted over my shoulder.

And then I pushed off, dropping into my chair once again and letting myself sail backward to the finish line. I held up my hands, gloating.

"And let that be a lesson to you." I smiled ahead at her playful scowl.

But then her eyebrows shot up, and her mouth fell open.

I looked over my shoulder and immediately put my feet down on the floor, stopping myself.

"Mr. Marek," I said, looking up at him leaning against the wall next to my classroom door.

What is he doing here?

My chest rose and fell from the exertion, and he tipped his chin down, cocking an eyebrow at me.

I shot up, smoothing my dress down and glancing over at Kristen. I only caught her smirk before she disappeared, pushing her chair into her classroom down the hall.

I turned back to Marek. "Excuse me," I said, feeling heat spread over my cheeks. "We were just . . ."

I trailed off, leaving it there. He knew what we were doing.

His three-piece black pin-striped suit looked crisp and dark against his fair skin, and his white shirt and slate-gray tie shimmered in the glow of the light overhead.

I took a few steps forward. "What are you doing here?" I asked.

His eyes shot down to my feet, and I followed his gaze, remembering that I'd forgotten to put my heels back on.

"Always losing your shoes," he commented, a smile curling his mouth.

I pursed my lips and turned around, snatching my heels off the seat and slipping them back onto my feet. Grabbing the back of the chair, I pulled it behind me and entered my classroom, knowing he'd follow.

"You came to my workplace unannounced," he stated behind me. "I thought I would return the favor."

I replaced my chair behind my desk and looked up, seeing that he had closed the door behind him.

"And?" I prompted.

"And I came to apologize," he admitted, stopping a few feet in front of my desk. "I've been unfair, and I'm sorry. Christian has his phone back, so we'll see how this goes."

I stilled, my heart galloping in my chest, and I almost smiled.

Really?

I opened my mouth but had to swallow the lump before I could speak. "Well, that's great," I said, surprised. "Thank you."

I guess I got through to him at his office.

He slid one of his hands into a pocket and narrowed his eyes on me, looking a little surprised.

"You seem very knowledgeable and determined." His voice sounded genuine. "You're an impressive woman, Ms. Bradbury, and I should've taken the time to understand your methods."

I kept my shoulders squared, but my eyes dropped, embarrassment warming my cheeks.

"Thank you," I mumbled, turning around to grab a dry-erase marker to start writing the schedule on the board for when the kids came back on Thursday.

"Christian talks about your class," he said behind me. "I can tell your teaching interests him, even if he would never admit it."

I uncapped the marker and rested my hand on the board but didn't write anything.

"He really can't stand me, can he?"

I dropped my hand to my side and spun around slowly, surprised by his question.

And feeling terrible all over again. I should never have said that.

No matter how much I thought I knew about him, they were nothing more than assumptions. Who was I to insinuate his son didn't care for him or vice versa? And what gave me the right to say anything at all in the first place?

He breathed deeply, and for the first time since I'd met him, he looked unsure of himself.

"I was twenty when he was born," he told me. "That's no excuse, but it's the only one I have."

Twenty.

I was twenty-three, and I couldn't imagine having a child right now.

I watched him and waited, not wanting to say anything or interrupt because I found I kind of liked it when he talked.

"I know what you think of me." He looked me dead in the eye and then dropped his gaze, speaking in a voice close to a whisper. "And what he thinks of me."

And then he let out a bitter laugh, shaking his head. "I don't know why I even care what you think. You don't give a shit about me, but I guess that's what's so intriguing." He moved forward, his soft eyes turning to steel. "You're so cold and distant," he charged. "I guess I wouldn't think anything of it if I hadn't seen you so different at one time."

I inhaled a shaky breath, looking down at his right hand. The same one that had held my waist while we danced.

I licked my lips, barely noticing him advance.

"You were flirty and fun." His voice turned husky, and I looked up, seeing him round my desk slowly. "And you keep pissing me off, but it feels good," he whispered, playing with me, drawing me in.

I knew that look in his eyes. I may not know much about him, but I knew that look.

And we were in my classroom.

His son's classroom.

I may have had little shame, but he had none.

"Mr.—"

He cut me off. "Why won't you ever say my name?"

I shook my head, confused. "Why do you care what I think?"

"I don't," he maintained. "I care that you don't think of me at all."

I narrowed my eyes on him, clenching my teeth. "That's not . . ." I trailed off, plastering my back against the whiteboard as he hovered over me.

"That's not what?" he pressed, his voice sounding strained.

He stood so close that I had only to lift a hand and I could touch him.

"That's not true," I finished.

He leaned in. "You look at me like I don't matter." His eyes searched mine. "And I don't like it."

"I . . ." I shifted my eyes, avoiding his gaze. "I . . ."

Did I look at him like that?

"The masquerade, Shaw's office, my office . . ." he went on. "You've completely held my attention in any room we've been in together," he admitted. "Whereas you make me feel like I'm not worth your time. How do you do that?"

My body vibrated with his heat, and it was like being with him at that ball all over again. My eyelids fluttered, and I couldn't look at him.

"I . . ." *Fuck, why can't I speak?*

I cleared my throat, forcing my eyes up to his. "I don't mean to be cold." I spoke softly. "You are worth my time." And then I added, "Like all of my students' parents."

He dropped his eyes, speaking softly as well. "It's not often I let people speak to me the way I let you," he confessed. "Nor should I enjoy it as much as I do."

My heart hammered in my chest, and I wanted to tell him all of that was true for me as well. He dominated my attention when he was around, and I felt like he didn't see me or think anything of me.

And even though he pissed me off and riled my temper, I kind of enjoyed it.

In fact, I wanted to run toward it.

"Why you?" he questioned. "Why have I been thinking of you ever since that Mardi Gras ball?"

He pressed his body to mine, and I shook my head slowly.

"Mr. Marek," I pleaded, but it was useless. My eyes fell to his mouth, and then I glanced to my closed door, knowing that even though the students were gone for the day, there might still be staff around. "Please."

"There was something that drew us together that night," he maintained. "Something that got under my skin, something that's still there."

His mouth was an inch from mine, and I breathed hard, needing to push him away, but at the same time, that was the last thing I wanted.

"Easton," he whispered, and reached down behind my thigh, lifting it to press himself closer against me.

I groaned, feeling the ridge of his cock nestle between my legs.

"We can't do this," I told him.

My clothes felt like sandpaper on my skin, and I wanted them off. I wanted his shirt open and to know what he felt like under my fingertips.

"I know," he answered.

But while his left hand held my knee up, his right hand slid between my legs and rubbed my clit through my panties.

I sucked in a sharp breath and clutched his shoulders, letting my eyes fall closed as my head floated away from me.

"Mr. Marek," I begged.

But his breath fell against my mouth, and he whispered, "I told you there would be no stopping me when we finally ran into each other again."

And before I could open my eyes, he'd captured my bottom lip between his teeth and then kissed me, sending me reeling until I didn't know which way was up.

I couldn't fight it. His tongue dove into my mouth as he pressed me against the whiteboard and kissed me hard. I circled my arms around his neck, knowing I was getting myself into a shit ton of trouble, but I didn't care at the moment.

My body needed him. That's all it was.

I wouldn't get involved emotionally—I never did.

He grabbed me underneath both thighs and swung me around, planting my ass on the desk.

I groaned, his mouth working strong and fast over mine, stealing my breath as pleasure swarmed in my chest. It spiraled downward like a cyclone low in my belly.

I tightened my legs around his waist as his fingers slid under my dress, raking down my thighs.

I grabbed the back of his neck, cocking my head and returning every inch of his kiss. He tasted like coffee with vanilla, and I felt a hint of stubble on his face under my fingertips.

Dropping my hands down his body, I started unbuttoning his black vest. It was too thick, and I couldn't feel him.

I pulled my mouth back, then dove back in to flick his tongue with mine.

"Jesus Christ," he groaned, eating me up with quick kisses and nibbles. "Why does it have to be you, huh?"

I fumbled with the last button and finally tore open the vest, running my hands up his stomach and chest, covered only by his fine white dress shirt.

But even through the shirt, I felt the dips of his abs and pecs and of his toned waist and back.

Something screeched to my right, and I twisted my head to see the flailing branches of the tree outside scraping against the windowpane. The leaves blew, and I knew the storm would be here soon.

But I turned back to him, both of us breathing heavily, and I loved the storm in Tyler Marek's eyes even more.

He slid his hands inside my panties and leaned his forehead into mine. I whimpered and grasped the back of his neck with both hands, my pussy throbbing at the thick ridge of his cock pressing against my leg.

He leaned down, his teeth nipping at my jaw as my eyes fluttered closed.

"Tyler." I let my head fall back, craning my neck for his lips. "Mr. Marek, please stop," I begged.

His hot breath fell across my ear, and I shivered.

"I thought about you all weekend," he whispered. "How do you make me do that?"

I snatched up his lips again. I liked what he was telling me too much.

He grabbed the hair at the back of my head and pulled, exposing my neck again as he dived down and whispered against my skin, "When you walked in, dressed in that short little skirt, my fucking hands wanted these thighs"—he raked his fingers down my legs again—"almost as much as my mouth did," he admitted.

I squeezed my eyes shut, the need becoming agony. "Mr. Marek," I quaked. "Oh, God."

I didn't want to stop him, but . . .

I bit my bottom lip, feeling his fingers slide up and down my pussy, dipping and bringing out the wetness, spreading it over my clit.

And then whimpered, feeling two long fingers plunge inside of me.

"Shit," I moaned, squirming against his fingers. "Please stop," I pleaded. "Tyler, please."

But he just added another finger, staring down and watching the pleasure of what he was doing spread across my face.

"Say it again," he ordered.

I blinked, opening my eyes, even though his thumb rubbing circles on my clit was driving me wild.

"Tyler," I said gently. "Please stop."

His mouth curled into a smile, and he stole a kiss, nipping at my bottom lip. "You don't want me to, do you?" he breathed out.

He increased his speed, flicking my clit faster and harder and curling the fingers inside of me, making me suck in air quicker and quicker and making me so needy I damn near gave in and begged to ride his cock.

"Tyler, oh, my God," I cried, squeezing my eyes shut again and feeling my insides swirl and tighten.

"On second thought, call me Mr. Marek," he insisted, and I popped my eyes open, seeing the devil in his grin.

I bit my lips between my teeth, groaning as I leaned back on my hands and slid my ass back and forth, fucking his fingers.

"Yes, Mr. Marek," I breathed out, dropping my head back as the whole fucking world started to spin.

One of my heels dropped to the floor, but I couldn't care less.

He continued staring down at me, looking like he was completely captivated with my face.

"You going to be nice from now on?" he challenged in a hard voice, rubbing harder.

"Yes, Mr. Marek," I rushed out.

"You going to keep your temper in check?" His long fingers filled me up again and again.

I nodded frantically, feeling the orgasm coming. "Yes, Mr. Marek."

"And I'm not done with you yet," he warned. "Just so you know."

I breathed in and out quickly, my body tensing and shaking. "Yes," I cried out.

And then the orgasm exploded, spreading down my thighs and through my belly. I dropped my head all the way back, plastering my hand to my mouth to stifle the cry as I squeezed my eyes shut and let him rub my clit, bringing the orgasm to an end.

My legs, suddenly as shaky as Jell-O, released their grip on his waist and dangled off the side of the desk.

He kissed me, holding my lips for a few moments, and for just a few moments I felt like I did on Sunday mornings. When I woke up and realized I could stay in bed.

Content.

A small smile spread across my mouth, and I felt high from him.

He withdrew his fingers, and I was almost sad at the loss until he brought them up to my mouth, resting them against my lips. I opened, and I sucked each finger, my lips wrapping around him and cleaning off the proof of what he'd gotten out of me.

His thumb dragged out of my mouth, tugging gently at my lip, and I watched him watch me.

I blinked long and hard, letting out a sigh.

What the hell are we doing?

I couldn't get involved with a parent, and even if I did, it couldn't be him.

I enjoyed him too much.

I leaned up, planting my feet on the ground, both heels having fallen off. I straightened my underwear and smoothed down my skirt as he slowly buttoned up his vest and straightened his tie.

"I hope it's smooth sailing for us from now on," he commented, buttoning his jacket.

I nodded absently, smoothing my hands down my hair. "Yes," I said, focused more on my messed-up appearance.

But his finger hooked under my chin and lifted. I raised my eyes, meeting his.

"*Yes*, what?" he prompted, looking stern.

My clit pulsed and started throbbing again, and I bit back the excitement warming up my chest.

"Yes, Mr. Marek."

He leaned in slowly, kissing my lips once more, and then pulled back and looked down at me.

"Is my tie straight?" he asked, changing the subject.

I couldn't contain the small laugh that escaped. It amazed me how he could go from hot to boyish in a matter of two seconds.

I reached up and fixed his black and gray tie and then straightened my back, again checking my dress and my hair.

But he tipped my chin back up, locking eyes with me. "You're perfect," he assured me. "Everything about you is perfect."

But then I gasped as he spun me around and forced me to bend over. I had time only to twist my head to see what he was doing behind me before he yanked up my dress and slapped me on the ass.

"Wha—!"

He pulled me back up, my ass pressing into his groin as he smoothed my dress down and palmed my behind, breathing against my neck.

"Except that little episode at my office on Saturday," he growled low in my ear. "Don't ever mouth off to me in public again."

And then he let me go and walked for the door, stopping once he'd put his hand on the door handle.

"I'll see you soon, Ms. Bradbury." He smirked and walked out, the sound of the janitor's cart rolling down the hallway outside my door.

I stared at his back as he left, my stomach churning at his commands and confidence, and I shot out my foot, kicking the leg of my chair.

He had spanked me.

He'd spanked me!

I looked over at the windows, the angry sky dark with the promise of rain and the trees' leaves dancing wildly.

Smooth sailing, my ass.

EIGHT

TYLER

"Hey," I greeted Christian as I walked into the dark kitchen. "How did practice go?"

He was sitting at the granite island, leaning back in his chair with his thumbs jutting out furiously on his phone.

"Fine," he replied, not looking at me.

His eyebrows were pinched together, heavy in concentration on whatever he was doing, or maybe he was just trying to look like he was busy.

He grabbed a piece of popcorn out of the bowl in front of him and tossed it into the air, catching it in his mouth.

I glanced down at the floor, shaking my head and smiling at the evidence that he wasn't a perfect shot every time.

I walked around the island and opened the refrigerator, grabbing a beer.

"The rain is starting," I told him. "Do me a favor and make sure the shutters in your bedroom are drawn and all of your windows are locked."

"Mrs. Giroux already made the rounds to all the rooms," he told me, continuing to type on his phone.

"Good." I nodded, twisting the lid off my longneck. "I don't think the hurricane will hit us, but I want you to stay inside unless you're in school or with me."

The storm had entered the Gulf, but its trajectory showed it heading toward Florida, so, at most, we were looking at a tropical storm.

"There is no school."

I swallowed the beer and gave him a questioning look. "What are you talking about?"

He looked up at me as if I was supposed to know. "They canceled school until Thursday," he announced. "They're anticipating some flooding, so I'm off for the next two days."

I set the beer down with a *clunk* and placed my hands on the island, staring at him.

"Do they send home notes letting parents know this sh—" I stopped myself. "Stuff?" I corrected.

"Yeah," he answered, sounding sarcastic as he put his hand on the paper on the island and pushed it over. "They also e-mailed the parents, if you cared to check."

I picked up the light blue piece of paper and read the notice.

The school sat in a depressed piece of land, and due to the heavy rains expected, they didn't feel it was safe for students or teachers to be traveling the streets to and from the school.

"Oh," I mumbled, calming down. "Well, that's a nice surprise, I guess. I used to love surprise days off as a kid."

"I'm not a kid," he shot back, grabbing his Dr Pepper off the counter and taking a drink. "You missed that part, remember?"

I set the paper down, loosening my tie and slipping off my jacket.

What was he trying to accomplish with this behavior?

I took a deep breath and let it roll off me.

"Well, the Saints are playing tonight," I said, looking over my shoulder at him as I grabbed a sandwich off the plate in the refrigerator. "I was thinking we could hit Manning's for a bite to eat and watch the game."

He hopped off his chair and picked up his soda. "Marcus's dad is taking him to their cabin in Mississippi to fish for a couple days to get away from the rain. They invited me." He started to walk out of the kitchen. "They'll be here to pick me up in half an hour."

What?

I slammed the refrigerator door closed and charged after him.

"Stop!" I barked, following after him down the hallway. "I didn't give you permission to go anywhere. Do you even know how to fish?"

He rounded the staircase and stopped to look at me, disdain written all over his face.

"My dad has taken me fishing," he pointed out, talking about his stepfather. "Many times. And I've been to Marcus's cabin. Many times since elementary school. I wonder why you don't know this," he sniped, and continued jogging up the steps.

"Christian, stop!" I ordered again, my fist wrapping around the banister as I glared up at him.

That prick was not his father. I was.

"Goddamn it, Christian," I gritted out, talking to his back. "I know nothing about you. I know that." I tried to slow my breathing. My pulse was raging. "I messed up a lot," I added. "And I was never there. I never put you first, and I'm sorry."

I lowered my eyes, knowing he had every reason to hate me. Who was I to him anyway?

"I need you to start letting me in." I spoke quietly. "Let me get to know you."

I heard footfalls and looked up to see him continuing up the stairs away from me.

"When you start trying, maybe I will," he called back before disappearing around the corner.

I started after him, but then Jay's voice came from behind me. He'd just stepped out of my office.

"Just let him go," he urged.

I stopped, looking up at the top of the stairs. "I've been letting him go."

"So what are you going to do?" he challenged. "Keep him from going, so you can take him fishing instead?" I heard the teasing note in his voice. "Or hiking?" he suggested, knowing all too well that I didn't have time to do either. "We have work to do, Tyler."

I closed my eyes, feeling fucking defeated.

Jay was right.

I could chuck everything and spend the weekend fishing with my kid with my phone turned off and the laptops abandoned at home, and we'd have a great time.

But then e-mails would back up, production would stop because I wasn't there to hold hands and make decisions, and Mason Blackwell would have more endorsements, because he'd stayed home and kept working.

I could tell my kid that things would calm down after the campaign.

And then I'd promise him I'd be there after the election.

And then there'd be this trip or that, and he would realize as well as me that the choices I refused to make still had consequences. They already did.

I walked back down the stairs, refusing to look at my brother as I passed him.

"Go home," I told him.

Christian left around six, and I spent the rest of the evening in my office, going over quarterly budgets and making calls to set up new contracts.

I e-mailed my assistant, Corinne, to make flight arrangements first thing tomorrow for a trip to Asia in late November and to begin making arrangements for a luncheon I wanted to host at the house in a couple of weeks.

We could try to make it a family affair. Christian might like being able to invite friends.

It would probably be the only way I could get him to attend.

Then I researched some information online and faxed Jay my notes to add to the speech he was editing for me for a city council meeting later in the week.

"Mr. Marek."

I glanced up from my desk to see Mrs. Giroux, the housekeeper, standing in the doorway.

"Hi." I stood up, walking to the bar to fix a drink. "What are you still doing here?"

She entered, carrying something under her arm. "I went out for supplies, just in case." She smiled, her blond hair—graying around her face—tied back in a low ponytail.

"We weren't stocked with batteries or water, among other things," she added. "You should be good to go now if the storm intensifies."

"Okay, good," I commented. "Thank you."

I was glad she had thought ahead. Most residents of New Orleans—especially people like me, who'd lived here their whole lives—knew to keep bottled water, canned goods, and things like flashlights, batteries, and first aid supplies on hand. We were used to storms and torrential rains, so when we could stay in the city and weather it, we did.

When we couldn't in safety, we left.

The rain wasn't terrible yet, but it would be a monsoon out there tomorrow.

And by Thursday we'd have streets full of leaves, trash to clean up, and mud puddles to avoid.

I replaced the cap on the Chivas and walked with my glass back to my desk.

She approached. "I was just heading out, but I found Christian's laptop in the TV room." She handed it over. "I'm not sure where his charger is, and I didn't want to leave it on the floor."

I took it and set it down on top of my closed one.

"Thank you." I smiled. "Now get home before your husband comes down on me," I teased.

She rolled her eyes and waved me off. "All right. I'll see how the weather is the day after tomorrow. If you need anything, let me know."

"Will do."

I watched her leave and then picked up the laptop, ready to set it aside, but then I stopped, hesitating for a moment.

Social media groups.

Letting my curiosity get the better of me, I set the laptop back down and opened it up.

I powered up the computer and brought up the Internet. Facebook was the home page, and I held back, feeling guilty about invading his privacy.

But I wasn't prying unnecessarily. I was researching. I wanted to know what my son was like.

There was a shit ton of selfies, mostly young girls, and I immediately scrolled quicker, suddenly feeling like a perv for nosing around their adolescent world.

I caught sight of his groups on the left and saw MS. BRADBURY FIRST PERIOD and clicked on it.

Scrolling down the posts, I saw photos of student work, discussion threads about what they had talked about that day, and even parents commenting with their opinions on a historical event.

The participation was widespread, and everyone seemed excited.

I couldn't help feeling like shit.

Christian was in this group, interacting with his peers, their parents, and his teacher, and I was nowhere.

I saw a message from Ms. Bradbury posted about two hours ago, wishing the kids a pleasant and safe few days off and to not forget to work on their assignments which were still due Friday.

Some of the students commented with pictures or jokes all done in good humor. They seemed to like her.

And I still knew almost nothing about her.

I closed the laptop and set it aside, opening up my own again.

I hesitated for only a moment, and then brought up my web browser, typing in “Easton Bradbury.”

NINE

EASTON

I tore open the bag of microwave popcorn, a steam cloud full of the scent of butter and salt bursting forth as I shook the contents out into a large glass bowl.

"Always" by Saliva played on the iPod, and I bobbed my head to the music. Tossing the bag away, I grabbed two Coronas out of the refrigerator.

"All right. Your windows are all secure," my brother called as he pounded down the stairs. "I'm surprised you don't have shutters, though. I thought you'd think of that, Miss Self-Sufficient."

I shook my head, handing him a beer. "Well, consider it my next project."

He grabbed the bottle opener out of the drawer and popped the top. "There's no way you're hanging out the windows to install them yourself, Easton. You're hiring someone to do that job."

I shook more salt onto the popcorn. "I was going to."

"No, you weren't," he deadpanned.

I laughed to myself. *No, I wasn't.*

Installing shutters sounded fun. Of course, I'd have little knowledge of what I was doing, and by the time I was done, the house would probably look like something out of a Dr. Seuss book, but it'd be something new to learn.

And it would get Jack off my back.

I think it honestly bugged him that I didn't need his help more, which was why he reveled in situations such as these. It gave him the opportunity to hover even when I'd assured him the house was ready for a storm. Windows and doors secure, batteries and flashlights stocked in the kitchen drawer, and food and water shelved in the pantry if need be. That was about all we could do.

The ominous clouds this morning had turned into a light rain this afternoon, and after considering the forecast for the next forty-eight hours, most schools in the parish had decided to close. E-mails and letters were sent home to parents, and I posted in the Facebook groups, reminding students that the chapter test was still set for Friday and to continue with their reading to prepare.

I'd come home, changed into some pajama shorts and my Loyola Wolf Pack T-shirt, and then downloaded some scary movies. Jack had rushed over to make sure I was safe.

"Maybe I should stay here," he offered, leaning against the counter behind me.

I picked two cloth napkins out of the drawer and then popped the top on my Corona. "Jack, when was I born?" I asked, not looking at him.

"November seventh."

"What year?" I pressed.

"Nineteen ninety-one."

"Which makes me how old?" I ran my hand over the napkin, smoothing the folded rectangle as I waited.

"Twenty-three." He sighed.

I turned and looked at him, his contrite expression telling me he understood everything I didn't say. He didn't need to hold my hand during a rainstorm or worry that I'd cross paths with a black cat.

"I'm twenty-three," I reiterated. "I don't worry that you can take care of yourself."

"I haven't gone through what you've gone through," he said, sounding defensive but sad. "You were sixteen when he started . . ."

I looked away, swallowing the lump blocking my airway.

"When he started following you, texting you, terrorizing you . . ." Jack went on, looking pained.

I shook my head. "Jack," I warned, wanting him to stop.

"You never knew what was coming." He squeezed the neck of the bottle in his hands. "You never knew whether he was going to show up in—"

"Jack, stop," I gritted out, cutting him off.

"I know you have guilt about Avery and our parents . . . about that night—"

I snapped my eyes up to his. "Enough!" I ordered.

He held my eyes, both of us frozen in the kitchen as the sound of fat raindrops pounded the roof and windows.

His expression hardened, turning from sad to challenging, and he set down his beer and powered into the living room, going straight for the bookshelf.

My arms heated with fear, and my throbbing heart pounded harder as I watched him reach onto one of the shelves and unearth the small wooden chest nestled there.

He turned around, gesturing to the locked box.

"What are you keeping in here?" he demanded.

But I clamped my jaw shut. He was invading my privacy, and I refused to give in.

"Open it," he ordered, knowing that I had the key.

I tipped my chin up and tried to calm my racing heart. "No," I answered calmly.

"Easton." His jaw flexed. "Open it."

I looked away. How the hell had he known something was in there?

My eyes burned, and I blinked long and hard. *I can't open the box*. I wouldn't. It hadn't been opened in five years, and this was none of my brother's business.

"No."

He stared at me, shaking his head, probably not knowing what to do.

He walked over, speaking quietly. "You keep the past too close. You're not moving on." His eyes searched my face, almost pleading. "I don't know what's in there, but I know it's too heavy a weight for you to carry around with you. You're twenty-three. You say you're a woman, but you still live within the lines as if you were a child." He dropped his eyes, whispering in a shaky voice, "You don't step out of the box, Easton."

I let out a breath and turned, walking back to my popcorn. "That's not true."

"Do you have any friends?" he challenged, following me. "Who was the last person to make you laugh? When was the last time you went to bed with someone more than once?"

I ground my teeth together, picking up the snacks and walking back to the living room.

But Jack kept pressing, "Has anyone other than me ever been in this apartment?" he asked.

I slammed my food down on the coffee table and picked up the remote.

"I'm tired of seeing you alone," he burst out. "I'm ready to burn this fucking place down and everything in it, so you're forced to leave the safety of your little shell!"

"Ugh!" I grabbed a handful of popcorn and flung it at him, the popped kernels hitting his face.

He jerked back, struck dumb by what I'd done.

Dropping his gaze, he arched an eyebrow, looking down at the white puffs on the floor.

I snorted, trying to contain my laugh, and he couldn't keep from smiling either, as he looked up at me.

"Ask me how old you are again," he grumbled. "I think I'd like to change my answer."

He brushed off crumbs from his shirt as I kept laughing.

But then we both jerked, a knock on the front door catching our attention.

Jack looked to me, a question in his eyes, but I shrugged. I had no idea who would be knocking on my door. He was right, after all. I had no friends.

I walked into the hallway, my bare feet quiet against the hardwood floor.

"Who is it?" I called, leaning up on my tiptoes to see into the peephole.

And my stomach instantly dropped. I fell away from the door, landing back on the heels of my feet.

What the hell?

"Easton?" he called through the door. "It's Tyler Marek."

I pinched my eyebrows together and shot up, peeping through the hole again.

How does he know where I live?

He was still dressed in the same suit from today, although his tie was loosened and his hair was wet, probably due to the rain. His head was cast downward as he waited, and I dropped to my feet again, realizing I was breathing a mile a minute.

I couldn't have a parent from school at my house. What did he think he was doing?

I unlocked the dead bolts and chain but opened the door only enough to fit my body between it and the frame.

"What the hell are you doing here?" I demanded. "This is my home."

He leaned a hand against the door frame and raised his eyebrows, a cocky smile dancing across his face.

"I made you come on a desk this morning," he pointed out. "I can't stop by your house?"

A snort that turned into a quiet laugh escaped from behind me, and I peeked over my shoulder to see my brother leaning against the frame between the living room and the entryway, smiling.

"Is someone here?" Tyler stood up straight, narrowing his eyes on me.

I inhaled a deep breath. "What do you want?" I asked, getting to the point.

He pushed his wet hair back over the top of his forehead and stuck his other hand in his pocket, all of a sudden looking nervous.

He cleared his throat, raising his hesitant gaze up to mine. "I want to apologize."

I let out a bitter laugh. "Don't worry, Mr. Marek. This morning is our little secret. Just go away."

I moved to close the door, but he shot out his hand, keeping it open.

"Easton," he called out, sounding unusually gentle. "I should never have been rough with you today, and I'm sorry."

Rough with me?

I narrowed my eyes, suspicious. "Why?" I asked.

"What do you mean?"

"Why are you sorry?" I demanded, forgetting my brother standing nearby.

Tyler Marek was never gentle, and I'd never given him the impression that I had a problem with that. Why did he suddenly feel bad?

He opened his mouth, looking like he wasn't sure what to say. "I . . ." He cleared his throat again. "I just don't feel like I've treated you as well as you should be treated," he admitted.

I stood there, frozen in place and staring at him suspiciously. What the hell was going on?

When had I ever given him the impression that I couldn't take what he dished out? And now he was worried about me?

"All right." My brother grabbed the door and opened it completely, breaking me out of my daze. "I'm out." He leaned down to kiss my cheek. "Be safe and . . ." He looked at Tyler as he slipped past both of us and through the door. "We'll meet another time."

He jogged down the steps, his dark green T-shirt slowly turning black in the rain as he ran for his Jeep.

Tyler looked after him and then turned to me, cocking his head. "I'm not a jealous man, but for you I might make an exception."

Huh?

And then I realized he'd never met my brother. He thought Jack was a lover.

"No need to be jealous," I reassured him. "You're the parent of a student and nothing more."

He looked away, shaking his head at my audacity.

But then his expression cleared and he looked at me pointedly. "Why didn't you tell me you played tennis professionally?" he asked.

My face fell. "You had me investigated?" I accused.

"No. I know how to Google, thank you," he retorted. "You're as much of a mystery as my son, so I looked you up."

My hand fell off the door handle, and I searched my brain for a way to deter him without making him more curious.

He stepped through the door, and I backed away, letting him in.

"There wasn't so much on Easton Bradbury, the Loyola student or teacher," he told me, closing the door behind him. "But there were thousands of hits and pictures on you as an athlete." He inched closer to me, not giving up. "Tennis player, close family, promising future that crashed and burned when . . ." He trailed off, and I looked up, seeing the uncertainty in his eyes.

I smoothed my hand down my T-shirt and shorts, steeling my spine.

Now he knew everything. Nearly everything.

There were articles, video footage, interviews . . . My rise had been highly publicized, and so had my fall.

When my parents and sister died on that rainy night in a vicious accident, I'd lost everything. My routine, the world as I knew it, and my desire to play.

Who was I if I wasn't the star in their lives, and why the hell did I want to play tennis anymore anyway?

It was my fault they'd been driving that night, and when it was time to get back on the court, my will to play was gone. Even now, on the rare occasion I tried, my game had gone to shit.

My magnificent exit and display of temper were forever digitized. I'd forfeited the match and walked off the court, pushing cameras and microphones out of my face as I left for the last time.

"Easton, I'm sorry." Marek reached out and touched my cheek

But I pushed his hands away and stepped back. "Stop apologizing."

How dared he act like I needed to be put back together?

"Don't handle me, Tyler," I growled. "I'm tired of everyone hovering and sticking their noses in. You don't matter," I shot out bitterly, "so stop trying to push your way in."

I charged into the living room, but he grabbed my arm and swung me back around, pulling me to him. I crashed against his chest, the rain on his clothes like ice against my arms and legs, and my breath caught.

"Yeah." He nodded. "I don't matter. I don't matter so much that there was no way in hell you could say no to me today," he charged. "And I'd be willing to bet I'm the first man you can't say no to, because it's the same way for me."

He bent his head down to mine, our noses brushing. "You're strong and proud, resilient and capable. I can see that." His voice was thick, like he was feeling more than he was saying. "I value those qualities in a person, Easton. You don't give anyone an inch, and it's like looking into a mirror, because it's the same independence I value." He looked at me like a dare and wrapped an arm around my waist, pulling me closer and whispering, "And when I touch you, I can't explain what I feel, but I know you're feeling me, too."

I closed my eyes, inhaling his sweet scent of cologne and

leather—probably from his car—and even the cold rain on his clothes couldn't cool me down now.

I let my head fall to the side against his chest as I spoke, closing my eyes. "Everyone watched me all the time." I trembled. "The cameras, the crowd, my parents . . . Everything I did was under a microscope."

I slipped my arms inside his jacket and wrapped them around his waist.

"If my lips were tight, then I was angry," I told him, reminiscing about the commentators' assumptions as they watched me on the court. "If I hesitated, I was scared. If I didn't smile at the camera, I was a spoilsport . . ."

I dipped my nose into his shirt, inhaling a long breath before I looked up at him. "Everything was judged." I shrugged. "And when my parents and younger sister died in a car accident, it only got worse. Everyone was in my face."

I pulled away, turning around and crossing my arms over my chest.

"So I started over," I told him. "Jack and I moved to New Orleans, went to college, and let the past go."

I turned and locked eyes with him. The room looked so small with him in it, and I realized that he was the first person, other than my brother, who'd been in my apartment. Droplets of rain spilled down his temple and neck, and I licked my lips, trying to keep the libido that was beginning to heat low in my stomach chained.

I cleared my throat. "But after five years, my brother still tries to hold my hand. He still worries about me. Am I happy? Do I smile enough?" I approached Tyler, dropping my arms to my sides. "He forgets that I'm a grown woman."

I slipped my hand against his, resting it there lightly. "But you don't," I whispered, seeing his fist curl, holding mine inside it.

"I didn't know," he said softly, his breath fanning across my forehead. "I should've treated you—"

I cut him off, looking up. "I like how you are with me. You're not careful with me. You see more of me than anybody else does."

I pressed my body against his, arching up on my toes and leaning toward his lips. His breath hitched, and I slipped my hands inside his jacket again and gripped his waist.

"Don't be careful with me, Tyler," I whispered, catching his bottom lip, sucking it quickly and then letting it go. "Please," I pleaded.

And he groaned, closing his eyes and diving in.

He held me to his body and captured my mouth, moving over my lips slow but hard. He tasted cool and fresh, like water, but then he pulled away and dove for my neck.

I gasped, his hot breath on my skin causing chills to spread over my body as he kissed and bit me gently.

"Don't be careful," I reminded him in a whimper as I reached up and circled his neck with my arms, holding him to me.

He picked me up, and I wrapped my legs around his waist, kissing him with full force on the mouth.

"Your clothes are all wet," I rushed out between kisses, breathless. "Get them off."

"Are you sure you want to do this?" he asked, nibbling at my mouth.

"Do what?" I played, licking and biting his jaw, hearing him suck in a breath. "Fuck like animals in my bed upstairs?"

His fingers dug into the skin of my ass, and I went to town with my tongue. I attacked his neck, his jaw, and his lips, squeezing my thighs around him.

"Fuck." He stilled, holding me tight. "Just wait. Hold on," he gasped, dropping me back down to my feet and letting me go.

"What's wrong?" My voice trembled. I was so fucking turned on, and he'd just stopped.

His shoulders slumped slightly, and his face was twisted as he breathed in and out. "Shit, that's painful," he cursed, the bulge in his pants hard and ready.

What was he waiting for?

"What's wrong? Is it Christian?" I asked gently, feeling guilty.

He shook his head. "No," he choked out. "He's away for a couple of days." He jerked his chin to the stairs. "Go get dressed."

"Why?"

I curled my toes into the floor, my clit pounding like my heartbeat during a run. I didn't want to leave. What the hell?

"Now," he ordered, his voice hard and pissed off. "I'm taking you to dinner. Go get dressed."

TEN

TYLER

I knew her kind.

It was like looking in a mirror, and I had no doubt that everything she'd told me was true. She was too brave to lie.

But I also knew she was trying to distract me. She didn't want to open up too much or take off the mask.

Easton Bradbury was a survivor, and she'd ride me to kingdom come if it would get me to stop asking questions.

I'd love every minute, but I didn't like how she kept me at arm's length.

I'd always set the boundaries, not the other way around.

She'd gone upstairs, without argument surprisingly, and came back down dressed in a pleated black miniskirt.

It was sexy but tasteful. Her top was off-white and off the shoulder, and it felt like water when I placed my hand on her back and guided her to the car, beneath an umbrella I'd found right beside her door.

Every bar in the Vieux Carre was open, and the streets were flooded with people, despite the heavy rain.

The French Quarter was the highest point in New Orleans, so

it rarely flooded, not that flooding would stop the residents. The electric charge in the air only incited the already thick lust for life that flowed in their veins.

Just give them an excuse and there was a party.

Patrick dropped us off at Père Antoine on Royal Street, a block off Bourbon, and I rushed her inside, doing a piss-poor job of not ogling her beautiful legs, decorated with drops of rain, as she followed the hostess to a table and I followed behind.

I sipped my Jameson neat and watched her trail her fingers along the edge of the tablecloth in front of her, her lips moving slightly. The cloth was white with small flowers sewn into the design.

"What are you doing?" I asked.

She looked up, her eyes wide.

"I . . ." She closed her mouth and then opened it again. "I was counting," she admitted. "It's kind of a habit I've been working on stopping, but sometimes I still find myself doing it."

"What do you count?"

Her head turned, her eyes scanning the room as she spoke, as if she was afraid to look at me. "I count my steps as I walk sometimes." She looked down, smoothing her clothes as she went on. "My strokes when I brush my teeth. The number of turns when I use a faucet. Everything has to be an even number."

I set my drink down. "What if it only takes three turns to get your desired temperature with the faucet?"

She glanced up. "Then I do shorter turns to get to four," she shot back, a hint of a smile on her face.

I narrowed my eyes, studying her.

She blushed, looking embarrassed as she leaned her elbows on the table and took a drink of her gin and tonic.

Why couldn't I get a reading on her?

Her face was oval shaped with high cheekbones, and she had big blue eyes that always seemed covered by some kind of filter. I couldn't look at her and tell what she was thinking.

Her top lip curved downward, making her bottom lip look pouty, both the color of a sullied pink that I wanted to feed on.

Her shoulders were squared, and her jaw was strong, but she wouldn't meet my eyes, and her breathing was shaky.

So much like a strong woman, but the vulnerability and temper were that of someone who worked very hard to never really face the world.

She wanted me but acted like I could easily be replaced.

I thought about her when we were apart, and I wanted to know that she thought about me too.

"So why do you do it?" I pressed.

She shook her head, shrugging slightly. "It's soothing, I guess," she placated.

"Have you talked to anyone about it?"

She met my eyes, holding the glass in her hand as she leaned on the table. "I have. Sporadically," she added. "Most people like me function just fine, and when I'm busy, I forget about it. But at certain times"—she paused, watching me—"I regress."

Certain times? Did I make her nervous?

"It just makes me feel better," she explained. "And sometimes, it's just a habit."

I nodded, understanding. "So you count things. What's your favorite number?"

"Eight."

I laughed a little. "Didn't have to think about that, huh?"

She blushed, giving me a timid smile.

Licking her lips, she reached for the container of sweeteners and pulled some out, setting them side by side on the table.

"Can't have two," she told me, looking at me with amusement as she explained, "because if they separate, then they're alone." She slid the packets apart, proving her point.

Then she grabbed two more, lining them up with the others.

"Can't have four, because even if there's two in each group, it's still only *one couple* in each group."

Her voice turned playful, and she seemed to relax as she got caught up in explaining her secret obsession.

She took out more packets, making two groups of three. "And you can't have six, because if you separate them into two groups of three like this, then there's three in each group, and that's an odd number."

Her eyes widened, looking like that would be the worst thing ever, and I laughed.

She took out two more packets, making two groups of four each. Eight packets total.

"Eight is perfect." She grinned, fingering the packets to make sure they were straight. "Two groups. Four in each group making two couples in each group."

And she looked up, nodding once as if everything were perfect with the world.

I couldn't help it. My lips curled into a smile because she was the fucking epitome of intriguing. So sexy, but if you blinked too long, she was transformed and you realized everything you thought you knew about her barely touched the surface.

She hooded her eyes and looked away, smiling to herself. "I'm crazy," she admitted. "That's what you're thinking."

I let my eyes rake down her bare neck to where her shirt fell off her shoulder. The hardened point of her nipple poked through the thin fabric, and I knew she wasn't wearing a bra.

The shirt was the only barrier, and that turned me on more than the idea of her naked did.

I raised my eyes to her. "I'm thinking you're beautiful," I said in a low voice. "And if you need everything in eights, it could be a long night."

She held my eyes, not moving, but I could see the excitement trying to break out across her face. Her hitched breathing, her stillness . . . I loved that I'd shut her up for once. She was fun, and I enjoyed peeling away her layers.

The waiter came over, setting down the crawfish étouffée for Easton and my blackened catfish and left to get us another round of drinks.

She took her spoon and pushed it through her stew of rice and peeled crawfish tails. I grabbed my fork and knife, ready to cut into a meal I wasn't the least bit hungry for, but I stopped, seeing her take a small piece of bread and dip it into the stew. She brought the bread up, dripping with creole sauce, and caught it with her mouth, sucking the tip of her thumb before starting to chew.

Glancing up, she caught me staring. "What?" she asked more as an accusation.

I cut into my food. "You're only allowed finger foods when we go out to eat," I deemed.

I heard her snort. "*If* we go out again," she corrected.

She picked up her spoon and we both started eating. I ate the fish with the sauce and all of the rice, quickly realizing I was hungrier than I'd thought. I rarely just sat and ate, unless it was with Christian, and more often than not, we were both interrupted by phone calls or texts at the dinner table.

Business dinners were a lot of talking and drinking, so Mrs. Giroux's home-cooked meals were much appreciated. It was my fault I chose to eat them at my desk as I worked.

I raised my eyes, watching her eat and loving the sight of her sitting there: her dark hair spilling over her shoulder, her skin glowing in the light of the ostentatious chandelier hanging above her, her downcast eyes as she licked her lips after taking a drink.

I wasn't thinking about work or home. At the moment I wondered only what she was thinking.

"Why do you want to go into politics?"

I stopped, looking up. She watched me silently, waiting.

I shrugged slightly, setting down my silverware and relaxing into my seat.

"I have money," I pointed out, picking up my drink. "Now I'm bored, and I want power."

She set her spoon down, sitting back and crossing her arms over her chest. She cocked her head, unamused.

My chest shook with a laugh before I took a sip and set down my drink. She didn't take any bullshit, did she?

"I've been on top of the world my whole life," I told her, fingering the glass. "I grew up attending private schools, and my father made sure I had everything I could ever want. College was a blast. Being on my own, money I didn't earn or question where it came from sitting in my pocket . . ." I trailed off, staring at the table and narrowing my eyes.

"I didn't concern myself with anything that brought me down," I confessed. "I was arrogant."

I stopped and smirked at her. "Well, more arrogant than I am now," I added. "I was self-serving and selfish."

The waiter stopped and set down the drinks, leaving just as quietly when neither of us looked at him.

I raised my eyes, meeting hers. "When I was nineteen I got a girl pregnant." I swallowed the lump, remembering that day I'd wished so many times I could go back and redo. "She wasn't even really my girlfriend," I added. "It was new, and it was casual, and then all of a sudden my connection to her was permanent."

Easton's expression was emotionless as she listened.

"And you know what?" I continued. "I still didn't change. I threw money at her so she'd go away, and after a year or so, she married someone else."

I looked away, feeling ashamed. "A great guy who wanted her even though she had another man's kid, a guy who was there for my son."

My throat tightened, and I forced my breathing to slow. I'd worked very hard over the years not to think about Christian waking up in the middle of the night or having stories read to him by someone else. Times when he was small and helpless and needed me and I was nowhere around.

I was never there.

"I thought I was a man." I spoke quietly. "I wasn't even close."

She dropped her eyes, looking saddened, and I wasn't sure if that was a good thing or a bad thing. Did she think less of me now?

Of course she did.

"When I was twenty-two," I went on, "I was in my last semester of college and ready to be done. I had to take this social science course to fulfill a requirement. I forget what it was called," I told her, "but I remember, very well, arguing with the professor one day. He was giving us some prison statistics. Percentages of the inmates' races, percentages of repeat offenders . . ."

I tipped back the drink, finishing it off, setting the glass down, and clearing my throat.

"Everyone thought that the inequalities in prison culture were shocking, but I didn't care. It didn't seem like a big deal."

A smile escaped me as I remembered that day. "The professor got in my face and told me to look harder." I looked at her point-blank, imitating his deep, gruffly voice. "'Mr. Marek, if you're not angry, then you're not paying attention.' And I shot back with 'Well, I don't want to be angry all the time. Ignorance is bliss, and I don't care about fuckups who got sent to prison for their own mistakes' and all that bullshit. I thought I was so smart."

I felt utterly ridiculous, quoting my twenty-two-year-old self. Back when I thought I knew everything.

I continued to explain. "He wanted us to question the how and why, and I couldn't have cared less. I wanted to make money"—I shrugged my shoulders—"go to parties, and have fun."

She continued listening, not moving a muscle.

"And then," I continued. "I remember like it was yesterday. He looked me in the eye, and he said, 'Tyler, if you're going to be a burden on the world, then just die now. We don't need you.'"

She blinked, looking a little shocked. "Wow," she whispered.

"Yeah." I nodded. "He shut me up. And he made me open my eyes," I added, remembering the moment my outlook on life changed.

"I was a nobody," I explained. "Expendable and useless . . . I was a loser who took and never gave."

I glanced up, seeing the waiter approach, and waited for him to take the plates away.

"Would you like coffee?" he asked.

I shook my head, waving him off.

"And so"—I looked at her again after he'd gone—"in my last year of college, I finally started studying. I read books about prisons, poverty, religion, war, gangs, economics, even agriculture," I explained, "and the following fall I went back to school for my graduate degree, because I wanted to make more than just money. I wanted to make a difference and be remembered."

Her eyes dropped, and a small, thoughtful smile peeked out as if she understood just what I was talking about.

"I realized that if I wanted to effect change," I told her, "and be a person others could count on, then I needed to start with my own kid. He was two years old at that point and had seen me . . ." I shook my head. "Very rarely," I confessed. "Brynne, his mother, didn't want to have anything to do with me, though."

I took in a hard breath, the weight of regret making it hard to talk. "She took the money my father sent every month for Christian's sake, but I'd burned my bridges with her. She told me that our son had a father who loved him already and I'd only confuse him."

"And you agreed with her," Easton ascertained.

I nodded. "I was scared off," I admitted. "I was working hard to contribute to the rest of the world, but when it came to my kid . . ." I dropped my eyes, shaking my head at how easily I'd talked myself out of his life back then. "I was too afraid of failing." I raised my eyes, meeting hers. "So I didn't even try. I saw her husband with my kid, and I didn't know how the hell I was going to compete with that. I wanted to be in his life, but I'd still just be the weekend daddy."

At the time, it had made sense.

I'd wanted him to know me, but what if I didn't live up to his expectations? He'd already had a full-time father and a life that was familiar.

What if he still hated me?

No, there was time. Later. When he'd grown up enough to understand. Then I could be his father.

"As he grew, I tried to keep in contact with him," I consoled myself out loud. "I never pressed for any kind of custody, because my traveling was sporadic and unpredictable, and Brynne let Christian go with me from time to time as long as that's what he wanted," I explained. "But he started having friends, sports, extracurricular activities, and so I let him have his life. We grew even further apart."

"But he's with you now," she pointed out, sounding hopeful.

But I couldn't summon her optimism. Under the same roof, I felt more distanced from my son than when he wasn't there.

"I was supposed to pick him up for dinner one night last June," I explained, "and he stood me up. He went to a baseball game with his other father." I accentuated the word "other."

"I got pissed and went to collect him, and Brynne started yelling at me on the phone to leave them alone," I went on. "I was just making everyone unhappy, she told me, but he was my son, and I wanted him with me that night."

I blinked away the burn in my eyes, remembering how fucking sick I'd gotten of her telling me he wasn't mine.

"And I was pissed, because I had no right to be pissed," I told Easton. "Brynne was right. I was the outsider. I'd given him up. And I was making everyone unhappy."

The waiter brought the bill, and I dug my wallet out of my breast pocket and handed him a couple bills.

"Keep the change," I said, and didn't watch him leave.

Easton leaned her chin on her hand, her eyes never leaving me.

I picked my napkin off my lap and dropped it on the table.

"When she said they were going to Egypt for a year," I continued, "and that she was taking Christian, I said no. I told her I wasn't letting my son leave the country, and we fought. A lot.

"But I was done being a coward. I wanted my son with me." I didn't know why, but I wanted Easton to understand that. "I thought it was too late when he was two. I thought it was too late when he was ten. And now that he's fourteen I've finally fucking realized that it's never too late," I told her.

I swirled the brown liquid I had yet to drink, knowing that I was still failing with my son and wondering what Easton was thinking of me. Maybe she'd learned too much, and I'd fucked up.

I'd gone to her apartment tonight because, after what I'd seen online, I didn't want to bring her any unhappiness. I wouldn't be so arrogant as to think I could make her life better—she seemed to be doing pretty well—but I was reminded that what others let us see is very little. There's a lot I didn't know about her, but I did know she was hiding something.

She deserved to smile, and for some reason, I wanted to give her that.

But telling her my own shit might've pushed her away.

Women didn't tend to like weakness and mistakes in men, but when she'd looked so interested, something compelled me to spill everything.

I guess I hadn't really told anyone all of that before.

She sat there, watching me, and I tipped my drink at her, blowing off the whole thing with a smile and suddenly feeling like I'd made a huge mistake in telling her.

"Anyway," I joked. "That's why I want to be in politics."

ELEVEN

EASTON

What is he doing to me?

I'd sat there, silent nearly the entire time, and listened to the things that had brought him to where he was now. The mistakes of his youth, the teacher who'd pushed him, the son who thought nothing of him, and all the things he didn't know how to fix.

And all I wanted in the world was for him to keep talking.

I liked how his experiences had shaped him and how he was committed to succeeding. He didn't give up. When I saw the moments he'd looked away from me or heard the hesitance in his voice during his story, I knew he still felt like that twenty-two-year-old kid down deep.

The midthirties construction mogul who dominated conference rooms and crowds still didn't think he was a man.

I had no doubt that Christian's mother had every reason to be angry and not to trust him. She'd been young, too, I was sure, and he'd left her holding the bag.

But I could see the regret and pain Tyler tried to hide on his face at all the lost years with his son.

And he wouldn't give up again.

A man who endeavored to be better was already superior to the men who claimed to be great.

He took my hand, leading me out of the restaurant, and I threaded my fingers through his, holding back the smile at the chills spreading up my arms.

We stepped out of the restaurant and onto the sidewalk, stopping to take in the sight of the rain pouring down in buckets and yet doing nothing to deter the party in the street.

The heavy drops hit the ground in sheets upon sheets, and I had to squint to make out people's faces, dancing in the midst of the celebration.

Trumpet music played off to my left, and I looked over, seeing an older man with graying hair swaying to and fro under the canopy as he played "When the Saints Go Marching In."

Peering back out to the crowd in the streets and lining the sidewalks, their black and gold football jerseys glued to their drenched skin, I realized that it was Monday-night football. The Saints must've won.

I couldn't care less about football, but I envied how something so insignificant in the scheme of things could make people so happy.

Women adorned with beads around their necks clutched the long green necks of the Hand Grenade drinks in their fists and twirled, kicking up the water that had accumulated on Royal, while men smiled, nearly tripping over their own steps. All laughing and probably enjoying one of the best moments of their lives, because they felt truly free right now. Chaos lost in chaos. Liberty in being a small part of a larger madness.

When you weren't seen, you weren't judged. There was a desirable freedom in that.

"You think less of me." He spoke at my side, still watching the rain. "Don't you?"

I narrowed my eyes on him and shook my head. "No."

"I'm not the same man I was back then, Easton." He looked down at me. "I take care of what's mine now."

His hard stone eyes held mine, and there was nothing that I didn't want him to prove. Would he be rough but never hurt? Get me to want more?

Make me never want to leave?

I turned away from him and stepped off the sidewalk, instantly pummeled with heavy raindrops as I walked into the street.

Water filled my flats, and my skirt and shirt instantly stuck to my skin. I closed my eyes, feeling him behind me, watching.

The cool rain soaked my hair, and I threw back my head, letting it cool off my face.

Why him? Why had he been the one to push his way in, and why had I allowed it?

A wall of warmth hit my back, and I felt his hand take my hip. I turned my head, and he caught my face in his hand and covered my mouth with his.

Tyler.

I darted out my tongue, brushing it against his and feeling my breath catch in my throat. My skin buzzed, desire pooled between my legs, and I snaked my hand up, holding the side of his face as I dived in, kissing him greedily.

I flicked his top lip with my tongue and dragged out his bottom lip between my teeth, taking time to let him do the same to me.

His hands fell down to my stomach, pulling me back and holding me to his body as his lips worked mine, leaving me breathless.

The rain spilled over us, plastering our clothes to our bodies, and his tongue darted out, licking and sucking the water off my jaw and chin.

"Tyler," I gasped, squeezing my eyes shut, because he felt so good it almost hurt. "Tyler, this is wrong."

I pulled away from him and turned around, breathing hard.

It wasn't easy to say no to something you wanted, but I was taught that while some mistakes can be overcome, others should never be made. In our hearts, we always know what's right and wrong. That's not the struggle.

The struggle is wanting what's wrong for you and gauging whether or not the consequences are worth it.

"I like your kid," I told him. "And I love my job. You're in the public eye. We can't do this."

By now my arms hung at my sides, weighing a thousand pounds. I wasn't tired, but for some reason I felt exhausted.

He tipped his chin down at me and inched forward.

"Easton, you're coming home with me," he stated as if it were a done deal.

My weary heart pumped harder, begging me to agree. *If you don't give in, you'll always want him.*

Go home with him. Get in his bed. Self-destruct, because some rides can't be stopped.

But I couldn't.

What if things turned bad? I couldn't just not see him.

And New Orleans might be a large city, but there were almost no degrees of separation from you and the stranger on the street. Someone—anyone—was bound to see us together, and it would be only a matter of time before we were found out.

No.

I looked up at him, speaking softly. "Take me home, please," I told him. "To *my* house."

His eyes narrowed and his jaw hardened, but I didn't wait for an argument. Spinning around, I dashed across Royal and continued walking down the quieter side street, toward the parking garage.

The rain had drenched my clothes, and I folded my arms over my chest to ease the chill seeping through my skin.

I could hear his footsteps behind me, and I walked quickly to avoid any further discussion, speed-walking past a hotel entrance and continuing down the sidewalk.

If he pressed me further, I knew I'd be tempted to give in.

But he hooked my elbow, bringing me to a stop as I twisted around to face him.

"I like you, okay?" he said, letting his gaze fall and looking like it was hard for him to admit that.

He stepped closer. "I like you a lot, and I don't know why, because you're fucking miserable to me half the time," he mused. "You rarely smile. You never laugh, but you love to argue, and for some reason I want you around. I want you to know things about me, and I like telling you shit. Why do I feel like I'm in the wrong here?"

I bowed my head, hoping he wouldn't see the smile his words had caused. He was absolutely right. I was a miserable person half the time, and it was odd that he liked me as much as he did.

And in a different situation, maybe I'd give him a shot. Maybe.

"Marek?" I heard a voice boom through the storm. "Is that you?"

Tyler and I pulled away from each other, and I peered around him, seeing the group of men standing underneath the canopy of the hotel entrance we'd just passed.

Tyler twisted his head, his face immediately turning stern at the sight of the four men in suits, smoking cigars.

He took my hand and walked us back to where the men were standing, and I noticed he kept me slightly behind him instead of at his side.

"Blackwell." Tyler's deep voice sounded impatient.

Mason Blackwell—whom I recognized from TV and his involvement with city council—looked completely at ease and in good humor, something I'd never seen from Tyler.

His black tie was loosened, and his hand rested in his pants pocket. He wore an easy smile, and I could smell the odor from the cigar hooked under his pointer finger as he grinned at Tyler.

But from Tyler's rigid stance, I could tell he wasn't as comfortable with Blackwell.

"They've instituted curfew on the Westbank," he told Tyler. "But the party still goes strong over here."

His white teeth disappeared as he brought the cigar to his mouth and puffed away.

A few young women, dressed in short cocktail dresses, came bursting out of the hotel doors, giggling and stumbling, before they stopped at the group of men, each cozying up to a different gentleman.

A young brunette, her hair a shade lighter than mine, put her hand on Blackwell's chest as she hugged his side, looking intimate.

Tyler cleared his throat. "How's your wife, Mason?" he asked, hints of both amusement and disdain seeping out of the comment.

Blackwell's hand was in his pocket, so I didn't notice a wedding ring, but the young woman's left hand was draped over his shoulder, and she wasn't wearing one.

Blackwell stared at Tyler with a smile that didn't reach his eyes, and the tension in the air between the two men thickened.

His gaze shifted from Tyler, finding me at his side, slightly behind him.

"Hello?" he greeted, cocking his head and letting his gaze rake down my figure.

He sucked in a breath through his teeth and he half grinned at Tyler. "I envy you," he said, bringing the cigar up to his mouth. "For once."

My stomach rolled, and I swallowed, tasting something bitter. Perhaps the cigar was a turnoff, or maybe it was his blatant arrogance, but I felt a sudden urge to shut him up.

Mason held out his hand to me, a lascivious look in his eyes. "Mason Blackwell," he introduced himself.

But Tyler stepped in front of me, blocking Mason's view.

"She's cold," he shot out. "I'm taking her home."

And without a goodbye, he grabbed my hand and pulled me back down the street so briskly that I had to jog to keep up.

"He's not your favorite person," I mused, blinking away the rain in my eyes. "I can see why. I like him better on TV."

Tyler crossed the street, dragging me in tow as he turned down another street.

"You don't like him at all," he bit out in a low voice.

The sidewalk dipped, and I stumbled. Picking up the pace, I jogged a few steps and continued to follow him down the dark, vacant street.

"Tyler, I wasn't going to introduce myself," I assured him, wondering why he was so brusque all of a sudden.

Is that why he'd blocked Mason from shaking my hand? I hadn't planned to tell him who I was. I knew he and Tyler were rivals, vying for the same Senate seat. He could use me against Tyler, and I wasn't stupid.

I held tight to his hand, because he was going so fast. "This is exactly what I was talking about," I maintained, standing my ground. "We're bound to run into people you know. What are you going to do? Slink into my apartment at night after Christian's gone to bed?" I shot out. "Take me to hole-in-the-wall restaurants buried in the Marigny? I don't want to be your secret, Tyler. This is too dangerous."

But then my breath caught in my throat as he yanked me off the street and through a wide-open gate that led to a darkened driveway, immediately backing me up against the wall next to the gate.

Only just a hair away from prying eyes.

The doors of the huge wooden gate opened for cars to come in and out, and I knew that the driveway would lead into the living area, giving way to a large courtyard.

So far, though, there was no sign of anyone.

"What are you doing?" I gasped.

His forehead pressed against mine, and his hands moved urgently, holding my face. "Dark spaces, quiet places," he whispered over my mouth. "That's all we need, Easton."

And I sucked in a breath as he dove in, taking my lips, moving fast and making it sting so sweetly when he sucked and bit my bottom lip like he was starving.

I moaned, feeling the thick ridge of his cock as he ground into me.

His hands dropped, lifting me by the backs of my thighs and pinning me to the wall as he continued. I tightened my legs around his waist and held him close.

He moved his hands up, squeezing my ass in both of his greedy hands, and he was going at my mouth again and again so fast I couldn't think straight.

"Tyler, please," I rushed out, gasping for breath. "We can't."

He was making it impossible, and I knew I was lost.

Fuck!

He lifted me higher, holding tight as he pulled down my off-the-shoulder blouse enough to expose my naked breast.

The hardened skin of my nipple begged for his mouth, but I wrapped my hands around his neck, drawing him closer to me.

He caught my nipple in his mouth, quick and rough, and I shivered as he dragged his teeth and sucked, making it burn. I closed my eyes, arching my back to give him more.

He came up, hovering over my lips, while his fingers slipped between us and into my underwear, finding my pussy wet.

"I don't give a damn who you introduce yourself to," he growled, sliding his finger in and out of me, "as long as it's not that piece of shit."

"Tyler . . ." I squeezed my eyes shut as he pumped his finger.

"He's always so fucking smug," he gritted out, biting at my jaw, "always getting the upper hand. I thought I'd like having something he wanted, but I don't." He slipped in a second finger, stretching me. "I don't want him looking at you, Easton."

He grabbed the hem of my panties, and I bit my bottom lip to stifle the cry as he ripped them clean off my body.

"I was jealous. I never get jealous," he charged, pressing me against the wall and grinding his hips against my bare pussy. "You make me insecure. Why do you do that, huh?"

I groaned, my thighs aching, the heat between my legs unbearable.

"Because you covet something you can't have," I taunted. "And you're afraid someone else will get it."

I rolled my hips, rubbing myself against him. Against the only part of him I wanted.

But instead, he slowed, looking at me with mischief.

He leaned in toward my ear and whispered, "You poor thing." He sounded sinister. "You actually think there are things I can't have?"

I smiled, tightening my arms around his neck, and brushed my lips across his jaw to hover over his lips. "Make it worth the risk," I challenged. "Show me how you take what you want."

He breathed out a quiet laugh against my cheek and palmed my tit, squeezing it possessively.

"I'm burning," I gasped.

He flashed me a smug smirk, and my pussy clenched as I moaned, feeling his hand work between our bodies, unfastening his belt. "I'll make it better," he promised.

The warm flesh of his cock crowned my entrance, and he slid it up and down my slit to spread my wetness.

"Wait," I panted, trying to pull off his jacket. I wanted to see his body.

But he slammed his hips into mine, and I cried out, that sweet pain of the first thrust spreading through my belly as he slid into me.

"Oh, God," I groaned. "I fucking hate you."

Why couldn't he wait? I wanted to feel his skin.

"As long as you fucking fuck me, I don't care."

He reached down between my legs and hooked an arm under my left thigh, holding me in place, and I closed my eyes, letting my head fall back, as he thrust his cock inside of me again and again, going faster and faster until all I could do was grab his jacket in my fists and hold on for the ride.

He gripped my ass in one hand, while his other wrapped around my thigh, and yanked me to him, demanding that I feel every inch.

The cool, wet air filled with the smell of earth surrounded us, and I heard laughter coming from off in the distance.

People were coming down the sidewalk, and here I was, skirt around my waist, getting fucked by a man I wasn't even sure I liked.

But—I whimpered, rolling my hips and fucking him back—I damn well liked what he did to me.

"Tyler," I cried out, my back stinging from the friction of the wall as he thrust into me.

I looked at him, seeing his eyes on mine, and we both watched each other, our lips barely an inch apart as he lowered his forehead to mine.

My pussy clenched around his cock, loving every inch he put into me and feeling that high every time he rubbed my G-spot.

He bit my bottom lip. "Is that it?" He slid in and out of me, raw and rough. "Do you like how I take what I want?"

The amused tone was so fucking smug, I wanted to teach him a lesson.

"No," I answered. "You're being careful with me."

"Am I?" he repeated, feigning concern.

And before I knew it, he'd dropped me to my feet and spun me around. He lifted my skirt again, and I bent just a little, planting my hands on the wall as he gripped the curve of my hips and impaled me with his cock.

"Ah." My breathing shook and my legs tingled. "Tyler, God."

I reached back and snaked an arm around his neck as he pushed me gently against the wall, still driving into me. The rough, cool bricks bit into my chest, and he seemed to realize it, because he placed a hand against the wall for my face to rest on.

My eyes rolled to the back of my head, my orgasm cresting deep inside. "You feel so good," I said in barely a whisper.

He took my face and turned me toward him, dipping his tongue into my mouth and kissing me long and slow.

I felt my insides tighten and clench, and while his body didn't slow down, it was his lips that captivated me the most.

Soft, sweet, and gentle with me.

"Easton," he breathed against my mouth.

I opened my eyes to see him looking at me.

His gaze turned thoughtful. "I've been with enough women to know when it's right and when it's wrong"—he bit my bottom lip and released it—"and when I have you in my hands, it feels more right than anything."

I moaned, holding his eyes as I pushed against the wall and backed up into his thrusts.

"I still haven't felt your skin on mine," he said, his voice turning harder as he lowered his hands, kneading and squeezing my hips roughly. "And I still haven't tasted you."

I dropped my head, struggling to catch my breath. "Please," I begged, though I wasn't sure what for. "Tyler, please."

I didn't want him to stop what he was doing and I didn't want him to stop what he was saying, but I knew he should.

"I'm going to strip you down and get you in a bed," he breathed into my ear, "so I can see this beautiful body fuck me from on top,"

I dug my nails into the brick, scratching the hard surface. "Yes," I groaned. "So good."

He leaned in until there was absolutely no space between us. "I hope you're on the pill." His thrusts grew harder and faster, and I backed up into it, my moans, his grunts, and our skin meeting over and over again the only sounds in our little space. "I'm taking you home with me, and we're doing this all over again."

I spoke into his ear, smiling. "But I have schoolwork," I played. "You and I have a parent-teacher conference soon, and you're not the only parent I have to take care of."

His eyes flared before falling closed. He was close.

"Your schoolwork and the other parents can wait," he ordered, grabbing my hair, his breath falling on the side of my face. "You're still taking care of me."

My pussy tightened around his cock, and I opened my mouth, gasping and moaning.

"Tyler," I cried out.

He breathed hard, squeezing my tit as he moaned. "Oh, fuck."

And I hunched over, crying out as my insides exploded and his dick rammed my sweet spot, bringing me home.

"Oh, God," I groaned.

Warmth spread through my belly, and my legs shook from the tingles spreading down my muscles.

My whole body continued to jerk, and my head bobbed back and forth as he kept pounding me from behind.

"Ah," he growled, and I winced from how hard he gripped my hips.

He yanked me back again, my neck jerking twice as he slammed his cock deep inside me and came. The warmth of his come filled me up, and his ragged breathing fell across my shoulder blade as he bowed his head, trying to catch his breath.

He stayed inside me, and I made no move to separate us.

Holy shit.

The slow realization hit me of where we were and that anyone could have seen us. My body—hot only moments ago—began to cool from my wet clothes, and the soreness between my legs started to feel heavier by the second. My back probably had scratches on it, my ass and hips probably had bruises from his hands, and my panties were a torn scrap on the dirty ground.

But I didn't care.

I tilted my head, finding his sweet lips and getting lost in his soft kiss.

No, I didn't care.

Shit.

TWELVE

TYLER

The constant rain pummeled the windows, and I blinked awake, the only light in the room coming from the blue glare of the digits on the alarm clock.

Sitting up slowly, I combed my fingers through my hair and wiped away the sweat on my forehead.

Shit, it's hot in here. The humidity from the rain always made everything so miserable.

Glancing to my side, I noticed the small form underneath the sheet, and I slowly leaned down on one elbow, my heart racing with pleasure at the sight of Easton Bradbury curled up on her side, her hand—palm up—resting next to her face.

Her eyelids, with their thick, brown lashes, rested calmly, with none of her usual little scowls tightening her pretty face. She looked peaceful.

I inhaled a heavy breath, suddenly feeling like the air was too thick.

What the hell was she doing to me?

I hadn't felt like this in a long time.

Not since the first time I realized I wanted my son and I was losing him.

Christian had barely been a toddler the first time I'd seen him. And for the first time in my life, I finally started to realize there were things I might not be able to have.

And I'd been scared. Exactly like I was now.

Christian smiles so wide his eyes close as he kicks the beach ball with his little legs. His mouth makes an O when he sees how far the ball travels, and he takes off, running after it.

I look between Brynne and him, playing in the park and unaware that I'm there. My heart aches.

My son.

I can barely breathe.

I was driving down St. Charles when I'd spotted her car. I'd glanced around for only a few seconds before I saw her.

And him.

I don't know why I did it, but I'd pulled over. We hadn't spoken lately, and I hadn't seen my son since he was born. I thought about him, but it still didn't feel like he was real.

Not until now.

I swallow, seeing her pick him up and hold him over her head. He's only about a year and a half, and I smile, noticing how happy and playful he is.

He looks just like me.

Life was scarier—and harder—when you had things you were afraid to lose.

Reaching out, I ran my thumb down her golden cheek, the skin as smooth as water.

She pursed her rose lips, her soft breathing sweeter than music, and I let out a breath, running my possessive hand down her side and over her ass.

What the hell was I doing? Why was she so damn addictive?

She reminded me so much of myself—the pride, the independence, the stubbornness . . .

But I rarely ever spent the night with a woman, much less brought them to my house, so why the hell had I done so with her?

I struggled with too many expectations from other people on me, as well as my own, to bring a woman into the mix.

This was a mistake.

She'd start getting demanding, I'd start disappointing her, and she'd eventually realize that she would never come first.

At least that's the way it had always been.

Pushing away my warring thoughts, I slowly pulled down the sheet, exposing her perfect breasts, full with hard nipples that begged for my mouth.

My cock began to rush with heat and harden, and my chest swelled with the need to be something for her that I had never been for any other woman. I wanted to give her everything. I wanted to never disappoint her.

Reaching down, I took myself in my hand and stroked as I leaned over and flicked her nipple with my tongue and then caught it between my teeth, dragging out the sensation.

She moaned, and the sheet over my cock tented. I loved that little sound of hers.

"Do that again," I begged, opening my mouth and sucking in as much of her tit as I could handle.

Her hand went to my hair, and I could feel the vibrations of her groan against my mouth as I kissed her body.

Fuck.

I let out a breath, feeling my groin tighten even further. "You got me hard again."

And I grabbed her hand, laying it on my steel cock.

She mewed like a satisfied kitten, and I looked up to see her eyes still closed but a little smile peeking out.

I didn't wait. I never fucking waited with her.

I rose and climbed on top of her, nestling between the warm legs she so graciously opened for me.

I grinded up and down her slick heat, feeling her wetness on my cock already.

"Jesus, you're wet," I whispered against her mouth as I laid my chest flush with hers with my forearms resting on either side of her head. "Is that what I do to you? Huh?" I teased.

But rather than her usual smart-ass comebacks, she blinked awake and gazed at me, looking so fucking innocent and dreamy.

"Yeah." She nodded.

My fists balled above her head, and I covered her mouth with mine as I thrust my hips, sliding into her tight body.

What the hell was I doing?

The hot spray cascaded over my head and down my neck and shoulders, sending chills over my skin as my body finally relaxed. I'd woken up again during the night with another erection and realized it was because her mouth was wrapped around my cock under the sheets.

I leaned a hand against the black tiled shower wall and bowed my head, letting out a breath.

Biologically, neither one of us was at our sexual peak, but you wouldn't know it. I was practically in high school all over again, with an insatiable young woman I couldn't get enough of, and all she had to do was look at me or breathe and I was as hard as a steel pole.

I hadn't felt an urge to go more than twice a night in years, and here I was, four times in the last eight hours, with muscles I'd forgotten existed aching.

I couldn't be more satisfied. Or less.

Plus, I had a shitload of work to do—I shouldn't have overslept—but if I took her home, I knew I'd only be running back to her in a matter of hours.

I turned off the water and grabbed the towel hanging off the hook. After drying off my face and hair, I wrapped it around my waist and stepped out of the shower.

But as soon as I walked back into my bedroom, I stopped and hardened my glare.

"What are you doing?"

Easton was fully dressed in her wrinkled skirt and blouse from last night and sitting on the edge of the bed, bending over as she slipped her feet back into her flats.

She glanced over at me briefly before turning away again.

"I need to go home."

I ground my teeth together to prevent myself from shouting at her, instead walking over to yank a pair of dark-washed jeans out of my closet.

"You got a dog?" I asked, ripping off the towel and tossing it.

"No."

I peered over at her as I slipped my legs into the pants. "A cat? A kid? You left the stove on?" I went on.

She pursed her lips, knowing I was mocking her. Turning away, she ran her fingers through her hair, trying to tame it.

"Take your clothes off, Easton. They're dirty," I ordered, buttoning my jeans. "I have a T-shirt you can wear."

Her posture straightened, and I could see she was taking a deep breath. I combed my fingers through my wet hair as I walked over to her.

"I'm a gentleman only when I need to be," I warned. "It's a monsoon out there. You're not walking out of here."

She spun around, her worried eyes pulling at my heart.

"I shouldn't have come back here." She crossed her arms over her chest. "Christian could come home unexpectedly, or . . ."

"Christian won't be home," I cut in. "Trust me. This is the last place he wants to be."

She shifted on her feet, refusing to meet my eyes.

I tipped her chin up, making her look at me. "I want you to spend time with me," I told her. "I'm not saying I want a relationship. God knows, I suck at that. But I'd like us to relax for a day, okay?"

She looked away, letting out a sigh. "I hate not knowing what to expect." She gave a sad little laugh. "I hate not seeing what's coming at me, and I get nervous when things go off course. I—"

"You're on the pill, right?" I shot out, but I managed to keep my voice light.

She blinked, straightening her back at my sudden change of subject.

"Excuse me?" she blurted out, looking confused.

I almost laughed. "I haven't been pulling out, and you never answered me last night."

"Well, you didn't really ask," she reminded me. "And you didn't seem too concerned about it, either."

"In the moment, no," I agreed, walking over to my chest of drawers and getting her a white V-neck. "And after feeling you without one, I doubt I'll want to start now." I walked back over to her and handed her the shirt.

"You are on the pill?" I asked again. "Right?"

Her eyebrow quirked, and the mischievous grin she offered delighted me.

"Easton." I gave her the warning tone I usually reserved for my son and my employees.

Her smile spread wide, actually revealing teeth. "Of course," she soothed. "I would've stopped you if I wasn't."

I shook my head, taking her shirt and lifting it up over her head. Whether or not getting involved with my son's teacher was a huge mistake, getting her pregnant would definitely be a disaster.

"You see?" I told her. "Problems can always be bigger."

I undid her zipper and let her skirt fall to the ground. She was completely nude underneath, and I felt my heart pick up its pace when I remembered her lacy underwear were probably still lying somewhere in the French Quarter.

I slipped the T-shirt over her head and then reached down and grabbed her ass, bringing her closer.

"You distracted me on purpose," she accused, a hint of amusement in her eyes.

Yes, yes, I had. Her head had been starting to work again, just like last night, and I didn't want her worrying about half a million things that wouldn't happen today.

Or to start counting things, for crying out loud.

"Yes." I trailed my lips across her cheek and down to her neck. "Because you can't go home," I whispered as her arms circled my neck and held me close.

"Why?"

I squeezed her ass, pressing her to my hardening cock. "Because your pussy is like gold, and in a matter of hours, I'll want more of it."

"Ugh," she growled, pushing me away but smiling. "I see men in their thirties are no tamer than men in their twenties."

I pinched her chin between my thumb and index finger. "Lucky you," I replied.

She shook her head at me, probably deciding to pack away her escape plan for now. She was stuck.

"I'm going to go make some phone calls," I told her, backing away. "Feel free to use the shower, and there's food in the kitchen if you're hungry."

THIRTEEN

EASTON

Arguing with Tyler Marek was a waste of time, especially when you didn't really disagree.

I *should've* gone home.

I had work to get ahead on, an oven that I could've been cleaning, and lots of updates to be made to my website for the students and parents. Not to mention, I had leftover homemade bread in the freezer that needed to be eaten before the end of the month. I had a responsibility to Christian, and if I were his mother, I'd . . .

I let out a deep breath as I walked up to the vanity in his huge bathroom, having put back on his T-shirt after my shower, I rubbed the back of my head with a gray towel and shook my head.

I should go home.

But he kept wanting me.

He kept tapping at my shell like I was an egg he needed to crack. And while I constantly felt like goo that would spill everywhere if not protected by my hard outer armor, he made me feel like I didn't need it.

Like he was going to take care of everything.

Here, in his cave of a house, with its shutters drawn and big, empty rooms, the serene glow of the soft lamps and the pitter-patter of rain on the roof, I'd finally relaxed.

He made me feel safe, and while I didn't need a man to protect me, I kind of enjoyed letting some of the worry go. For the first time in a long time, I'd closed my eyes and fallen asleep last night without a struggle, peaceful in the feeling that someone was next to me.

And when I woke up, I hadn't had the split-second moment of panic I always had before I registered that I was safe.

Instead, I'd woken up this morning, and rather than quickly scanning the room and taking inventory, my eyes had immediately fallen on Tyler's back as he walked to the bathroom and winked at me over his shoulder before disappearing into the shower.

I found his hairbrush on the expansive sink counter, along with a hair dryer. After combing out my hair, I blew it out, threw the used towel in the hamper, and made up his bed. I also folded my clothes neatly, placing them on the chair in the corner, and scanned the room to make sure everything was in its place.

Or in its place as well as I could tell.

Stepping out of the room and into the hallway—if you could call it that—I slowly turned my head, taking in the surroundings that I had failed to notice last night as Tyler practically hauled me upstairs.

The landing was circular with a railing, so you could lean over and peer downstairs. Bedroom doors—or I assumed that's what they were—lined the edges, and there was another staircase, leading to a third floor. The dark teak floors glimmered in the gentle lighting from the chandelier hanging above, and all of the wooden furniture surfaces shined. The lemon scent of wood polish, leather, and cologne filled my lungs, and it brought a smile to my face.

Men lived here, and those scents brought back memories of growing up with Jack and my father.

Trailing down the stairs, I stepped hesitantly, poking out my head with a watchful eye. I was still afraid Christian or someone else might appear and I wouldn't have the slightest idea how to explain myself.

Peering to the right, I spied the foyer, so I turned left, heading toward the back of the house, figuring I'd find the kitchen. At the sound of Tyler's voice, I stopped at the entrance to another hallway and caught a glimpse of a light coming through another door.

I couldn't make out what he was saying, but he had that deep, frigid tone that he'd tried using on me in his office last Saturday, so I deduced he was probably on a business call.

I continued looking for the kitchen, my stomach swimming with butterflies at the image of him conducting business and issuing orders with his scary arched eyebrow while wearing nothing but those jeans.

When I found it, I rummaged through the refrigerator, craving carbs and protein.

I'd want him again when he was done with his big, bad call, so I needed energy.

When I switched on the radio, Rihanna's "Only Girl" filled the room, and I started bobbing my head as I padded around the kitchen in my bare feet. I chopped up some leftover potatoes I'd found in the refrigerator and fried up some bacon. After mixing up some eggs, chives, salt, and pepper, I poured the mixture into a pan, scooped the bacon pieces and potatoes on top, and then placed the dish in the oven to bake for a country French omelet.

Before I knew it, I was happily lost in fixing place settings at the granite island with coffee and orange juice and chopping up fresh pineapple, strawberries, and blueberries for a salad, as well as drawing hot biscuits from the oven. I figured they were homemade, since I'd found them in a plastic container in the refrigerator, so all I'd needed to do was heat them up.

I wasn't sure who kept the kitchen so well stocked or who'd originally cooked the biscuits I was reheating, but I guessed it wasn't Tyler. I couldn't picture that.

I grabbed the pot holders and switched off the oven, leaning down to retrieve the pan.

"Goddamn," I heard behind me. "You're never allowed to wear underwear again."

I peeked over my shoulder, still leaning down to the stove, and saw Tyler standing on the other side of the counter with his eyes nowhere near mine. His forearms rested on the island, and his head was cocked to the side as his gaze swept over my bottom and down my legs. And since he'd torn away my underwear last night, I wore nothing underneath.

I grabbed the pan and straightened, smiling as I placed it on top of the oven.

"How's business?" I asked, using a knife to cut the large omelet in half.

"I've still got a bit to do," he answered, and I heard him pouring coffee, "but I'm not allowed to touch you until it's finished, so I'll get it done quickly."

I twisted my head around to narrow my eyes on him.

He must've seen the question in my eyes, because he laughed to himself. "On the rare occasion I have something I'd rather be doing instead of work, I have to bargain with myself," he explained, and locked his gaze on mine. "And I can't put my hands on you until I'm done with my work. That's the bargain today."

I smirked. "We'll see," I taunted.

He arched his damn eyebrows at me and set the coffeepot down.

I slid half an omelet onto a spatula. "You like omelets, I hope?"

"Yes," he rushed out, sounding relieved as he slid onto the stool. "I'm starving. You didn't have to do this, but thank you. It looks great."

He immediately started digging into the omelet, and I had a hard time not watching him as he ate everything on his plate and downed his glass of orange juice, quickly pouring himself another. The fruit and biscuits in front of him disappeared just as fast, but I, on the other hand, had to force myself to take bites, because I was having more fun watching him wolf down his breakfast.

He kind of ate like he screwed. In the moment, it was the only thing he needed, and while it was happening, it was the only thing he was thinking about.

His hair was devoid of any product and fell casually to the side, while his jeans hung loosely, just above the curve of his ass. I set my fork down, hungry but not for food anymore, as my heart rate picked up, and I devoured him with my eyes.

"Easton," he growled, making my name sound like a warning. "I mean it. I need to work."

I snapped my eyes up to see him sipping coffee and staring ahead, a hard expression on his face. He knew what I'd been thinking.

"Can't keep up with the appetite of a twenty-three-year-old?" I teased.

He looked affronted. "You're going to pay for that."

Oh, I hope so.

I was half tempted to put more effort into distracting him. I liked making him angry.

But I decided against it, realizing it would divulge to him how much I was enjoying his company.

I let my eyes trail down his thick, corded forearms, wide chest, and toned stomach, almost wishing Tyler were twenty-two again. Maybe if I'd slept with the cocky asswipe he'd been in his youth, I wouldn't have grown to like him as much as I had already.

He was still an asshole, but it came off endearing most of the time, and he completely turned me on. He was also patient, as eager to please me in bed as he was to please himself, and confident in what he wanted.

And today that was me.

I cleared my throat and tried to continue eating. "Are you sure you're not expecting anyone home today?" I asked.

"I just called Christian to check in," he assured me. "He's a hundred twenty miles away and already out fishing for the day."

I winced and returned to my fruit.

"What?"

I looked up at him, not having meant for him to see my reaction.

"Ah, well . . ." I searched for the words. "I guess it seems boring. For me anyway," I added.

"I agree." He nodded, surprising me. "I'm not much of a country boy."

I grinned to myself, happy to hear that I hadn't offended him. Or maybe happy to hear we had that in common, as well.

I'd never been interested in hunting or fishing, although I didn't think I'd be averse to camping and hiking if I ever got the chance to try them.

Reaching over and grabbing the iPad, I laid it on the island between our plates.

"I'd say the wilderness you brave is far more dangerous, anyway," I commented, gesturing to the *Times-Picayune* article I'd found about him online.

He rolled his eyes at the headline: *Marek and Blackwell Vying for Senate?*

"You investigated me?" he accused, eyeing me playfully as he repeated my words to him from last night.

I licked my lips, trying to hide the smile. "I know how to Google," I retorted.

I brought up the notes I'd made on the iPad, shoving it over to him as I hopped off my stool and began clearing dishes.

"What's this?" he asked about what I'd written.

"I made some notes on your platform," I told him, clearing off the plates and placing them in the dishwasher.

While the food had been in the oven, I'd scanned some articles about him and browsed around his website, taking a look at random press conferences he'd given concerning news in his company or his interest in running for senator.

"Who writes your speeches?" I asked.

"I do."

My eyebrows shot up, but I didn't turn away in time. He'd seen my face.

"What?" he asked, sounding defensive.

I dried off my hands and faced him, wondering how I would tell a man as insistent and stubborn as Tyler Marek that he kind of stunk at something.

He watched me, and I gave him an apologetic smile. "No offense," I inched out, "but your speeches are lacking. You're about as heartwarming as a meat locker."

His back straightened and his chin dipped, and for a moment I thought I was in for another spanking.

"And your online presence needs work," I added. "You're kind of dull."

His eyes narrowed. "Get in my lap. I'll show you how dull I am."

I rolled my eyes, ignoring his threat as I circled the island and came to stand at his side.

"Here, look." I tapped the screen, bringing up his social media."Your Twitter followers." I pointed to his number and then brought up another profile. "Mason Blackwell's Twitter followers."

I eyed him, hoping he saw the huge difference. Mason Blackwell had five times as many followers, but he didn't have nearly the influence of Tyler Marek.

Tyler owned a multimillion-dollar worldwide corporation. So why did he come off looking like a hermit?

I went on, scrolling through the iPad, pointing things out. "You tweet—or the person you hired tweets—once every other day. And it's boring," I told him. "Retweets of articles, 'have a nice day everyone,' Blah."

Tyler looked up, clearly not appreciating my attitude.

I continued. "He tweets every other hour, and it's photos, family funnies, mundane crap, but it's engaging," I explained, meeting Tyler's eyes.

He sighed, sounding stubborn. "I already hear this from my brother. I don't need it from you," he argued. "Twitter won't put me in office. People vote for—"

"Whoever's popular, Tyler," I cut in, not sorry that I sounded curt. "Sorry to say, but not every voter makes informed decisions."

And then a thought crossed my mind, and I grinned, grabbing the iPad and snapping a picture of his nearly empty bowl of fruit, save for a strawberry half and two blueberries.

Attaching the photo and adding a caption, I posted it under his profile. Lucky for me the device was already logged into his account.

Handing over the iPad, I let him take a look.

He read, "'Having breakfast on lockdown. Stay safe out there everyone!'"

I blew on my fingernails and brushed them over my shirtsleeve, pleased with myself.

His eyebrows nose-dived. "Wait," he bit out. "You can see my stomach in that picture."

"Mmm-hmm," I cooed, nodding.

He glared at me. "My bare stomach, Easton," he pointed out, as if I were blind.

I held up my pointer finger and thumb, measuring an inch. "Just a sliver."

The small white ceramic bowl was sitting near the edge of the island. The picture showed not only the bowl, but a nice slice of his tight stomach.

He shoved the iPad at me. "Delete it."

I grabbed it, feigning nonchalance. "Sorry. No can do." I shrugged and then looked at the iPad when I heard a notification alert. "Oh, look! It's already been retweeted twice, and it's probably been screenshot by ten other users," I explained. "If you delete it now, it'll look weird."

"Give it to me." He stood up, holding out his hand. "I'll figure it out myself."

"No!"

I ran around the island, stuffing the iPad into the microwave, and moved to turn around, but he was already at my back, stopping me.

I breathed out a laugh, the heat of the chase filling my lungs with excitement.

"You can't have it," I whispered, plastering my palms against the microwave.

His body blanketed my back, and his lips nuzzled my neck, making my eyelids grow heavy.

His fingertips grazed up over my hips, and I realized that he was pulling up the T-shirt.

"Maybe that's not what I want anymore." His gravelly voice was filled with promise, and I immediately groaned at the rush of heat between my legs.

But I wasn't fooled.

"You're trying to distract me," I assessed, although I didn't mind it in the least.

His quiet laugh tickled my ear, but his hands continued to roam, and I let my head fall to the side, feeling him immediately bury his nose in my neck.

"What is that?" he asked, popping his head up.

I blinked as his attention shifted, the tingles his hands were bringing dissipating. I listened, hearing beeps and whistles, and I turned around, smiling.

"Favorites, retweets, replies," I listed, gloating. "The sounds of victory."

He pinned me with a familiar stubborn look, but I caught the hint of amusement underneath.

"Go finish your work." I jerked my chin in the direction of the hallway. "You can thank me later."

FOURTEEN

TYLER

When I was her age, twenty-three, she was twelve, for Christ's sake.

Not to mention that Brynne would have my head—and deservedly so—if she ever found out about the things I was doing with Christian's teacher.

What the fuck was the matter with me?

Every time I had the opportunity to take the high road in my personal life, I didn't. I'd put my kid on the back burner for the sake of my career, and now I felt like I was taking advantage of a young woman.

Sure, she was just as complicated as I was and she gave as good as she got, but I'd learned to assess the road ahead before taking steps. With her, I had no idea what the next hour held, much less the next week or month.

She was unpredictable and entirely too addicting. It wasn't so much the woman she tried to be that I liked but the girl she tried to hide. The one who needed to be held.

I sat at my desk, trying to work through the laundry list of e-mails I'd accumulated since leaving work yesterday as her music played in the background and she sang along a few feet away. Something about "drown" or "drowning." It had been so long since I'd listened to music, but thanks to her and Christian, I was getting up to speed.

Despite the fact that I was swamped, as usual.

Production had stopped in Brazil due to rain, and a contract I'd already secured in Japan now had a lower bidder, so I was trying to put out fires, but my head just wasn't in the game today.

The storm outside had lightened, but it was still too heavy to enjoy leaving the house.

Not that I wanted to anyway.

I glanced over, seeing Easton standing at the bookshelves in my office, the hem of my T-shirt rising up her thigh and over the curve of her ass as she reached to the third shelf.

Jesus.

I blinked and refocused on my computer screen, mentally hitting myself for inviting her in here. I didn't want her to be bored, so I'd told her to hang out, grab a book, and read or work on the spare laptop if she needed.

However, she'd quickly turned into a woman on a mission, unable to resist alphabetizing my small personal library.

"This doesn't drive you crazy?" she'd complained, wincing at the sight of my messy shelves. "This would drive me crazy."

Yeah, so I let her off her leash to have at it.

As long as she didn't incorporate the entire fucking Dewey Decimal System into her organization, I had no problem watching her cute little behind while she reached for books.

However, I wasn't getting much done.

She'd been quiet, concentrating on her own work, but when a five-foot-seven brunette with gorgeous golden legs is crawling around on your floor, organizing stacks of books and looking cute as hell, watching her is an irresistible enjoyment.

"Are you almost finished?" She stood on the small ladder, reaching up and replacing the last few books.

I blinked, refocusing on my screen. "Not yet," I answered. "About ten more e-mails to respond to."

I wiggled my fingers, trying to remember what I needed to type and realizing I'd forgotten what the damn e-mail I needed to respond to had said.

Out of the corner of my eye, I noticed her stepping down from the ladder, barely making a sound.

"Tyler?"

I looked up, seeing her standing on the other side of my desk with a sweet look on her face. I narrowed my eyes.

What is she up to?

"I'm getting bored," she said.

"The kitchen cabinets need organizing," I shot back.

But she let out a sigh. "I think I'm just going to go take a bubble bath in your huge tub and wait for you," she chirped. "And think about you. Maybe."

I raised my eyes, swallowing down the thought of her wet and covered in suds.

"Sit down," I commanded, pointing to the couch. "This was an hour's worth of work that's turned into two, because you're distracting me."

"You told me to come in here!"

"And you're not taking a bath," I shouted, ignoring her interruption, "because I'm going to damn well come with you, so don't move! You understand?"

"I'm bored," she repeated, "and I don't like not to be doing things."

"Tough."

And I dropped my eyes back to the screen, typing I-have-no-idea-what just to get it done. My fingers worked without thinking, and

I was probably coming off less polite than I normally made the effort to appear in my business communications, but there were better things to be doing.

She stood on the other side of my desk, watching me. "All right," she said. "I'll make you a deal."

I tapped the keyboard, trying to ignore her. The sooner I could finish, the sooner we could spend the rest of the day in bed.

"If you finish your e-mails before I'm done, I'll stay," she challenged. "If you don't finish those ten e-mails before I'm done, I'm leaving, and I don't care whether it's raining or not."

What?

I shot my eyes up to her, scowling. "Before you're done?" I shot out. "Done with what?"

A twinkle flashed in her eye, but she didn't smile.

Instead, she walked over to the coffee-colored leather sofa and picked up the black pin-striped suit jacket I'd left there days ago, when I'd come home from work. With her back to me, she slipped my T-shirt over her head, dropping it to the floor, and brought my jacket up to her front, covering herself.

Every inch of me felt like I'd climbed into a hot, soothing bath, but my racing heart was anything but soothed. I fisted my fingers, seeing her long, naked back, smooth and toned, and I wanted to touch every part of her, including that perfect, heart-shaped ass she was flashing me.

Lying down on the sofa, she spread my jacket over her naked body, one hand rubbing the fabric over the inside of her thigh while the other slipped underneath the jacket.

My breath caught, seeing her fingers move under the coat, while she rubbed my jacket over her pussy, rolling her hips into the cloth.

Before I'm done. She was masturbating.

"Oh, you fucking bitch," I whispered, meeting her heated eyes.

She blinked, and I expected to see her looking amused and playful, but she looked beautifully desperate.

"It has your smell on it." She ground my jacket between her legs, closing her eyes and arching her neck back.

The jacket covered her as if I were wearing it and lying on top of her, from the neck to the tops of her thighs. Her legs were bent at the knees, and the bottoms of her feet were touching, making a diamond shape. That hand that I was so jealous of played slowly and softly, judging from the little movements under the jacket.

The idea of my clothes on her naked body was driving me fucking insane.

My jeans were tight, and the ache between my legs was growing.

"That's a two-thousand-dollar suit," I pointed out, trying to sound unaffected.

She dragged her bottom lip between her teeth, groaning as she clutched the fabric resting between her legs. "Worth every penny," she taunted. "God, it feels like you."

The corner of my lips turned up. I loved the idea of showing her that I felt a hell of a lot better than some piece of cloth she was dry fucking.

"Move the jacket," I told her.

She opened her eyes and peered over at me, a rose-tinged blush falling across her cheeks.

"I don't think that's a good idea." Her body shifted and squirmed under the jacket as she continued fingering herself. "It'll distract you."

"Move the fucking jacket, Easton."

A smile flashed across her eyes, and she slid the jacket off her body, letting it fall to the floor.

Jesus.

I tipped my chin at her. "Drop your foot to the ground and open your legs wider."

She did it, letting her right foot rest on the hardwood floor and spreading her thighs wide. My view was perfect.

She grazed her clit with her middle finger, rubbing over it and playing as she watched me.

"You better get typing," she teased, tapping her clit three times. "Type, type, type . . ." she taunted.

I scowled, ducking my head and typing furiously and then punching the backspace button fifteen times because of all the mistakes I was making.

I tried not to look at her, but it was like she was the only thing in the room, completely dominating my senses. I kept typing, but I would blink and dart my gaze over to see her rubbing her hard little nub in circles faster and faster. The flesh was dark pink, and I couldn't stop wishing my mouth was buried in it.

I finished the e-mail, clicked *Send*, and double-clicked on another one. Some VP in the South American office whining about delayed production on the new line of equipment.

Fuck you. Fuck you. Fuck you. Get it done.

I didn't really say that. Only the last part, but . . .

Her little moans carried across the room and vibrated over my skin, and I groaned, feeling my dick grow steel-rod straight. She wasn't loud or exaggerated, and that made it hotter, because it was real.

I clicked *Send*, and then I opened up another e-mail. "Don't come," I ordered, looking up to check on her.

Her left hand was gripping the back of the sofa next to her, and her head was up, so she could watch her fingers move softly in and out. Her mouth was open, and her face looked pained as she let out little cries.

Shit.

I typed faster.

"I wish you were here," she breathed out, teasing me. "Your kisses drive me crazy, so I wonder what your tongue would feel like between my legs."

I grunted, shifting in my seat, and clicked *Send*, opening up another e-mail.

"God, I can see your cock through your pants," she mewed. "It's making my mouth water, baby."

I blinked long and hard.

Type, type, type . . . My fingers worked hard, making constant mistakes, but I kept my head down, scowling, every muscle in my face as hard as iron.

Open, type, send, open, type, send . . . I grunted, shifting in my seat, her little moans getting higher and higher and making my body ache like hell.

"Please tell me I can have it," she begged. "Please."

"Are you trying to make me come?" I growled. "You said I had to finish 'before you were done,' so masturbate and shut up. I can't concentrate with that talk."

I opened another e-mail—only two left—but then I heard her small, taunting voice, sounding innocent.

"Yes, Mr. Marek."

Fuck.

I glared at her, barely hesitating before shooting out of my chair. I slammed the laptop closed and rounded the desk, holding her eyes as excitement flashed across her face.

"You asked for it," I gritted out.

I pushed my pants down, letting them drop to the floor, and then I came down on her and nestled my hips between her thighs.

I groaned, my heart racing as I grabbed my cock and ran it up and down her pussy. "This is what you do to me."

She bit her bottom lip, squirming as she moaned.

I grabbed the backs of her thighs and pulled her into position. "You get me all worked up, and this is what happens."

I pressed my hand into the armrest behind her head and thrust hard, sliding into her hot little pussy.

"Ah, ah!" she gasped, her eyes pinching together in sweet pain.

"Goddamn it," I moaned. "You feel so fucking good."

The first fucking thrust is always the best.

I held myself up with one hand on the sofa behind her head, and I slid my other hand under her ass, keeping her where I wanted her as I pulled out and slid back in again, hard and deep, up to the hilt.

"Oh, Tyler." She swallowed, moving both hands to my back and spreading her legs even wider.

I slid into her again and again, faster and faster every time, until I was pounding into her so hard that I couldn't see straight.

Her pretty tits bounced back and forth as sweat started to glide down my back.

"Ah, oh God." She moaned, breathing hard and arching her head back.

Her cries filled the room, and her skin was glued to the leather of the sofa, but her pussy was hot and smooth, and I darted down, catching her bottom lip between my teeth.

"You're bad for me, and I love it," I breathed out, grinding between her legs, not letting up for a second.

She kissed me deep, pushing her head up and putting everything into it. Her tongue tasted sweet and sexy, just like her, and we were both moaning, like animals that couldn't get enough.

She fell back on the sofa and held on to my back, letting me have my way with her.

"I love your body, Tyler." She ran her fingers lightly down my chest and stomach.

I gave her a small grin, liking the sound of that. I was usually the one complimenting a woman's body. I didn't know why, but it wasn't something women often thought to say to a man, and I loved her for it.

Especially since I wasn't the twentysomething she was probably used to being with. I didn't mind being older than her, but I didn't want to seem old.

"I don't want anyone else to have it while we're doing this, okay?" she asked, looking up at me.

I laughed and circled my arms around her waist, flipping us both over so that I sat up against the back of the couch with my feet on the floor, and she sat on top, straddling my hips with my dick still inside her.

"You laying claim?" I teased, gripping her ass as she immediately began rolling her hips, riding me.

"I mean it," she stated firmly. "You've seen my temper."

I smiled at her, arching my head back and closing my eyes as she slid up and down my cock. "Don't worry," I soothed. "This dick is yours."

Sex had never been this good with anyone in my life, and there had been plenty to compare her to. The thing I'd learned about sex was that for it to be good, it had to be more than just fucking. Playing, teasing, talking—the pair up of the right two people—and you had the difference between an act that you'd forget in two minutes and something that you wanted again and again.

Easton Bradbury kept me wanting more.

She seemed to like my answer, because she leaned down and trailed kisses over my neck and jaw. "Same goes for you." I squeezed her ass tighter with my other hand and threaded my fingers through her hair, pulling gently and raising her head to face me. "You got that?"

She licked her lips, looking at me with a sudden serious expression, almost sad. "You're the only one I want," she spoke softly. "Right now."

That made me jerk my head up and narrow my eyes on her.

Tightening my grip, I grabbed and lifted her again, tossing her back down on the couch before pinning her wrists above her head.

"That wasn't exactly reassuring," I barked, thrusting good and hard.

She squeezed her eyes shut, moaning, "Oh, God. Tyler." She cried out, "Fuck, I'm coming!"

I felt her pussy clenching around my cock, and I showed her no mercy. Diving into her mouth, I tasted her tongue and let her cries drown out in my kiss.

She grabbed my ass and held tight, the bite of her nails stinging my skin as her body tensed beneath me.

She spasmed, her short, fast breaths echoing around me as her body shook with the orgasm.

"You make me want to ignore my work," I accused, loving how wet she was after coming, "and I'd rather have you here at my beck and call than let you go home. Now, if you liked that," I bit out, referring to the orgasm I'd just given her, "then I think you can assume you're going to be coming back for more for the foreseeable future."

She blinked her eyes open, looking desperate and confused. "All I know"—she breathed hard, searching for words—"is that you're the only one I want."

"For today?" I asked gently, placing my elbows on either side of her head and grazing my lips over hers, before whispering, "Or can I at least get a week out of you?"

She opened her mouth, trying to catch my lips for a kiss, but I pulled back just far enough to tease her.

Anger flashed in her eyes, and I smiled, loving that she liked getting kissed by me.

"What's your track record, Easton?" I looked down into her eyes, keeping my voice calm. "How many boyfriends have you had? How long did they last? How long before you're ready to jump into a new bed?"

Her eyebrows shot up, and she pushed at my chest. "Get off me," she gritted out.

But I continued my smooth, even rhythm as pleasure started to course through my groin. "How long?" I taunted.

"What about you?" she snapped, pushing at my chest. "You can't tell me you don't have another woman somewhere."

"Oh, I do," I replied, keeping my voice light. "Several, actually. One on every continent."

"Go to hell." She slammed her palm into my chest. "And get off me!"

But I grabbed her hands and pinned them up above her head.

"There's one in France and another in London. And they have beautiful women in Buenos Aires."

She pinched her lips and pushed against my chest. "Ugh!"

I rolled my hips as I continued to move in and out of her while I tried not to laugh. "But you know why I want the hot little teacher in New Orleans?" I taunted, looking down into her eyes. "Because she fucking gives me what I want better than anyone else."

The two small wrinkles between her eyes deepened, and her jaw hardened as she tried very hard to look angry when she wasn't.

"You've got a hell of a body, Easton," I breathed out over her lips. "You've also got a sharp tongue, and your temper is a hell of a lot of fun. It's not just about sex."

I dipped down, kissing her neck as I released her hands and grabbed the armrest to anchor myself. I began moving faster again, her small whimpers in my ear growing more desperate as her body took control.

I grunted, feeling the pleasure course down my cock.

God, I needed to come.

She squeezed her eyes shut. I could tell she was about to come again, too.

"So you wanna have fun with me for a while?" I asked.

"Yes," she gasped, pleading. "Yes."

I arched up, peering down at her closed eyes and her chest rising and falling with heavy breaths.

"Please, what?" I thrust into her harder, seeing her come apart.

God, she was beautiful. For one second she was stripped down, bare, and gorgeous, without any of her armor—and it made me feel like she would die without the one thing I could give her. But I also hated that those moments came so rarely, because I lived for them now.

"Please kiss me," she begged.

I covered her mouth with mine as I went at her with everything I had.

"Yes!" she cried, then pulled away to shout, "Fuck! Harder!"

I gripped her thigh and gave her everything I had, completely lost in her moans and cries, smell and taste. Her sounds got higher and her skin was drenched.

"Fuck," I gasped out, closing my eyes, letting the moment overtake me.

"Ah!" she cried out, then stilled, holding on for the ride.

I thrust into her again, my body jerking as I finally spilled inside of her.

"Jesus Christ," I groaned, sliding out of her before slowly lowering my body back down on hers and kissing her collarbone.

My back started to cool, and my body buzzed with exhaustion.

I swallowed, trying to catch my breath. She was stunning.

"What are you doing to me?" I asked, breathless.

Her hands came up, threading through my hair and grazing down my neck. She trailed sweet kisses across my cheek and then wrapped her arms around my neck, damp with sweat, and held me in place.

But when I tried to arch up to look down at her, she tightened her hold, not releasing me.

"I can't look at you and say this," she said quietly, her soft voice sounding sad.

I stilled and averted my gaze, ignoring the apprehension building in my chest.

"My track record isn't good," she started. "I've never had a boyfriend. I've never wanted anyone again and again," she admitted. "But when I think about you, I get excited."

I stayed, listening, even though a smile started to spread my lips.

"You feed on me like food," she went on, "and it makes me happy, because you exhaust me to where I can't think." She placed a light kiss on my neck, sliding her hands down my back. "You like that I'm difficult, and God, I love your body, Tyler. I definitely want more."

She started breathing hard again, and I felt the hair on my arms stand up when she ran her feet up the backs of my legs and began sucking on my neck and kissing my ear.

My eyes closed. "Don't," I groaned. "I think my dick is dead."

I felt her shake with laughter beneath me.

"Let's go get in the shower," she whispered. "We'll see if your dick likes my mouth as much as my pussy."

FIFTEEN

EASTON

I stared out the window, seeing the early-morning joggers hop over streetcar tracks and puddles glistening with light from oncoming headlights.

This was the time of day when I liked the city most.

Predawn, before the sun burned off the blue-gray clouds, when the city was heavy with the memory of whatever fun had been had the night before but quiet and peaceful as most still slept.

My favorite time.

"Stop looking at me," I chastised as I gazed out the window, inhaling his scent as he sat next to me, trying to keep the smile off my face.

"No," he shot back.

I wasn't used to someone else being forefront in my mind, but I was always hyper-aware of him now. It kind of sucked. In an attempt to calm myself, I smoothed my hands down my wrinkled skirt and pushed up the sleeves of his white button-down, feeling completely out of order.

"Stop fidgeting," he commanded.

I turned my head to look at him, arching an eyebrow.

"You're all sleek in your pressed suit," I pointed out, "and I'm doing the walk of shame in no makeup and men's clothes."

He was taking me home before he headed into the office. Christian was due back later today, and although he'd told me I could sleep in and he'd have Patrick drive me home later, I didn't feel right about being there without him. I'd wanted to go home last night, but he'd talked me into staying again.

Today, though, I had work to catch up on, and he had a company to get back to now that the rain had subsided.

He smiled over at me and reached up, pushing the button to raise the privacy glass between Patrick and us.

"You're stunning," he said in all seriousness, giving me that look of his that made me hot. "And you shouldn't be embarrassed. I'm lucky people can't see the scratch marks on my back," he joked.

It made me laugh as an image of the marks on his back in the shower this morning flashed through my mind.

Butterflies fluttered through my chest, and I released the breath I'd been holding. Maybe that was the ticket. Picture him naked, and he wasn't so formidable.

"If you'd like," he started in his smooth voice, "I can offer you an opportunity to rebuild your self-esteem."

I cocked my head, peering over at him. "Oh?"

He nodded. "I'm hosting a luncheon at the house this Sunday, and I want you there," he stated, and then blinked. "I *would like* you there," he corrected, as if remembering he wasn't addressing an employee.

I shook my head, even as a grin escaped. The gesture thrilled me, though I would never admit it to him. I looked back out the window, lifting my chin.

It didn't unnerve me that he wanted to see more of me. But it did unnerve me that I liked that he wanted to see more of me.

But at his *house*? During the day, with other people there? If I were social—which I wasn't—it would still be awkward. And make what we were doing even less tactful.

"Tyler, we can't—"

"Not together," he interrupted, reassuring me. "But I like to see you and not be able to touch you. It adds to the fun."

When I turned toward him, expecting to see a mischievous smile, instead I saw a serious, even expression that made me rethink my smart-ass comeback. His eyes were pinned to mine, and I turned forward again, taking a deep breath and resisting the urge to crawl into his lap.

I cleared my throat. "What kind of luncheon is it?"

"Networking," he answered. "The city elite, a few politicians . . ." He trailed off, sounding bored. "Christian will be there."

"Thanks." I shook my head. "But I think—"

He cut me off. "You can bring a friend, if you like. Or your brother?"

I sat up straight, steeling my jaw.

I didn't want to decline the invitation, but I knew I had to. Even if we weren't romantically involved, it was a conflict of interest to attend parties at a student's home.

"You don't have to be nervous," he teased. "I'm sure you can handle the company."

I couldn't help the laugh that escaped.

"I'm not nervous," I argued, turning my head to regard him again. "And I know what you're trying to do."

He thought I couldn't handle myself around his crowd. I'd played tennis with movie stars in the stands.

The car slowed to a stop, and I glanced outside to see that we had arrived in front of my house. Leaves and fronds from a few palm trees in the neighborhood littered the ground, but the rest of the house seemed to be fine, despite my lack of shutters. The ground was still wet, the light sprinkle still falling rippling the puddles that had accumulated on the ground.

I picked up my blouse from next to me on the seat and moved to get out, but he caught my arms, stopping me gently.

"Noon," he said softly, not really demanding but not really asking, either. "I'll leave you alone the rest of the week, so we can both get some work done," he explained, taking his hand away and sitting back, "but if you're not there, I'll come to get you myself."

Despite my best intentions, I smirked, rising to his challenge. Then I leaned over the console and placed an innocent kiss on his cheek.

Whispering against his skin, I teased, "I love it when you play predator. It's so cute."

But then I yelped when he grabbed me under the arms and dragged me over to his lap, wrapping his arms around me and cutting off my breath with a kiss as he held me tight.

I moaned, but I couldn't fight. His tongue swirled with mine and his hand slipped up my thigh, grabbing my ass cheek.

His lips moved over mine, eating me up and sending me reeling. My head spun, and I wanted him again.

And if what I could feel poking into my behind was any indication, he wanted me, too.

Tyler and I were one and the same. Both of us hated to be handled.

Until now.

I liked his dominance, and I think he liked mine.

He pulled away, and I felt like the air had been ripped out of my lungs.

He placed his hands on his armrest and breathed hard.

"Now get out of here," he ordered, his tone turning clipped. "And if you don't show on Sunday, I'll never do that again."

Arrogant, confident, son of a . . .

I hopped off his lap and pounded on the window for Patrick to let me out. I didn't have to turn around to know that Marek was smiling.

And when Patrick opened the door, I stepped out, not once turning around for Tyler to see my grin.

Once I'd stepped inside the house, I heard his car pull away, and I closed the door, slipping off my flats.

Catching myself in the large square mirror on the wall perpendicular to the door, I took in my appearance, feeling completely disheveled but not out of sorts. My deep brown hair was clean, but it was a little frizzy, since it hadn't been blow-dried properly, curled, straightened, or styled in any way. I always thought I looked bland without makeup, but my skin was glowing, and there was a natural blush across my cheeks that I'd never seemed to have before.

The top two buttons of his shirt were open, and I wasn't wearing a bra, so I could feel the smooth, soft fabric against my sensitive skin. Everything touched me like it was a new feeling. Like my skin had come alive, tingling with frenzy.

I pulled the collar over my nose and inhaled, the smell of a spice, wood, and leather filling my chest.

Twisting around, I hit all the locks on the door and then rounded the entryway into the living room.

I stopped, spotting my brother sprawled out on the couch.

"Jack?" I called, walking up to the couch.

He shifted, lying there in his jeans with no T-shirt as his eyes slowly blinked awake. I looked over at the clock, seeing it was still only six oh four. He must've been here overnight.

"What are you doing here?" I rounded the couch to stand next to him.

He opened his eyes and focused on me. "Easton, what the hell?" he grumbled.

Sitting up, he planted his feet on the ground and hunched over, putting his elbows on his knees as he rubbed his eyes.

"Did you just get in?" he asked, peering up at me with worried eyes.

I tossed my blouse on the chair off to the side. "Yeah. What are you doing here?" I asked again.

He yawned. "The power went out in my neighborhood yesterday, so I let myself in," he explained, raising his arms above his head to stretch. "You have cable, so . . ."

I exhaled a laugh and leaned down to start tossing his soda cans and napkins inside the empty pizza box. I never cleaned up after him, but I was in a good mood this morning.

"Where were you?" he pressed again. "I texted."

I picked up the pizza box full of his garbage and shoved it to his chest. "I was out," I answered.

He cocked an eyebrow and set the box aside. His eyes fell down my clothes, and he reached up, rubbing the hem of my shirt between his fingers.

"Expensive," he commented, realization crossing his face as he turned away.

He closed his eyes and ran a hand through his hair, but I didn't care what he was going to say. Jack watched over me too closely, and I was done with it.

"I want nothing more than to see you with someone," he appeased, "but don't you think you're playing with fire?"

I leaned over, picked up the box again, and pushed it against his chest harder this time.

"I like fire," I stated, and stepped up onto the couch and sat down on its back.

"Yes, you're a risk taker," he teased, "but only when you're sure of the outcome, Easton. Hate to burst your bubble, but those aren't really risks."

I shook my head, rolling my eyes at him. "I'm not falling in love with him. We're both way too complicated for that."

"Do you want him to?"

"What?" I heaved a sigh.

"Fall in love with you."

I stared at my brother, trying to keep a hint of a smile on my face to hide the fact that I was actually thinking about it.

Did I want Tyler Marek to love me?

No, no, of course not.

I wanted someone to love me. Eventually. But I didn't want it to happen yet.

I thought I'd have years to build a relationship with someone. Years to get my life in order. To feel comfortable letting someone in. But not now and not him.

He was too caught up in his own life—as I was in mine.

He was also twelve years older and at a different point in his life. He probably had too many obligations to take time to travel and explore. And he probably had too many hang-ups about his own parenting abilities to want more children. I wasn't entirely sure if I wanted to have them, either, but it wasn't something I was ready to rule out.

No. Tyler Marek was a fling.

I licked my lips, flashing my brother a smile. "He makes me laugh and he turns me on," I taunted. "And I love it when he does this thing with his tongue—"

"Okay!" he burst out, turning away. "We're not that close."

I shook with quiet laughter, sinking down onto the couch.

"You want to know the best part?" I asked, and he looked at me.

"I haven't counted anything since yesterday morning," I told him.

He looked at me like he didn't believe me. "Really?"

I nodded, standing up and crossing my arms over my chest.

"I'm keeping my expectations reasonable," I assured him. "But for now, I feel relaxed for the first time in forever. I'm going to enjoy it while it lasts."

He seemed to give up his objections, because he slowly started nodding and taking deep breaths. My brother was a contradiction, and I still had trouble understanding him. He wanted me to move on, but he seemed to get antsy whenever I picked up a racket. He wanted me to date—not just have dalliances—but apparently someone like Tyler Marek wasn't what he had in mind.

If anything, I would've thought my brother would entertain the idea. Tyler was successful, connected, and political, everything my brother wanted to be.

I knew what my brother *said* he wanted for me, but on the rare occasion—like lately—when I seemed to go after it, he would try to pull me back, and I didn't understand why.

"Well." He heaved out a sigh and shot me a nudging smile. "Since you're in such a good mood, I have been dying for some of your bacon and mushroom quiche."

"Quiche?" I winced. "Do you have any idea how long that's going to take?"

He widened his smile, looking more comical than sympathetic, with both rows of teeth showing.

But I couldn't deny him. Being needed kept me busy.

I rolled my eyes. "Fine, but I'm playing music, then. Use the headphones if you want to watch TV."

I rounded the couch and walked into the kitchen, halting immediately when I spotted three cabinets and a drawer open.

Seriously?

"Jack!" I called, walking over and closing everything. "If you're going to hang out here, at least close the cabinets and drawers after you've opened them."

"Now, in the decades between the American Revolution and the Civil War"—I paced down the aisle in my classroom the next day—"our country experienced the First Industrial Revolution," I told the students, summarizing the reading from the storm break.

"What kind of inventions sprang forth?" I asked, snapping my fingers. "Let's go. Come on."

"The cotton gin!" Rayder Broussard shot out.

"Which did what?" I continued, listening as I stared at the tile and paced back and forth.

"Uh," a girl stuttered, and then shouted, "Cotton fibers separated from seeds, enabling clothing to be more quickly produced!"

I looked up, seeing it was a student from Team One, so I jetted over to the board and tallied a point for her team and one for Rayder's.

"What else?" I called out.

The students flipped through their notes and charts, working vigorously and still going strong despite being worked like machines from the moment they'd stepped into the room today. They sat or stood scattered around the room in organized chaos with their groups and with their noses buried in their research. I would've loved this level of participation if my intentions were noble.

But they weren't. I'd needed the distraction ever since my brother's visit yesterday. He'd denied leaving my kitchen a mess, and now it was all I could think about. If Jack hadn't left the drawer and cabinets open, then who had?

He should've known. The minute he'd walked into the apartment the night before and seen the kitchen out of sorts, he should've known something was wrong. I never left things out of place.

Four cups in a stack in the cabinet, two turns to close the toothpaste, closet organized—blouses, shirts, pants, skirts, dark to light—everything was always in order.

But upon further inspection yesterday, I'd found my shower curtain also open and two skirts I hadn't worn lately hanging on the back of my bedroom chair.

My heart started to pound again, and I swallowed.

While I arranged and organized things as a way to achieve a small sense of control, it had begun as a way to tell if anyone had been in my space.

At sixteen, when I'd started obsessing, if something was mussed, crooked, or out of place, I would know that I wasn't safe.

And while now I still did it for a measure of peace, I hadn't felt unsafe in five years. Not since the last time I'd seen him.

Maybe I'd taken the skirts out two nights ago, when Tyler had wanted to take me to dinner. Maybe I'd opened the cabinets and drawer before that, when I was arguing with Jack.

I hadn't counted anything lately, so maybe I was starting to loosen my grip on the order I'd once needed. Maybe my brain was so preoccupied with my class and with Tyler that I'd started to do what I'd needed to do for years: move on and let go.

Or maybe my brother did open the cabinets and drawers and just forgot.

Maybe.

I blinked, the class's commotion growing louder.

I took a deep breath, forcing myself to relax. "Come on!" I clapped my hands, rejoining the class. "Team One is in the lead here!"

I looked to Christian, who sat with his team but was not participating. "Christian?" I prompted. "Any ideas?"

He didn't answer but only flipped through his notes absently, not attempting to even look like he was trying to work.

"The steam engine!" someone shouted.

I let my aggravation over Christian's continued defiance go as I met Sheldon's eyes and mentally tallied Team Three.

"Which did what?" I called out, walking for the whiteboard again.

I heard a chair screech behind me as someone shot up. "It allowed a wide range of machines to be powered!"

I recognized Marcus's voice and placed another point for Team One and one for Team Three on the board.

"What else?"

"The telegraph!" someone called.

"And what was its purpose?"

"To um . . ." The girl's voice drifted off, while everyone else whispered in their groups or flipped through their notes.

"Come on," I urged. "You're heading for Earth, and your spaceship is out of control. You're going to crash!" I shouted, a smile tilting my lips.

"Communicate over long distances using Morse code!" Dane called out, his eyes wide with excitement.

"They already could communicate over long distances by writing letters," I challenged.

"But the telegraph was quicker!" he shouted, pointing his finger up in the air as if declaring war.

I laughed. "Good!" I praised, walking to the board and marking points.

Turning around, I walked back down the aisle, paying special attention to Christian.

"Now," I started. "Imagine that you need a ride home, and cell phones don't exist. How do you get home?" I asked.

"Find a phone," Sidney Jane answered.

But I shot back. "The school's closed, so you can't use theirs."

"Go to a business and use their phone," Ryan Cruzate called out.

I shrugged. "No one answers when you call."

"Walk home," Shelby Roussel continued the problem-solving.

I nodded. "Okay, you got there, but you don't have a key."

"Sit your butt outside," Marcus joked, a few kids joining in the laughter.

"It's raining," I argued again.

Trey Watts locked his hands behind his head. "Go to a friend's and wait," he suggested.

"They're not home, either." I winced with fake sympathy.

"Call someone—"

I stopped her with a head shake about the same time she realized we'd already been through that. The class laughed when they remembered that they don't have cell phones in this scenario. How easy it was to forget that we no longer had something we didn't realize we relied on so much.

And there really was no solution. You adjust and cope, but you can't make it the same again.

I paced the aisle, feeling Christian's silence like a deafening weight to my left.

"Now, we can survive without cell phones and microwaves," I explained, "but advances in technology have obviously made life easier. To the point where, in some cases, we don't know what we'd do without them."

"If your mom—or dad—had a cell phone," I went on, "you could've reached them wherever they were, no matter that they weren't home. Now, we know what some of the big inventions during the Industrial Revolution were, and we know what they did, but what was the impact on our country and our daily lives after they came into existence?" I asked. "How did they make life easier? Or more difficult? How does new technology"—I raised my voice for emphasis—"forever change the course of our lives?"

I gazed around the room, seeing their contemplative expressions. I hoped they weren't merely blank and that they were actually thinking.

Maybe I'd asked too many questions at once.

I glanced to Christian, who stared at me, looking very much like he had something to say but was holding back.

"Make a T-chart," I ordered. "Label pros and cons and then put your pencils down."

The students did what was asked of them. They opened their notebooks to a blank page, drawing one line down the middle and one across the top and labeling the two sections.

After they'd replaced their pencils on their desks, I went on.

"Revolution usually means quick, dramatic change," I pointed out. "Do you think the Industrial Revolution was aptly named? Were the changes in production and distribution fast, or were they a steady development over time?"

I walked up the last aisle and stopped. "Christian, what do you think?"

He shook his head, looking bored. "I think it was fast, I guess."

"Why?"

He dropped his eyes, mumbling, "I don't know."

I got closer. "You don't have to know." I kept my voice light. "Tell me what you think."

His eyes shot up to mine. "I don't know," he repeated, his voice turning angry.

"It was decades," I shot out, knowing I was close to overstepping my bounds. One of the first things you learn about classroom management is to never call out a student in front of the class.

But I needed a reaction out of him. I needed him to do something. To say something.

"Is that fast or steady, Christian? What do you think?"

"It's all about perspective, I guess!" he barked. "Humans are, like, two hundred thousand years old, so yeah, a lot of advancement in only a few decades would be fast," he argued. "Some civilizations in history barely made any progress in generations, while others a lot. Everyone's frame of reference is different!"

I held his angry blue-gray eyes—the same as his father's—and elation flooded my chest. I let out a breath and gave him a small smile, nodding.

"That's a good point," I told him, and then turned around to walk away.

"But then it may not be fast, either," he continued, and I stopped.

Spinning around, I watched as he crossed his arms over his chest and tilted his chin up, more confident.

"I would say the past two decades have seen even more advancement in manufacturing and technology than during the Industrial Revolution," he debated. "The phones, the iPads, automobiles, the Mars rover . . ." He trailed off. "It's about perspective."

It felt like those moments when you get exactly what you want and then you don't know what to do with what you got.

I stood there, wondering what the good teachers do when a student opens up, and I was clueless. Christian Marek was an angry kid. He was difficult and defiant and so like his father and yet so different. Whereas I gathered Tyler always felt he had something to prove, Christian seemed like someone who never needed to prove anything to anyone.

"So was it fast or steady?" a student called out to my left.

I bowed my head, smiling as I turned around and walked to the front of the classroom.

I cleared my throat. "You're not being graded on what you think," I told the class. "You're being graded on why you think it. Defend your answers."

I turned off the Smart Board and placed my hands on my hips.

"Complete your T-chart with the pros and cons of the impact on life by the inventions of the Industrial Revolution. Then tweet what you learned today—hashtag Bradbury2015—and then you may get online and start adding primary sources to your folder for the Deep South project," I instructed.

I turned, grabbing a dry-erase marker, and finished adding points for the class.

"Aw, yeah!" I heard Marcus bellow when he saw the points I added to Team One. "We got fifty points. Good job, Marek!!"

Team One clapped, celebrating their success and the final point Christian had earned for them, bringing them to a total of fifty before all the other teams.

"So we get Song of the Week, right?" Marcus asked, already working his laptop to find his song, no doubt.

"Yes." I nodded. "You have five minutes."

"It's my choice, everyone!" he shouted, clicking his computer and standing up as the song began playing.

The entire class stopped what they were doing and joined in the fun as the song came out louder and louder from Marcus's computer. Soon there were hands in the air, voices singing along, and people standing up at their desks, moving to the music.

I laughed at the sight, loving the amount of work they put in to succeed just so they could have these five minutes as often as possible. Even Christian was laughing as he watched others dance to the music.

And then my face fell and I sucked in a breath as I finally realized what song was playing, Afroman's "Because I Got High."

"Wait!" I blurted out. "That song has profanity."

Marcus jerked his shoulders in moves probably only he thought were cool.

"How would you know, Ms. Bradbury?" he singsonged.

And I just planted my face in my hands as the entire class joined in on the chorus so loudly the entire school probably heard.

SIXTEEN

TYLER

Two days later and I was still thinking about her. What the hell was wrong with me? The luncheon was the day after tomorrow, and I couldn't wait. I hoped she wasn't going to chicken out, because it would throw off my entire fucking day.

I pulled back the pen, noticing I'd been retracing notes I'd already made as I sat at the head of the conference table, vaguely aware of Stevenson, one of my vice presidents, updating everyone on distribution figures from the last quarter.

I wasn't even listening.

Every time I sat still, my head would drift back to her. Her body, her lips, her hunger . . . She was driving me crazy, and I knew right then and there that I hadn't lied to her.

I might actually have a crush.

And I dropped the pen to the table, knowing that was the last thing I needed.

Easton Bradbury was beautiful, educated, and strong. She was built for challenges. But she was also complicated, difficult, and moody. She wouldn't make friends easily.

Even if she weren't my son's teacher—even if I weren't about to enter a campaign, knowing that going public with a love interest could put me further under the microscope—Easton could still fuck me up.

Damaged people were survivors, and they survived because they always put themselves first. Self-preservation demanded it.

I didn't like realizing I might not be the first one to walk away.

I had to enjoy her for what she was and not let her mean more than that. She was fun company, good in bed, and a welcome distraction when I had time for one. And I had every confidence I was the same for her.

Other than that, she needed to be pushed out of my head.

I came back, refocusing on the table in front of me. "All right," I said, cutting off Stevenson midsentence. "Everyone go to lunch. We'll continue this later."

I didn't wait to see if anyone had any questions before I got up and moved back into the main office to continue the work that was doubling before me, no matter how many hours I spent at it.

Everyone slowly drifted out while I got on the computer and started reviewing messages from Corinne.

There was a stockholders' meeting in the evening, but I was going to send Jay in my place, and some new contracts to delegate to regional vice presidents.

Jay was right. I couldn't handle everything myself. With the campaign—and the Senate, if I won—I was going to have to learn how to hand off more work to others.

Then I looked around, seeing that my brother had left the meeting. Picking up my phone, I speed-dialed him.

But Corinne walked in. "Mr. Marek? Ms. McAuliffe is here to see you," she said.

"Five minutes," I commanded.

She nodded, knowing that it was her job to come in and scurry out whoever I needed gone, so I could get on with my day.

Corinne walked out, and Jay picked up his phone.

"You just told us to go to lunch," he pointed out, knowing I needed him back here.

"Not you," I shot back. "I want to be out of here by four, so get back in here."

"Four?" he blurted out, but I hung up the phone without responding.

I never left the office that early, and he knew it. But slowly I'd started to try to manage my time better. I could take a break, eat dinner with Christian, and then work in my home office while he went to his room to do homework or over to a friend's house.

I began clicking on the messages on my computer when I saw Tessa stroll in, a casual smile brightening her face and her beige suit jacket and handbag hanging in her hand.

She was dressed in a burgundy blouse and a beige pencil skirt, and as usual, she had a relaxed sway to her hips and determination in her steps, as if she were always comfortable, no matter the room or the company.

Such a contrast to Easton's stiff posture and the black curtain that seemed to hang over her eyes.

I don't want anyone else to have it while we're doing this, okay?

I inhaled a deep breath and hardened my jaw.

"Close the door," Tessa instructed Corinne a few feet behind her, turning her head only enough to be understood but not enough to see her.

Corinne shut the door, and Tessa tossed her things onto one of the chairs opposite my desk.

She smiled. "I thought you were away on business," she said sweetly, but I knew she was scolding. "Or perhaps detained with no way to communicate." She circled the desk, making her way to me. "Or maybe you lost my number and, knowing how anti–social media you are, you didn't think to tweet."

Twitter? Was she kidding?

Tessa and I were never the type to check in with each other, and while I knew she was playing it cool, it was unlike her to show up at my office without calling.

Or put herself on my side of the desk, interrupting my day. That was what I liked—or did like—about Tessa. She respected our careers, and she didn't get territorial.

Not like Easton. I started to smile at the thought of her but stopped myself.

"Tessa—"

"I'm seeing someone?" she interrupted, finishing for me. "Is that what you're going to say?"

I sat down, watching her as I ran my finger over my lips. I knew what was coming.

She looked at me, all business, calm and levelheaded. "Here's the thing, Tyler." She sat down on the edge of my desk, crossing one leg over the other. "I don't care. Her, me . . ." She shrugged. "You get two for the price of one. Which works for me, because I don't want anything more anyway."

And then she leaned in, running a finger down my light blue tie. "But I don't want to lose what I already have," she clarified.

I looked up into her eyes, wondering why she was really here. A few months ago she'd insisted on having our lunch date in my office, but we'd never eaten. She'd walked in, pulled up her skirt, and straddled me in my chair.

And while I'd enjoyed it, I was simply wondering now if the five minutes I'd told Corinne to give us were up yet.

I let out a breath and cocked my head. "You haven't been waiting around for me to call," I challenged.

"No," she allowed, pulling back with a smile. "But I would've canceled any plans I'd made if you had."

I grinned, appreciating her candor. She was useful, and I'd rather keep her on my side if I could. We'd enjoyed each other, and there was mutual respect for the other's position and connections in the city.

But the thing was . . . I'd never craved her.

And I no longer wanted her.

It's not that I was callous or that I thought women were disposable. I only involved myself with women who knew the score and wanted the same thing as me.

Easy fun.

Now everything felt different.

Because of Easton.

Her sharp tongue spouted words that cut, but it also tasted like a cool lake on a hot day.

I remembered her whispers in my ear, waking me up Wednesday morning before she slipped a leg over my stomach and climbed on.

I inhaled a sharp breath, refocusing on the current situation.

"It turns out," I confided, "maybe I do want to complicate my life a little."

Her eyes widened, and she smiled big. "Dish," she demanded.

I let out a bitter laugh. "Not a chance."

"It's off the record," she assured me, holding up her hands in innocence.

"You're never off the record."

"Oh, come on." She waved a hand at me. "You're bound to take her to dinner sometime. The press would kill to see someone unknown on your arm. You can't hide her away forever."

That's exactly what I wanted to do. If anyone found out, we'd be done, and I wasn't ready.

I let out a sigh. "I can do whatever I want," I replied, aware I sounded a little cocky.

She pursed her lips in a plotting smile. "I'm intrigued."

"But not disappointed, I see," I shot back.

"*Psh.*" She laughed and hopped off my desk. "I would be disappointed if I thought it would last."

I narrowed my eyes, watching her walk back around the desk to the chair and pick up her jacket and handbag.

She cocked her head, looking coy. "But you, Tyler, are a bachelor for life," she asserted. "I only hope you marry her. It'll make our little interludes all the more fun."

And with a confident smirk, she spun around and walked for the door, calling one last time over her shoulder, "You'll call me when you're done with your shiny new toy?" But she didn't wait for an answer.

Swinging the door open, she disappeared, and I let my eyes fall closed as I pinched the bridge of my nose. I wasn't quite sure if there was a man alive in this city who could match that woman's set of balls.

"Jesus Christ," I breathed out.

"Well, that was quick."

I looked up to see my brother strolling back in, his attention half on me and half on his phone.

"She'd make a good politician's wife," he hinted. "No matter what, she always looks cheerful."

I cocked an eyebrow and stood up, getting ready to sort through what I needed him to handle today.

Cheerful. And then I snorted, thinking how much that word and Easton would never go hand in hand.

My phone buzzed, and I immediately stopped, reaching into my top drawer for it.

Since Easton's little lesson to all of my VPs the other day, I'd set out to prove her wrong by leaving my phone out of reach at certain times. There was no such thing as an information addiction. It was simply an excuse so she could manage attention in an easier way.

But when I saw a text from her, liquid heat rushed in my veins, and I couldn't possibly ignore her like I did others when I was busy.

How many politicians does it take to change a lightbulb? she'd texted.

How many?

Two, she answered. One to change it, and one to change it back.

I laughed, causing Jay to peer up from his phone with an inquiring look.

Tweet that, she ordered.

I shook my head but did it anyway.

"What are you doing?" Jay pried as I clicked on my Twitter app and began typing.

"Tweeting," I said in a low voice.

"Oh," he said, sounding surprised. "Good. Your breakfast tweet earlier this week was exactly what I've been talking about. People eat that shit up."

I finished the tweet, tossed my phone down on a pile of folders at the edge of my desk, and ran my hand through my hair.

"I need you to make sure Corinne has everything set up for the luncheon," I told him, "and can you set up a conference call with Mexico City for one o'clock today?" I asked but didn't wait for an answer as I grabbed a sheet from the printer, handing it to him. "Also, here's the speech for the veterans benefit. I made some changes, so just look it over for me."

I sat back down, straightening my tie and grabbing the remote. I turned on the TVs on the wall, a barrage of news stations coming to life and their chatter filling the room as I turned to my computer and jumped online.

Trying to organize my day to allow for more time for Christian was kicking my ass.

"Are you okay?" Jay asked.

"Where the hell are those deeds to that land in California?" I barked, ignoring him as I scanned my e-mails.

The lawyer was supposed to scan them and send them over, so we could get on the land, and I knew there were at least fifteen other fucking things I was forgetting to do.

"Corinne, get in here!" I shouted.

"All right, I'm outta here. I'll take care of this," I heard him say, holding up the speech I'd run through last night. "Is Tessa coming to the luncheon?"

"Yes, of course," I answered. "She's influential, isn't she?"

"And Ms. Bradbury?"

I stopped, looking up at him and sitting back in my seat. How the hell did he know?

He smirked, shaking his head at me. "Give me a break, Tyler," he scolded. "It was pretty clear you weren't the one taking that picture of your breakfast, and judging by the sparks in your office last Saturday . . ."

He stood there, probably waiting for me to say something, but I didn't.

Jay was younger, but I knew he never took it to heart that I was the boss. He liked working here and working with someone who took his bullshit.

Working together had never been a problem. Until now.

An average assistant would know their boundaries. A brother had none.

"Look," he started, "I'm not saying you can't—"

"That's right." I cut him off, nodding. "You're not telling me anything."

I let his expertise drive the invitations I accepted, the platform I created, as well as guide my campaign, but I would keep Easton separate.

It wasn't that my brother didn't have a right to ask. I just didn't care to hear what I knew he would say.

"Tessa McAuliffe is *our* business," I clarified. "Whoever I fuck is *mine*."

I'd gathered in my short and limited experience as a father that being a parent was like tossing marbles up into the air and seeing how many would land in a shot glass.

I'd read enough and seen enough to know that kids could grow up in the worst hell and become valedictorians and doctors. Or they could be raised in privilege with two parents and Christmas trees stocked with gifts and still die of overdoses or by suicide.

One irrefutable fact about parenting that I knew even before I was one was that there was no "right" way. No set list of proven methods to follow if you wanted your kid to captain a submarine or conduct orchestras or be president.

If you pushed them to succeed, they could resent you. If you didn't push them enough, they could still resent you. If you gave them what they needed, they would complain about not having what they wanted, and if you gave them what they wanted, they may only want more.

How much was too much? How much was too little? How hard should you push to be able to call it encouragement, because if you pushed too hard, they'd call it bad parenting?

How do they know that you love them? How do you know if they love you?

How do you know if they're going to be okay?

I stared out the car window, watching Christian talking to a couple of girls, and there was an ocean of regret for the years I'd missed. I could tell myself that he'd turned out well. Maybe if I had been in his life, he wouldn't have become this strong or confident, but I knew I was making excuses. I should've been there.

Easton stood at the bottom of the stone steps, smiling as she talked to a parent, her arms crossed. The students had just gotten out of school, and although Patrick usually picked Christian up, I'd decided to be here as well. I'd worked through lunch, even stopping Corinne from ordering food, so I didn't waste time eating. I still had a few loose ends to tie up for the day, but I could get to that after Christian and I had dinner.

"Patrick?" I leaned forward and handed him a small black bag. "Would you please take this to Miss Bradbury?" I told him. "And hurry Christian up, please."

"Yes, sir." He reached around and took the bag, then hopped out of the car, leaving me alone.

I watched as he traipsed over to Easton, interrupting her conversation. Politely, I was sure, knowing Patrick.

She smiled at him, and the parent waved goodbye to her as she took the bag Patrick offered. Her face was a mixture of surprise and something else I couldn't place. Curiosity, maybe?

She knew Patrick, so she had to know it was from me. He bowed his head quickly, saying goodbye, and she dipped her head, peering into the bag.

I watched her, my heart starting to beat faster, and I had to remind myself that I'd see her Sunday.

She slipped her hand into the bag and picked out the small box. Opening it up, she plucked out the smoky gray Lamborghini lighter I'd stopped to buy on the way here.

Her eyebrows pinched together as she cocked her head, studying it. I almost laughed, because she looked intrigued but utterly confused. Easton, I already knew, wasn't a woman who liked to be caught off guard, and I enjoyed gaining the upper hand this once.

She pushed the button and jerked a little, breaking out in a smile as the flame appeared. Reaching back into the bag, she plucked out the small white card and read my message.

Don't set any fires without me, it read.

She smiled to herself, the genuine kind of smile she always tried to hide. I knew if I were next to her I'd be able to see her blush.

Finally looking up, she met my eyes, and I saw the need there that I was hard-pressed to ignore as well.

The car door opened and Christian appeared, climbing in and dropping his bag before he sat down. When I looked back, Easton was just disappearing back into the school.

I loosened my tie and set my phone down on the console. "How was your day?" I asked.

"Fine," he responded.

Yes. Fine.

Okay, yes, no, maybe, whatever . . . His usual responses.

"Was that Sarah Richmond you were talking to?" I inquired. "Clyde Richmond's daughter?"

He took out his phone and started scrolling with his thumb. "Yeah, I guess."

"I talked to your mother today." I crossed my legs, resting my ankle over the top of my other knee. "She would like you to go to Egypt for Christmas to spend some time with her."

I didn't want him to go. My father and his wife were planning a huge party, and Christian could get to know my side of the family better, not to mention that I'd never spent a Christmas with him.

But he sat there, focused on his phone, and nodded absently. "Yeah, whatever," he mumbled.

I shook my head.

Picking up my phone, I texted him. Right there, two feet away from me, because he wouldn't talk to me, so I had to text my kid to have a fucking conversation with him.

I would rather you stay. I clicked *Send.*

I heard his phone beep and watched his lips tighten when he saw it was from me. He started to look up but stopped, instead typing out a response, I assumed.

I don't like you, he texted back.

I stared at it, hating those words and feeling my chest tighten like a rubber band was wrapping around my heart.

I know, I responded.

His phone beeped, and he hesitated, looking like he was wondering if he wanted to continue the conversation.

But he did.

You piss me off, he admitted.

I nodded as I typed. I do that to a lot of people.

I'm not a lot of people, he shot back immediately.

I paused, feeling guilty that I'd made him think he was no more important than anyone else in my life.

I know, I agreed.

He started typing, and I waited, but when he kept going and I hadn't received a text, I stilled just as much out of gratitude as out of fear.

I was afraid he had more to say that would be hard to hear, but I was also elated that he was talking to me. Albeit texting, but it was still communication, and it was about as much open dialogue as we'd had since he'd moved in.

Patrick turned onto St. Charles and headed east toward the CBD when my phone buzzed.

I opened Christian's message.

I used to see you on TV or in the newspaper, he wrote. You had time for everyone but me. I used to wonder what was wrong with me, and then I realized that you were just an asshole.

I gritted my teeth as I held the phone and tried to figure out what I was going to say to him. He was right, after all. There was no excuse and no reason good enough.

And I'd known this was coming.

Come on, Tyler. You've had fourteen years to figure out how to make this up to him. *You got nothing?*

My phone buzzed again.

You're an asshole.

I texted quickly. I know.

A huge asshole! he shot back.

I know, I replied again.

That was all I could do.

He was right, and if I didn't stay calm, I'd push him farther away.

And I'm sick of this jazz shit! he texted.

I forced away the smile that pulled at my lips. Patrick kept the music light—with no lyrics—per my request, since I often made phone calls or worked on my laptop in the car.

I texted back. What kind of music do you like to listen to?

Rock.

I licked my lips and looked up, calling out to Patrick.

"Patrick, could you put on a rock station, please?" I asked.

Without answering, he began spinning the dial in search of a different station. Finally, once he settled on a tune that sounded angry and talked about "home," I leaned back in my seat and took the opportunity to push Christian further. He was talking to me—or yelling—but we still hadn't accomplished anything.

We've got a party on Sunday, I texted. You could invite friends.

His phone beeped, and I glanced over out of the corner of my eye to see his eyebrows furrowed. Finally, he started typing.

I don't want to go to a party.

I continued. Food, music, swimming . . . You and your friends can enjoy the pool before it gets cold.

He sat there, staring at the text and wiggling his thumbs over the screen, looking like he wasn't sure how to answer. He hadn't said no, so I sent another text before he found a way to say no.

I invited Clyde Richmond. His daughter may come. I hoped like hell that enticed him.

The luncheon was for business, but families and significant others were coming. Some bridges needed to be built, but it was supposed to be a relaxed occasion, as well. If Christian liked the girl, as he appeared to—and he had the safety of his friends—maybe he'd brave it.

He began typing, but it was a while before I got another text.

I invited a few people, he wrote.

My jaw ached with a smile, and I looked out the window, letting out a breath. He must've sent a mass text to his friends. He was giving me a shot, at least.

I had one foot in the door.

"Are we going home, sir?" Patrick's voice came drifting back.

And I blinked, realizing I hadn't told him where we were going.

"Ah, Commander's Palace," I told him. I was starving.

"Not again," Christian blurted out, startling me.

I twisted my head to see him scowling.

And I laughed to myself, because I liked it. *Give me anger. Give me annoyance. Just give me something.*

I raised my eyebrows in expectation and waved my hand, inviting him to reissue the order to Patrick.

"Camellia Grill," he told Patrick.

And I slipped my phone into my breast pocket, hoping I wouldn't need it at dinner.

SEVENTEEN

EASTON

Letting Tyler Marek push me into corners and whisper into my ear right under the noses of everyone around us was going to get me into trouble.

And him.

He had a lot to lose, too.

So why wasn't I ending it?

I was standing in the middle of a burning room, daring myself to stay as long as possible before it was time to run.

"Are you ready?"

Jack looked over the hood at me, straightening his navy blue and pink polka-dot tie over his pink pin-striped shirt. Not many men would brave such a color, but New Orleans men were a different animal, and it looked good on him. Especially with his matching navy blue slacks.

I smiled lazily. "Ready for what?" I asked, glancing at Kristen Meyer as she climbed out of the back of Jack's Jeep.

Tyler had said I could bring a friend, and I thought it would be more comfortable—or comforting—to have backup when I knew Jack was going to spend his afternoon schmoozing.

"Are you ready for the party?" Jack repeated. "You're Miss Antisocial-Constantly-Uncomfortable-Wants-to-Be-Home-Instead-of-at-a-Party-Ever, so I guess I shouldn't worry, right?"

His lips were spread from ear to ear, pleased with his own assessment of me, and I just rolled my eyes.

"Ah." Kristen spoke up, smoothing down her sleeveless knee-length peach dress. "So it's not just me. She's always difficult."

She shot me a joking glare as she put her hands on her hips and grinned.

Apparently she thought we were close enough to insult each other in good humor.

I cocked an eyebrow. "Just because I don't bounce around like I'm in a Skittles commercial doesn't mean I'm difficult."

And I walked off, hearing their snorts behind me as they followed.

I almost went for the side door, next to the covered driveway, but I caught myself just in time, remembering I had to keep up the pretense that I'd never been here and most guests wouldn't use that door. Of course, my brother was informed about how close Marek and I had gotten, but that didn't mean I could be careless.

Before we even reached the front door, though, it opened, a butler I hadn't seen before greeting us.

"Good afternoon."

"Hello." I nodded, taking a few steps into the entryway and stopping.

Kristen and Jack strolled in behind me, and the sunlight fanning across the floor slowly fell away as the door closed.

I inhaled and instantly dipped my head, trying to hide the smile caused by the flutters in my stomach. I loved his smell, and I suddenly realized my new favorite place was being curled up in his sheets, where that scent covered me.

"Ms. Bradbury," I heard a voice say from above.

I looked up, seeing Christian descend the dark hardwood stairs with one hand on the cast-iron railing, and I immediately felt a light layer of sweat break out on my forehead.

Yes, this was definitely inappropriate. I shouldn't have come.

"I didn't know you'd be here." He looked at me quizzically as he reached the bottom of the stairs.

Yeah, I shouldn't be, should I?

I forced a smile, taking him in. I was glad to see I hadn't over- or underdressed.

He wore black slacks with black shoes, and while he hadn't put on a tie, he still looked dressy in a light blue oxford with his sleeves rolled up. I'd decided to take advantage of the warm October weather and wore a sleeveless dress that fell just above my knees, but while it was mostly white, it was filled with a spatter of pink and blue flowers in the middle that looked a lot like a watercolor painting. It was vintage, and I loved it.

"Hi, Christian," I greeted in a light voice. The pleasant-teacher one I used for the students. "Yes, your father invited me. This is my brother, Jack." I waved my hand, joking, "He's nicer than me. I promise."

He nodded but didn't smile.

"And you know Ms. Meyer." I gestured to Kristen.

Christian gave her a half smile, but there was something that still wasn't right. I didn't know if he'd already been put off before we got here, or if it was my overactive sense of guilt that he might not want me here, but he seemed displeased about something.

We'd made some progress in class, and his work outside of the classroom was excellent. Whatever was bothering him wasn't getting in the way of his performance, so I could only hope it had nothing to do with me.

The quiet butler in his white jacket and black tie approached us. "Everyone's out back," he told us. "Down the hall and you'll see the glass doors."

"Yeah," Christian spoke up. "Follow me."

And he turned around, leading us to the back of the house. The echo of mine and Kristen's heels drowned out any other sound as Christian took us across the white marble floors of the entryway to the slate tiles of the kitchen toward the French doors leading out to the patio.

"Wow. Look at this place." Kristen's whisper was filled with awe.

But I refused to look around. If I did, I'd see the door leading to the study where he'd mauled me four days ago or the stove where I'd made breakfast wearing only his shirt.

"It's a large house," I commented to Christian ahead of me. "I mean for just you and your dad."

We all walked through the doors, and Christian turned around, regarding us casually.

"He's my father, not my dad," he pointed out, looking around. "And this is his house, not mine."

Reaching over, he grabbed a bottle of water from the neatly lined-up beverages on the refreshments table and offered a cocky smirk. "Have fun," he said, and then spun around, walking away.

My brother appeared at my side, shaking his head and watching Christian stroll away to his friends. "Pretty cold for a fourteen-year-old."

Yes, he was.

However, I couldn't help but envy him. Maybe if I'd known my own mind at that age as well as he did, I wouldn't have behaved so stupidly. He stood his ground, he knew who he was, and he held everyone to a standard. Christian wasn't denying himself good things because he was damaged. Rather, he was shielding himself against harmful things because he'd been disappointed.

Sometimes second chances were too much to ask. Or maybe he'd realize that his dad was still learning.

"Ms. Bradbury."

Speak of the devil . . .

Elation swept through my chest, and I couldn't keep the smile at bay this time.

Turning around, I held out my hand, keeping up appearances. "Mr. Marek," I greeted as he took my hand, a mischievous look crossing his face.

He was dressed in a black suit, cut to flow with the shape of his body.

And even though the suit was dark-colored, his white shirt and light blue tie gave off a casual and bright appearance for a luncheon set outside.

He took longer than necessary, holding my eyes just enough to tell me I was on his mind, and then he turned to my brother, holding out his hand.

"Jack, right?" he asked.

My brother held out his hand, taking Tyler's. "Yes, sir. Jack Bradbury."

"Hi, Mr. Marek." Kristen held out her hand. "I'm Ms. Meyer. I teach—"

"Earth Science." He cut her off, nodding and taking her hand. "Yes, I know who you are. Welcome."

I glanced around, wondering how long I should stick around before I left. Jack would undoubtedly stay until the party ended. The amount of suits here, all important people in New Orleans, was a social buffet for my brother, and I was sure he couldn't wait to start making the rounds.

Kristen had the personality to fit in anywhere. She probably made friends easily. I was different.

Not difficult, just different.

And right now I was sure I'd have more fun at home repotting some plants or sharpening my new steak knife set.

"Well, make yourselves at home," Tyler told us, gesturing with the rocks glass he held in his hand. "Food and refreshments are over there, so feel free to help yourself and mingle."

He spared me a quick glance before addressing my brother again. "There are some people I'd like you to meet," he told Jack, taking him away.

"And, Ms. Bradbury?" He turned back around, leaning in. "The ladies are over there."

He nodded to the clique of beige and pink congregating around the tables, laughing and talking.

"It's probably safer," he said, and I jerked my eyes back up to him just in time to see his smug smirk before turning away.

Safer?

As in, I'll be less intimidated?

I snorted, following Kristen over to the refreshments. Maybe he was teasing me. Maybe he was challenging me, but I wasn't bored anymore.

Picking up a champagne flute filled with some kind of orange liquid, I floated around the party with Kristen, taking in the lively atmosphere and the beautiful day. The backyard was paved with more slate tiles, similar to the ones in the kitchen, with sparse sections of lush grass here and there. There were a few trees, as tall as one-story houses, and around the perimeter a cast-iron fence and a vast offering of foliage, including ferns, rosebushes, and neatly trimmed hedges.

There were tables with hors d'oeuvres and refreshments, as well as a full bar, because New Orleanians drink for everything. Even funerals. Lunch would most likely be served at the tables instead of buffet style, because, well, Tyler Marek didn't do business half-assed.

And this luncheon was business.

The centerpiece of the backyard was a rectangular-shaped pool with deep blue tiles, which made it look like the Mediterranean Sea. Or so I believed. I'd actually never been there.

And then, glancing to the left, I instantly paused, seeing a single tennis court. I narrowed my eyes.

Why hadn't I noticed that this week when I was here?

It wasn't like I'd spent any time outside, but I'd taken a look through the doors at least and noticed the pool and the beautiful landscaping.

My feet and legs tingled with the desire to get on the court and break a sweat. I suddenly wanted to hold a racket and chase the ball again. For years I'd try—sporadically—to get back on the court and feel comfortable, but it never worked. Now I wanted to.

A love of tennis may have been "beaten into me," so to speak, but it was still love.

The guests had separated into factions, it seemed. Christian, along with a few friends I recognized, had plates loaded with food and were disappearing back into the house, probably for a movie or video games. I couldn't imagine this scene was a lot of fun for them.

The ladies—or wives—had grouped off, and while they appeared to be enjoying themselves, I didn't want to surrender to whatever mold Tyler challenged me with. Many of the ladies, I was sure, ran charity organizations, wrote successful blogs, and had careers of their own; however, there was still a good-ole-boy mentality in this city that kept women on the sidelines.

I set down my empty glass and picked up another of the same drink. It was nonalcoholic but still a delicious concoction of orange juice, pineapple juice, and Sprite, I believed.

With Kristen following, I headed over to Jack as he chatted with a small group of men, including Tyler, Mason Blackwell, and a few others I didn't recognize. I couldn't imagine why Tyler had invited Blackwell—I knew he didn't like him—but I was sure it had everything to do with business and nothing to do with pleasure.

"The other party has already endorsed Evelyn Tragger," one of the gentlemen said casually, speaking to Blackwell. "She's plain-spoken and hard-nosed. She has a good reputation north of Baton Rouge, and she's very popular with certain circles here."

"And she is not happy with you, Mason," another guest joked before taking a sip out of his rocks glass.

I stopped behind Blackwell, no one noticing my presence.

"Of course she's not," Blackwell asserted. "Most unmarried women are disgruntled."

The group broke out in laughter, some nodding in agreement, and their ignorant, pasty, self-satisfied smiles suddenly irritated me.

Straightening my back and crossing my arms over my chest, I cocked my head. "And because you're male that makes you worthy of office?" I retorted.

Everyone turned to face me, suddenly noticing I was there, except Jack. He simply let his head fall back as he sighed, probably bracing himself for my antics, which he knew all too well.

Blackwell looked at me with a half smile and definite amusement in his eyes. The three gentlemen I didn't recognize regarded me with interest, appearing surprised but not the least bit offended. I had no idea what Tyler was thinking, but I could feel his gaze on me.

"Uh, gentlemen." I heard the laughter Tyler kept contained. "This is Ms. Easton Bradbury. She's a—"

"Voter," I finished for him, pinning Blackwell with a stern stare. "And I'd like to know, Mr. Blackwell, why it is that with one hundred senators in this country, only about twenty are female?"

I didn't so much care either way about the gender of our leaders, but I was interested in hearing his answer.

"None of them are from Louisiana or from the South, for that matter," I added. "In fact, Louisiana has elected only one female senator throughout history."

That was a lie. There'd been three, actually, but I wanted to see if anyone would correct me.

He stood there, one hand casually sliding into his pocket and the other holding a glass of something brown.

"The job goes to whoever is qualified," he answered, and I almost laughed.

"Twenty-eight percent child poverty rate," I pointed out, "and one of the largest prison inmate increases in the country."

Politics and history went hand in hand. I couldn't love one without being informed about the other.

I held his stare. "We're also the unhealthiest state in the union, based on obesity, suicide, alcohol consumption, and teen pregnancy."

His stare faltered for a split second, and I deduced either he was unaware, aware but didn't care, or he had no response.

The problem with people like Blackwell was that they treated public service as an extension of their careers. It was a means to gain influence and change laws that kept them from making money in whatever manner they chose. Their public service wasn't about the public at all.

And I wasn't so sure Tyler had a nobler agenda, either.

I took a deep breath, lifting my chin. "I just told you that much of your future constituency is underfed and undereducated," I clarified. "Now, I would never base my vote on someone's race or gender, but you can be sure my vote isn't guaranteed simply because you have a dick."

Tyler choked on his drink, coughing, and the other gentlemen broke out in snorts and laughs that were quickly concealed with a hand over the mouth.

Kristen cleared her throat, and I could tell she wanted to laugh, while a smile tugged at Blackwell's lips.

Leaning in, he whispered in my ear, "But you haven't seen it."

His smooth voice was filled with sexual innuendo, and I stilled, feeling the hair on the back of my neck stand up. This guy was disgusting.

"Tyler," a woman said behind me. "Aren't you going to introduce me?"

Blackwell pulled back, still smirking, and I turned my head, seeing a beautiful blonde in a red wrap dress walk up from behind.

And I tensed, remembering her. She was the blonde from the Mardi Gras ball last year.

She came to stand at Tyler's side, and I instantly felt heat rush to my cheeks.

"I'm Tessa McAuliffe." She smiled, holding out her hand. "And you are?"

I opened my mouth to speak, but Tyler cut me off.

"Tessa," he interrupted, stepping up to me. "I need to speak with Ms. Bradbury." He smiled politely, but it didn't reach his eyes. "Please excuse us for a moment," he told everyone.

I narrowed my eyes, ready to object, but he grabbed my elbow and led me away from the group so fast I nearly stumbled along the brick path.

"What are you doing?" I whispered as he moved his hand to my back, continuing to lead me off the patio and into the house.

But he didn't answer.

Most of the guests were outside, but there were a few scattered about, browsing around the house, as well as servers gathering food and supplies to refresh the tables.

"Tyler, someone will see us," I whisper-yelled this time, trying to dig in my heels and stop him.

But once we were past the bustle of the kitchen, he took my hand and pulled me down the dimmed hallway and past the foyer to his den.

He opened the door, dragged me inside, and slammed it closed. Releasing my hand, he walked behind his desk and crossed his arms over his chest, locking eyes with me.

What the hell was wrong with him?

The woman simply wanted an introduction. Did he think I didn't know how to be discreet? She couldn't possibly have recognized me.

Or maybe he was angry about my behavior before she arrived. I guess I wasn't so discreet.

"What did he say to you?" Tyler barked out. "When he whispered in your ear?"

I cocked my head, choosing to be stubborn.

"Does it matter?" I played.

He shook his head, letting out a bitter laugh. "Not everything that's in your head needs to come out of your mouth," he scolded.

Ah, now we were getting somewhere.

"Are you angry because of what I said or because I drew attention to myself?" I inquired, crossing my arms as well. "Maybe I shouldn't wear any short skirts either."

He placed his hands palm down on his desk and glared at me. "That's not what this is about."

"Right." I smiled. "Let me guess. I forgot my place. Legs open, mouth closed, right?"

He pulled up, slowly circling the desk and looking down at me. "Don't be dramatic."

My skin tingled, and my heart sped up. "What are you really mad about?"

"What did he say to you?" His full bottom lip was tight with tension.

"I forgot." I shrugged. "Something about his dick."

His entire face hardened. "I should've hit him."

"Then why didn't you?"

"Because I'm not a child!" he bellowed. "I'm an adult who picks his battles. I don't just run off, half-cocked, no matter how much I wanted to see him bloody for even getting near you."

"Too bad," I taunted, a slight smile on my lips. "If you had, I'd be in here on my knees, sucking your dick right now instead of thinking about his."

His eyes flared, and he bared his teeth. Grabbing me by the jaw in one hand and hovering his lips just over mine, he slowly swung me around and slammed my ass against the desk, the small tray of file folders on the corner spilling to the floor.

My blood raced. *Yes.*

I hopped up, planted my ass on the desk, and wrapped my hungry legs around his waist as he moved his hand to the back of my neck and came down on me, his lips hot and strong.

I whimpered, his tongue sending thrills down my body, spiraling in my stomach, and throbbing between my legs.

His hands were everywhere, underneath my dress, inside my panties, and gripping my ass.

"Tyler," I groaned, nibbling and kissing his lips.

"You drive me crazy," he breathed out, sounding angry as he sucked and bit my lip.

One of his hands left my ass and shifted to grip my breast through the dress. The other moved to my hair, holding my head back by the scalp.

He ripped his mouth away from mine, and I whimpered at the sting.

He glared down, tightening his hold on my breast. "Tonight you will be on your knees," he whispered, kissing me, "and I'm going to like the sound of you shutting up. Now, get out there and make me jealous." He pulled away, grabbing my upper arm and yanking me off the desktop. "It'll make your punishment more fun."

He walked around his desk, and I tightened the muscles in my legs to keep them from shaking. The fierce heat between my thighs ached, and I winced with the discomfort.

But I wouldn't give him the satisfaction of knowing how worked up he'd gotten me. I could get what he gave me anywhere. At least that's what I'd lead him to believe.

Standing tall, I pivoted on my heel and walked for the door.

"And, Easton?" I heard him call.

I spun around to see him eyeing me with the phone to his ear as he made a call.

"Louisiana has had three female senators throughout history, not one," he said with a cocked eyebrow before looking away and dismissing me.

I let the corners of my mouth turn up before I walked out.

He might just have my vote, after all.

"All right." I held the racket in my right hand and the yellow tennis ball in my left. "Stand between the center mark and the sideline, and you have to serve into the opposite service court," I instructed Christian. "You can hit the lines, but if the ball shoots outside of those boundaries, you've lost that point."

He nodded, the same little scowl on his face that his father often wore. It was funny, because I think that look intimidated most people. It looked like he was angry, but it was just the look of him paying attention. I'd been getting it more and more in class lately.

Most of Christian's friends had already left the party, only a few still sticking around because their parents were still here. When I'd inquired about his tennis court, he'd said it had come with the house when his father bought it years ago. But to his knowledge, it was never used.

Still, it appeared well kept, though the net could be changed. It was stained from the heavy rains over the years and frayed.

I tossed the ball into the air above my head and swung the racket from behind, the dull popping sound of impact sending shivers up my arms. The ball flew over to the other side and landed in the other service court, bouncing several times before it finally came to rest against the fence.

"And then is it the other person's turn to serve?" he asked, his hands in his pockets.

I handed him the racket and walked over to the side in my bare feet, grabbing a new can of balls he'd brought out.

"No. You serve the whole game," I called back, looking over to the garden and seeing more guests begin to leave.

"The whole game?" he blurted out, sounding daunted.

I tried not to laugh. "Not the whole match," I pointed out,

emphasizing the different vocabulary. "Just that game. Men's singles generally have two sets per match, a third if needed."

I peeled off the lid from the can and popped the sealed top, instantly dipping my nose in and smelling the new-ball scent. It reminded me of summers and sweat, Gatorades and sore muscles.

"Do you play any sports at school?" I asked him.

He reached his arm up, dipping his racket behind his head and throwing a practice swing.

"Yeah," he breathed out. "I play soccer, but . . ."

"But what?"

He shrugged. "I don't know. I just get . . . pressured, I guess," he confided, attempting more practice swings. "I don't think I'm very good. The other team or everyone watching sometimes gets in my head, and it's all I'm thinking about."

I smiled to myself, knowing exactly what he was talking about. It was very common for athletes to feel the crowd's expectations, and winning was as much mental as it was physical.

"Do you know what I realized when I played tennis?" I asked him. "I realized that you're playing a part in a way. When you put on that uniform or grab that ball, you sometimes have to become someone else to play the game. Braver, harder, tougher . . . When you're in a competitive situation, you're you times ten."

His eyebrows pinched together, like he understood what I was saying but wasn't sure what to do with the information.

"An easy way to put on that new mask is to do something to your appearance," I suggested. "I used to create elaborate braids before pulling my hair back into ponytails for a match. It kind of helped me get my head into the game and feel tougher," I told him. "Other athletes paint their faces . . ."

He nodded, looking pleased with that idea.

"Hello." A woman's voice interrupted, and I turned my head to see the blonde from earlier, Tessa McAuliffe.

I narrowed my eyes but quickly recovered. I'd thought she'd left.

Many of the guests had filtered out, and I was getting ready to grab my brother—who was deep in conversation with one of the mayor's assistants—and Kristen—who was chatting with the son of someone important from somewhere important—as well, to leave. Tyler had been in and out of the party, talking to a few people and making eye contact, probably to make sure I was having fun.

But I'd been fine.

I'd spoken to several guests, and my brother was in his element. Tyler had been on my turf a few times, so it was only fitting that I got to invade his.

And it had been eye-opening to see the people he surrounded himself with. Blackwell, other politicians, and members of the elite.

And then Tessa McAuliffe, who I remembered also hosted a morning news show. It was reasonable to believe Tyler had invited her due to the influence she held or her media connections, but I still didn't like the way she said his name.

Or the way she was so familiar with him.

"I tried to introduce myself earlier," she said, holding out her hand, "but he swept you away so quickly."

She gazed at me with a twinkle in her eye.

I nodded once and took her hand. "Easton Bradbury."

"Tessa McAuliffe."

"Yes, I know," I responded, turning away to hand Christian the can of tennis balls before facing her again. "From the morning show, right?"

She grinned, squinting her eyes playfully. "Not a fan?"

"Oh, no," I shot out. "I'm sure I would like it well enough, but pop culture isn't really my thing."

She nodded, and I let my eyes fall down her body for a moment. She looked like everything I wished I was.

Her red dress stood out against the other female guests' beiges and pinks, and she walked with grace in her tan heels. Her hair was neatly coiffed in an up-do, with locks of rich blond hair falling around her face. Her makeup was soft, and her posture was confident.

My dress seemed childish now, and the dark blue heels I'd rushed out to get to match the splatter of flowers on the dress were cheap compared to hers. It wasn't that I didn't have the money for designer things. I'd made a small fortune playing tennis and even modeling in ads for clothes and tennis shoes. I simply had no interest in spending my money on things I considered impractical.

Until now.

She was a woman, and I felt like a girl next to her, with my hair hanging in loose curls instead of up, looking sophisticated. I should've done something with it.

What does Tyler prefer? Does he think she's prettier? More presentable? I—

And then I cleared my throat, stopping myself.

Ridiculous. How the hell did I get filled up with all of these insecurities all of a sudden? All that mattered was me. How I felt comfortable and what I liked.

And Tyler certainly seemed to like something about me.

"And what do you do?" she asked, interrupting my thoughts.

I took a deep breath, stepping over to the side to slip back into my heels. "I teach at Braddock Autenberry."

"Where Christian goes to school?" she inquired. "What do you teach?"

My toes ached as I pushed them back into the tight-fitting shoes. "American and World History," I replied.

And then I stopped to look at her. "Are you here in support of Mr. Marek's campaign?" I asked, ready to find out exactly what she was about.

"Mr. Marek?" she joked. "Doesn't he allow you to call him Tyler?"

I straightened my shoulders, glancing at Christian to see him running to collect all of the balls he'd hit.

"He's the parent of a student," I clarified. "I wouldn't be so familiar."

"Not even when you two are alone?"

I held her eyes even though my pulse raced in my chest.

Was she really that perceptive?

Or had Tyler confided in her?

No, he wouldn't do that. It would be a betrayal to confide in another woman about his relationship with me.

She let out a small laugh. "It's not hard to figure out, Easton," she gloated. "I know most of the guests at this party, and none of them are teachers at Braddock Autenberry."

I heard Christian's footsteps off to the side as he ran back over to this side of the court. She must've seen him, because she inched closer.

"And judging by the way he scans the party from time to time, in search of you, I'd say he's very territorial," she pointed out, looking over her shoulder to the party.

I followed her gaze, seeing Tyler around a group of men, and as if on cue, he twisted his head and locked eyes with me at once, already knowing exactly where I was. Then his eyes narrowed, and his jaw tightened, making it clear he didn't like Tessa and me talking.

She turned back around, looking smug. "He's been doing it all day, you know?"

No. I hadn't known. And while I liked knowing I was on his mind, she might not have been the only one to notice. My brother, now Tessa—how long before others knew there was something going on between us?

Hell, Mason Blackwell probably recognized me from the Quarter the other night, too. My job, Christian, and Tyler's campaign . . . there was too much risk.

She smirked and turned around, walking away, obviously successful in doing whatever it was that she'd set out to do. Maybe she wanted me out of the way, maybe she intended to out us, or maybe she was just having fun, but one thing was clear: She wasn't on my side. She enjoyed making me squirm.

I quickly glanced back over to where Tyler had been and noticed him gone.

"Shit," I mumbled under my breath.

I looked over at Christian. I loved seeing how hard he was working. I wished I could stay on the court longer with him, but it was time to get out of here.

And never be anywhere in public with Tyler again.

After saying goodbye to Christian, I traipsed across the lawn and stepped back onto the walkway. I entered the house and searched out Tyler, starting with his den.

Peeking inside, I saw no one, but when I heard voices coming from the next room, I quietly pushed open the door and saw Tyler with three other men around a pool table.

An older man in a slate-gray suit hit Tyler on the back as he bent over the pool table to take a shot. "There's not enough money in the world to buy you charm, Marek," he stated, letting out a laugh.

Tyler shook his head and took the shot, slamming the six into the side pocket. His brother, whom I'd already met, leaned on his pool cue, while another man, a few years older, puffed on a cigar off to the side, all of them smiling and looking relaxed.

I straightened my back. "Mr. Marek, I'm sorry to interrupt." I opened the door fully and took a step inside. "My brother and I are heading out, and I wanted to thank you for the invite."

He stood upright, and I didn't miss the way his eyes drifted down my body.

The cigar guy let out a laugh. "Can I invite her to my next party?" he asked. "She's a pretty little thing. And pretty entertaining, too," he added, and I realized he must've been in the group of men outside.

And then Jay smiled. "Yeah, I've never heard anyone speak to Blackwell that way."

"You see?" Tyler turned to me, looking playful. "You can't go. Your charms are in demand."

"They're not charms," I shot back. "It's called an education. And I can't stay, unfortunately. I have plans this evening, so again, thank you for having me."

I turned to leave, making it only a few steps before a hand hooked the inside of my elbow and spun me back around.

"Wha—" But my protest was cut off.

Tyler's mouth covered mine, his hands holding my waist and pressing my body to his.

I squirmed, pushing against his chest even as the taste of him sent tingles down my thighs.

What the hell?

I grabbed his bottom lip between my teeth and bit, feeling him jerk back and break the kiss. But he didn't let me go.

"Gentlemen"—he spoke to them but looked at me—"would you excuse us, please?"

I heard some amused, low voices as they walked past us, out the door, but I was too embarrassed to look. My face felt flushed, and I wanted to hit him.

They closed the door behind them, and I didn't wait a second longer.

I slammed his chest, finally getting him to step away. "How dare you demean me like that in front of others!"

"You liked it," he retorted, turning around to replace the cue on the rack.

"They could tell someone!"

"The one in the tan suit is sleeping with his kids' nanny. The other one has his secretary keeping track of his mistresses, and the other one was my brother," he replied. "Most of us are gentlemen—outside of the bedroom anyway," he added, "and we don't share each other's secrets. You wanted me to claim you. So I did."

I hadn't wanted him to claim me.

Okay, maybe I had hoped he would've said or done something when Blackwell made an advance, but I didn't want to be treated like his personal piece of ass in front of a group of men.

I crossed my arms over my chest. "You just compared me to their illicit affairs."

He let out a sigh, dropping into a high-back leather chair. "What got you pissed off—again—that made you want to leave?"

I pressed my lips together and turned around, walking for the door.

"Tessa McAuliffe," he called out, and I stopped in my tracks.

Spinning around, I glared at him. "I couldn't care less," I told him. "And I'm not angry."

"No, but you're a hell of a lot of trouble," he retorted. "I think that's what I like most about you. You're worth every second of fucking frustration you give me."

He relaxed into the chair, his head resting on the hand he'd laid on the armrest.

I inched closer, swallowing the lump in my throat. "Have you slept with her?"

"Yes."

I let out a quiet breath. I didn't like that.

"When was the last time?" I asked.

He kept his eyes on mine and spoke calmly. "A couple months ago."

I got closer, hating everything I was hearing but unable to stop the conversation. Of course he'd slept with her. She was beautiful and sophisticated, and I was a hot mess.

I cleared my throat, my gaze faltering. "Were you exclusive with her?"

"No."

I moved my lips, barely getting the words out. "How many are there at one time?"

"Many."

I felt my chest shake, and I looked away, feeling my eyes burning.

So he didn't do monogamous relationships. No one kept his attention for long.

But that's what I wanted, right? I was the same. We were the same.

So why was what he told me so hard to hear?

"Jesus, you're stupid."

I shot my eyes up, seeing him shake his head and look down on me like I was pathetic.

He rose from the chair and walked toward me. "You're young and naive."

I breathed hard, pinching my eyebrows together and scowling.

"You ask the dumbest questions, and you're having the tantrum of a child," he charged. "It bores me."

I growled low, ready to leave, but he took my face in his hands and spoke hard, his voice and the heat of his breath taking me over.

"Yeah, I've had women," he admitted, baring his teeth. "Lots of women. I'm thirty-five fucking years old, for Christ's sake." He shook my head slightly. "Tessa McAuliffe is a beautiful woman, and we've enjoyed each other many times."

I rammed my palm into his chest, but he didn't budge. "Many times?" I raged.

He nodded, getting in my face. "Yeah, many times."

But as I felt my eyes pool with tears, he came closer and grazed my lips with his. "All before you," he whispered, making my breath stop. "There hasn't been anyone since you."

I stayed still, needing to pull away but wanting to stay.

"That's why you're stupid." He grabbed the backs of my thighs and lifted me onto the pool table. "Why the hell would I want her or anyone else when I've got this?"

And he pulled up my dress, pulled my panties to the side, exposing my pussy, and dove down, capturing my clit in his mouth.

My eyes rolled and my head fell back as his hand pushed the top half of my body down to the table.

"Tyler," I cried out. "You have to stop."

I squeezed my eyes shut, trying to keep the tornado low in my belly from building further, but he was going too damn hard.

His lips covered my clit, sucking it in between his teeth and warming me with his hot breath against my entrance. He was sucking so hard.

And then he began dragging his tongue up and down my length, switching between that and more sucking as I slowly fell backward on the table. Reaching behind my knees, he pushed them up to where they nearly touched my shoulders, opening me completely for him.

My thighs instantly tensed, wanting to close, because I felt so exposed, but he started kissing and biting and do everything that drove me mad.

"The door's not locked," I pleaded.

But then he plunged his tongue inside me, and I cried out.

"Oh, God," I gasped, my pussy pulsing so hard I could barely think of anything except the need to fill it.

"Tyler, the lock," I gasped, whimpering. "Please."

I felt his mouth leave my skin, and I looked down to see his eyebrow cocked.

"I thought you liked standing in the middle of burning rooms," he challenged.

Asshole.

He smirked and walked over, turning the lock on the door. Striding back to me in long steps, he slid his arms under my thighs and pulled me to the edge of the table. He then hooked his fingers in my panties and slid them down my legs, my heels having long since fallen off.

He dipped back down, lapping at my clit and swirling his tongue around the nub as he worked to unfasten his belt.

"When Tessa's happy, she smiles," he commented against my skin. "When she's angry, she smiles."

I threaded my fingers through his hair, listening.

He rose and pulled me up, reaching behind me and unzipping my dress. "You're the complete opposite," he said, staring into my eyes. "You say what you think and you refuse to indulge people you can't stand. You're like a ball of fire I can never hold for too long."

He pulled down the top of my dress, bra straps with it, and pushed me back down to palm my breasts and rub his thumbs over my nipples.

I groaned, letting my eyes fall closed.

"You belong in my bed every night, and I fucking hate that I can't have you there," he gritted out, his hands working between our bodies. "I want to buy you shit just to have you throw it back in my face, and I want to fly you to Fiji just so I can rip a bikini off of you." I felt the hot tip of his cock at my entrance, and I could feel the wetness between my legs.

"I said my dick was yours, and I meant it," he breathed out, grabbing hold of my hips as he slammed his dick inside of me.

I cried out, feeling the sweet ache of him stretching me. He clamped a hand over my mouth, pounding into me harder and harder. I loved the feel of him, how he fit me so perfectly. I loved the smell and taste of him, both of which excited and calmed me.

But what I loved most was his eyes watching me as he stood above me.

"You've been a bit of a brat today," he scolded.

I nodded, squeezing my eyes shut.

"You were jealous, weren't you?" he asked.

I bit my bottom lip, groaning as he took his hand away from my mouth and began to rub circles on my clit.

"Yes," I breathed out.

"Why?"

I swallowed, my mouth like a desert from the exertion. "She talked to me about you," I started, my breasts bouncing back and forth with his thrusts. "She talks about you as if she knows more about you. She gets to touch you in public and call you 'Tyler.'"

He came down, never once breaking pace as his face hovered over mine.

"She's not getting any of this, baby," he whispered. "She's not the one I can't stop watching or thinking about."

I gave a weak smile, and his knuckles grazed my cheek.

My pussy began to tighten and clench, and he rose up, thrusting harder and faster.

"Oh, God," I panted.

"Now are you going to be good?" he challenged, holding my hip in one hand and my breast in another.

I arched my neck back, taking everything he was giving me and closing my eyes. "Yes," I whispered.

But as the orgasm exploded between my legs and floated up to my belly, I smiled, knowing I could never keep that promise. And he didn't want me to, either.

EIGHTEEN

TYLER

Life never follows your plan.

The truth was you could spend countless hours planning and preparing, and the only thing you could count on once you'd got your plan set was that it would be the one way things *won't* happen.

This year was supposed to be about Christian—creating a relationship with him—and my future in the Senate.

But all it takes is for one woman to look up at you, her eyes saying everything that she doesn't want to admit out loud, and all of a sudden she's all you're thinking about.

Easton was jealous last weekend, not only of Tessa McAuliffe, but also of having to hide our relationship. She would never admit it, because she was too damn stubborn, but she wanted more.

The relief in her eyes and the weak little smile she gave me when I admitted how much I wanted her was tearing me up, because what I'd told her was the truth, and I didn't know what the hell to do about it.

I was thirty-five and had never been married, so why shouldn't I want something permanent? She was young, beautiful, smart, and well educated, and while her temper was a pain in the ass, she was also a force to be reckoned with. I liked the idea of having her at my side in life.

Patrick opened the door, and I stepped out of the car, buttoning my black pin-striped suit coat as I headed over the grass to the sidelines of the soccer field.

I'd missed the reminder for his soccer game on my calendar and had zoned out when the secretary had reminded me during a meeting, because I was trying to multitask too much at once, so now I was late.

As usual.

My father had always attended my games, on time, ready to cheer for me. He was also a busy man—and still was—but he'd managed to show up anyway.

He would tell me that I just didn't know how to prioritize, and that came from selfishness. I wanted what I wanted, and I didn't want to give up one thing in order to have another.

He never went easy on me and still regularly called me out as if I were twenty-two again and not a grown man who had built a worldwide corporation without any of his money giving me a head start.

I had big shoes to fill, and I wasn't measuring up.

Never measuring up.

"Tyler!"

I heard a stern voice cut through the cheers and whistles, and I turned, immediately inhaling a ragged breath.

Speak of the devil . . .

Tipping up my chin, thankful that my undoubtedly annoyed expression was covered by my sunglasses, I walked down the sidelines to a group of parents who had set up a couple of tents with a small buffet spread out and cushioned lawn chairs. Aluminum trays were heated by candles underneath, and an array of salads and other sides adorned the tables. Balloons and tablecloths in the black and forest-green school colors blew in the light wind, and women toasted with their mimosas, trying not spill anything on their designer scarves.

I strode up and scanned the field for Christian, seeing him stop the ball with his chest and then begin to kick it in the opposite direction before passing it off. He wore black and green face paint like a mask over his eyes, and I smiled, seeing that he was the only one daring to be different.

I wondered what had made him do that.

"So how are you doing, old man?"

I laughed, shaking my head. Matthew Marek was thirty years my senior, and yet he'd called *me* "old man" since the first day I'd stepped into his classroom fourteen years ago.

As my professor, my father didn't treat me with any gentler a hand at school than he had at home. He'd said I must be ancient to have such a cynical world view, and I'd absolutely hated having him as my teacher.

Until, of course, nearly the last week of the course, when his advice had changed my life forever.

I understood then that, despite the old money and Marek family expectations, my father had been right to follow his calling to academics. He knew a thing or two.

I pushed my sunglasses back up the bridge of my nose. "I'll let you know once this day is over."

I could hear the smile in his voice. "Yeah, they all start melting together eventually," he agreed. "And judging by that gray"—he ruffled my hair—"I'd say time is moving faster than you."

"Bite me," I grumbled, smoothing my hair back down. "My hair is as black as yours was thirty years ago."

He snorted, crossing his arms over his chest, and I did the same, both of us watching Christian run back and forth on the field.

I quickly scanned the rest of the area, finally spotting Easton at the small concession stand, filling containers of popcorn.

I lingered on her, and the temptation of her bright smile as she exchanged snacks for cash was absolutely brutal. I bit the corner of my mouth to stifle the desire running hot in my veins.

She looked gorgeous. Her tan pants were tight, not inappropriate but definitely becoming, and showed off her form very well. She wore a long-sleeved white blouse buttoned up to the neck, and her wavy brown hair was pulled back in a ponytail.

I loved her teacher clothes. They gave a false impression of innocence and purity, like her lips weren't wrapped around my cock two nights ago when I'd called her at midnight, telling her to open her front door for me.

"I checked out your recent developments with Marek Industries," my father said. "Hiring local workers in the East with the same pay they would've made in the United States. That's positive change, Tyler."

I continued watching Christian as I spoke. "And in the meantime, my competitors are paying slave wages in those third-world countries and spending three times less."

"How much money does a man need?" he shot back.

I glanced over at Easton, her hands on her hips, chatting and smiling with Ms. Meyer.

"There's always more world to conquer," I said in a low voice. "Always things I want. There's never enough money."

"And that pursuit will take you away from everything that truly matters," he retorted.

He was always the teacher and never just my father. I faced the field again, barely seeing Christian as I braced myself.

"You still fight that battle," he went on. "Your conscience knows what's right, Tyler, but your ego keeps telling you to advance. It's not about speed. It's about direction. Clarify your goals."

"I want everything." I turned back, shooting him a cocky grin. "Those are my goals."

"But it's not about getting what you want." He shook his head. "It's about wanting what you get. In the end, is it going to make you happier? Was it worth it?" he asked. "You've got a thriving corporation that employs thousands of people worldwide. You've got a healthy son, but for some reason you're not content."

I gritted my teeth, seeing Christian score a goal, but it didn't even register, and I didn't clap.

Why did everyone want to fuck with me?

I managed real estate and relationships, dealt with banks and thousands of workers around the world, and I did a damn good job.

And I had noble intentions for the Senate. It wasn't some scheme to further my business interests.

I did my best. I managed everything to the best of my ability.

I just wanted more. I didn't want to have to live up to anyone else's expectations but my own.

"I just . . ." I searched for the words. "After all these years, I still feel like . . . like I haven't proven anything. I still feel like I'm twenty-two."

My father loved me, and I always knew that. But I guess, growing up, I resented the teacher in him. The one who couldn't say "Good job" or "That's okay; you did your best." No, the teacher always expected better, and after years of giving up and giving in to mediocrity, because I was afraid to fail him, he'd finally told me off in front of the whole class when I was forced to have him as a professor during my last year in college.

He'd handed me my ass and told me that success is earned and not given. A winner fights for it, and I'd been a loser.

"I know I can do better," I said, my voice turning thick.

I felt his eyes on me and then his hand on my shoulder. "Which is exactly why you have my vote if you ever get there," he added.

He turned and walked back to his friends, who'd probably invited him, knowing his grandson was playing today, but then I heard his voice again.

"Tyler, try to remember one thing," he insisted, and I kept my back to him but listened.

"You can do a couple things and succeed," he pointed out, "or you can try to do fifteen things and fail at all of them. Clarify your goals. What are you doing? And why are you doing it?"

And then I heard him walk away, leaving me with his rhetorical questions.

He was right. Every ounce of me knew that something had to give, and I'd end up having to let go of something I very much wanted just so everything else in my life didn't suffer. I was one person with limited hours in a day and too much desire to fill it.

And too many people with their own expectations.

I wanted Marek Industries to grow, because it was something I had built from scratch. I was proud of the work we did, and I could see its effect around the globe in the structures it had built and the people it employed.

I wanted to sit in a Senate seat in Washington, D.C., because I'd read too much and seen too much to trust anyone other than myself. I couldn't watch the news or read a paper without thinking about what I would've done differently.

I wanted my son to smile at me and joke around with me. I wanted to tell him stories about me as a kid, for us to watch football games together, and I wanted to teach him things. I had loved him since the first time I saw him, and I was desperate for him to know that my decisions weren't his fault. They were mine, and I regretted them.

And I wanted Easton.

I wanted to see her in a beautiful dress across a crowded room, knowing those clothes would be on my bedroom floor later that night.

I wanted some of these things more than others, but I didn't want to give up any of them.

"Ms. Bradbury!" someone behind me called. "Please have a seat."

I glanced to my side, my arms still crossed over my chest, and spotted Easton handing a rack of water bottles to one of the coach's assistants.

She twisted back around, sparing me a quick glance before turning to the small party where my father sat.

"Oh, no, thank you," she replied to Principal Shaw. "I'm just making the rounds. Helping out . . ."

She stood not five feet away, but it felt like much closer. I could feel her heat, and my whole body buzzed with awareness of her.

She looked at me again, nodding politely. "Mr. Marek," she greeted.

I nodded to her, seeing Shaw rise from his chair out of the corner of my eye.

"Ms. Bradbury has been doing wonderful things in her class," he told everyone. "We were all very hesitant at first, but it's working phenomenally. Mr. Marek," he called from behind, "Christian seems to be doing well. You must be pleased."

I twisted my head, eyeing Easton through my sunglasses but speaking to Shaw. "Yes, I'm very happy with her." I tried to keep the smirk off my face. "She has a very hands-on approach."

Her eyes widened ever so slightly, and she glanced at Shaw, looking half nervous and half enraged.

I snorted and focused back on the soccer match, letting my lips curl into a smile. But before I could enjoy that one too much, she retaliated, getting me back.

"And Mr. Marek has graciously accepted an invitation to speak on Career Day," she announced, sounding unusually cheerful. "I may have dangled a nice lunch to sweeten the deal," she told Shaw.

What the fuck?

"Well"—he laughed—"we beg, borrow, and bribe around here. Easton's catching on quickly."

Yeah, no shit. Career Day?

"Ms. Bradbury," I cut in, "may I speak to you about Christian's project, please?"

She nodded, her small smile saying she knew she'd gotten me, and I walked down the sideline with her following behind me.

Stopping just far enough that we were clear of listening ears, I faced the soccer match and spoke to her at my side.

"I meant what I said." I spoke softly. "I am very happy with you, you know? Especially with the way I woke up the other night."

I caught her sharp intake of breath and saw her thumbnail go immediately between her teeth. She was trying to hide a smile, and I found it endearing and frustrating. Hiding what was going on between us had an element of excitement and turned out to be great foreplay for later. We were living two different relationships, so it kept things constantly new and unpredictable.

However, I wanted us to have liberties that we couldn't have in public. I wanted her to smile at me and to be able to reach out and touch her.

But I couldn't, and that part was getting increasingly annoying.

"I want to do that to you again," she said softly, her breathy voice turning me on.

"Do you?" I played, remembering waking up and how my hands instantly went into her hair as she took me into her mouth.

"Yes," she responded, dropping her voice to a small whisper. "I've been thinking about it all day."

And I looked down at her, seeing her eyes locked on the match and an innocent blush cross her cheeks as she bit her nail.

Damn. I blinked, turning back toward the field, realizing I didn't know when I was going to see her again. And I needed her soon.

"Good job!"

She suddenly broke out in a yell, clapping her hands, and I shifted, refocusing my attention and seeing Christian and his teammates celebrating on the field.

I let out a frustrated sigh and clapped as well, feeling like a bigger asshole because I'd missed it.

You can do a couple things and succeed, or you can try to do fifteen things and fail at all of them.

My son's black hair was shiny with sweat, and I smiled, seeing him enjoying the win with his friends.

"Mr. Marek, may we have a picture?" a woman asked, holding some high-tech digital camera.

I nodded, but Easton pulled out of the picture before she took the shot, adjusting her ponytail and trying to act nonchalant.

The woman shrugged with a polite smile and walked off.

I narrowed my eyes, studying Easton. "It's just a friendly shot for the school paper," I assured her, having seen the woman's school sweatshirt. "A parent and teacher talking isn't scandal-worthy, Easton."

She didn't make eye contact or say anything, and before I could pry, she smiled widely, seeing Christian heading over.

"Hey, great job," she exclaimed. "You did amazing."

"Yes, you did great," I told him, seeing his smile fall when he looked at me.

"Were you even watching?" he shot back.

I dropped my eyes, thankfully disguised behind my glasses. I didn't think he'd realized I was here, since I'd been late. But he'd known, and he'd seen that I was, again, distracted.

Inhaling a deep breath, I lifted my chin. "I thought we could go to Sucré for some dessert before dinner," I suggested. "To celebrate."

He shook his head, brushing me off. "I'm going to hang out with friends."

"Your friends can wait an hour," I pressed. "If Ms. Bradbury came, would you be less bored?"

No sense in coddling him with a softer approach. My son wasn't an idiot, and I wouldn't try to play him like one.

"Thanks, but I need to get home," Easton interrupted.

"Christian?" I prompted him for an answer, ignoring Easton's protest.

He looked between his teacher and me, seeming to consider it. "Can I drive?" he asked.

The corner of my mouth lifted, actually liking his boldness.

When I didn't answer right away, Easton stepped in, urging me.

"No, he can't drive," she answered for me. "Ty—" She stopped and corrected herself. "Mr. Marek, he doesn't have a permit," she pointed out.

I eyed Christian. "Have you ever driven before?"

"Not in the city but yes."

I nodded, giving in.

He turned and started walking for the parking lot, and I followed, glancing behind me to a baffled Easton.

"Get in the car," I ordered. "Don't act like you're thinking about saying no."

"No, wait," Easton burst out. "That's a light!"

"Shit," Christian cursed, and I shot him a glare. I didn't have a huge problem with swearing, and I didn't mind him working me a little, but I didn't want him taking advantage. Fourteen-year-olds shouldn't swear, especially not in front of their parents.

He'd stopped at the red light, just like a pro, but after a second he started to go through it, thinking it was just a stop sign.

"It's confusing," he barked. "There are so many stop signs, it throws me off when they have a light instead."

"And half the streets are only one way," Easton added from the backseat.

"And land in the wrong pothole," I contributed, "you could total your car. My car," I corrected, shooting him a warning look. "So be careful."

After Patrick had tossed the keys to Christian, we'd offered to give him a lift home for the night, but he'd said he'd rather take the streetcar, so the three of us just left together. Christian drove with me in the passenger seat, and Easton sat in the rear-facing seats behind Christian. All I had to do was look to my left and there she was.

"So many issues with the streets." She shook her head. "I don't suppose fixing any of these problems are on your platform."

"No, but I can get you in touch with the mayor," I replied, resting my elbow over the back of the seat.

The light turned, and Christian pulled forward, cruising the streets easily but looking a little nervous. I suspected he'd driven four-wheelers out in the country but never a big SUV on busy city streets. Thankfully, we were off the main avenues and coasting through the quieter, less-populated neighborhoods.

I glanced back at Easton, seeing her watching the road as well. With both of us, we were probably making Christian more nervous, but she was right. He was only fourteen, and if he got into trouble, he might find being Tyler Marek's son finally somewhat useful.

"There's no parking." He scowled, scanning the space in front of the shop.

Easton pointed to the right, just a few yards ahead. "Right there."

Christian jerked the wheel right and slid into the spot between two cars, his front end in the clear, but the back end still sticking out into the street. I turned away, not wanting him to see my smile at his attempt at parallel parking.

This was a big car. For a space that tight, he'd have to back into it.

"Shit," he cursed again. "This is ridiculous."

I shook my head. "First, stop swearing," I ordered. "And second, you've lived here your entire life. Haven't you ever paid attention to your mother while she drove, or were you too busy playing on your phone?"

"And what do you do while Patrick carts you around town?" Easton blurted out.

Christian laughed, and I pursed my lips in annoyance.

"Hey, how'd you know our chauffeur's name?" Christian asked, looking at Easton through the rearview mirror.

I caught Easton's eye as she clearly realized her mistake.

But she blew it off and changed the subject. Looking out the back window and seeing a car go past, she instructed Christian, "Okay, back out and pull up right next to the car ahead of you."

Christian gripped the wheel, looking worried. But he followed her instructions. After backing out, he pulled ahead and lined up with the car next to him.

"Okay—" Easton started, but Christian cut her off.

"But I'm in the driving lane," he protested. "There are people behind me waiting."

"And they'll wait," she assured him patiently.

I watched as she instructed him and led him back into the parking space with ease, and I was surprised by how different she was with him from with me.

Not that our interactions were bad, but she was almost never calm. With him, she stayed controlled and relaxed, easing his nerves about the cars behind us waiting to get by and stopping and correcting him without sounding brusque.

She was good with him and slid into her role with ease. I smiled to myself.

It was funny that I liked her being so calm with him while hoping she would never be that way with me.

Christian put the car in park and broke out in a huge smile. "I did it."

I shot Easton an appreciative glance and turned to Christian. "Good job."

He shut off the car and took the keys out of the ignition. "Thanks," he said quietly, handing me the keys.

He didn't look at me, but it was a start.

After entering the shop and picking out a selection of macaroons and homemade marshmallows, we took our desserts and drinks to a small table perfect for watching clientele breezing in and out of the quiet atmosphere.

Easton had picked out some gelato, and I loosened my tie, drinking some coffee.

"I got an e-mail from your mother today," Easton told Christian, and I narrowed my eyes, not realizing that they were in contact.

I didn't know why I hadn't thought of it. Of course Brynne would be in touch with all of Christian's teachers to make sure she stayed abreast of his progress. I guess I had figured Christian was keeping her informed during their weekly video chats.

"She's thrilled with your progress," Easton went on. "We thought you might like to test for an AP class."

Advanced placement?

"Really?" Christian's eyebrows pinched together as he thought about it.

"Like an honors class?" I asked.

"Yes." She nodded. "It would be with a different teacher and the class would be even more demanding, but I think he'd be challenged more."

"You're pretty challenging," Christian retorted, and Easton laughed.

"Well," she inched out. "It's also about being with *peers* that challenge you. Braddock Autenberry has an excellent student body full of students that excel, but there are always a few who could use a more stimulating environment."

Why hadn't I known about this? I'd stayed up on all the social media groups and e-mails from all of his teachers. I may have been late to his soccer game, but I wasn't dropping the ball on everything.

And it's not like I hadn't seen Easton. She'd had opportunities to tell me.

"Thanks." Christian shook his head. "But I like being in classes with my friends, and I like your class. The activities are fun."

She tried to hide her smile, but I could tell she liked hearing that. And I wasn't so sure I wanted Christian out of her class.

Of course, if she were no longer his teacher, our relationship wouldn't be such an issue, but I wasn't willing to sacrifice a good teacher that made him happy just so I could have what I wanted. If I had to make the sacrifice, I would. But not him.

"You could just take the test," Easton offered. "To see where you stand in case you change your mind."

"Does my mom want that?" he asked.

Easton's eye flashed to mine for a moment, and I knew she felt awkward talking about Christian's mother as if my thoughts didn't matter.

But I guess Christian had every right to trust his mother's opinion more than mine.

"Your mother wants to see you reach your full potential," she answered.

Christian sat silently for a moment, staring at the table as he chewed his macaroon.

And then he looked to me, his eyes thoughtful. "What do you want me to do?"

My eyebrows shot up, and I opened my mouth but nothing came out. He'd just asked for my opinion.

I searched my brain, trying to think of what he wanted me to say. Or maybe what my father would say.

This was an opportunity to not fail, so I struggled with what to tell him, because I honestly didn't feel strongly about the advanced-placement class. He'd have a bright future no matter what classes he took. I only wanted him to know that he was free to choose, and in my eyes, I'd be okay with either choice.

I locked eyes with his and spoke with certainty. "I want you to do what you want," I told him. "Just remember, you're the only one who has to live with the decision, so whatever you decide, just have a good reason for it."

And that was all I wanted him to learn. Bad decisions were made from either not thinking them through or for the wrong reason. As long as he had a good one, he'd feel confident about his choice.

He let out a breath and looked to his teacher. "I'll do the test," he told her. "Just to see what it says."

"You did a good job today," I told Christian, grabbing a couple of Gatorades out of the refrigerator and tossing him one.

I'd driven us back to the school tonight and watched while Easton got safely into her car and drove away. Bringing her home with me had been all too tempting, but it was impossible.

"Would you like to practice again tomorrow?" I asked. "Driving, I mean."

He twisted the cap and turned away, heading out of the kitchen. "I'll be busy."

Shit.

He was pulling away again.

I rounded the island. "You forgot you hated me for a little while today," I reminded him.

He stopped and turned around, his eyes faltering as if he was trying hard to stay angry because his pride wouldn't let him forgive.

"Come on," I urged, brushing past him down the hallway.

I pushed open the door to the den, hearing his reluctant steps behind me, and I headed straight for the cue rack, taking out two sticks.

He hovered in the doorway, slowly inching inside as he took in the large, darkened room. I'd told him my den was the only place off-limits when he moved in. It was two rooms joined, my office and the billiards room, great for entertaining and bullshitting with guests over cognac and cigars.

But I rarely used it, since I almost never had people to my home; last Sunday's luncheon was the first time in more than a year.

I racked the balls and then grabbed the pool cues and handed one to Christian.

He reached, looking annoyed as he took the stick.

"This is stupid," he grumbled.

"It's what I know," I told him. "My father always talked to me over a pool table."

Men and women were different creatures. My mother, before she passed away when I was fifteen, tried sitting with me and talking to me about her being sick. About the fact that she wasn't getting better and she wouldn't be around for very much longer.

She kept wanting me to react, to say something or tell her what I was feeling and how she could help, and all I remembered was feeling uncomfortable, like the walls were closing in.

So my father took me into his den, and we played pool. After a while, we started to talk, and by the end of the night, I'd let it all out. My anger and my sadness . . . how she couldn't die and how much I loved her.

In that respect, I knew my son. Forcing him to sit down and bare whatever was in his head would be just as uncomfortable for him as it would be for me.

We needed to be moving and doing something. We needed to have an activity together without the pressure of conversation. The communication would eventually come.

I started off, taking the first shot, the fourteen in the corner pocket and then the twelve, but missing.

Christian pocketed the one and then the six. I was pleasantly surprised and relieved. He wouldn't want me trying to teach him how to play right now, so I was glad he could hold his own.

Moving around the table, he shot the four but missed the two.

We took turns, and he won the first game. When I asked him if he wanted to play another, he simply nodded and stood silently by as I racked the balls again.

"I know why you're mad at me," I started after he took the first shot.

"You don't know anything," he threw back, taking the next shot and missing. And then standing back upright, he scowled at me. "Why do you even care all of a sudden?"

I bowed down to the table, aiming for the nine. "I always cared."

"You have a crap way of showing it," he shot out.

I pocketed the shot and moved around the table to take aim at the eleven. "You're right."

I'd helped support him, and I'd wanted to do good by him, but he was ultimately right. I couldn't argue that, and I didn't want to.

It was his turn to shoot, but he didn't budge. "It was kinda fun tonight, you know? We could've had that all the time. Why were you never around?"

I forced myself to meet his eyes. "I was a dumb kid, Christian. I didn't want to care about anyone but myself. And then later, I didn't want to fail, so I didn't even try."

"You still failed."

"No. I just haven't done it right yet," I replied, a small smile playing on my lips.

He rolled his eyes, but he wasn't leaving.

I wanted to be a man Christian could look up to. I wanted to show him that mistakes can be made but so can amends. I would never not look him in the eye again, and I would never let him think he wasn't wanted.

"I'm not asking you to forgive me or act like the past fourteen years didn't happen," I told him.

He pinned me with stern eyes. "Then what do you want?"

For a moment I blinked long and hard, hating that question. I knew exactly what I wanted, but I feared there would come a day when I had to admit I couldn't have all of it.

But he was first. He always had to be first. Before anything or anyone.

He may not want me as a father, and he may never forgive me, but what I had right here, right now, I had to keep.

I looked at him and spoke gently. "I want to play pool."

NINETEEN

EASTON

Patrick held the door to the Range Rover open for me, and I climbed inside, adjusting the short dress Tyler had sent to me this morning.

But then I shot out my hand, pressing against the door to keep it from closing. "Wait, please."

Stepping back down out of the car, I jetted up the stairs to my apartment and twisted the doorknob, pushing at the door to check its security. Inserting each of my keys into the three separate dead bolts, I double-checked to make sure they were all locked.

I'd come home from school yesterday to find an upstairs window open, and I'd been running through the house all day, doing my Saturday cleaning and checking the rooms two or three times to make sure everything was in its place. Pillows sitting two to a corner on the couch, cabinet contents in alphabetical order, shoestrings tucked neatly inside my tennis shoes.

Maybe I'd left the window open. We'd had a nice evening after I got home from Sucré with Tyler and Christian. Maybe I'd opened it.

But no, I wouldn't have left it open while I slept.

I climbed back in the car, Patrick shutting the door behind me and walking around the back to the driver's door.

I rubbed my hand over my heart and took some deep breaths. The fact was, I'd gotten careless. My head was either on school and my work or it was consumed with Tyler. The flirty text he'd sent me or the glimpse I'd caught of him picking up Christian at school . . . I was constantly distracted, and I may very well have left the window and cabinets open.

But it still didn't make sense. Returning things to their place, taking a last glance around a room before I left to make sure nothing was out of order—these habits were second nature to me. I did them without having to think about it.

Could someone have been in my house?

Fear gripped me, thinking about all those years ago, when very much the same thing had happened.

It wasn't possible.

I forced myself to sit back in the seat and smooth my hand down my dress, willing the worried expression off my face as I relaxed my muscles.

No. Everything was fine.

I looked down at the dress that hugged my thighs, concentrating on how good it felt, and tried to be excited for the evening ahead.

I didn't often dress up for nights out, and the outfit was like a second skin. I was surprised Tyler knew my size.

But of course he knew my body.

This morning Patrick had delivered a box with the dress and a note saying he'd have Patrick pick me up at ten. I'd been annoyed on several levels. For one, he didn't ask; he directed. And second, he had bought me an outfit to wear.

The dress was black, long-sleeved, short and tight. It also featured goldlike jewels around the neck and on the straps running vertically down my naked back. I'd pulled my hair up in a sexy bun, and even though the dress was provocative, it wasn't distasteful.

After realizing that this meant he was taking me out, I gave in and kept the dress, telling Patrick I'd see him at ten. Which gave me plenty of time to finish tidying up the apartment, run errands, and work out before I had to get ready.

I held the clutch purse in my lap and looked to Patrick, who was making his way toward the French Quarter.

"Where are you taking me?" I asked, knowing Tyler wouldn't have had me get dressed up to go to his house.

"Veil," he answered over his shoulder.

Veil?

I'd heard of it, but it was the high end's version of a high-end club. *Tyler is taking me to a nightclub?*

I bit back my smile, having a hard time picturing it. Not that he gave off the vibe of being a drip, but—okay, yes, he did.

But that's one of the things I liked about him. I couldn't claim to know him all that well, but I could guess that there were ten other things he'd rather be doing than spending time in a club. There was only one place he let himself relax, and that was usually wherever he could get me alone.

"Will Tyler be waiting there?" I inquired.

I could only see the side of Patrick's face as he spoke, as he kept his eyes on the road. "He got stuck on a conference call overseas, but he shouldn't be too long," he explained. "He asked that I take you inside and stay with you until he gets there."

"No need," I assured him. "I can take care of myself."

"Sorry, miss." I could hear the smile in his voice. "Those are the orders."

I sat back and stared out the window, letting it go. I wouldn't be able to convince Tyler I didn't need protection, because I'd learned karate moves on YouTube. Yeah, right.

After Patrick navigated through the Quarter, slowing for the pedestrians and tourists constantly in the streets, we stopped on Toulouse Street, in front of a large black building with wide windows on the second and third floors. Neon blue and pink light flooded through them, and I noticed a barely visible sign on the front of the building next to the door that read VEIL. It was etched onto a plaque in black and then mounted into the black brick of the establishment, making it anything but obvious. Which I guess would account for its name.

I knew the club was members only, but obviously Tyler could invite guests.

Patrick handed the keys to the valet and circled the car to open my door. I took his hand, stepping out and tucking my small handbag under my arm.

The doorman opened the door and Patrick let me go first. I entered the arcane darkness with him following closely behind.

I stepped slowly, taking in my surroundings, because who knew when I'd ever get to see a private club again.

It was like stepping into a different world.

Of course, everything in New Orleans was old, aged, decrepit, and ruined, but walking past those doors, my eyes widened, and I felt like I'd left the city and entered some secret world hidden right under our noses.

Not that I didn't like what made this city, but it was a nice surprise to see something so out of place and new-looking.

It was dim but not dark once we entered, and as I walked over the slate marble floors, I suddenly realized why Tyler had bought me the dress. With the way everyone looked here, I certainly fit in.

The men wore sleek, dark suits, some with ties and some without, while the ladies wore tight dresses that showed off bodies they presumably paid for with three Spinning classes a week. I didn't like the idea of Tyler dressing me up to be like them, but he would've known the club had a dress code.

The long bar curved down the wall, looking like a white wave, and the walls were an architect's dream. Curving in and out in a cubed, geometric pattern, it made you feel not only as though you were in another world but another time. It was sleek, chic, and most of all, expensive-looking.

The massive oval-shaped columns in the middle of the room had to be four feet wide and were made of glass and filled with water that gave off a purple glow from a light hidden somewhere in the tanks.

I sat down at the bar and patted the seat next to me, urging Patrick to join me. He was always so quiet, and it felt awkward having him stand behind me like a bodyguard.

I ordered a gin and tonic, while Patrick settled for a Coke and insisted on paying for mine as well.

"Why does Tyler employ you?" I asked, twirling my straw around my drink. "Does he really need a driver?"

Tyler was very self-sufficient, but I wondered why he felt the need to be chauffeured most places.

"He says it saves time," Patrick answered, his Adam's apple bobbing up and down as he took a drink. "He can get work done in the car while I drive."

I curled my lips in a smile, thinking that made perfect sense for Tyler.

I spoke as quietly as I could over the beat from the speakers. "Do you think he'll make a good senator?" I broached.

"Of course." He answered quickly, his face never faltering as he smoothed his blond hair back over the top of his head.

"Is that a paid answer?" I challenged, and immediately regretted it.

His eyes narrowed on his drink, and he cocked his head to look at me.

He knew Tyler. Probably better than I did. His loyalty wouldn't allow him to betray his employer even if it was a paid answer.

We sat silently for a few moments, and I felt like I should apologize, but then he spoke up.

"I've driven him around for more than five years," he told me, his hazel eyes locked on mine. "Do you know how many calls he's made, deals he's negotiated, and people he's spoken to during those drives when he thought I wasn't listening?" he asked rhetorically.

"Being invisible has its perks." He went on, crossing his arms over his chest. "I've gotten to see all the arguments he's had with his father, with his brother . . . when they try to mold him into something he doesn't want to be."

He chewed the corner of his mouth, looking like he was thinking. I waited and listened.

"I've seen the frustration on his face when he worries about his kid," he continued. "I've seen how he responds to women, and I know when one means more than all the others." He paused, staring at me, his insinuation clear.

He took a deep breath. "I've had the privilege of seeing him more closely than probably anyone else, and I can tell you, his character isn't just for the camera," he disclosed. "Yes, I do think he would make a great senator."

"Patrick." A deep voice cut through the room, and we both jerked around to see Tyler standing behind us.

Patrick hopped off the bar chair and tucked it in. "Sir."

Tyler's eyes darted from him to me and then back to him, and I knew he'd heard at least part of what we'd been talking about.

"Thank you." He nodded at Patrick, but he looked and sounded curt. "I have my car, so you're done. Have a good night."

And Patrick left without another word, leaving me in Tyler's hands.

I decided not to feel bad about plying Patrick with questions. Tyler Googled me, after all.

I tilted my head and took in his appearance, surprised to see a difference. He wore a coal-black suit with a black shirt open at the collar and no tie. His short black hair shined in the light, and for some reason he looked younger than he usually did. Maybe it was the surroundings.

"You wore it." He let his eyes fall down my body as he commented on the dress.

I stood up, grabbing my bag and my drink. "You sound surprised."

He smirked, leading me away. "With you, always," he joked.

With a hand on my lower back, he guided me toward the elevator.

The doors opened, and we stepped inside. As soon as he pressed the button for three, the doors closed, and he hooked an arm around my waist, pulling me in.

"Hey," he whispered and then captured my lips, completely taking me over. His soft lips were gentle but fast and playful. He dipped in, nibbling and kissing, and then cocked his head the other way, going back for more as he grabbed my ass in both hands.

My knees buckled, and thank goodness his arms were wrapped around me, holding me up.

"You look beautiful." He spoke in a husky voice, pinching my chin between his thumb and fingers.

He kissed me one last time, then let me go just as the doors opened, and I clutched his arm, feeling like my muscles had turned to Jell-O.

A host stood outside the elevator and smiled as soon as he saw us.

"Mr. Marek," he greeted, bowing his head just a bit. "Right this way."

He led us through a spacious lounge, complete with a small dance floor and several square arrangements of sofas, sparsely filled. The third floor of Veil was much like the first floor, but what was white downstairs was black upstairs, which made the ambience darker and more cavelike.

The water-tank columns glowed purple and the black curved

bar had an array of different bottles along the wall, each glowing with the light built into the backsplash. Several semiprivate booths lined the perimeter of the room, and it appeared right away that guests in here were on a different plane from what I was used to. Nearly all of the men had young, beautiful women with them, and champagne was everywhere. The chandeliers glittered in the dim light, and I had the strangest feeling of being in a dream.

"Marek," a man's voice called, and we both stopped, turning around.

A gentleman, about the same age as Tyler, approached him with a smile and shook his hand. "How are you? Haven't seen you around in a while."

Tyler rolled his eyes. "Busy as usual. What do you think?"

He quirked a smile at me and placed his hand on my back again. "This is Easton Bradbury," he told the man, and I felt a momentary shock that he'd introduced me so freely.

"Easton?" Tyler said. "This is James Guillory."

I shook the man's hand, narrowing my eyes as realization dawned. "As in oil?" I asked, shocked again.

The Guillorys owned half the oil rigs in the Gulf.

He winked at me, clearly interested in neither confirming nor denying it.

He slapped Tyler on the arm. "Keep in touch," he told him, and walked back to his table, packed with his buddies and their ladies.

Tyler led me to where the host had stopped and let me slide into the booth first. Our table was set in a semiprivate space with drapes on both sides, a three-sided couch, and a low glass table, making it easy to get up and move around.

Tyler sat down, ordered some champagne and began to relax, resting his elbows on the back of the sofa.

"So this is where the millionaires come to play with their secrets?" I looked around at the heavy flow of liquor and the pretty women who probably weren't their wives.

But Tyler had a different take on it. "It's where men and women who lead very controlled lives come to lose control," he clarified, looking around the room. "Everyone here is in the same position, Easton. They want to cut loose once in a while like everyone else, but someone is always watching."

And then he locked his eyes on mine. "This is one place where no one cares. We all have something to lose, so privacy is respected."

"I hope," I added with a smirk.

No one knew who Easton Bradbury the schoolteacher was, so I was grateful he'd brought me here. I was tired of quiet, secluded dinners and catching stolen moments whenever we could. It was fun to be out with him in public and in plain sight.

"Do you like the dress?" he asked.

I set my drink down and nodded. "Yes, I do."

"I'm surprised you weren't insulted." He laughed. "You always dress beautifully, but this place is a little different. Not to mention I wanted to see you in something short again."

Yeah, again. Every time I wore a short skirt or dress, he ended up inside me.

I leaned in, taking advantage of being with him somewhere where I could openly touch him, and slid my hand inside his jacket, rubbing his chest.

"I'll tell you what," I bargained. "You can dress me as long as you promise to undress me."

And I slipped my leg over his and kissed him, holding his smooth face in my hand and shivering when he ran his hand up my thigh.

"Do you like to dance?" I whispered against his lips, having seen a few couples and some women on the floor.

He ran a thumb over my cheek and held my face. "It's been a long time," he admitted. "College, I think."

"You were a lot different when you were my age, weren't you?" I pressed.

He shook his head, smiling as he took the champagne the waiter handed to him. "When I was your age, huh?" he repeated. "Way to kill the mood."

I shrugged. "Just keeping it real. You're only ten years younger than my father would be."

His eyes flared, and I gasped as he grabbed me, planting me in his lap so that I straddled him.

Gripping my hips, he growled against my mouth. "You're going to pay for that," he threatened.

I laughed quietly, meeting his lips as he dove in.

"Such a brat," he whispered before going deep and swirling my tongue with his.

I could feel him everywhere, and even though I liked being out with him, I felt a sudden need to leave.

"Easton?"

I pulled back and looked up, feeling my heart crash into my stomach.

I swallowed the lump in my throat. *Oh, no.*

"Kristen?" My voice was barely audible, and I licked my parched lips.

This isn't happening. Of all the places to run into someone. *Here?*

"What . . . what are you doing here?" I blurted out.

Her eyebrows shot up, surprise written all over her face. "Um . . ." she stammered, looking like she was searching for words as she bit back her smile. "I'm tagging along with a friend who's here for a private party."

I looked at Tyler and slowly slid off his lap much too late to hide what had been going on.

"It's okay." She nodded, holding up her hands before I had a chance to say anything. "I actually think I'm too shocked to see you at a club to worry about who you're with."

Tyler snorted, and I scowled.

I know how to have fun, thank you very much.

"Mr. Marek?" Kristen put her hands on her hips. "I'm taking Easton onto the dance floor. You stay."

She reached over and grabbed my hand, and I stumbled over Tyler's legs, trying to keep up with her as she pulled me out of the booth.

What the hell?

I cast a worried glance at Tyler, but he just jerked his chin to the dance floor. "Go ahead. I want to watch you."

As I followed Kristen, the slow beat of "You Know You Like It" vibrated under the floor and through my heels. There were only about six other people on the small floor, so we had plenty of room. I stood tall, smoothing my hands down my waist and thighs, suddenly a little nervous. The dance floor sat in the center of the room, so we were on display for anyone who cared to look.

Kristen turned around, facing me, and immediately began moving her hips and flipping her hair as she raised her hands into the air.

I looked down at my heels, arching an eyebrow, and then turned, kicking my shoes off to the edge of the floor. Glancing up at Tyler several feet away, I saw a smile spread across his face and his chest shake.

Laugh it up, dude. You'll be thankful you aren't carrying me out of here with a broken ankle.

I started to move, closing my eyes as I reached up and pulled the pin out of my hair, letting it fall down my back. Swaying my hips slowly to the beat, I let the music guide my body.

When I looked over, I saw James Guillory take a seat across from Tyler, and they started to chat, but Tyler constantly looked up, watching me as we danced.

"I knew it," Kristen yelled in my ear over the music. "When he came to your room that morning, my panties practically lit on fire with the way he was looking at you. How long has it been going on?"

I wasn't sure what to tell her. Of all the damn places to run into someone we both knew, this was supposed to be the least likely.

She was very friendly, but that didn't mean we were friends. I had no reason to trust her. This was my job, Christian's stability, and Tyler's future on the line.

But he didn't seem worried to have run into her, and I kind of wanted to talk about it with someone. I was happy, and I hadn't been able to share it with anyone besides my brother.

I took a deep breath and admitted, "A couple of weeks."

Maybe three, but she didn't need every detail.

Nodding, she grabbed two shots of something brown off a waiter making the rounds and handed me one.

"Well, be careful," she insisted, actually looking serious for a change. "I'm sure he's great, but men like that take what they want, and what they want changes like the wind."

She tipped back her shot, and I hesitated a moment before shooting back mine.

I winced at the burn as my tongue felt like it had been bitten.

We handed our glasses back to the waiter, and he left. I guessed the rounds must have been complimentary.

I blew out a breath, trying to cool off my mouth. "What makes you think he doesn't need protection from me?" I challenged.

She threw her head back, laughing. "That's the spirit," she cheered.

Her black halter-top dress hugged her body as she moved, and I let my eyes follow her hands as they glided down her body.

Her red hair fell in waves, and I realized for the first time how pretty she was. I hated to admit it, but every time I looked at her, I assumed she was flighty and carefree.

Would Tyler find her attractive? I suddenly felt small, trying to figure out what the hell I offered him that he wanted so much. She was happy. I was discontent. She was playful. I was serious.

She moved in closer, and I almost moved to back up, but she put her hand around my neck and pulled me in, speaking in my ear. "So how is he?" she asked. "In the bedroom?"

I couldn't help the little smirk that escaped as I looked away, my skin heating up at the thought.

"Ohhh, I see," she cooed knowingly.

She didn't need it spelled out, but I was sure my face confirmed that Tyler Marek was keeping me very satisfied.

"Well, I'm completely bummed." She pouted. "You're having great sex with a handsome millionaire, and I'm here with a friend who's the friend of some pop singer I've never heard of."

I laughed, and we both turned our heads to the side, seeing Tyler with his elbows hooked behind the seat again, watching us as Guillory talked to him.

"Don't worry." I leaned in to Kristen. "I'm enjoying this for what it is and while it lasts. We'll eventually move on from each other."

She cocked her head, and I couldn't ignore how close we were as her eyes turned mischievous.

"I'm not so sure about that," she argued. "As long as you both keep finding ways to make it interesting."

And then her hands went to my hips, and I slowed my body, instantly feeling the heat of Tyler's stare on my back.

She licked her red lips and breathed against my face. "Let's play with him."

At first I narrowed my eyes, confused, but then I understood when I felt her hands run up my sides, in a slow and possessive gesture.

My pulse sped up, and I had a hard time keeping my breathing steady as her fingers dug into my hips and pulled me closer, her thigh fitting between my legs as she continued to move slowly to the music.

What the hell?

"Watch his face," she instructed in my ear.

But I was afraid to look. On the one hand, I liked playing games and turning him on, but on the other hand, I was scared he would get ideas.

Twisting my head to the side, I raised my eyes, instantly drifting to Tyler. Guillory had left, and he pierced me with that stare. I knew how he looked angry, and I knew how he looked relaxed, but shivers ran down my arms, and I felt myself growing wet as he watched us with his heated gaze.

I knew that look.

He was two seconds from bending me over in a bathroom stall.

I started to move more, rolling my hips into Kristen and running my hands over her waist and hips.

She took the back of my neck in one hand and dipped her head under my ear as we lightly grinded our bodies for him.

"I don't know whether he wants to see more or wants to tear me apart for touching you," she joked.

But I knew the answer. Tyler wanted a lot of things. He wanted everything. But he would never choose one over the other. It was what it was, and he would never claim me like that. I knew as much.

"How far are you willing to go to find out?" I asked, challenging her.

She raised her eyebrows, giving me a "try me" look.

I took her hand and led her back over to the booth, slowing and dropping to my knees to the sofa as I inched over to him.

He narrowed his eyes on me, and I could see the shallow breaths that he was trying to hide.

"Did you like what you saw out there, Mr. Marek?" Kristen crawled over to him on the seat cushions.

He ran a finger over his lips as he looked at me. "What's not to like?"

"I don't know," she answered, stopping and sitting back on her heels. "You looked . . . tense."

Her sexy voice was filled with desire, and I suddenly felt like I wasn't sure of what I was doing. This was a game. Someone was going to stop it.

Right?

"I was tense." Tyler looked over to her, tipping her chin up. "You two are beautiful," he allowed. "As long as you know she comes home with me."

"How about we both go home with you?" she suggested.

Had I wanted her to say that? I couldn't swallow past the lump in my throat.

Tyler didn't answer, and before I knew what I was doing, I dipped my head to his neck, kissing the soft skin under his ear.

I heard his sharp intake of breath, and I caught his skin in my mouth, dragging it between my teeth.

"Kiss her," I whispered. "Please."

I saw him out of the corner of my eye as he hesitated, and then, slowly, he reached out and took her by the neck, bringing her in, their lips meeting.

I squeezed my eyes shut and took hold of him, trailing deep kisses over his neck and across his cheek, trying to own what was happening.

The sounds of their kissing and her moaning turned my blood cold and made my heart ache.

Kiss her, I thought. *This needed to happen.*

I would force myself to watch the whole damn thing and take any desire I had for him—any need—and twist it into knots to where nothing good could be made from it and no part of what I felt for him could ever be recognizable again.

I couldn't have him. Not for good. He was sex, and he'd hurt me.

I'd have to let him go eventually. Why increase the inevitable pain on my heart when I could end it right now before he got a chance?

I didn't want to love him. This needed to happen.

A tear fell down my face, and I quickly wiped it away as I pulled back and watched him. Not them, just him.

His hand was on my thigh as he kissed her, and he tried pushing it under my dress, but I slowly inched away, out of the scene.

"Keep going," I urged. "Let me watch you."

His tongue was in her mouth, and his other hand palmed her breast over her dress, and I envisioned it. Him taking her home, pulling the top of her dress down as he planted her ass on his desk and fucked her rough and dirty.

Or maybe he'd take her to bed. Let her ride him as he watched her body move.

I inched far enough away that his hand lost contact with my thigh, and I just sat there on my knees, watching him make out with another woman while I felt like he was slowly getting farther and farther away from me.

His eyes were closed; he wasn't seeing me. My composure cracked, and more tears pooled in my eyes.

He didn't even know I was here. He didn't see me.

All he saw was her.

But then his hand started reaching across the sofa in search of me, and the next thing I knew, he pulled away from Kristen and pushed her off, glaring at me.

I stopped breathing, realizing that he was pissed. He was really pissed.

He looked at me like I'd betrayed him.

"I'm sorry," I gasped, nearly in tears. "That was stupid."

And I crawled back over into his lap, straddling him, ready to apologize.

"What the hell are you trying to do?" he barked, the vein in his neck bulging.

I shook my head, taking his face in my hands. "I don't know," I cried. "Just don't let me go, okay? I shouldn't have done that."

And I kissed him softly, my whole body shaking with the sobs I tried to hold back.

I didn't want to let him go. I was falling for him.

His angry breaths slowly calmed, and after a few moments, he wrapped his arms around me like a steel band and kissed me back.

I heard Kristen clear her throat next to us and then felt her shift off the sofa.

"Well, I'll just excuse myself," she said in a light tone, as if nothing had happened.

But then I felt her lean in and whisper in my ear, "And if you haven't noticed, he's in love with you, too."

I gripped his jacket, not even hearing her walk away as I closed my eyes and saw only him.

TWENTY

EASTON

"You messed up my books," I commented, lying on my back on the floor of his study and gazing up at the bookshelves I'd so tirelessly organized a few weeks ago.

"Yes, I did," he admitted without hesitation.

I wore one of his long white shirts with the sleeves rolled up and was supporting a glass of Scotch on my abdomen with my feet crossed.

"Did you do it on purpose?" I pressed.

"Yes."

A smile spread across my lips, and I leaned my head up, taking a sip of the hearty liquid.

Christian was apparently spending the weekend with his grandfather across the lake, so Tyler brought me home with him from the club. It was one a.m., and neither one of us was the least bit tired.

I'd felt guilty about ruining our night out, but Tyler had said he didn't give a shit. He didn't like clubs anyway but had wanted to take me out.

After pulling me out of the club, he'd raced home, damn near getting into an accident on the way, and stripped off all of my clothes as soon as we'd gotten in the door. He'd carried me upstairs, my legs wrapped around his waist, and kept me good and occupied for more than an hour.

He'd gotten a few calls while we were busy, though, and since neither of us was sleepy, he'd come downstairs to take care of some business while I got drunk on his alcohol.

He stood behind his desk in gray lounge pants and no shirt, sorting through some papers.

"You're not going to fix them?" he suggested.

I tapped the glass with my fingers, staring up at the hodgepodge he'd made of the books.

"I'm considering it."

I heard his quiet chuckle. "Maybe you no longer need to be soothed," he suggested. "Or maybe you found something else equally effective."

"Cocky," I shot back, teasing.

But actually, he had a point. A few weeks ago, those books, sitting there out of order, some facing the wrong way, had driven me bananas, and I could not concentrate on a damn thing until I'd gotten them sorted.

Now it just kind of bugged me. I still felt the pull, but there was something else in the room tugging at me, too.

"It's such a strange feeling," I mused. "Suddenly abandoning a habit I've had for seven years. I feel more peace now than I ever had doing it, though."

"Seven years?" he repeated. "I thought you started when your parents died five years ago."

I let out a breath and closed my eyes. "Shit," I whispered under my breath, not loud enough for him to hear.

I'd forgotten that he didn't know.

"Easton?" he prompted, clearly waiting for an answer.

I swirled the glass in a circle, watching the brown liquid coat the inside. "Yeah, that story was never in the media, was it?"

In his Googling, he wouldn't have come across it, because my family had kept it under tight wraps.

"What story?"

I took a deep breath and set the glass down on the floor, tucking my hands behind my head as I started.

"I wasn't always the sophisticated, capable, and charming woman you see now," I joked.

He walked around the desk, leaning against the front of it and staring down at me.

"No?" He played along.

I looked up at him and, after steeling myself, opened up to him. "When I was sixteen, I was very naive and sheltered," I told him. "I didn't know how to make decisions or question anything. I had never even been on a date, and if my parents had had their way, I never would've been."

I stared ahead at the bookcase, remembering my perfect white house and my perfect pink bedroom and my perfect, strict schedule posted on the refrigerator.

"I was a twenty-four-hour tennis player, and the only people I spoke to were my family, newscasters, and my coach, Chase Stiles." I looked at Tyler. "He was twenty-six at the time."

His expression turned guarded. "Chase Stiles? Am I going to like where this is going?"

I gave him a soothing smile and continued.

"He was so devoted to me," I admitted. "Always encouraging me and spending so much more time working with me than what he was paid for. He would buy me things, and I liked it, because I thought he was the only one who cared about who I was on the inside. He asked me about my interests outside of tennis."

Tyler stayed quiet, and I hesitated, feeling my stomach knot as the old fear started to surface.

But I forced it out, keeping my eyes downcast. "I didn't see it as wrong when he started buying me outfits." I went on. "Tight shorts and sports bras to train in. And I didn't think it was such a big deal when he took pictures of me posing in the outfits he'd bought."

"Easton," Tyler inched out, apprehension thick in his voice. He didn't like where this was going.

I swallowed through the tightness in my throat, still not meeting his eyes. "But then he started getting familiar," I explained, chewing on my bottom lip. "Patting me on the behind when I did well or hugging me for too long." I blinked, pushing away the shame I felt creep up. "A couple of times he came into the locker room while I was showering, pretending it was an accident."

At the time, I'd felt like it was my fault. Like I was enticing him, or that what he was doing was normal. We'd spent a lot of time together. Training, traveling . . . We were close, so maybe he was just a really good friend or someone, like my parents, whom I should trust to never hurt me.

"I didn't tell anyone what was going on, and I didn't confront Chase about any of it," I told Tyler. "I just started getting more stressed, and I became angry. Very angry," I added.

"I started refusing his gifts," I continued. "And I threw fits when my mother would try to leave me alone with him on the court. After a while, I finally broke down and told them about his behavior."

"Did he force himself on you?" Tyler bit out, his voice turning angry.

I shook my head. "No. But the behavior was escalating," I explained. "My parents fired him, but they didn't press charges. They didn't want America's next tennis darling tainted with a scandal forever preserved in the newspapers."

I looked at Tyler and could see his fists balled up under his arms.

"And then, on top of that," he deduced, "you lost your parents and your sister two years later. That's a lot for a young person to go through."

I nodded. "It was."

Chase's abuse, and my parents' and sister's deaths, had almost killed me five years ago. I dove into a world of turning chaos into order and building such a tough outer shell that nothing bad could hurt me again.

It wasn't until recently that I'd realized, looking up at Tyler, that my shell protected me from all the good stuff, too.

"I started arranging and counting things as a coping mechanism, a way to have consistency," I told him. "To know what I could count on. Awareness of my surroundings, everything in its place . . ." I went on. "I didn't like surprises."

"You needed control," he assessed.

I nodded. "Yeah. After Stiles and then the accident, Jack and I tried to keep it going, but as you saw online, I couldn't get it together. My game fell apart. We sold our house and moved here, so I could have a fresh start and my brother could pursue his own dreams finally."

Tyler pushed off the desk and approached me, standing tall above me and looking down intently.

"And what's your dream?" he asked.

I inhaled a long breath and took my hands out from behind my head. Running one up his leg to the inside of his thigh, I whispered, "To not want you as much as I do."

The next week flew by, fall conferences having started, and I needed to get ahead on revising lesson plans that I'd already completed last summer.

I'd expected that to happen, as classes don't always go according to schedule and certain changes I'd decided to make at the last minute needed to be accounted for later. I didn't mind how my personal life had changed or even how unpredictable it had become, but I didn't want to lose control of my career. Being a good teacher was acceptable. Being a great teacher was my mission.

My sister, Avery, had wanted to teach, but I'd finally realized that I, too, was made for this. I enjoyed seeing my students engaged and interacting, and the rush of finally seeing them make a connection, discuss it, and ultimately teach one another fed my desire to do this every day.

Tyler had been out of contact a lot, being held up in constant meetings and campaign planning. He'd also had to take a day trip to Toronto on Monday that turned into two days away. His brother had stayed with Christian, and although I knew Tyler hated leaving him, he called and texted him regularly to check in.

In my classroom, I set up the laptop, positioning it in front of the three chairs at the table. Christian sat in one chair, playing on his phone, and I checked my watch, seeing it was four oh two, past time for our parent-teacher conference.

I then glanced at my phone, seeing no missed texts, so I hoped Tyler was on his way.

Bringing up Skype, I decided not to wait for him. I dialed Christian's mother, knowing that she was expecting my call.

I was in no rush to see her face-to-face, though. We'd spoken on the phone and had e-mailed several times. She seemed like a great parent and wanted to be kept informed of everything that was happening with Christian. She even belonged to the social media groups and participated.

I threaded my fingers together, trying to push down the uneasiness I felt at facing her.

"Hello?" she chirped, coming on-screen, and I forced a smile.

Of course she was beautiful.

Her long black hair was pulled back in a neat ponytail, and her ivory skin looked impeccable.

"Hello, Mrs. Reed," I greeted. "I'm Easton Bradbury, Christian's American History teacher."

"Nice to finally put a face with the voice," she commented with a bright smile.

"We're still waiting for Mr. Marek," I told her, "but he should be along shortly."

She nodded, an aggravated look crossing her face, but she recovered quickly.

"Put down your phone, Christian. I want to see your face," she ordered her son.

He rolled his eyes and set it down.

"I miss you," she singsonged.

"I know," he sang back, and we both broke out in a laugh at his sarcasm.

They chatted for the next few minutes, and I updated her on what we were currently studying and what we hoped to have covered by the end of the year.

Christian and his mother got along great, and I started to wonder a lot of things as I sat there, observing them. I'd never had so many insecurities as I had with Tyler, and I didn't like it at all.

Did he ever regret letting her go? Had he once loved her? What would she think of me if she knew how I felt about him?

That one scared me the most. Christian was my student, and every day I hated myself even more for doing anything that threatened his stability and happiness. I was supposed to make his life better, and I was very close to turning it upside down.

Clearing my throat, I looked at the clock and saw that it was nearly four fifteen. Where the hell was Tyler?

I smiled, trying to keep the mood going.

"You look like you're having wonderful weather there," I noted, seeing the white curtains blowing in the breeze coming through the open windows behind her.

"Oh, it's hot but beautiful," she clarified. "There's so much land to explore. I invited Christian to spend the holidays here, but he hasn't answered me yet."

She shot him a hinting smirk, and he sighed, shaking his head.

"I don't know," I teased. "Teenagers are hard. You might have to sweeten the deal. Ensure him he'll have Wi-Fi."

She laughed and turned her eyes to Christian. "We'll have Wi-Fi."

He tried to hide the smile, but I could see it.

I wasn't sure if Tyler wanted Christian home for Christmas, but a trip to Africa would be a wonderful experience for him.

I glanced at the clock again and picked up my phone. "I'll give Mr. Marek another call," I told her. "If he's running late, we may have to start without him."

I dialed Tyler's cell, knowing he would answer if he saw it was me. I called rarely, so he would know it was important.

"Hey, I'm on my way to a meeting. Can I—"

"Mr. Marek," I cut him off, putting on my teacher hat. "I'm here with Christian and his mother on Skype. Would you like us to wait for you?"

"Wait for me?" he shot out.

I gritted my teeth and smiled, keeping my voice even for Christian and his mom. "Christian's conference," I reminded him.

"Shit!" he bellowed. "Goddamn it!"

I let my eyes fall closed, hearing Christian laugh under his breath and shake his head. He'd heard that.

Tyler's heavy breaths poured into the phone. "I'm only a few blocks away," he gritted out. "I'll be there in five."

And he hung up, leaving me there feeling like an idiot.

I set my phone down. "He's on his way," I assured her. "But I think we can go ahead and start by looking at Christian's first-trimester test scores."

Over the next few minutes, I covered Christian's rough start at the beginning of the year, assuring his mother that I had every confidence it had to do with his transition from moving homes and starting high school. He'd caught up and continued to excel now, moving beyond several of the students in class.

Tyler blew into the room, and I stopped talking, taking in his appearance. He looked like a wolf that had lost its prey.

Some of his hair fell over his forehead, and his tie was wrinkled and hanging loose around his neck. The weight of a mountain rested on his shoulders, and I turned away, refocusing on the documents in front of me instead of worrying about him.

He took the seat next to Christian and glanced at me on his son's other side.

"Excuse me," he apologized.

And then he turned, nodding to Christian's mother. "Brynne."

"Tyler," she replied curtly.

Christian sat quietly, his eyes downcast.

"Mr. Marek, we already went over Christian's test scores and discussed some of his homework," I told him, handing him the documents. "You can take those home and review them in your spare time."

I looked to Christian's mother, careful not to make eye contact with Tyler, too afraid I would give something away.

I continued. "Christian will be given the opportunity to choose some of his assignments now," I informed them. "It's a technique I like to use for students I feel have earned the privilege. For unit projects and some daily assignments, he'll be able to choose from a selection, which will all be worth the same percentage of points, providing he puts in the same excellent effort," I explained, hearing a phone vibrate and seeing Tyler take it out and look at it.

My irritation grew, but thankfully, he put the phone down, ignoring it.

"Sounds wonderful," Brynne agreed. "Christian, would you like that?"

He shrugged. "Yeah, sounds fine." And then he looked at me.

"When do I take the test for the AP class?" he asked, seeming more interested in it than he'd been at Sucré. After some time to let it absorb, he must have grown more interested.

"Thank you for reminding me," I burst out, taking out the permission form. "I'll schedule you for—"

But Tyler's phone buzzed again, interrupting my chain of thought, and I dropped the paper to the table, shooting Tyler a stern look.

"Mr. Marek, would you please turn off your phone?" I chided, not really asking.

He shoved it into his breast pocket, and I didn't care that he looked the worse for wear. He could be present for this.

"Excuse me," he apologized again.

Christian snorted, and I continued, explaining the class and that Christian was doing well in several subjects and might qualify for more than one advanced course. Then Tyler signed the permission slip, authorizing us to test his son, and I wrapped up any last questions they had. Tyler didn't have any, because his head was clearly somewhere else today.

"Thank you, Ms. Reed, for joining us from so far away." I smiled at her and tapped my folders on the table, making sure they were stacked neatly.

"Yeah, with the time difference, she still managed to be here," Christian jabbed, shooting his father a cold look. "I'll wait in the car."

And he walked out.

"Tyler," Brynne said flatly, "we'll talk later."

And she clicked off, no happier with Tyler Marek than their son.

I stood up and dropped the folders onto my desk, letting my anger show now that we were alone.

"You have secretaries," I pointed out. "A calendar of appointments and meetings on your phone." I turned around, seeing him stand and straighten his tie. "How could you forget?"

Out of all the things to be present for at school . . . It's not like his presence here was required often. He couldn't make this a priority?

"It was a simple mistake," he explained. "There's too much going on. I'm running around everywhere, and my head is crammed full with a million things. I'm doing the best I can."

"For you?" I threw back. "Or for Christian?"

TWENTY-ONE

TYLER

My father's words of advice were a constant refrain in my mind lately: *You can do a couple things and succeed, or you can try to do fifteen things and fail at all of them.*

I jetted down the stairs of the school, feeling my cell vibrate from my inside breast pocket and ignoring it.

Damn phone calls all day. The fucking loggers in Honduras were in the middle of a battle with the environmental activists over clear-cutting, which shouldn't have had anything to do with me other than it was my equipment they were using to cut down the trees. Now Jay was in a fit over the guilt by association.

After that I'd been forced to a waste time having lunch with the mayor just to maintain the connection, and then I'd gotten stuck on call after call all afternoon. That was, until all hell broke loose down at the docks, when my shipment of buckets for the dozers and loaders making their way up the Mississippi for the final assembly at the factory in Minnesota turned out to be several tons of coal that wasn't mine.

Everything that could go wrong was going wrong lately, and I didn't know what the hell to do. My head was almost never on work anymore, and I kept dropping the ball. When I wasn't worrying about Christian, I was thinking about Easton and when I could see her.

I'd been going over last weekend again and again in my head. Her stunt at the club and how she'd tried to push me away. I'd been enraged.

I didn't want Kristen Meyer.

The woman was a void, like every other woman I'd come into contact with since Easton.

But I would've played ball if Easton had wanted it. If she'd been a part of it.

I didn't need the excitement or the experience, but I'd enjoy it. Sure. What man wouldn't? Especially with how hot she'd looked on the dance floor, another woman's hands on her. However, I didn't want to go into it without her. There was no point if she wasn't involved. It was about us experiencing something together.

But then she'd pulled away, disconnecting herself from the scene, so that I would find pleasure in another woman and she could walk away, convincing herself that anything we had wasn't special.

There's no amount of red sufficient enough to explain the rage I'd felt when I reached out for her hand and found only air, then realized what she was doing.

But then she'd crawled into my lap and cried and kissed me, and Kristen had instantly disappeared.

There was nothing but Easton.

And then, later that night, when she'd told me her story and how that lowlife had victimized her, I'd wanted to erase it all from her life and make sure she had the best of everything. Happiness, love, consistency . . .

And then I wanted to find him and erase him. It made me sick to think of him out there, walking around. Did he know where she was?

Climbing in the back of the car, I unbuttoned my jacket and

looked to Christian sitting across from me, staring out the window. "Room to Breathe" blared on the radio, and I reached over, turning it down from the controls in the back.

Leaning forward, I gave him my full attention. "I'm sorry I was late," I told him, tired of seeing that look on his face. For every step forward we took, it was another two steps back.

"You forgot." His sharp tone cut, his eyes still turned out the window. "You forget, because it's not important to you."

I sat back in my seat, hooding my eyes. "Is that what your mother tells you?"

"Yes," he stated matter-of-factly, twisting his head finally to look at me. "And then in private she tells my stepdad that you're a shitty, self-absorbed father."

I hardened my jaw, feeling like everything was slowly slipping through my fingers. I was losing everything.

Christian turned his head, speaking to Patrick.

"I want to walk," he said.

Patrick met my eyes in the rearview mirror, and I hesitated, not wanting him to get out of the car.

But dealing with Christian was like climbing a rope with one arm, and I was tired. Let him cool off, and I could think.

I finally nodded.

Patrick pulled over, letting him out. It was only a few blocks to the house and it was still light out, so I didn't worry.

My phone buzzed in my pocket as Patrick pulled away from the curb, and I closed my eyes, exasperated.

Yanking it out of my pocket, I saw Brynne's name on the screen and squeezed the phone, hearing it creak under the pressure.

Answering it, I held it up to my ear. "I don't need to hear it," I shot out.

"I was sitting there on a computer screen, Tyler," she barked. "You couldn't be there in person for Christian? You already missed one other conference this week."

"I'm not making excuses," I explained, "but it's not that I don't care. The campaign, the company . . . I'm very busy right now."

"All of which Christian couldn't care less about," she threw back. "I agreed to this, because you truly seemed to want to get to know him, and I didn't want to uproot his life while he was in school, but you're a mess! He knows he's not the most important person in your life, and he's wondering why. Do you have any idea how much he wants you to love him?"

"I do love him!"

"You're going to lose him forever!" I could hear the tears caught in her throat.

I rested my elbow on the door, holding the phone to my ear as I bowed my head and closing my eyes.

"That is, if you haven't already," she added, sounding somber. "Tyler, there comes a point when you've been disappointed or hurt too much that the bonds can never be repaired. You always wait for tomorrow. But let me clue you in. Tomorrow was yesterday."

I clasped the phone in my hand, staring out the window, deep down knowing she was right. When would I wake up and realize that it was finally time to make my son a priority?

My first priority.

I shook my head, my throat swelling with regret. I wouldn't realize it until it was too late. That's what it would take for me to wise up.

"If you can't get it together, I'm coming back to get him," she told me.

I swallowed and spoke quietly. "It's harder than I thought it would be," I lamented. "Trying to balance everything alone."

"I know," she replied. "Thanks to you, Tyler, I know that very well."

And she hung up, leaving me on my own just as I'd done to her all those years ago.

The weekend had passed slowly. More slowly than I'd thought it would, unfortunately.

I'd had a site in southern Florida to check out, so I'd taken Christian with me, handing over my social media and e-mails to Jay for the weekend just so I wasn't distracted.

Christian had joined me out in the heat and mud as we walked around, going over the plans for a plant to be built. Some of the workers had shown him how to handle the machines and even how to drive a loader. I don't think he understood exactly what I did, getting to see only the suits and clean offices at home, but on-site, it was dirty and loud, the ground being dug up and bulldozers roaring in every direction.

After a spell of trying to act disinterested, he'd joined in the fun, finally taking in the full impact of what Marek Industries was all about.

Sunday happened to be my birthday, so we'd spent it on a boat, fishing with some of my colleagues. I enjoyed seeing him smile so much that I'd decided not to press him about anything or to try to talk to him. Instead we would ease into it, learn how to be together comfortably, and let things happen naturally.

I knew one trip wasn't going to win him over, but I was glad for the opportunity to spend some time with him away from the day to day of the company and other distractions in New Orleans.

No matter how much I was still thinking about her.

I'd texted Easton to let her know I'd be out of town for the weekend, but other than that, I hadn't talked to her. She'd responded with a *Be safe*, and I hadn't called after that.

And it wasn't that I didn't want to.

But it was time to face reality. It was still only October. She'd teach Christian for another several months, so was I going to continue to sneak around with her all that time?

And not to mention that, if Christian found out, I'd lose him instantly.

"Mr. Marek?" Corinne came over and poked her head in my office door. "Ms. Bradbury is here to see you, sir."

I turned around in my chair, from where I had been gazing out the windows, and felt a rush of heat. It was late Wednesday afternoon, and I hadn't seen her since the conference last Thursday.

Why is she here?

I nodded. "Send her in."

Corinne left, and I turned down the TVs on the wall

A moment later, Easton walked in wearing a long black coat, tight at the waist but flared at the legs, and her hair windblown beautifully around her face.

My breath caught. God, I'd missed her.

Her skin glowed, and her rose lipstick made her lips look plump and edible.

Corinne closed the door behind her, and I blinked, regaining focus as I tried to force nonchalance.

"You coming to my office can't be a good thing," I teased, remembering the last time she'd been here.

She clasped her hands behind her back, looking vivacious and flirty. "I missed your birthday this weekend," she pointed out. "And I wanted you to know I was thinking about you."

A smile played on her lips, and I leaned back in my chair, taking her in.

"You look beautiful," I told her. "How's school?"

She leaned forward, placing her palms on my desk and pinning me with a smirk. "Wouldn't you rather have your present, Mr. Marek?"

My pants instantly got tighter.

Jesus.

I cleared my throat and played the game with her. Looking her up and down, I simply shrugged. "I'm not seeing it. Where is it?"

She stood upright and held my eyes, the blue hue of her gaze turning sensual and dark. She slowly began unbuttoning her coat, and my cock immediately stiffened with need for her.

She pulled the coat off, letting it slide down her arms, and then she dropped it on a nearby chair.

My lungs emptied, and I suddenly felt starved.

She wore black stockings with lace trim, a black necktie around her neck, and absolutely nothing else.

I groaned as I took her in. The beautiful olive skin of her hips and upper thighs looked soft and smooth, and I wanted my mouth on her flat stomach and full breasts. Her nipples were hard, and her hair floated across her chest, making me want to bury my hands in it.

"Just my size," I said in a low voice.

One corner of her mouth turned up. "Oh, this isn't your present," she admitted, turning around to take something out of the coat pocket.

My eyes landed on her ass, and I saw the little bruise she still had from the pool table.

Looking up, I saw her tear off a piece of duct tape from a roll and meet my eyes. "This is." She gestured to the tape. "No backtalk."

And she placed the strip over her closed lips and batted her eyelashes at me.

I started laughing, loving her ingenuity. If only she knew how much I really loved her mouth.

She rounded the desk, stepped out of her heels, and straddled me, slowly lowering her body down and resting her arms over my shoulders.

I reached out and ran both hands up her sides, kneading her skin, unable to help myself.

She moaned behind the tape, and I threaded my hand in her hair, grabbing a fistful of it and burying my lips in her neck.

But then I stopped. I let my forehead fall to her chest, wondering what the hell I thought I was doing.

Christian.

He came first. He had to come first.

And this would hurt him.

I was thirty-six. What was I doing with a twenty-three-year-old teacher who taught my son?

I couldn't have this no matter how much I wanted it. Brynne was right. I was a mess.

Looking up at her, I saw the question in her eyes. She was wondering why I'd stopped, and then she ran her fingers across my forehead, pushing away the hair that had fallen forward, and I knew that I was in too deep with her.

I would hurt her, disappoint her, and throw away any chance with my son along the way.

I dropped my hands to her hips and gripped them hard, my resolve ready to cave, because I didn't want to choose.

Sitting back, I raised my weary eyes and slowly peeled the tape from her mouth.

"I'm sorry. I have a meeting," I told her. "I don't have time."

She sat still for a few moments, probably trying to figure out if I was really kicking her out when she knew I just wanted to keep her here.

I'd never not had time for her.

And that was the problem. I'd put her before everything else.

She rose off me, looking everywhere but at me, and walked around the desk, slipping on her coat as fast as she could.

I tightened my hands into fists, feeling like everything inside of me was hollowing out.

She turned to leave but then spun back around. "If you're pushing me away, just say it. Don't leave me guessing."

I clenched my teeth together as I stood up and forced a glare. "I said I have a meeting," I bit out. "I don't show up in the middle of your workday, do I?"

Her eyes widened, looking surprised. "Tyler"—she held up her hands—"when a naked woman sits on your lap, offering herself up, you take it. And if you can't—for whatever reason—you at least say sweet things to her. I can't believe I—"

"You want to know why I'm aggravated today?" I grabbed my phone and brought up Twitter. "Look at the negative comments on the tweets you've been telling me to post," I shot out. "And this morning someone wrote a blog post calling me 'immature' and 'unprofessional.'"

I tossed my phone down on my desk, feeling like the walls were closing in. She blinked several times, and I could tell she was caught off guard and hurt.

"You've also gained just over five thousand new followers in the past couple of weeks." Her voice cracked. "The more you put yourself out there, the more negativity you'll see. That comes with the territory. I was trying to help."

I planted my hands on the desk and steeled myself, forcing my eyes to stay on her despite the hurt I could see in her eyes. "I didn't want your help. I just wanted you in bed."

She pulled back, instantly straightening her posture.

The pain on her face disappeared, her expression turning to stone. "I see."

She looked just like the Easton at the open house. The one who was cold and distant and far away from me.

"I guess I'll see you, then," she said, sounding cordial.

But this was goodbye.

I nodded, forcing myself to meet her eyes. "Yeah."

She turned and walked out, and I immediately shot out from behind the desk, ready to go after her. But I stopped myself, planting my hands on the desk and bowing my head, trying to calm myself.

Fuck.

I wanted her.

I needed her!

I slammed my fists down. “Goddamn it,” I growled under my breath.

“She really is gorgeous,” I heard behind me, and I recognized Jay’s voice. “Just don’t do it at the office, okay? Be more careful.”

I brought my head up, scowling at him. He must’ve seen her leaving.

“Relax,” I snapped. “It’s over.”

“Why?” he challenged, actually looking concerned. “You were definitely happy. I don’t see anything wrong with it as long as you’re both discreet.”

He slipped some file folders onto my desk, and I shook my head, unable to admit to my brother what I could barely admit to myself.

I looked forward to her. More than anything else.

And I couldn’t put her first anymore.

TWENTY-TWO

EASTON

The cool breeze blew down St. Ann, and I closed my eyes for a moment, enjoying its caress in my hair.

Laurel's "To the Hills" drifted like a heartbeat through my earbuds, and I soaked in the sun and the wind blowing my off-the-shoulder blouse against my skin.

I'd been strolling all day, playing tourist and enjoying the atmosphere that I rarely took the time to experience even though I'd lived here for more than five years.

It was funny. I'd woken up this morning with a list and a plan. Clean the inside of the stove, work out, and then research field trips for my classes, since we'd been discussing so much war history, and New Orleans had some wonderful sites to visit.

But when I'd gotten dressed, I'd realized I wasn't in the mood.

I'd crumpled up the list, tossed it in the trash, and grabbed my little bag, which now hung at my hip with the strap across my chest, and walked out of the house.

I took a streetcar to Canal and hopped off, disappearing into the Quarter.

Around the corner from St. Louis Cathedral, with its madness of artists, musicians, and palm readers, I traipsed a block or two to Maskarade, a little shop I'd discovered last Mardi Gras when I was searching for my first mask.

I wasn't interested in the gaudy souvenirs sold in the French Market or tourist shops. I'd wanted handmade work by real mask makers, and I'd always intended to come back, perhaps to start building a collection for my wall.

When I stepped in, the rough wooden floors creaked under my sandals, and the woman behind the counter smiled at me before returning to her paperwork.

That was one thing I liked about New Orleans.

Merchants didn't jump on you the second you walked into their establishments.

Masks covered all of the walls but were divided into categories. Leather to the left, then animal-inspired masks and feathered work to the right. Many of the masks were styled simply for male customers, while others were jeweled, glittered, and ornate for even the most audacious buyer.

"It's almost Halloween," I told her, looking around and seeing the place empty. "I thought you'd be busier."

"It goes in spells," she explained. "Mardi Gras is the really busy time."

Yeah, I could imagine. I couldn't believe it was only about four months until the next carnival season began.

Nearly a year since the first time I'd met Tyler.

And—I let my eyes drop for a moment as I walked around the shop—it had been more than a week since the last time I'd talked to him.

I'd seen him—once.

He'd picked up Christian last Monday from school, and even though I wasn't sure, because I'd refused to look for him, he was most likely there every day this week to get his son.

I'd smiled at the parents, wished the students a good afternoon every day when they left, and returned to my classroom, closing my door and blaring Bob Marley as I worked late and didn't think of him.

Or tried not to think of him.

But then I'd see the bra in my drawer that no longer had matching panties and remember that they were left in an alley in the Quarter. Or I'd wake up hot, the sheets chafing my naked skin, and let myself fall apart, wishing my hands were his.

He was right, though. What we were doing was careless and selfish.

I turned back to the clerk. "Where are your metal masks again?" I asked.

She pointed behind me. "Through there on the left wall."

I saw the French doors in the middle of the room and gave her a small smile. "Thank you."

Walking into the next room, I gazed at the walls, all adorned with masks, much like the first room, and went straight for the small selection of metal masks they carried. Some looked very much like the one I had purchased here last winter, but that was another perk of this place. No two masks were alike.

I picked up an ornate gold one, shining with crystals built into the center part that sat in the forehead. Along the sides, curling designs traveled up both temples, and exotic eyes gave it an erotic look, like a mixture of sex and mystery.

A smile I actually felt crept out for the first time in a week.

I loved the black one I'd worn all those months ago. I didn't know where I would wear this one, but I was buying it.

I picked out a mask for my brother as well, since he had mentioned he had a Halloween ball to attend for his new internship at Greystone Bridgerton, letting her wrap both up and bag them before heading back up to Canal to catch a streetcar.

It was after three in the afternoon, and even though I hadn't accomplished anything useful today, I'd promised Jack I'd make him dinner.

The only things he cooked were Hot Pockets and scrambled eggs.

Carrying my bag, I walked under the fragrant lilac tree in my quiet neighborhood and crossed the street to my apartment.

But as I jogged up the steps to the porch, I slowed, seeing my front door open.

What the . . . ?

Fear attacked me, slicing across my chest like a giant claw, taking everything in its grasp, and I instantly backed up, stepping down the stairs.

But I locked the door.

I remembered locking it, because a neighbor had greeted me, and I'd turned around to say hello before clicking the lock and jiggling the door handle to make sure it was secure.

I shook my head. *No. I am not going through this again.*

I charged up to the door, pushing it open with my hand.

"Who's here?" I shot out, trying to keep the shakiness from my voice.

Air rushed in and out of my lungs as I quickly scanned the room, looking for any movement. The interior was dark. I'd turned off all the lights before I'd left, but the day's last light was coming through the windows.

"Who's here?" I shouted again, dropping the bag to my feet. "Come out right now!" I dared.

The cabinets, the window, the shower curtain . . . They weren't my imagination or lapses in concentration.

Someone had been coming into my house.

I forced down the lump in my throat and inched into the foyer, searching the area for anything out of place.

And then I widened my eyes, seeing the pile of wreckage in the center of the living room.

I rushed for the debris and fell to the floor, the skin of my knees burning on the area rug.

"No," I gasped.

Someone had broken into my house, and they'd known right where to go.

My shoulders shook as I cried silently.

My treasure box—the one Jack worried about—lay shattered on the floor, its contents scattered about and ripped to pieces.

I squeezed the scraps of papers in my hands, feeling the agony that I'd felt all those years ago when I'd locked them inside the box.

Chase.

All of his letters. His threats. Everything he'd sent me after my parents fired him as my coach. Everything they'd hidden from me.

After they died, I'd found the file in their home office with his "love" letters to me. From the dates, he'd been mailing them since he was fired.

I'd found them and read them, and my instant reaction was to want to self-destruct. They made my skin crawl and made me hate my parents for never pressing charges. They'd confiscated my phone not long after the stalking began, and also cut off my e-mail, so these letters were the only proof of what he was doing. Hard proof to give to the police. Why keep this from me instead of using it to protect me?

How could they have read these letters—some of them disgusting and perverted—and not done anything?

And then I remembered that they were dead because of *me*—because of what I'd done that night—and I didn't want to be rid of the evidence.

Jack would've burned them, but I kept them locked in this box, never opening it and yet keeping it in plain sight, as a constant reminder of what losing control of your own life does to you.

Never again.

"Easton?" I heard a voice come from behind me.

I forced a deep breath.

"Easton," Jack's voice repeated. "What the hell happened?"

"You need to leave," I demanded, hurriedly taking the handfuls of paper and stuffing them into my arms.

"Easton, what are you doing?" He stopped next to me, but I ignored him.

Dropping to his knees, he grabbed a piece of paper and studied it as I took my armful to the kitchen to find a gallon bag to keep them in for now. This pile of trash had kept me on a straight track for five years.

"Easton, stop!" Jack called. "How did you get these?"

I charged back into the living room, grabbing more scraps from the floor, pushing the pieces of wood out of the way to get every bit of paper.

"Easton." Jack grabbed my arm. "You can't keep them!"

I pulled away, gritting my teeth as I marched back into the kitchen and stuffed everything in bags.

But Jack dove around me, taking the bags out of my hands.

"Leave me alone!" I shouted.

"Like hell!" he bellowed. "You're not keeping all of this. It's sick!"

My whole body felt tight, and I growled, shoving at his chest.

But he just dropped the bags and pulled me into his arms, wrapping them around me.

I instantly closed my eyes and shattered.

My chest shook, and I collapsed against him, sobbing. "Jack, please," I begged.

"I'm sorry, Easton," he nearly whispered, and I could feel his short breaths as his chest shook. "I'm so sorry."

I hated this. My brother had suffered enough. Suffering he shouldn't have had to go through if it weren't for me, and here I was again, center stage with the drama.

No more.

I pulled away, pushing at his chest to distance myself. "I don't need to be taken care of."

I stared up into his eyes and narrowed my own, forcing my tough outer shell into place. "Stop worrying about me and stop interfering," I demanded.

And I circled around him, picked up the ziplock bags, and ran upstairs.

On Monday I left school after the bell, having changed into my workout clothes, and crossed into Audubon Park for a jog. It was something I did every Monday and Wednesday, but instead of hanging around school a few extra minutes like I'd done the last week in some pathetic hope that Tyler would seek me out, I just left.

I'd spent the entire day yesterday filing a police report about the break-in, and then I'd cleaned the house from top to bottom, removing any trace that someone had been in my home.

This morning, before I'd left for school, I'd remade my bed twice, checking the corners, and then checked to make sure the windows were locked and all of the cabinets were closed.

Four times.

I'd pushed my car locks eight times, and I'd counted my steps into the school.

And then I'd sat down at my desk and laid my head in my arms, crying my eyes out before first period, because I didn't want to be scared anymore.

I didn't want to be like this.

I wanted to be how I was with him.

Not that Tyler could save me, but I'd been happy.

I was in love with him.

But I refused to miss him.

Tyler couldn't make me feel better anymore, and I wouldn't let him fix me.

So I dried my eyes and decided *no more*. I didn't know who had been in my apartment, but I would be the one to deal with it. I'd called the police and reported it, deciding that I wouldn't try to handle it quietly like my parents had. Instead, I'd be proactive and not sit and wait for anything.

I pounded the pavement, sweat running down my back as I completed my eighth lap and kept going. Shaman's Harvest's "Dangerous" charged my muscles, giving me the energy that my mood had depleted, and I started to feel more like myself for the first time in a long time.

It was a little chilly today, but I wasn't feeling it, despite the white workout tank and black shorts I wore.

I stuffed my earbud back in my ear, as it had started to fall out, but then something slapped me on the ass, and I jerked to a halt, yanking both earbuds out.

"Hey." Kristen jogged in place next to me. "You actually do this for fun?"

She smiled sweetly, looking a little comical, because she was losing her breath but trying to hide it.

I shook my head at her and continued jogging, not caring if she kept up. "What are you doing here?"

"Well," she breathed out. "I always see you run out of school at the end of the day in your workout clothes to go jog, and I think to myself . . . I could do that," she mused.

I couldn't help it. I snorted, my chest shaking.

"Made you laugh." She gloated. "You haven't been smiling the past few days—actually the past week—so I consider that my special skill."

"What?" I grumbled, trying to sound annoyed.

"Making you crack a smile," she pointed out. "I'm sure not everyone can do it. I might be like your hetero soul mate. Your other half."

I rolled my eyes, the breeze flying under the canopy of trees cooling my skin.

"I'm fine," I stated. "The honeymoon is over, is all. Teaching finally got hard."

"Amen, sister," she shot back. "But if I had your technique in the classroom, I'm sure I'd be very happy with my class. At least you're not dealing with behavioral issues up the butt."

No. I wasn't. And what I'd told her hadn't been the truth. Teaching was always hard, but that wasn't the reason for my mood.

I just didn't feel like telling her about everything.

Despite what had happened at the club, I liked her. It wasn't her fault, after all, and with the way she'd handled herself at school afterward, and her discretion, I'd grown to trust her.

And she seemed to like me, though I had no idea why.

"I heard Shaw asked you to conduct a lesson for the teachers at Staff Development on engagement techniques," she continued.

I nodded, draping my earbud cord around my neck. "I said no."

"Why?"

"Because I think it would rub other teachers the wrong way for someone as inexperienced as me to tell them how to do their jobs," I explained.

"Screw 'em." She waved her hand at me. "Just like the students, the teachers have to be willing to change in order to succeed." And out of the corner of my eye I saw her lean in, playing with me. "And you're so capable, I think you could get them to want to."

What did she know? Teachers usually hung on to their jobs for a lifetime, and they became creatures of habit. The idea that I could swoop in and tell them—people who had years of experience—how to improve was presumptuous.

Why would she care what I did?

I regarded her with a sideways glance. "Why are you so nice to me?"

She twisted her lips. "Skeptical much?"

"No," I answered. "I mean, I haven't really let you see anything about me to like."

She giggled. "Not true. You're a wonderful dancer. You do great things with your hands."

I knocked her on the arm, letting out a snicker as I slowed to a walk and headed for the grass.

She smiled wide, following me. "I like you," she panted, out of breath. "You do your job as if procedures weren't already in place. You're inventive. You do what you want, how you want."

I dropped to my ass and pointed to my feet for her to hold as I crossed my arms over my chest and immediately started curling into sit-ups.

"People respect that," she told me, kneeling down to hold my feet with her hands. "I respect that."

I shot up, keeping my abs tight as I leaned back and curled up again.

Why shouldn't she be my friend? I didn't have many.

Or any, really.

And it had been a long time since I'd had one.

She was messy, and I could tell she enjoyed disorder. Everything I was against.

"I'm shy," I warned her.

"You're intolerant," she corrected. "There's a difference."

I gave her a small smile. "I'm cynical," I pointed out.

"Ohhhh, cynics are so cute," she cooed, and I shook my head in amusement.

"And I don't really like to party," I told her, laying down the law.

"And I do," she threw back, shrugging. "We'll meet in the middle."

TWENTY-THREE

TYLER

Hearing the cheers outside the auditorium, I dug my phone out of my breast pocket and pressed the button, turning it off.

I'd learned a little something over the past couple of weeks. The world would wait.

I swung the doors open and entered, a flood of battle cries and high-pitched instruments surrounding me as I walked in and let the heavy door slam shut behind me.

Jesus. How the hell was I going to find Christian in all of this?

The entire gymnasium was packed, bleachers filled to capacity on both sides of the basketball court with parents, staff, and students, some forced to stand on the sides for lack of seating.

The Friday pep rally, normally held during the morning on days there would be football games in the evening, was being held in the afternoon this week due to testing earlier in the day. Christian had texted, asking me to come.

Most of the parents would be here, and over the past several days he'd been more and more interested in me seeing things that went on at school and meeting his friends.

I'd instantly agreed. I'd come for Christian, but I was doing a piss-poor job of ignoring the small hope that I'd see Easton. I'd looked for her every day I picked up Christian from school, trying not to but fucking failing miserably.

No matter how much I tried to ignore the pull, I always scanned the school grounds for her after school, but she was never there. She didn't come outside anymore to see the students on their way, and the only glimpses of her I got were online in the social media groups.

I scanned the bleachers, forcing myself not to look for her, but there was no way I was going to find Christian in this mess, either. I almost dug my phone out to text him when I spotted Jack, Easton's brother, watching the dance performance taking place in the center of the court from the sidelines.

I debated whether to greet him, but not saying hello would prolong the awkwardness.

"Jack." I stepped up to his side, folding my arms over my chest. "How are you?"

He twisted his head toward me, giving me a genuine smile. I guessed that Easton hadn't confided in him, or he might have reacted differently.

"Very well," he replied. "I'm taking Easton to dinner after this. I only hope she doesn't have to stick around to clean up the mess."

He laughed, and I just nodded, wishing I didn't love hearing even the littlest thing about her.

"Thanks for the introductions at your luncheon a few weeks ago," he said.

"No problem," I told him. "I hope it was helpful. I know how hard it can be to break into the right circles here."

"Do you?" he threw back, an amused look on his face.

I breathed out a small laugh, looking him in the eye. "I used my family's money to receive a good education, but I built my company on my own."

He seemed to take that in stride, because he turned back to the court and didn't say anything else.

We stood in silence for a few moments, and I caught Christian's waving hand from the bleachers.

I held up my hand, waving back, and he sat down with his friends, continuing to clap with the audience as the cheerleaders took the floor.

I let my eyes swing from left to right, but I still didn't see her.

I inhaled a long breath through my nose. "How's Easton?" I broached.

"She's good. *Newsweek* wants to interview her."

"*Newsweek*?" I shot him a look, surprised. "Why?"

"For her teaching methods," he responded. "She's gaining some great publicity." And then a look crossed his eyes, and he turned back to the court. "As always."

I'd been in *Newsweek* once. When I was a twenty-five-year-old entrepreneur, as part of a feature on twenty-four other up-and-coming entrepreneurs. She was being interviewed personally?

Jack shook his head. "No matter what she does, she's always a winner."

"And how does she feel about that?" I asked, suddenly worried. "After everything that happened, being in the press again, is she okay with it?"

Jack looked at me, suddenly appearing tense. "What did she tell you?"

I shrugged slightly. "She told me about your parents and sister." And then I dropped my voice. "And that she had a coach who was inappropriate and then fired."

"That's it?" he asked, pinching his eyebrows at me. "He was more than inappropriate. He stalked her."

"What?"

He dropped his arms, sliding his hands into his pockets. "My parents fired him, but that was only the beginning." He spoke quietly. "For two years, he terrorized her. E-mailed, called, left messages, showed up at her matches . . . He threatened her, broke into her hotel rooms, ransacked her things . . . My parents had to take away her phone, her e-mail, and eventually her freedom."

I looked away, wondering why she hadn't told me any of that.

No wonder she was so damn tough.

No wonder she hadn't looked for me like I'd been looking for her these past two weeks. Turmoil and disappointment were nothing to her anymore.

"She didn't tell me any of that." My voice was barely audible.

"Not surprising," he stated. "Easton hates talking about her problems. She thinks it makes her look weak." Then he added, "The fact that she told you anything is something."

I narrowed my eyes, knowing that was true. For Easton to open up to me meant she trusted me.

She *had* trusted me.

He continued. "She was sixteen and in a constant state of stress," he said. "But it wasn't just him. It was me, our parents, our sister . . . All of us hurt Easton."

"What do you mean?"

"No one even considered going to the police," he explained. "My parents didn't want her name associated with a sordid mess, so rather than deal with Stiles, we just did our best to shield her."

He shook his head, gazing out at nothing. "But all we did was cage her in," he confessed. "She barely had any contact with her friends. She slept with the lights on, and she always had to wonder if he was in the stands, watching her play. She was disconnected from life, and she was lonely."

His eyelids fluttered, and I could see the regret he had for her.

"How could your parents let her go through that?" I charged.

"My parents loved Easton," he rushed out. "They always had her best interest at heart. They thought it would pass and didn't want the press causing more harm."

"Does she at least have a restraining order against him?" I shot out.

The last thing I wanted was this guy trying to come back into her life.

"Wouldn't be much point," he replied flatly. "He's dead."

"Dead?" I questioned, hoping I'd heard him right.

His Adam's apple bobbed as he swallowed. "Two years after the stalking began, when Easton was eighteen, she'd finally had enough," he told me. "She got bolder. She started sneaking out for late-night jogs, leaving her hotel room door unlocked, getting a phone behind our parents' backs . . ." He looked up, meeting my eyes. "She was daring him," he clarified. "She was tired of being afraid, and she wanted her life back."

How long would you stay?

Longer than anyone else.

"Standing in the middle of a burning room," I mused, remembering how she liked a dare.

"What?" he asked, confused.

I shook my head. "Nothing. Go on."

"One night," he continued, "Stiles left a note on her car, promising that she would never forget him."

I turned my head, trying to hide my anger.

"Later that night, Easton disappeared, and my parents were frantic." He leaned in, lowering his voice as much as he could manage with the noise. "They took Avery with them but left me at the house in case Easton came home, and they drove around looking for her, not knowing that she had gone to Chase's apartment to confront him."

What?

"When Chase never showed up, she came home, but the police were already at our house, giving us the news," he told me. "My parents had lost control of the car in the rain and swerved into the path of a semi."

"Jesus Christ," I whispered under my breath.

Easton and Jack had gone from a family of five to a family of two, and now I understood. Not so much in what Jack told me but in everything Easton hadn't.

She'd had her heart broken too much and didn't gamble on uncertainties.

But she'd opened up for me. Even just a little. She had shown me that she cared.

"Why wouldn't she tell me all of this?" I asked him.

"I'm sure she would've," he assured me. "Eventually."

"And Chase Stiles? How did he die?"

Jack hesitated, taking a deep breath. "He . . . committed suicide earlier that day," he admitted. "I'm guessing the note he left for her was a suicide note."

So Easton had gone to wait outside his apartment, and he was already gone. I was tempted to inquire how he'd killed himself, but if it didn't directly concern Easton, then I didn't want to know anything else about him.

"Easton died a little that night, too," Jack added, getting ready to leave as the music stopped and Principal Shaw wished everyone fun tonight.

I held Jack's eyes as he continued. "It's not that I don't like the woman my sister's become, but since that day, her heart is a machine," he cautioned. "She can start and stop it at will."

"Dad?" Christian called, running over to the car, his light blue button-down hanging out of his uniform dress slacks. "Would it be okay if Patrick picked me up after he takes you back to the office?" he asked. "I want to have some friends over."

I slid my phone back into my pocket. "I'm not going back to the office."

His forehead creased with surprise. "Really?"

I nodded, pushing up from where I leaned against the car. "I thought we could order pizza and watch the fight."

There was a match on Pay-Per-View I wasn't interested in seeing, but I definitely enjoyed spending time with Christian, so . . .

"Are you sure you don't want to work?" he pressed. "I mean, I appreciate the effort you're putting in, and it's the thought that counts, but . . ." He trailed off, glancing back to where his friends were joking around.

"But . . . ?" I inquired.

His arms hung at his sides, and he looked severely displeased. "Well, I wanted to have some friends over tonight without my dad hanging around, you know?"

I scowled. "You're fourteen."

And then it dawned on me.

"Are you inviting girls?" I exclaimed.

A nervous smile spread across his face, and he glanced behind him again. I noticed Clyde Richmond's daughter shifting her gaze over to us, and I immediately started shaking my head at my son.

"I may not be father of the year," I chided, "but I'm not stupid, either. You're not allowed to make me a grandfather for at least another fifteen years. Understand?"

He rolled his eyes, his shoulders dropping.

"But nice try," I allowed.

"Okay." He groaned. "Can I still have friends over, though?"

"Yeah," I allowed. "Let's see how many we can fit." And then I pointed to him, stopping before I turned for the car. "And no touching my pool table this time."

Last time he'd had friends over, I'd found a pizza stain on the ten-thousand-dollar table.

"Dad," he whined.

"I mean it," I shot out. "I'll have Mrs. Giroux order pizzas, and you and your friends can have the media room, but no one in my den. And don't even think about trying to break through the parental controls on Pay-Per-View."

"How come you can watch porn?" he blurted out sarcastically, and I heard a mother nearby gasp.

I leaned in, pulling him close by the back of the neck. "A. The controls are for R-rated movies, not porn," I lied. "B. Who says I even watch porn? And C," I continued, "I went to college, so I can do whatever the hell I want. Now, go get your friends."

He smiled, brushing me off as he left to go round up his classmates.

I moved to head for the car, but then I looked up and I stopped.

Easton was in her classroom, walking by the window, but as soon as I spotted her, she disappeared.

I tilted my chin up farther, trying to see her again, but she wasn't near the windows anymore, and I didn't know what to do.

Leave her alone. For her sake and for mine.

It wasn't even about Jack and what he'd just told me in the auditorium. I'd always known that Easton was a strong woman and she would be fine.

But my heart was racing, and I refused to think about what I was doing. I walked toward the school and climbed the steps, needing more than anything to look at her for just one moment.

Stopping at her classroom door, I watched her pad around in her bare feet, her heels lying next to her desk, and arch up on her tiptoes to stack books on top of a wardrobe cabinet.

Coming up behind her, I reached up and pushed the book into place for her.

She sucked in a sharp breath and whirled around, the long, sexy bangs of her deep brown hair falling over one eye.

"Mr. Marek." Her small voice sounded out of breath.

Her red blouse was only one inch from my chest, and her little black pencil skirt only reminded me of how well I'd feel her if I took her in my hands right now.

But I backed up, forcing some distance.

"I owe you an explanation," I told her.

Her expression turned emotionless. "No, Mr. Marek," she replied stiffly. "You don't."

I had never told her our relationship was over. I'd never warned her I wouldn't call again. I'd simply stopped. I owed her an apology and an explanation, and I wanted her to hear it.

"My son needs to come first," I explained.

She walked around her desk and turned to face me, her back and shoulders straight. "Of course he does," she agreed. "Christian is what's most important, and we were wrong. You made the right choice."

I narrowed my eyes on her. Why was she acting like that? Where was the sharp tongue? The temper?

At least yell at me when you tell me you don't care.

"Are you attending the Greystone Ball on Halloween?" I inquired.

She shook her head. "No. Why would I?"

"Your brother is interning with their firm, right? I thought he'd be taking you."

"How did you know about the internship?" She squinted her eyes at me.

But I ignored the question. I wouldn't tell that I'd made the call after the luncheon to get him that position.

She waited for me to answer, and when I didn't, she sighed. "I'm not going."

I watched her, wanting her to know so many things. That I thought about her every day, nearly all day. There was hardly a minute when she didn't cross my mind.

That I couldn't smell her in my bedroom anymore, and that I wanted to touch her.

If nothing else, I needed her to know how much she had mattered to me and still did.

Stepping up behind her desk, I hovered over her, seeing her breathing turn shallow. "Being a man is making hard choices and living with them," I told her, "no matter how much it hurts."

And then I reached out and ran my thumb across her cheek. "I miss you," I whispered.

Her cold expression slowly started to crack, and her face turned sad.

Looking up at me, she shook her head. "You're wrong," she argued. "Being a man is having the wisdom—and the courage—to make the *right* choices."

And then she took my hand off her face and evened out her expression.

"And you have," she told me. "You're a good father, Mr. Marek."

So cold.

Her heart is a machine.

She turned away, but I reached out and pulled her in to my body, hearing her breath shake.

"Say you miss me," I begged, whispering in her ear. "If you say that, then I can leave you alone. I can stop risking my relationship with my son, who is standing right downstairs, and my campaign, knowing that it wasn't just sex."

As I spoke, I held her cheek with my hand, turning her lips to meet mine. "Say you miss me," I whispered against her mouth. "And that you won't forget me. Ask me if I think about you and miss you every day."

She softened and let her lips fall to mine, kissing me gently, and then looked at me with pity in her eyes.

"Oh, Tyler," she lamented, speaking quietly. "I don't ask questions I don't want the answers to."

And then she pulled out of my arms and calmly walked from the room, away from me.

TWENTY-FOUR

EASTON

I finished writing out Twitter handles for the students to follow for homework and capped my dry-erase marker, turning around and calling to the students, "Flip."

"Wait, wait, wait!" Marcus shouted, keeping his head down and holding up his left hand while he continued writing with his right.

The rest of the students flipped their papers over, protecting their work from wandering eyes, and then Marcus sat back, putting his pencil down and finally turning his paper over as well.

"Stand," I instructed.

The students stood up, some rubbing their eyes and others yawning.

"Stretch." I locked my hands above my head and pushed up on my tiptoes, leading by example.

The rest of the class did their own stretches, getting their blood moving after sitting with their constructed response questions. I made them stand every fifteen minutes to keep them alert.

"Jump," I commanded, and we all started hopping or jogging in place.

I stopped, strolling up the aisle. "Now sit."

They took their seats, the desks shifting under their weight.

"Attack," I finished, issuing the last instruction and hearing their snickers and snorts as they continued with their tests.

"You have ten minutes left," I warned them, and locked my hands behind my back, strolling up and down the aisles.

They'd had a selection of ten different constructed response questions and had to pick three to answer. Judging from the amount of writing going on, I was going to have a very long weekend of reading.

Normally, we completed a lot of assignments online or with a Word document, which they e-mailed to me when they were done. With tests, though, I liked to keep it old-school. There was too much at stake to run the risk of losing a document in cyberspace.

Christian held his paper up, pencil in hand, and appeared to be rereading his work. This was the last class I would have with him, since he'd been transferred into AP History starting next week.

Principal Shaw told me he had e-mailed his father to let him know, but I hadn't heard anything from Tyler.

Christian's mother was thrilled, and Christian himself seemed to just roll with it. He'd gotten the assurance from me and Principal Shaw that if he didn't like it, he could come back to my class.

Part of me hoped he'd hate it. I wanted him back.

It didn't escape me that with Christian out of my class, seeing his father wouldn't be as much of a problem publicly—but that was never really our problem. Not really.

Tyler took what he wanted but cut loose what he didn't need. His upcoming campaign, his son, and his company were his priorities, as they should be, and he'd made a choice. While there may have been space enough for me in his life, he was too afraid to fail at anything else to make the room.

I had offered myself up, naked, in his office, and he'd let me go. We had come too close to the point where it was going to hurt too much to ever let go of each other. And then last week, I'd let him go. He'd been in my classroom, and I'd walked away from him.

Checking the clock, I turned and faced the class. "Is there anyone not done?"

Isabel Savers raised her hand, and I looked to the boy in front of her.

"Loren, can you take Isabel to Ms. Meyer's room?" I requested. "She can finish there. Thank you."

Once they walked out, I collected the test papers, and the students opened their laptops to continue gathering research for the simulations they were planning. It was a new teaching technique I'd discovered, where students re-create—live—what it was like to experience everyday life on, say, the *Mayflower* or in a wigwam. I was excited to see what they'd come up with.

"Ms. Bradbury?" Christian approached my desk as I started grading the papers. "Since we have the rest of class for private study, can I watch my father's interview? It's streaming online."

"Um . . ." I shot up my eyebrows, for a split second thinking of telling him no because I wasn't sure I wanted to see Tyler.

But that was selfish. The fact that Christian was at all interested was fantastic.

I nodded quickly. "Sure," I told him.

But then I stopped. "Actually . . ."

I turned on the projector, my laptop screen appearing up on the front board.

"What site is it?"

"You don't have to put it on for everyone to see," he interjected, and I could tell he was embarrassed.

I switched off the projector, not wanting to make him uncomfortable.

"Okay, but I'd like to see it," I added.

"KPNN," he called over his shoulder as he walked to his desk.

I brought up the site and turned down the volume, grabbing my green pen, a rubric for grading, and the first student paper, listening as I read.

Tyler's face flashed on the screen, and I had to force my expression to stay as hard as stone. He looked so large and commanding, and I was afraid the shot of lust coursing through my body, making it hard to breathe, would be written all over my face.

He wore a black three-piece suit with an emerald-green tie, and I wished the camera would back up so I could see all of him. His jet-black hair had been cut since I'd last seen him and was styled up and off to the side, shiny, with every hair in place.

He sat at the conference table in his office, and I knew the expression on his face. The one that said he had better things to do.

Tyler hadn't officially announced his candidacy yet, but the whole city knew it was coming. I was interested in seeing how he handled the interview, knowing his aversion to prying eyes in his private life and his inability to indulge people and play nice.

And then I steeled every muscle in my arms and legs, seeing the camera flash to Tessa McAuliffe as the interviewer.

Son of a bitch.

"Well, yes, Mr. Marek," she went on, continuing a conversation that I was catching the middle of. "But you employ no consultants. Your company has interests in the economy, agriculture, and construction, but what qualifies you to vote on legislation for, say, education?" she challenged.

"The fact that I go to the source and talk with teachers," he answered without hesitation. "Ms. McAuliffe, I don't need a conference table full of consultants and lobbyists advising me or influencing me on a topic from which they're also isolated," he explained, leaning back in his chair with one hand resting on the table. "To learn about construction, I visit my sites. To become aware of issues prompted by poverty, I can find that a block from my home. To know about education, I'll talk to teachers. Go to the source." He laid it out. "Ask questions. Read. Research. Find the answers you need in the purest form." And then he narrowed his eyes, speaking with command and certainty. "I learn some things from second- and thirdhand accounts, but even more from firsthand accounts."

I looked down at my paper, twisting my lips to hide the smile.

"What changes would you like to see in education?" she asked, unfazed.

He took a deep breath, and then a thoughtful look crossed his face as he thought about what he was going to say.

"A teacher's job is undoubtedly hard," he started. "They struggle with less and less funding and ever-growing class sizes." He looked at her, tipping his chin down. "They need support, and the curriculum and the methods need to change," he stated.

I put my paper and pen down, unable to concentrate on anything else.

He continued. "Teachers are finding it difficult to compete with increased technology use in the home but then are unable to use that same technology to maintain their students' attention in the classroom," he explained, and I smiled, a shocked breath expelling from my lungs at his statement. "They need cell phones, iPads, laptops . . . We're educating students for jobs that don't yet exist, and we're still using tools that are fifty years behind the times. It's long past time that those teachers got those tools and learned how to use them to engage students."

I felt my body flood with heat, and I closed the laptop, unable to keep the elation from making my stomach flutter.

He'd practically quoted me.

I felt something tighten in my throat. I couldn't believe he'd done that. Not only had he remembered what I'd said, but he was using it in his platform.

No matter how much I told myself that I didn't need him, I'd never thought that he might have need of me.

He'd hurt me by not choosing me, but it had never occurred to me that he was suffering from his decision, too. Even after he'd visited the classroom to see me, I'd still thought it was merely about sex.

I blinked, looking up, and found Christian sitting at his desk staring at me.

I straightened, evening out my facial expression, but he just sat there watching me like the wheels were turning in his head.

How long had he been looking?

The bell rang, and the students started stuffing their backpacks and jetting out the door.

"Okay, don't forget," I shouted, shooting up out of my chair. "Check out the new follows on Twitter in addition to your reading tonight!"

All of the students filtered out, and I sat back down, turning on "Paralyzed" by In Flames as I started looking over the tests.

"Ms. Bradbury?"

I looked up, seeing Christian standing on the other side of my desk with his laptop bag slung over his shoulder.

"Yes, Christian?"

He looked serious, and I took inventory of the room, seeing everyone else was gone.

"I don't like Tessa McAuliffe," he told me.

I tilted my head, studying him and wondering why he was telling me that.

"The TV commentator?" I clarified, and he nodded.

"But I like you," he said matter-of-factly.

And something about the way he just stood there, holding my eyes, made dread creep into my chest.

Oh, no.

"I saw you and my dad in here that day after school at the beginning of the year," he stated, a bitter edge to his voice. "I'd gotten done with soccer practice and saw that Patrick was here to take me home, but my father's car was also outside, so I came to look for him. You were fixing his tie."

Fixing his tie? I let my eyes wander as I searched my brain for that, and then I remembered. The first time . . . on the desk more than a month ago.

A month!

I opened my mouth, but every damn hair on my skin stood up, and I was scared. Shit! What the hell did he see?

I wanted to crawl under the desk. Had anyone else seen anything?

"You're not going to lie to me, are you?" he asked.

I lifted my chin, though my dignity no longer existed. "No."

"Good," he shot out. "Everyone tries to handle me, and I'm not a baby."

I licked my dry lips and stood up. "Did you see anything else?" I asked plainly.

I needed to know how severe the damage was.

He shrugged. "Just that it was obvious something was going on." He arched an eyebrow at me. "I see how he looks at you. His face gets softer."

I dropped my eyes and let out a breath. What a mess.

"I didn't really care what the hell my dad did." He sighed. "But I thought it was pretty shitty of you. You're my teacher," he pointed out. "*My* teacher."

I nodded right away, looking him in the eyes. "Yes, I am." I owned up to it. "You have every right to be angry."

"People are saying that a lot to me these days, as if that makes everything better," he threw back.

Christian was right. Mistakes can be forgiven but not always forgotten. And it was unfortunate that he was the one to suffer for others' shortcomings.

"Why aren't you seeing my dad anymore?" he pressed.

"Because it was wrong," I told him. "Because life sometimes has too many obstacles. We betrayed your trust, and you're the most important thing."

He pinched his eyebrows together, looking like he wasn't sure what to believe.

"Really?" he asked quietly.

"You're the most important," I repeated.

He turned for the door and started to walk away but then hesitated. "The thing is," he turned back. "I started to like my dad more. He was trying harder."

Was he insinuating that I had anything to do with that?

"He's around a lot now," Christian explained, "helping me with homework . . ." He nodded to himself. "But now he seems sad," he mused. "I'm not sure why I care."

Hearing that Tyler wasn't happy hurt. I couldn't lie to myself. I wanted him to miss me, and I wanted him to have given me up for a good reason. Christian was that reason.

Christian peered over at me. "When I go to the AP class, can you date my dad?"

I broke out in a small smile. "But then I wouldn't be your teacher."

"But you'd be around my house," he retorted, perking up.

I relaxed, seeing that he was no longer angry. I didn't know if he'd told anyone, but I wouldn't put the burden of a secret on him, either. If he talked, he talked, and I'd have to deal with the consequences.

Unfortunately, though, he thought his father had moved on because of my relationship with his son, when, in truth, it went far deeper than that.

"I'm always here for you," I assured him. "You always come first. Don't ever forget that."

TWENTY-FIVE

TYLER

I planted my hand on the ornate marble railing and took a sip of my whiskey, gazing out over the bustle of cars, carriages, and lights in the cool evening of the Quarter. Conversation and laughter drifted outside from the Halloween masque through the doors behind me, but I narrowed my eyes, watching the gutter punks in the doorway down on the other side of the street beg for beer money instead.

Their ratty clothes, stringy hair, and "fuck it" attitude were something I had never understood, mostly because I'd barely noticed them before.

I guess, on the rare occasion I'd actually looked, I'd presumed they liked their lot in life. They were smiling as they chatted, after all.

But now I found myself wondering—as I felt my clean, crisp tux against my skin and the fragrant smell of the rich food from the ball going on behind me—where would they sleep tonight?

How long since that dog they were petting had eaten?

Where the hell were their parents?

I'd slowed my life considerably, trying to do a few things well instead of fifteen terribly, like my father wanted, but the more I'd taken the time to notice the little things around me, the emptier I felt.

Maybe they wanted more out of life and were just trying to get through the day. Or maybe they didn't, because they didn't know everything the world had to offer.

But I did know they'd be grateful for whatever money they got right now. They'd be grateful for food, drink, and a cigarette—or anything that made them feel good.

I wanted a lot of things, but—I realized, looking down at them—almost nothing I wanted would I treasure. Barely any of it would make me pause to feel grateful.

I'd missed what was truly important. I'd chosen wrong.

My phone vibrated from inside my breast pocket, but I just tilted the glass back up to my lips, ignoring it.

Jay was inside, constantly texting that I needed to get my ass in there and start chatting with people, but the luster was gone. It had slowly dwindled away the longer I went without her.

"Soooo," I heard a woman's voice say from behind me, and I looked to see my father and his wife smiling at me.

"When will you officially announce your candidacy?" she asked.

Rachel Marek was my father's second wife, and while I liked her, I barely knew her. My father didn't remarry for another ten years after my mother's death when I was fifteen. I'd long since moved out and started my own life by then.

I looked over, seeing Jay march through the French doors, clearly on a mission to find me and bring me inside himself.

I gave Rachel a halfhearted smile. "Somewhat redundant, I think. Everyone is aware of my intentions anyway."

But then I caught my father's "try harder" look, and I softened my response for her.

"Within the week," I assured her.

Jay stepped up next to me, and I nodded, telling him silently I would get my ass back into the party.

"Will you relocate to Washington, D.C.?" she asked, clutching my father's arm.

"Let me win first," I countered, trying to keep my expectations reasonable.

"Sorry." She laughed, glancing at my father. "We won't jinx you. We're just very excited for the next year. I love campaigns."

"We're all excited," Jay jumped in. "I've stocked up on PowerBars and Wheaties."

And I was still trying to figure out what the hell I was doing.

How the hell could my desires change so quickly? I'd planned for this. Dreamed of this.

And now everything in my life except Christian felt fucking worthless. Worthless and pointless.

"Give us a minute," my father said, and I looked up to see him hand off his wife to my brother.

They headed back inside, and my father tilted his head, gesturing for me to walk with him.

"Senators, in a way," he started, leading me back inside the dim, candlelit ballroom, "have more power than a president," he told me. "While presidents come and go, with term limits, a senator can be a senator for life."

I already knew that, and my father, having a doctorate in political science was also well aware.

"I've known Senator Baynor for more than thirty years," he explained. "He tried to hire me to work on his staff, but I turned him down."

"Why?"

We circled the perimeter of the ball, the other guests congregating around tables and on the dance floor.

"I wouldn't have found it rewarding," he admitted. "It's too glamorous a life for me."

I laughed under my breath, liking how candid he could often be. Most people didn't associate politics with glamour, but it most certainly was glamorous. Power, wealth, and connections with people who could make or break you.

Senator Baynor was from Texas, and while he and my father were good friends, I was glad he hadn't uprooted Jay's and my life here in New Orleans to pursue a political career.

My father didn't climb mountains for the sake of climbing mountains. His goals were clear and his reasons made sense. He'd made a good choice.

He stopped and turned to face me, pinning me with a hard stare. "Mason Blackwell has a lot of support, Tyler. He's very popular," he pointed out. "However, he doesn't have the endorsement of a senior senator like Baynor."

I nodded, but then my eyes flashed to the right, and I stopped listening.

I narrowed my eyes.

Easton.

She stood alone across the room, wearing a beautiful, fitted black gown with gold trim that showed off her arms and back. She was staring at a painting and looking so much like she had the night we'd first met.

My entire body warmed, and I felt her pulling at me like she had a rope tied around my heart.

"Is that what you'd like?" My father spoke up. "An endorsement?"

What?

I blinked, coming back to the conversation and looking over at him.

"You know better," I retorted.

I hadn't asked my father for anything, and I wouldn't.

He hooded his eyes, looking weary. "I thought so." He sighed. "You don't take anything you don't feel you've earned."

I pinned him with a stare. "You taught me that."

Taking a sip of my drink, I glanced over at Easton, noting that she was slowly making her way down the wall, taking in the paintings.

"I'm not your teacher anymore." My father spoke in a low voice. "I'm your father. A father who happens to believe you're one of the good ones."

At that I shot my eyes back to him.

He'd always been hard on me, which gave his rare compliments more of an impact.

"I'm proud of you," he told me, "and I would be proud to see you win this. I can get his endorsement if you want."

I inhaled a deep breath and shook my head gently. "You've never made anything easy on me. Don't start now."

And I set down my glass and walked away, leaving him to get back to his wife.

I didn't know what I was doing—as usual lately—and I didn't have a plan, but I knew where I wanted to be. And if I knew one goddamn thing about myself, it was that I wanted what I wanted, and right now I wanted to see her look at me.

Coming up behind her, I saw her holding a glass of champagne with her other arm folded over her chest.

I couldn't resist teasing her as I came to stand next to her. "Thinking of starting a fire?"

She twisted her head and met my eyes. Dark makeup accentuated her eyes, and I could see her shocked look through her gold metal mask before she regained her composure.

Letting her lips curl, she rolled her eyes. "I'm trying not to be so naughty these days."

Hallelujah. The idea of her getting naughty with anyone but me didn't sit well.

"Good." I nodded once. "I thought you said you weren't coming."

She shrugged, turning back to the abstract painting. "I didn't think I was. I knew I would see you, after all."

So she'd considered avoiding the ball because of me.

"So what changed your mind?" I pressed.

A stern expression crossed her face as she spoke in a low voice. "I decided I was tired of reining in my life because of men."

And then a little smile peeked out as she took a sip of her champagne.

I let my eyes fall down her body, where the straps of the long dress across her back only made her skin looked even more supple and glowing.

Her hair was in loose curls with half of it pulled up into pins and the rest hanging down, framing her face.

Her lips were red, her skin tan, and her scent exotic.

And I felt my desire steadily growing, as did my need to lead her away to somewhere dark and quiet.

"I saw your interview," she said, meeting my eyes again. "I thought it was wonderful."

I nodded, not really caring to talk about the interview.

She continued. "I don't know if you still feel like you have something to prove, Tyler, but I can tell you, even if I had never met you, I would vote for you."

In that moment, as I looked down at her, my lungs emptied.

I'd been told by friends and wives of friends, employees and colleagues, that I had their vote when election time arrived about a year from now, but I hadn't realized hers was the only one I'd wanted.

She actually thought I was worth a damn.

I couldn't keep the grin off my face as I stared at the Stricher in front of us. "The first moment I saw you"—I inched closer to her—"scowling at that Degas like it was shit on canvas . . ." I looked at her. "I wanted you more than I'd ever wanted anything."

The moment I'd set eyes on her, I had to have her.

A thoughtful expression appeared on her face. "A lot's changed."

"Nothing has changed," I shot back.

She turned to me and then looked around at something behind me. "Are you with Tessa McAuliffe tonight?" she prodded, and I glanced back to see Tessa in a beige evening gown happily schmoozing in the crowd.

I hadn't arrived with Tessa, nor did I plan to leave with her, but we'd had lunch before the interview last week and had spoken this evening.

"Some relationships need to be maintained," I pointed out. "Even though they're only professional."

"She needs you," Easton bit out. "You don't need her."

I reached out, grazing her cheek with my thumb. "I always loved it when you got angry," I mused, start to feel whole again.

She hesitated, letting me touch her, but then tilted her face away, breaking the connection.

"You must be proud of Christian." She changed the subject. "Transferring into AP History and also qualifying for advanced placement in Biology."

I dropped my hand, suddenly needing more air. "Yes." I sighed. "I'm taking him and some of his friends to an LSU game next Saturday to celebrate."

"He seems happy." She shot me a taunting smirk. "I think he's starting to like you."

I snorted. "I don't know," I grumbled under my breath. "Is one of the warning signs an aptitude for blackmailing me?" I asked. "Somehow he's weaseled a birthday bash at JAX Brewery out of me if he gets straight As this semester."

She breathed out a smile, shaking her head.

"Hello, Ms. Bradbury," Jay chirped, coming up next to me, and I inwardly groaned.

"Tyler." He leaned in, speaking in a low voice. "The archbishop is here."

I sighed, frowning.

Archbishop Dias was a big supporter, and I needed to at least greet him.

I glanced to Easton, torn between either taking her with me or telling her I'd see her later, but I had no right to infringe on her evening. I was the one to break it off, after all.

"Excuse me," I said, but she just turned back to the paintings without a word.

After saying hello to the archbishop and talking about the year to come, I moved from circle to circle, chatting with members of the media, local politicians, influential voters, and it was fucking painful.

I could do it. I wanted to do it.

But over the past few weeks I'd started to feel like I was trying to walk on one leg. Nothing came easy anymore, because something was missing.

I looked up every once in a while, scanning the party for Easton. She eventually moved from the outside of the scene to the center, sitting at a table with her brother and, I assumed, some of his fellow interns as they nibbled on hors d'oeuvres.

After a while I saw her in a group, laughing.

I looked at my watch, seeing that it was ten thirty, and I texted Christian to check in one last time for the night. He was crashing at a friend's house, since they had gone to the Krewe of Boo parade with his friend's parents.

How's it going? I texted.

I walked up to the bar and ordered another Chivas on the rocks.

We're hanging out, he texted back.

Where?

But after I'd gotten my drink and tipped the bartender, I continued to stand at the marble bar top, waiting.

Christian? I prompted again.

Taqueria Corona, he shot back.

I scowled, checking my watch again.

Are Charlie's parents with you? I typed, and hit *Send*.

Except I didn't get an answer, and heat rose from my neck up to my forehead.

Either get back to Charlie's, or I'm sending Patrick for you, I threatened, taking his silence as a no.

Taqueria Corona was a bar. A restaurant bar, but still a bar with a loud crowd, and how the hell did his friend's fucking parents not have them in the house yet? They were fourteen years old, for Christ's sake.

Come on! he challenged.

Are you arguing? I threw back to him.

The phone buzzed immediately. No.

I cocked an eyebrow, and another message came through immediately after.

Yes, he corrected, owning up. All right, we're heading to Charlie's.

I smiled, gloating, as I took a sip of whiskey.

Even though it's stupid early, he shot back.

I could practically hear his mope. My kid had an attitude, but I'd be lying if I said it bothered me. The fact that he got sarcastic meant he was comfortable with me. I saw it as a good sign. For now.

I jutted out my thumbs, typing quickly. The only way you can be outside of the house past ten at night is if you come to me at the ball. It's your choice.

I'd rather eat rats, his text read, and I broke out in a quiet laugh.

Shaking my head and still smiling, I typed, Ms. Bradbury is here. It wouldn't be that boring.

A moment later, his text came through. Really? he asked. Have fun with that.

My eyebrows nose-dived as I wondered what the hell he meant.

??, I typed, almost afraid to know.

My phone buzzed, and I set down my drink.

I'm fourteen, not stupid, he wrote. If you like her, I'm cool with it.

What? How did . . . ?

I dropped my hand to the bar and stood up straight, tensing.

Christian knew?

A million things ran through my head. *What did he know exactly? Did anyone else at his school know? Did he see something?*

And fuck! His mother.

But my main fear—my main reason—for backing off from Easton was Christian. Although I knew I couldn't be a good father, the head of Marek Industries, a senator, and her lover and balance all of those responsibilities well, my main concern was alienating Christian forever.

But he already knew. And he was fine with it.

Still perplexed, I typed slowly, my fingers shaky. Your friends might have something to say.

He could be ostracized.

Not if they know what's good for them, he replied, sounding cocky.

And then came another text.

I'm cool with it, Dad, he reassured me, and I smiled to myself in disbelief.

Running my hand down my face, I pulled at my collar, wishing I could figure out how to handle my personal life as well as I did business.

Clarify your goals. What do you want?

I placed my hands on the bar, bowing my head as my chest rose and fell harder by the second.

What do I want?

I pictured myself traveling to my work sites around the world, climbing the steps of Capitol Hill, accomplishing something that was supposed to be worthwhile and good for the world—and none of it held any luster.

None of it could replace her.

I clenched my fists and spun around, ready to charge over there and take her, but I stopped short, seeing Tessa standing before me.

"Dance with me?" she asked. "We haven't really talked tonight."

I glanced over to see Easton at the French doors, talking with her brother, when Mason Blackwell came up to them and shook her brother's hand.

Tessa followed my gaze, and I watched as he spoke to Easton. She didn't look like she was enjoying whatever she heard, but then he took her drink, put it down on the table, and I watched him lead her onto the dance floor.

I immediately snapped into action, brushing past Tessa, but she grabbed my arm.

"You were never photographed with her, were you?" she chastised. "Having an affair with your son's teacher would kill your campaign, Tyler."

I looked down at her, surprised to find that I didn't give a shit.

"Especially one as outspoken as her," Tessa sniped. "She's not built for discretion."

"But you are?" I inferred, catching her hint.

She licked her ashen pink lips with a hint of a smile on her face. "I think I'm everything you need."

And that's when it hit me. I had things I wanted but didn't need and things I needed but didn't want.

There were only two things I needed and wanted at the same time: Easton and my kid.

I spun on my heel and charged onto the dance floor, heading straight for Blackwell as he started to sway with Easton.

I stepped between them, forcing him out of the way.

"I'm leaving." I turned to Easton, telling her, "And I'm taking you with me."

Her worried eyes turned on me, and she shook her head. "Tyler, no," she urged, telling me I shouldn't be doing this.

But Blackwell stepped up, reaching for her.

"Keep your hands off of her," I warned, turning my scowl on him.

He backed off, crossing his arms over his chest. "I didn't realize she was here with you," he said calmly.

I was sure he was loving this, but I didn't give a damn anymore.

I took Easton's hand with my left and tilted her chin up with my right.

"Tyler, don't," she begged, looking around at whoever might be watching us.

Tessa's voice came up behind me. "Listen to her, Tyler."

I held Easton's eyes, seeing the tears pool there.

"You love me," I whispered softly enough for only her to hear.

"What's going on?" my father interrupted, stopping his dance next to us as he and his wife looked between Easton and me with concern.

Easton searched my eyes, still worried.

"I don't care," I told her. "I don't want to make trouble for you, but I don't care about the campaign if I can't have you. I don't fucking care."

Her desperate eyes pooled with more tears, and I cupped her face in both hands, caressing her cheeks.

"Aren't you the teacher that was featured in *Newsweek*?" my stepmother asked, inching forward in our tight circle as dancers moved around us. "You teach at Braddock Autenberry, right?"

"Braddock Autenberry?" Blackwell repeated, squinting at me. "Doesn't your son attend school there?"

And now it was done.

He knew, everyone would know, and Easton and I would have to weather this storm, but fuck it.

"Well, well, well," he mused. "My night just got better."

Easton started shaking her head, but I held her with my steady gaze, looking into her eyes.

"I don't care," I maintained. "I need you."

Mason Blackwell could ride this scandal to kingdom come. It would be a small price to pay to have her.

She clasped my forearms, and I grabbed her hand, ready to get her out of here.

"I almost feel sorry for you, Marek," Blackwell gloated when I turned around. "We all have our dirty little secrets, but most of us have the sense—"

"Yes!" my stepmother gasped, cutting Blackwell off. "You're the teacher who was a tennis player, right?" She gestured to Easton as my father listened with a stern set to his features.

"I was so sorry to read that part about your parents and sister. Oh, my goodness." She placed a hand on her heart, giving Easton a sympathetic look.

"Thank you," Easton choked out.

"What a horrible tragedy," Rachel consoled. "I can't imagine being eighteen years old and losing nearly your entire family."

Blackwell's eyebrows nose-dived as he listened.

Rachel continued. "And then you and your brother divided your parents' estate between several children's charities here in New Orleans?" she went on. "So generous when you had already lost so much."

I faltered, having not known that part.

"My brother must've told them that," Easton admitted, looking embarrassed.

I raised my eyes, locking on Blackwell's, and I saw it in his eyes. He could try to sling mud, but Easton's record and character spoke for themselves.

"You truly have given a lot to this city," Rachel stated, smiling. "I can't wait to see where your career goes, Ms. Bradbury."

Easton nodded, giving her a small smile. "Thank you."

"Excuse us for a moment." I grabbed her hand and pulled her away from everyone, rushing out.

Jay was somewhere. Her brother was somewhere. But we were leaving. I dug out my phone and quickly texted Patrick to bring the car around.

"Tyler," Easton urged as I jogged down to the stairs, holding her hand. "Tyler, what are you doing?"

I pulled her along, hearing her heels *clack-clack-clack* as she kept up.

Reaching the bottom, I pulled her around the banister and led her out of the hotel and onto the sidewalk.

The Quarter was filled with people, and photographers from a local news station waited outside, covering the ball.

I scanned the area, but I didn't see Patrick, so I continued to lead her down the street. She pulled her hand out of my grasp, stopping me.

"Tyler!" she burst out. "We can't—"

But I interrupted her, taking her face in my hand. "I love you, okay?" I rushed out. "I love you like crazy, and I've never said that to a woman before, but I'm completely in love with you, Easton Bradbury."

I breathed hard, moving my hands to her waist.

Bowing my forehead down to hers, I tried to keep my voice low. "You're going to get me into trouble with that mouth of yours, and I may not get everything I thought I wanted out of life, but if I don't have you and my son, then the rest of it means nothing," I told her. "You make me happy, my kid likes you, and I feel like I could do anything if I knew I was going to see you every day. I need you."

I layered my lips to hers, breathing in her breath and feeling her shake. I didn't know if it was from me or the chill in the air, but I pulled her in close and wrapped my arm around her waist.

The heat from her mouth and the way her lips quivered drove me wild.

She ran her hands up my chest and circled them around my neck. "People are watching," she whispered.

"Are you scared?" I grinned.

She laughed quietly, and her sweet smile made my blood rush.

"No," she answered, and I knew she was lying. "You?"

I shook my head, playing with her. "Not a chance."

We were both scared shitless, but that was the best part. If there was no gamble, there was no reward.

I heard a camera click, and then I heard a car horn sound. I reluctantly twisted my head, seeing the SUV in the middle of the one-way road.

Taking Easton's hand, I pulled her into the street and through the car door that Patrick held open.

I let her climb in first, and then I hopped in, Patrick slamming it behind us.

"They took our picture," she warned.

"Good. I'll frame it," I shot back, closing the glass between us and Patrick as he climbed into the driver's seat and drove.

"Tyler, those pictures will be online soon," she worried.

But I dropped to my knees in front of her. "I don't care," I whispered.

Reaching behind her neck, I unclasped her dress and pulled the top down, gazing at her gorgeous body and beautiful breasts. Grazing my fingertips down her flat stomach, I pulled the dress down farther, meeting her eyes, so she could see mine.

"I need you," I growled low. "Right now."

And I yanked the fabric until she got the hint and raised her ass off the seat, so I could get the dress off.

"Jesus Christ," I groaned. "You weren't wearing panties?"

I looked at her hard in the eyes, like she'd betrayed me or something. Why was she not wearing underwear?

Her dark eyes behind the mask flashed with excitement, and she plastered her naked body against me, wrapping her arms around my neck.

"I like the feel of clothes against my skin," she taunted, leaving soft kisses around my mouth. "Like your clothes."

And then she started rolling her hips against me in small circles, and I groaned.

"Fuck," I breathed out.

She slid her hand down my hardening cock, rubbing it slowly and teasingly through my pants. As I bit my lip, she grew more needy and demanding, taking my hand and slipping it between her legs.

"Tyler." She quivered when I slipped a finger inside of her.

"Yes," I answered, slipping in another finger.

She sucked in a breath and squeezed her eyes shut. "Those photos?" she pressed. "Call your brother."

I grinned and took out my phone, dialing Jay.

Easton pushed me back into the seat and knelt down, unfastening my pants and belt.

"What have you done?" Jay answered without saying hello.

Easton took my cock out, her eyes looking up at me through the mask as she slid it between her lips, taking all of it down.

"All right." I breathed hard. "Get out in front of this," I told Jay. "Easton Bradbury taught Christian, but he's now in an advanced class with a different teacher. I am simply dating a teacher from the same school my son attends."

She sucked hard, and I felt the muscles in my legs tense as my dick grew even harder.

"Fuck," I gasped.

"What?" Jay blurted out. "What are you—?"

But I zoned out as she took my dick out of her mouth and kissed and sucked down the sides, fucking worshipping me.

"I'll speak to her superior tomorrow," I told Jay. "Just build her up. Use the *Newsweek* article and her website. No interruptions until after nine tomorrow," I demanded, looking down and seeing the grin on her face as she licked the underside on one lone, taunting stroke with the tip of her tongue.

"Eh," I inched out. "Make that noon."

And I hung up.

Darting forward, I lifted her under the arms and put her on the seat across from me. Kneeling in front of her again, I pulled her hair gently, forcing her to arch her back so I could play with her tits.

Taking one in my mouth, I tugged at her nipple, drawing it between my teeth and kissing the skin around it before moving on to the other one.

"I love you, too, Tyler," she breathed out. "Don't be careful with me, okay?"

Bringing her back up, I threw off my jacket and ripped my shirt open, her hands going straight to my chest.

"I trust you," she told me.

I kissed her hard, kneading her ass. "You didn't tell me about the stalking," I charged.

"I know." She nodded.

"You'll tell me everything, you understand?" My hands were all over her, touching her like I would never touch her again. "No one else educates me about you, Easton."

She wrapped her arms around my neck, whispering against my neck, "Are you sure?"

"Of course."

But as I tried to gently push her down, because I needed to kiss every inch of her, she stopped me and raised her eyes.

So I narrowed mine on her. "What is it?"

She looked away, growing tense, and then so did I.

"There have been a couple of break-ins at my apartment," she explained, looking solemn. "I don't know who it is, and they don't appear to be taking anything, but—"

"What the hell do you mean someone has been breaking into your house?" I burst out, my skin growing hot.

"I reported it to the police," she assured me quickly. "And I added more locks. So far it's been minor stuff," she rushed out. "They've left my cabinets open, and they destroyed a display box my parents gave me when I was thirteen."

"And you have no idea who it is?" I rasped, fear making my breathing turn shallow.

She shook her head. "No," she nearly whispered, "and I don't want you to worry about it."

"Not worry about it!" I barked. "You're under constant guard now, you hear?"

But much to my surprise, she laughed.

"It's probably just kids, Tyler, and I'm not fighting with you about this right now," she maintained. "I just wanted to be honest. We'll handle it, but I won't be the prisoner my parents tried to make me."

I squeezed her hips, studying her hard. I didn't like this at all.

I dipped my head to hers, whispering close, "I need to have you safe," I confessed.

The idea of someone in her home—in her things—enraged me.

And what were the chances? After her coach did very much the same thing, it was happening again?

"I love you," I nearly begged.

A soft smile spread across her lips. "You love me? So what does that make us?" she taunted, suddenly changing the mood.

I laughed under my breath, shaking my head. *Always playing games.*

"I'm too old for girlfriends, Easton," I explained, nibbling her lips, satisfied that she was here with me now, at least, safe.

She moaned, and the taste of her skin started to make me hungrier.

I gently pushed her back and leaned down, sinking my mouth into her pussy.

"Oh, God," she panted as I licked and sucked her clit. "Tyler," she moaned.

"I want to talk about the break-ins more later," I warned her. "I want to know about your parents, your career, everything . . ." I demanded, stroking my cock as I kissed her heat.

"Tyler, please." She squirmed. "No more talking. Later, okay?"

"Always so hungry," I teased. "I love it."

"Then prove it," she fumed, arching her head up to look at me. "Or can't you keep up?"

I ground my teeth together, and my fingers tightened on her hip.

Little . . .

God, I fucking loved her.

Not thinking twice, I shot up and flipped her over onto her stomach with her knees on the floor. Yanking her thighs apart, I pulled her back to me and slid into her.

"Tyler!" she cried out, and I took a fistful of her hair, tugging slightly.

"You didn't want it slow, did you?" I pawed her breast possessively.

She shook her head. "Uh-uh," she whimpered.

I thrust into her harder and faster, groaning when she began backing up into it. Her pussy was so tight, squeezing my dick like a hand. I couldn't believe I thought I could do without her.

"Sir." Patrick came over the intercom, and I slowed. "Where am I taking you?"

I leaned down, turning Easton's head so her lips met mine. "You don't belong anywhere I'm not," I whispered.

She kissed me slowly, nodding.

I leaned back up, rocking into her and feeling her pussy clench and spasm.

"Home, Patrick," I choked out. "Take us home."

TWENTY-SIX

EASTON

Nothing good ever comes easy.

The picture of Tyler and me together was all over the Internet—the news of our relationship had become public knowledge now, and there was no turning back. Saturday night he'd claimed me, throwing his ambitions to the wind and risking what he wanted for himself to have me instead.

I had never felt so loved by someone.

Even my parents had never put me first, above everything else. My career was more important to them, not my sanity or safety.

Tyler and I had spent that night at his house, and when he woke up the next morning, I was the first thing he needed. He didn't check his phone, his e-mails, or explore the damage we might have done to our careers. We screwed and laughed and ate, and then we talked to Christian when he came home from his friend's house.

All in all, we were very lucky. The spin Jay had put on the story minimized the damage, and Tyler had called Christian's mother yesterday to talk about the situation. Not that she needed to know the details, but we wanted her to find out from us before she did another way.

She was livid. She already didn't trust Tyler, and she didn't know me well, so she took it exactly how I expected. As a betrayal.

Until she talked to Christian. I don't know what he said, but I had a definite feeling I was still unaware of the magnitude of Christian's abilities.

He seemed to calm her down enough for her to not rush home. Although he did have to sweeten her up by agreeing to spend Christmas with her and his stepfather.

There would be some growing pains as we adjusted to the ramifications and the public attention to our relationship, but I already felt like I was so much luckier than I should've been.

On Monday morning I stepped into the school office dressed in khaki skinny pants and a long-sleeved blouse with a romantic-looking tie collar. My interview about my teaching methods was this afternoon, so I'd chosen to dress conservatively but fashionably.

"Does he have a moment for me?" I asked Mrs. Vincent as I stepped up to her desk.

She popped her head up, and a look crossed her face when she realized it was me. I couldn't tell if it was good or bad, but it was clear she knew what was going on.

"I think so." She nodded. "Go on in."

I approached the principal's office door, knocking even though it was half open.

"Mr. Shaw?" I broached.

He glanced over his shoulder, standing with his hands in his file cabinet, and offered a tight smile.

"Easton, hello." He sighed. "Come in. I'm glad you stopped by."

I walked in, making sure to close the door behind me, because I didn't need Mrs. Vincent knowing more than she already did. I kept my back straight and my shoulders squared, even though I felt like I wore a badge of shame.

I'd screwed a student's parent. I was a slut who was a threat to all of the other families in the school.

That's how some parents and other teachers might see it.

They wouldn't see that I was in love. That Tyler Marek was the one man to break me open and love and need everything he saw.

That he was the one man I needed in the same way.

I sat down in one of the chairs opposite Mr. Shaw's desk and placed my arms on the armrests. I cleared my throat. "I wanted to speak to you about—"

"I know," he cut me off, dropping the file folders he'd retrieved from his cabinet onto his desk. "I already spoke with Mr. Marek, and I saw the photo online," he told me, and then asked, "When did this start?"

I lifted my chin, owning up. "We met at Mardi Gras last February," I explained. "But we didn't begin pursuing a relationship until this school year."

He squinted, studying me. "Even knowing that you could lose your job?"

I faltered, dropping my eyes.

But then I looked back and faced it head-on. "Mr. Shaw," I started.

But he held up his hand. "Ms. Bradbury—"

"Please, Mr. Shaw, let me say this," I rushed out, quieting him.

I needed to tell him the truth, so no matter what happened, he would know that I didn't take my actions lightly.

"I could never claim to be a person who was used to sacrificing what they wanted for the betterment of someone else," I confessed. "I've been selfish and defiant many times in my life, most of which I regret," I told him, remembering all too well my parents and sister.

"But I love what I do," I maintained, "and I do it with everything I have. I'm committed to my career, and that hasn't wavered. Mr. Marek" —I stopped and corrected— "Tyler is . . ."

I looked down, inhaling a long breath.

"I can't do without him." I stood my ground, owning my decisions.

"I don't want to. I love teaching, and I would hate to lose my job or your confidence, but I'm not sorry that I love him."

I folded my hands in my lap, knowing I would do it all again. "I'm simply sorry things happened this way," I admitted.

He sat there for a moment, looking like he was thinking about what I said.

I would hate to lose my job, hurt my reputation with the students and parents, or be the butt of someone's joke, but I wasn't tormented about the situation. Knowing that I would do nothing differently gave me peace.

He sighed and looked at me. "I'm not going to fire you." He smiled gently. "I wasn't going to."

My eyebrows shot up. "Really?"

He shrugged, leaning on his desk. "You're an excellent teacher," he pointed out. "Your methods are drawing much-needed publicity for the school, and if I can be frank, your . . ." He waved a hand at me. "Mr. Marek will quite possibly be a senator. I can't fire his wife."

I dug in, shaking my head. "Wife?" I repeated. "Oh, no, we're not engaged."

He laughed and looked at me like I was stupid. "He went public with a love interest during a campaign, Easton," he replied. "He may not yet realize he intends to propose, but his intentions toward you are definitely permanent."

Okaaaay.

"Christian has been reassigned to the AP class," he continued, standing up, "so there's no longer a conflict of interest there. He is aware of this development, I assume?"

I nodded. "Of course."

"Good." He nodded once. "You'll no doubt have to field some gossip with the staff and parents, but I think you'll find Mr. Marek's status and reputation will go a long way in making sure it passes quickly. Let me know if you need anything."

That was it?

He turned around and started rummaging through his file cabinet again.

I hesitated, feeling like there was still another shoe to drop, but when he didn't say anything more, I slowly rose and began to leave.

"Thank you," I said in a low voice.

"Easton," he called, and I turned around.

"When the news crew observes your class today," he instructed, "you represent this school and Tyler Marek now."

And then he turned back around, leaving my stomach flipping with his little hint.

Yes. I represented Tyler.

For possibly a while to come.

"Principal Shaw says that you'd been offered opportunities to lead some staff developments," the newscaster asked, "possibly taking days to go to other schools as well, but you turned him down?"

I smiled, the camera behind Rowan DeWinter, the Channel 8 anchor, fixed on me as I stood in front of the school.

The students had left for the day thirty minutes ago, and the interview was almost finished. They'd spent the last couple of hours observing classes and recording lessons before wrapping it all up with a final Q&A.

Jack, Tyler, and Jay all stood off to the side, observing and being here to support me. Jack knew I was apprehensive about being in front of a camera again, while Tyler and Jay were here to make sure I wasn't messed with.

"I enjoy my methods," I explained, "and I believe they work. But do I feel confident enough to teach other teachers?" I asked hypothetically. "No, not with only a few months' teaching experience. I think a teacher's place is in the classroom, and that's where I'll stay."

Tyler grinned, and Jay shot me a thumbs-up.

"So you're not taking any time off to help Tyler Marek with his campaign?" she queried.

But Jay stepped in, shaking his head. "This interview is about her—"

"It's fine." I held my hand up and met Ms. DeWinter's eyes again. "I will absolutely help Mr. Marek in any way I can," I assured her. "Even if it means stuffing envelopes. But he understands that I've made a commitment to my class and to Braddock Autenberry. If there's one thing I love . . ." I suddenly stopped, feeling like I shouldn't have given that away.

But then I started again, committing to it. "If there's one thing I love about him, it's that he's just like me. We're devoted to our promises."

She smiled, accepting that answer, and Jay winked at me as if to say, *Good job.*

I rolled my eyes, his praise making me feel like I was an act in a circus.

After the news truck left and the school had emptied of teachers and nearly all the staff, Tyler led me over to his car and opened the back door, digging out a bouquet of white orchids.

"I'm sure you've received lots of flowers in your short years"—he paused, handing them to me—"but I've never given them, so . . ."

I looked at the abundance of white flowers, their curved petals so soft and fragile-looking. I had received lots of flowers over my tennis career, from my parents and from fans, but I loved these the most.

I was even glad they weren't roses. I would've loved anything he gave me, but I'd definitely seen enough roses.

I peered up at him, cradling the bouquet like a baby. "You've never given flowers?" I teased.

"I've sent them," he rushed out, quick to clarify. "But I've never . . ."

He trailed off, laughing at himself, and I broke out in a smile, thinking that it sounded like him. Of course Tyler Marek hadn't taken the time to give flowers.

Until me.

He stepped up, a heated look entering his eyes as he pinched my chin. "I wanted to see the look on your face," he whispered.

I leaned in, grazing his lips. "Well, I love them."

"You should," he shot out. "Orchids are temperamental. Just like you."

I pushed him away, shoving the flowers to his chest as he laughed.

"Let me go get my things," I told him, unable to keep the smile from my face as I shook my head. "I want you to come to my apartment before dinner. There's something I need to show you."

I spun around and headed up the stairs, back into the school. We were taking Christian to dinner, but I needed to take care of one more thing before I moved on.

Even though there was still the unresolved issue of someone being in my apartment, I wasn't going to waste one more minute of my life being scared. I wouldn't move. I wouldn't sleep with the lights on.

And I wouldn't run to Tyler for protection.

I'd lock my doors, be aware of my surroundings, and never let anyone hold me hostage again.

If someone wanted to hurt me, they would find a way.

But what I really needed to do was get rid of the letters. And I wanted Tyler there when I did it.

Walking down the dim hallway, I veered right and slipped into my dark classroom, going straight for my wardrobe to retrieve my handbag and then to my desk for the folder of papers I needed to grade tonight.

But I glanced up and jumped, surprised.

"Jack?" I gasped, seeing my brother in the back of the classroom with his arms folded and staring out the window.

I'd thought he'd left.

Putting my stuff down, I slowly rounded my desk, watching him. "Jack, what are you doing here?" I asked.

He didn't move, only stared out the window, looking deep in thought.

"The cameras still follow you around," he mused. "Even now."

What?

And then I remembered the interview he'd been here for earlier and how strange it was to be back in front of a camera again.

I studied Jack, but it was already growing dark outside and there was no light in the classroom. I couldn't make out his face.

I inched toward him, shrugging. "I don't mind it so much anymore," I confessed. "It was to help the school."

But then he turned his face toward me, and I saw pain written all over his expression.

"Dad loved baseball." He spoke in a sad voice. "I was the oldest. Why didn't he name me Easton?" he challenged. "Or any name related to the sport for that matter?"

I narrowed my eyes, half confused about why he was talking about this now and half wondering where it was leading.

Our father had named me after the Easton baseball bat. I never told people that, because I found it embarrassing, but Jack was right. Our father loved the game.

He even wanted me to play when he started noticing I had a penchant for sports, but my mother thought tennis was close enough and had a wider range of opportunities for a woman. Instead of swinging a bat, I swung a racket.

"Well, at least you got to play baseball," I told him.

He shook his head and turned his gaze back out the window.

"I got that job at Greystone because of you," he bit out. "Marek put in a word for me. A perk when your sister sleeps with powerful people, I guess."

My heart began racing, and I froze. "Jack, what's wrong with you?"

My brother never said things like that to me. Plus, he looked like he hated me right now.

He turned, locking eyes with me. "I was happy," he told me. "When Chase Stiles drove you inward, started messing with your game . . ." he explained. "I was happy about that, Easton."

I felt my stomach roll, and I backed away.

"I hated seeing you hurt," he choked out, tears caught in his throat, "but I loved seeing your career go to hell," he admitted.

His face grew hard, and his eyes pierced me. "I loved seeing our parents lose their grip on you as you got more and more defiant," he bit out. "I loved seeing you fail."

"Jack." I could barely breathe.

I shook my head, trying to take short breaths, but barely any air was getting in.

He stepped forward. "I love you," he professed. "I do, and I want good things for you, but, God, Easton," he gritted out, tears pooling in his eyes. "I hated you, too."

I let my eyes fall to the ground. What the hell was going on? in Jack had always supported me. Always tried to protect me.

I thought he was okay. I thought the amount of attention I got or the fact that our parents treated me just a little bit better was something he'd moved past.

But deep down it was still there. I couldn't believe he'd never let on about any of this to me before.

I closed my eyes, feeling weary. "I'm sorry," I said, meaning it. If I were in his shoes, I'd no doubt have a lot of resentment, too.

He sniffled, evening out his expression. "It's not your fault," he maintained. "It never was. You didn't make our parents favor you. You didn't excel at tennis out of spite." And then he spoke slowly. "You're a winner, Easton. Everything I want to be."

I moved to go to him, but he backed up.

"It was me," he shot out.

"What was you?" I breathed out.

"The cabinets, the calls, the treasure box—it was all me," he confessed.

What?

Rage curled my fingers into fists. He'd opened all of the cabinets, the shower curtain, been in my closet, opened my window, and smashed the box, tearing up all of the letters.

"Why?" I cried. "I don't understand."

"Because it was supposed to be my turn!" he shouted, glaring at me. "For the past five years, it was my turn to have the attention. You leaned on me!" He hit his chest. "You needed me."

I slowly shook my head, backing away from him. My face cracked, and tears started streaming down my cheeks.

I swallowed, choking out my words. "How could you?"

"I wanted you to be okay." His voice was barely audible. "I wanted you happy with friends and loving the life you lived, but . . ."

"But?" I pressed.

He hesitated, looking up at me.

"He's going to be a senator," Jack stated. "If your relationship went the distance, you'd be back in the limelight."

"You were trying to get me to shrink away again," I cried, turning angry.

But he went on. "And then *Newsweek* and the interview today . . ." he pointed out. "It doesn't matter what you do, you'll always outshine me!" He hardened his jaw, scowling. "Why couldn't you just stay quiet? Why couldn't you just be normal like everyone else? Just be my sister! Let me have something!"

I continued backing away, thinking about him doing those things. He'd known it would hurt me.

"You made me think someone was in my home," I charged. "In my things! You terrified me!"

He closed his eyes, looking like he was ready to break.

"I often wondered what made Chase Stiles give up," he rasped. "Why did he take his own life?"

I stared at my brother.

"He knew he was going to hurt you," he concluded. "And he didn't want to."

Yes. The final stage of stalking was physical violence. Chase's abuse had been growing more and more threatening, and Jack was probably right. I didn't know why Chase killed himself, but I did know he was losing his grip. Or what grip he had left.

And my brother? Would he go that far?

He seemed to see the flash of awareness and understanding in my eyes, because he rushed forward.

"I would never hurt you."

But it was too late. Spinning on my heel, I ran out of my classroom and into the hallway with Jack yelling behind me.

"Easton!" he called.

But I raced down the hall, needing to get away from him.

I wasn't sure if he would hurt me, but up until this morning I wouldn't have thought he could've done any of the things he'd done. I had thought, next to Tyler, Jack was the person I could trust most in the world.

Why would he have wanted me to live in fear?

I ran outside, but Jack's voice was right behind me. "Easton, stop!"

He grabbed my wrist, and I cried out, stumbling in the heels and slamming with all my weight against the wrought-iron railing of the staircase.

"Jack, please!" I cried, grabbing on to his hand with both of my own as I screamed, falling over the side.

"Jack!" I cried out, again grasping at his hand with both of mine.

He hung over the railing, grunting as he tried to pull me back up, but my legs flailed fifteen feet above the cement ground below, and I gripped his hand so tightly, my knuckles turned white.

I twisted my head, seeing the distance to the ground below me and crying out as my arms felt like they were being ripped from their sockets.

Jack grabbed underneath my arm with his hand, fear in his eyes as he tried to pull me back up.

"Jesus Christ!" Tyler bellowed, swinging his torso over the side and grabbing me, too. "What the hell happened?"

I breathed as fast as my heart beat, and I cried out as both of them pulled me back up over the side of the railing.

I instantly fell into Tyler, both of us slamming to the ground.

He pulled my body in to his, holding me tight. I hugged him close, hearing his heart race through his clothes as I laid my head against his chest.

"Come here," he soothed, wrapping his arms around me.

I opened my eyes, seeing my brother on his knees by the railing. His broken eyes were filled with regret.

"Easton, please," he whispered. "I would never hurt you."

"What's going on?" Tyler shot out.

But I just looked at my brother, my tears making him blurry. "You already did hurt me," I told him. "You broke my heart."

And then I looked up to Tyler, his brows pinched together in concern.

"Take me home," I begged.

TWENTY-SEVEN

EASTON

Tyler's body shifted under me, and I opened my eyes to see him reaching over and switching on an iPod dock. The soft tune of Bush's "Glycerine" drifted out of the speakers, and I closed my eyes, hearing the light rain tap against his bedroom windows as well.

"You put an iPod in here," I said just above a whisper, nuzzling into the safe heat of his body.

His fingers grazed up and down my back as he kissed my forehead. "I've started taking time to enjoy the little things again," he answered. "Rediscover my youth . . ."

My body shook with a little laugh. It was all I could manage, I was so tired. Mentally and physically.

"Yeah," I joked. "I think I was two when this song came out."

He snorted. "Well, listen and learn," he shot back. "This comes from the last time music was good."

"Mmmm," I moaned, sliding my leg over his hip and laying my body on top of his.

I soaked up the sensation of his naked chest against my bare breasts, both of us completely unclothed under the sheets.

"Are you okay?" he asked gently, rubbing his hands up and down my side.

"Don't ask me that," I told him, lying on his chest with my eyes closed. "Ever."

"Okay," he replied quietly. "How do you feel?"

I laughed, loving how he'd gotten around that one.

I was sick of being worried about, coddled, and spending my time on things that didn't bring me happiness.

Tyler was my happiness, and at that moment I was exactly where I wanted to be and doing exactly what I wanted to do.

"Safe," I replied.

After we'd gotten home last night—and left my brother alone inside the school—we'd taken Christian to dinner at La Crepe Nanou. After I'd cried in Tyler's car, argued with him about just staying at home for the night, and then dried my eyes. I wasn't letting anything else get in our way. We'd promised Christian dinner out, and we weren't disappointing him.

I was heartbroken over my brother's betrayal, and I had no idea what we were going to do, how I would ever feel safe around him again, but I was done spending time holding myself back from life.

After dinner I'd dived into Tyler's shower, neither of us caring that Christian probably knew I was spending the night. It wouldn't be a habit, and we would be discreet, but Tyler wouldn't let me go home after the episode, and Christian seemed thrilled to have me around anyway.

"I don't want Jack around you," Tyler insisted, taking my ass in both hands.

"Neither do I," I assured him. "Not right now anyway."

"Easton," he warned, not liking the sound of that.

I opened my heavy lids and pushed myself up, my dark hair tickling my breasts.

"He wouldn't have hurt me," I said, staring down at him and running my hands up his chest.

"You don't know that," he pointed out. "He needs help."

"I know." I nodded. "I won't agree to even the possibility of being in touch with him unless he gets some help first."

I looked down at Tyler, ready to cry because I loved him so much. I touched him everywhere, my hands running over his chest and down his arms and then coming up to graze his face with my fingertips.

I rolled my hips, feeling him grow hard under me.

"Can you take me to my apartment in the morning?" I asked. "I need to take care of something."

He kneaded my hips and ass, his breathing growing labored. "Of course," he answered. "But I want you to stay here for a while."

I shook my head, giving him a gentle "no."

"Easton," he bit out, looking at me with less patience.

I fell forward, planting my hands on both sides of his head. "Yes, Mr. Marek," I sang out.

I heard his sigh.

"It's not that I don't want to be here," I rushed out, "but it's my apartment, and I'll come and go as I like."

"Then I want Patrick taking you to and from—"

But I got in his face and scowled at him as he tried to tell me what to do.

"All right," he bit out. "You're right. It just doesn't make it any easier."

I grabbed his lips, nibbling and kissing softly.

"Really?" I cooed. "Could you say that again?"

He chuckled. "Say what?"

"The part about me being right," I shot back.

"I didn't say that," he growled into my mouth as I began grinding on him.

I moaned, feeling his tongue flick my upper lip and then catch my bottom lip between his teeth.

"I love you, Mr. Marek," I teased, closing my eyes and kissing him back.

The wet heat of his mouth as I plunged my tongue inside sent me reeling, and I ground myself against him faster.

He whipped off the sheet and reached between us, grabbing his cock.

"Do you feel safe?" he asked me again. "I just need to make sure you're okay."

I arched my neck back and lifted up, positioning his cock at my entrance and slowly sitting back down, sliding him inside of me.

Smirking, I started moving up and down his dick. "My OCD hasn't kicked in, if that's what you're wondering."

He gripped my hips, dragging his bottom lip between his teeth as he felt me from the inside. "I kind of miss it," he breathed out. "It was cute."

I smiled, rolling my hips faster and harder.

"I'm all for eight orgasms tonight if you want," I told him. "Do you have Viagra?"

"Viagra?" He scowled and shot up, rolling me over onto my back and breathing against my lips as he ground between my hips. "You're going to pay for that."

After school the next day, Christian attended soccer practice, and Tyler took me to my apartment. The last time I had been there had been only a little more than a day ago, before the interview and before my brother's confession.

Tyler hadn't wanted me to deal with returning this morning before school for fresh clothes, so he had called a shop and had Patrick pick me up a new outfit.

But I needed to come back today. To rid myself of bad memories and move on.

Coming back downstairs, I met Tyler, who waited in the living room in front of the fireplace. Holding the ziplock bags in my hands,

I stared at the letters, seeing my former coach's writing peeking out from the mess of torn paper.

"They're all the letters that Chase wrote me," I told him. "His obsessions, threats . . ." I trailed off. "I had never seen them before my parents died, and it was only afterward that I realized the full extent of how he threatened me and my family."

"Why did you keep them?" he questioned.

I looked up at him, his navy blue tie loosened against his white shirt and heather-gray suit.

"My parents, my sister, Avery . . ." I began. "They died because I put them on the road that night. I took a risk I shouldn't have for my own selfish reasons, and I deserved to remember that."

"Did you think you would forget what you lost?"

I paused and then dropped my head, sighing. *No, I will never forget.* I felt the pain of their deaths every day. But back then, taking any kind of a risk made me feel like there was no control. There was no "careful."

For so long I had felt like I was in a stalemate with Chase, waiting for something to fucking happen, and when I finally chose to give up the control and say "Fuck it, let's see what happens," I liked it.

But I hadn't realized that I wasn't just risking myself. There were others I didn't think about.

"I deserved to be punished," I told him.

He touched my face, meeting my eyes. "You could never have known."

No, I couldn't. But carelessness brings consequences. I should've known that.

Which accounted for my behavior of making my life afterward as controlled as possible.

"Easton, there's no line you can walk that's safe enough," Tyler implored. "You didn't do anything out of malice. Crimes deserve to be punished. Mistakes deserve to be forgiven."

I nodded, finally understanding the truth behind his words. And I was ready.

Opening the bags, I dumped the contents into the fireplace and lit a match from up on the mantel. Leaning down, I lit the scraps on fire and stood back upright, both of us watching them turn to ash.

Taking his hand, I breathed out a sigh of relief, finally feeling better than I had since before I could remember.

"Are you ever going to be careful with me?" I asked quietly, watching the flames burn bright.

"No."

I looked up at him, my lips curling into a small smile. "Good."

EPILOGUE

"Chin up," the photographer instructed, smiling behind her camera.

I tilted my head up an inch, keeping it cocked slightly to the right, my relaxed smile still plastered on my face.

The shit I do for him.

I sat on the arm of a rich, brown leather chair, my legs crossed and my arm resting on Tyler's shoulder as he sat in the chair, both of us posing for our engagement photos.

Correction: engagement-slash-campaign publicity photo representing our perfect American family's high moral fiber. *Riiiiight.*

I dropped my eyes, feeling a blush heat my cheeks, remembering all the *immoral* things he'd done to me last night in our bed.

"Excellent," the photographer cooed, snapping a few more shots as she leaned down again behind her tripod.

I kept my left hand on my thigh, the round black onyx stone set in a platinum band and surrounded by freshwater pearls visible in the pictures.

Tyler had pushed for a diamond ring, wanting the best, but Jay liked my idea of environmental awareness as good publicity. So many diamonds came from war-torn countries, so I decided to go with something different.

Hell, Kate Middleton, the Duchess of Cambridge, rocked a sapphire engagement ring. The times were changing.

Actually, I just liked the pearls. It was Jay who was selling the war-torn story.

"You look incredible," Tyler commented, his white tie matching my cream-colored dress.

"Thank you," I whispered.

Over the past few months, we'd dived deeper and deeper into the campaign, but elections were still six months away, and I knew he was concerned that *his* life took too much of our time.

I looked down, running my thumb over the *fff* tattoo I'd gotten on the inside of my wrist when he'd proposed this past Mardi Gras at the very same annual ball where we first met the year before.

Family, fortune, and future.

He'd had the same letters tattooed, but his appeared on the outside of his wrist, right under where his watch sat.

To ensure that we never took our gifts for granted or lost track of what was truly important, we had promised each other to prioritize.

Family came first. Always first. We took care of each other and relied on each other. Without the family and without Christian, everything else would be worthless.

Fortune came next. It almost seemed shallow to have fortune before future, but we realized that fortune was more than wealth. It was health, goals, and maintaining what we had in the work we wanted to contribute to the world. Our fortune was the things for which we were thankful and the things we had to give.

Future came last. Private ambitions, plans for the years down the road, and other goals that could possibly take our attention away from each other and our jobs would be considered only if everything else was strong.

Christian had wanted to get the tattoo, too, but we'd told him that he had to wait until he turned eighteen.

And then Tyler took him to get the tattoo anyway.

That was fine. He could deal with Christian's mother when she came home in July.

Tyler's arm behind my back shifted, and I jerked, feeling his hand rub against my ass.

I cleared my throat, and I could feel his smile as he squeezed me.

Christian sat behind the camera, playing on his phone, while Jay stood off to my left, periodically instructing the photographer on what shots to take and what angles to shoot, as if she didn't know already.

Walking up to me, he tried to pin something to my chest, and I knew right away that it was a flag.

I shot out my hand, shooing him away.

"Easton, really," he chided.

"It's tacky," I burst out. "This is my engagement photo."

I wasn't turning it into a political statement. We'd already had that argument.

"Tyler." Jay groaned. "A little help, please?"

Tyler simply shook his head, probably sick of Jay's and my bickering.

"You're handling the publicity," I pointed out, glaring at Jay, "and I even let you pick the wedding date, because you whined about how good it would be for the campaign, but when you start to dress me, that's when we have problems," I snapped. "*Capisce?*"

"Everyone who's anyone has a personal shopper, Easton," he whined. "She can tell you which clothes are best for your coloring—"

But I yelped, cutting off Jay's lecture, as my fiancé's hands grabbed me and I fell into Tyler's lap. His lips came down on mine, and I moaned, holding his face in my hands.

We pulled apart, laughing at each other, and I heard the camera click.

"Ah," the photographer sang. "That's the cover of *New Orleans* magazine."

She looked at the screen of her digital camera, smiling.

"Now, Mr. Marek," she instructed. "Would you stand, please, and move to your fiancée's other side?"

Tyler rose from the chair and moved around to my left side, while I remained sitting.

She looked to me and asked, "Would you turn to him slightly and then cock your head a bit?"

I followed her directions, placing my arm around Tyler and leaning in to him as I tilted my head.

"Chin up," she chirped, and disappeared behind her camera again.

Tyler's scent invaded my head, and as much as I'd grown to love Christian, I was glad he was joining his friends in the country during spring break. Which started in a few days.

I still kept my apartment and would until the wedding in October, but it was getting harder and harder to stay there. Tyler and I found our time together when we could, and even though Christian wasn't stupid—he'd caught me there early one morning, probably figuring out I had stayed the night—we did make a huge effort to not make it obvious or inappropriate.

I was still a teacher at his school, after all.

And I'd decided to stay there, even taking on tennis coaching responsibilities for the girls' team for the next school year.

After the election, though, if Tyler won, we'd reevaluate whether or not we needed to relocate to Washington, D.C., for the length of his term.

For now, though, we simply worked on his campaign and planned the wedding, which we decided to have at Degas House to commemorate the paintings we discussed when we first met.

"I want my son in some photos as well," Tyler said, and the photographer nodded.

I looked over at Christian, loving how close he and Tyler had become. They didn't always have the same interests, but they'd found a lot of common ground and enjoyed doing things together.

Christian had even started tagging along with Tyler on some of his campaign trips around the state, touring factories and neighborhoods, and he was very interested in his father's business. Not the office work part of it, but when Tyler had to take a trip to see equipment or check out a building site, Christian loved to join him as much as his school schedule allowed. Tyler was a good father, and he hardly went anywhere without Christian now.

Which got me thinking . . .

"We still haven't talked about that," I said under my breath just to him.

"What?" He glanced at me.

I licked my lips, not sure how I would answer the question I was about to ask. "Do you want children?" I questioned, and then corrected myself. "I mean, *more* children?"

Tyler blinked, looking surprised, and then I saw his gaze go to Christian before turning back to me.

"Yes," he answered. "If it's with you."

My lips curled, and I felt strangely excited. A baby?

"You?" he hinted.

I inhaled a long, deep breath. "I think so." And then I looked at him, nodding as realization hit. "Yeah. I'd love to have one or two."

He leaned down and kissed me, his teasing lips making me promises for later that I couldn't wait for.

"Do you think we can balance it all?" I spoke against his lips. "Our careers, the campaign, children . . ."

He let out a sigh and stood back upright. "All we can do is try," he stated. "But we don't break our commitment. Family, fortune, future," he dictated. "None of it means anything without him or you."

I tightened my arm around him, not giving a damn that I needed him so much. I'd gotten very good at being weak, and I wasn't ashamed of it.

But in truth, I knew it wasn't weak to need people. To need love and connection.

You're only strong if you can stand on your own, right?

Nope.

The truth was, you're happier when you're needed and stronger when you're loved.

I could survive without Tyler, but why would I want to? Ever?

Nothing could replace him or erase him.

Except . . .

I opened my mouth, narrowing my eyes. "I forgot to ask." I looked at him with amused curiosity. "Which political party do you belong to?"

He broke out in a laugh, his chest shaking as he looked down at me.

"How is it that you don't know that?" he exclaimed. "You researched me online."

I shrugged. "I went to your website and social media, nosing around, but that was it."

Although we'd had discussions about his platform, and I'd accompanied him here and there, I realized it was the one thing that never came up.

He shook his head and stared at the camera.

"So?" I hinted.

"So what?"

I instantly hooded my eyes, unamused. "Which political party are you a member of, Tyler?"

"Does it matter?" he played.

"It might," I shot back.

But he just turned and wrapped me in his arms, bending me backward with the force of his kiss. I squealed under his lips and then let my eyes roll back, my head feeling dizzy, as his tongue entered my mouth.

"Ew." I heard Christian's complaint from across the room.

And then Jay. "All right," he chastised. "I'm getting the child out of here."

Tyler didn't break the kiss as he shot out his hand, waving goodbye to them, while I tried not to giggle.

He definitely knew how to shut me up.

ACKNOWLEDGMENTS

First, to all of the teachers in the world—the days are endless, the workload only increases, and you're not paid nearly what you're worth. But you're the greatest of all artists. Some paint with brushes, while others play guitars, carve wood, or perform onstage. But you work with living minds and diverse spirits and create dreams that cultivate futures. Thank you for everything you do!

Next, to the readers—this was the first book and the first characters I dived into after finishing the Fall Away series. So many of you have been there, sharing your excitement and showing your support, and I am continually grateful for your continued trust. I know my adventures aren't always easy, but I love them, and I'm glad so many others do, too.

To my family—my husband and daughter put up with my crazy schedule, my candy wrappers, and my spacing off every time I think of a conversation, plot twist, or scene that just jumped into my head at the dinner table. You both really do put up with a lot, so thank you for loving me anyway.

To Kerry Donovan and the rest of the team at New American Library—you've all been a joy to work with, and you've helped make one of my dreams come true. Every time I see my book in a book store, I know I didn't do that alone, and it makes me feel on top of the world. Thank you for helping me be the best I can be and for believing in me.

To Jane Dystel, my agent at Dystel and Goderich Literary Management—there is absolutely no way I could ever give you up, so you're stuck with me. I mean, I would literally wrap my body around your leg and chain myself to your hip. I hope you like the way I smell, because I'm with you to stay.

To the House of Pendragon—you're my happy place. Well, you and Pinterest. Thanks for being the support system I need and always being positive.

To Vibeke Courtney, who is always in my acknowledgments—thank you for teaching me how to write and laying it down straight.

To Lisa Pantano Kane—you challenge me with the hard questions.

To Ing Cruz at As the Pages Turn Book Blog—you support out of the goodness of your heart, and I can't repay you enough. Thank you for the release blitzes and blog tours.

To all of the bloggers—plain and simple, oh, my goodness! You spend your free time reading, reviewing, and promoting, and you do it for free. You are the life's blood of the book world, and who knows what we would do without you. Thank you for your tireless efforts. You do it out of passion, which makes it all the more incredible.

To Abbi Glines, Jay Crownover, Tabatha Vargo, Tijan, N. Michaels, Eden Butler, Natasha Preston, Kirsty Moseley, and Penelope Ward for their encouragement and support over the years. It's validating to be recognized by your peers, and authors supporting authors cultivates mutual respect. Positivity is contagious, so thank you for spreading the love.

To every author and aspiring author—thank you for the stories you've shared, many of which have made me a happy reader in search of a wonderful escape and a better writer, trying to live up to your standard. Write and create, and don't ever stop. Your voice is important, and as long as it comes from your heart, it is right and good.

READERS GUIDE

MIS CON DUCT

Penelope Douglas

READERS GUIDE

QUESTIONS FOR DISCUSSION

1. There is a twelve-year age difference between the protagonists of *Misconduct*. Do you believe the age gap made a difference as far as life experiences and maturity? How much of an age gap would be too much for you?

2. Easton fantasizes about standing in the middle of a burning room in chapter 1, but then she blows out the candle as she leaves the masquerade ball. Is there a significance in this action?

3. Tyler is stubborn about many things: social media, accepting campaign donations, taking on more responsibilities than he can handle. Why do you think Tyler is initially so inflexible? Is he naturally resistant or did he have good reasons for the fights he picks?

4. Why did Tyler question Easton's teaching methods? Do you believe he had a genuine fatherly concern?

5. Easton avoids intimacy, choosing to keep her distance from forming any real attachment to men. What's different about Tyler? Did she let him into her life, or did he force his way in?

6. So much of the city of New Orleans plays a part in this book. Have you ever visited the city, and, if so, what was your most memorable experience?

7. Had Easton's parents and her sister not died, would Easton have stayed with tennis, or would she have discovered her gift for teaching?

8. If Easton's parents had gone to the police about Chase Stiles, how do you think Easton's life would have been different?

9. Easton uses social media tools to teach her students. If you were a parent, would you embrace this practice in your child's school? What would be some of the advantages and/or disadvantages of using social media for instruction?

10. Tyler has a difficult relationship with his son, which he tries, throughout the novel, to fix. Given the demands in Tyler's life, do you believe his actions to improve that relationship were commendable, or would you have tried something different?

11. Easton has some fun at Tyler's house during the rainstorm, such as organizing his books in his study. Do you have any urges to organize something in other people's homes when you visit? If so, what do you find yourself needing to organize?

12. Tyler is ashamed of his role—or lack thereof—in his son's life when he was younger. Is what he said true, that it's never too late? Or do you believe what Brynne said on the phone call, that there comes a time when we've been disappointed too much to ever repair the bonds?

13. How do you think Christian felt when he would hear his mom and stepfather talking badly about Tyler?

14. Keeping in mind that Tyler promised he wouldn't hook up with anyone else, why did he entertain the idea when Easton presented him with Kristen?

15. In the end Easton and Tyler agree that Jack needs help. Knowing the amount of pain and stress Easton has suffered in her life, do you believe she'll be able to reconcile with her brother?

16. Based on the relationship that Tyler and Easton share, who is more dominant?

17. Were Tyler's reasons for ending the relationship in chapter 21 justified? Why or why not?

18. What do you think made Tyler finally see the light about what was truly important and helped him get his priorities straight?

19. As Tyler is running for office, and with politics filtered daily into our lives through the news and social media, do you believe Easton's statement of "the most popular wins" to be a true

statement? Do you research a candidate on your own without the influence of media before you vote?

20. Christian speaks his mind a lot in *Misconduct*, even showing up the adults in his life from time to time. Do you feel that he was right to hold Easton more accountable for her affair with his father? Why do you think her actions hurt him more than his own father's?

21. Why did Christian keep his knowledge of the affair secret?

22. Do you feel that we place too much pressure on our children to excel at too many activities such as sports? Do you feel that the pressure Easton felt with her tennis career exacerbated her OCD tendencies, not just the counting but the need for perfection, or did the trauma of her parents' and sister's deaths contribute more?

23. Easton did not know Tyler's political affiliation in his senate run. Which party do you believe she supports? Which party do you believe he supports?

24. Easton states to Tyler throughout their relationship not to be careful with her. What do you believe she means?

Don't miss Penelope Douglas's

FALLING AWAY

Available now.
Continue reading for a preview.

Three whole years.

I'd had a boyfriend for three whole years, and I still had more orgasms when I was by myself.

"Damn, baby, you feel good." His sleepy whisper felt wet on my neck as he dragged his lazy lips over my skin.

Packing. That was what I'd forgotten to add to my to-do list for tomorrow. It wasn't likely I'd forget to pack for college, but everything needed to go on the list so it could be checked off.

"You're so hot." Liam's fish lips tickled my neck in short, slow pecks. It once made me giggle, but now it kind of made me want to bite him.

And a pharmacy run, I remembered. I wanted to stock up on my pill so I wouldn't have to worry about it for a while. *Packing and the pharmacy. Packing and the pharmacy. Packing and the pharmacy. Don't forget, K.C.*

Liam thrust his hips between my legs, and I rolled my eyes.

We were still clothed, but I wasn't sure he realized that.

If I weren't so tired, I'd laugh. He rarely got drunk after all—tonight only because it was an end-of-summer bash. And although

I'd never been overwhelmed with a desire for sex, I did love that he tried to jump my bones at every opportunity. It made me feel wanted.

But it just wasn't happening tonight.

"Liam," I grunted, twisting up my lips as I pushed his hand off my breast, "I think we're done for the night, okay? Let's lock up the car and walk to your house."

We'd been in his car for over a half hour—me trying to indulge his fantasy of sex in risky places and him trying to . . . Hell, I didn't even know what he was trying to do.

I felt guilty for not being more into it lately. I felt guilty for not helping him get into it tonight. And I felt guilty for making mental additions to my to-do list while he was trying—keyword, *trying*—to get it on with me.

We hadn't made love in a long time, and I didn't know what my problem was anymore.

His head sank into my shoulder, and I felt the weight of his hundred and eighty pounds collapse on my body.

He didn't move, and I let out a sigh, relaxing into the passenger seat of his Camaro, my muscles burning from trying to support his body weight all this time.

He'd given up. *Thank God.*

But then I groaned, registering that his body had gone a little too still, except for the slow, soft rhythm of his breathing.

Great. Now he was passed out.

"Liam," I whispered, not sure why, since we were completely alone in his car on a dark, quiet street outside my friend Tate Brandt's house.

Arching my head up, I spoke into his ear that was nearly covered by his blond hair. "Liam, wake up!" I wheezed, since his weight was hindering my oxygen intake.

He moaned but didn't budge.

I slammed my head back onto the headrest and ground my teeth together. What the hell was I going to do now?

We'd gone to the Loop tonight for the last race before college started next week and then Tate and her boyfriend, Jared Trent, had thrown a party at his house, which just happened to be right outside, next door to her place. I'd told my mom that I'd be sleeping over at her house when I was really planning on spending the night with my boyfriend.

Who was now passed out.

Tate's house was locked, I didn't know how to drive Liam's car, and the last thing I was ever going to do was call my mother for a ride.

Reaching for the handle, I swung the car door open and pulled my right leg from under Liam. I pushed against his chest, raising him off me only as much as I needed to squirm out from underneath his body and stumble out of the car. He groaned but didn't open his eyes, and I wondered if I should be worried about how much he'd had to drink.

Leaning in, I watched his chest rise and fall in quiet, steady movements. I grabbed the keys he'd dropped on the floor and my wrist purse with my cell phone and slammed the door shut, locking the car.

Liam didn't live too far, and even though I knew it was a lot to ask, I was going to have to wake up Tate. If Jared was even letting her get any sleep at all.

I ran my hands down my strapless white summer dress and powered quietly down the sidewalk in my rhinestone sandals. Pretty dressed up for the race track earlier, but I wanted to look nice at the party. It was the last time I was going to see some of these people. For a while, anyway.

Squeezing my little purse—small enough for my phone and some money—in my hand, I traipsed up the small incline into Jared's yard and up the front steps of his house. No light shone from inside, but I knew there had to be some people still here, since the street was littered with a few unfamiliar cars and I heard the low beat of music still pouring out. Lyrics saying something about "down with the sickness."

I turned the knob, stepped into the house, and peered around the corner into the living room.

And stopped. Dead. *What the . . . ?*

The room was dark, not a single light showing other than the blue glow from the screen on the stereo.

Maybe there were other lights on in the house. Maybe there were other people still here. I couldn't say.

All I could do was fucking stand there as my eyes stung, and a lump stretched my throat, at the sight of Jaxon Trent damn near naked on top of another girl.

I instantly looked away, closing my eyes.

Jax. I shook my head. *No.* I didn't care about this. Why was my heart beating so fast?

Jaxon Trent was Tate's boyfriend's little brother. Nothing more. Just a kid.

A kid who watched me. A kid I rarely ever talked to. A kid who felt like a threat just standing next to me.

A kid who was looking less and less like one every day.

And right now he wasn't coming up for air. I jerked my body toward the door, not wanting him—or her—to see me, but . . .

"Jax," the girl gasped. "More. Please."

And I stopped, unable to move again. *Just leave, K.C. You don't care.*

I squeezed the doorknob, sucking in quick breaths, but I didn't move. Couldn't move.

I didn't know why my hands shook.

Chewing my bottom lip, I inched around the corner again and saw him and the girl.

My heart pounded like a jackhammer in my chest. And it hurt.

The girl—I didn't recognize her from school—was completely naked, lying on her stomach on the couch. Jax was sprawled on top of her from behind, and judging from his jeans pushed down below his ass and his thrusting hips, he was inside her.

He didn't even get fully undressed to make love to a girl. He couldn't even look her in the face. I wasn't surprised. With the arrogance he displayed around school, Jax could do whatever he wanted, and he did.

Holding himself up with one arm, he used the other to wrap around her face and twist her chin toward him before he leaned down and covered her mouth with his.

Liam had never kissed me like that. Or I'd never kissed him like that.

The girl—long blond hair fanning around her face and spilling over her shoulders—kissed him back with full force, their jaws moving in sync as his tongue and teeth worked her.

Jax's smooth, sculpted hips ground into her in slow, savory movements while his hand left her face to run down her back and then slide underneath her body to cup her breast. He didn't do one thing at a time. Every part of his body was in this, and everything he did looked as if it felt good.

And why wouldn't it? Jax was coveted by the girls in this town for a reason after all. He was suave, confident, and good-looking. Not my type, but there was no denying that he was sexy. According to Tate, he was part Native American.

His skin was like toffee—smooth, unblemished, and warm-looking. His hair was a deep brown, almost black, and it hung half-way down his back. He often braided pieces of it before tying it back into a ponytail midskull, which he did *all* the time. I'd never seen his hair hanging loose.

He had to be six feet tall by now and would probably be exceeding his brother in height in no time. I'd seen Jax on the lacrosse field at school and at the gym where we both worked out. The dips in his biceps and triceps flexed as he held himself above the girl and worked his body into hers. With the moonlight coming through the window, I could just make out the V in his torso as it descended to his abs and lower.

He didn't break pace as he whispered in her ear, and as if she were given an order, she dropped her foot to the floor, bent her knee, and arched her back.

Jax let his head fall back and bared his teeth as he sank deeper into her, and I stared, absently tracing the scar on the inside of my wrist.

I wanted it to be like that for me. I wanted to be breathless like her. Gasping and desperate. Passionate and hungry.

Liam had made me happy once, and when he messed up, I took him back, because I thought the relationship was worth it.

But now, seeing this . . . I knew we were missing something.

I didn't know when the tear spilled over, but I felt it drop onto my dress, and I blinked rapidly, wiping my face.

And then my eye caught something, and I blinked again, noticing someone else in the room. Another girl, nearly naked in her bra and panties.

I swallowed a gasp, sucked in air, and then swallowed again.

What the hell?

She walked across the room—she must've been over by the windows, because I hadn't seen her until now—and leaned down, kissing Jax hard.

Acid bile crept up my throat.

"Ugh!" I growled, and stumbled backward, hitting the opposite wall in the entryway. Scrambling, I yanked open the front door and flew outside without looking back.

Jumping the steps, I had hit the grass running when a deep voice commanded behind me, "Stop!"

I didn't.

Screw him. Screw Jaxon Trent. I didn't know why I was mad, and who the hell cared?

Running across the lawn, I bolted for the sidewalk, wishing I'd worn sneakers instead of sandals that flopped around on my feet.

"Stop, or I will take you to the ground, K.C.!" Jax's loud bellow threatened behind me, and I brought myself to a sudden halt.

Shit. My eyes darted from left to right, searching for an escape. He wouldn't really do that, would he?

I inched around slowly, watching as he stepped off the stairs and walked toward me. He was wearing pants, thank God. But I guess that was easy, since he never really took them off. The dark-washed jeans hung off his hips, and I got a damn clear look at the muscles framing his abs. He had a swimmer's body, but I wasn't sure if he was actually a swimmer. From the way the top of his jeans barely hung just above his hairline, I guessed he wasn't wearing boxers . . . or anything under the jeans. I thought of what was just beneath his pants, and heat warmed my belly. I clenched my thighs together.

I shot my eyes down to the ground, wondering how I could stand the sight of him. He was just a kid. Did he do things like that with a lot of girls?

He came up to stand in front of me, hovering down, since he was nearly a half foot taller. "What are you doing here?" he accused.

I locked my mouth shut and scowled at the air around him, still avoiding eye contact.

"You left with your dipshit boyfriend an hour ago," he pointed out.

I kept my hot eyes averted.

"K.C.!" He shoved his hand in my face, snapping his fingers a few times. "Let's process what you just saw in there. You entered my house uninvited in the middle of the night and witnessed me having sex with a girl in the privacy of my own home. Now let's move on. Why are you roaming around in the dark alone?"

I finally looked up and sneered. I always had to do that to cover up the way my face felt on fire at the sight of his blue eyes. For someone so dark and wild, his eyes were completely out of place but never seemed wrong. They were the color of a tropical sea. The color of the sky right before storm clouds rolled in. Tate called them azure. I called them hell.

Crossing my arms over my chest, I took a deep breath. "Liam's too drunk to drive, all right?" I bit out. "He passed out in the car."

He looked down the street to where Liam's car sat and narrowed his eyes before scowling back down at me. "So why can't you drive him home?" he asked.

"I can't drive a clutch."

He closed his eyes and shook his head. Running his hand through his hair, he stopped and fisted it midstroke. "Your boyfriend is a fucking idiot," he snarled, and then dropped his hand, looking exasperated.

I sighed, not wanting to get into it. He and Liam never got along, and while I didn't know why, I did know it was mostly Jax's fault.

I'd known him for almost a year, and even though I knew small details—he was into computers, his real parents weren't around, and he thought of his brother's mother as his own—he was still a mystery to me. All I knew was that he looked at me sometimes, and lately, it was with disdain. As if he was disappointed.

I tipped my chin up and kept my tone flat. "I knew Tate was staying with Jared tonight, and I didn't want to wake up her dad to let me in the house to crash. I need her to help me get Liam home and to let me in her house. Is she up?" I asked.

He shook his head, and I wasn't sure if that meant "no" or "you've got to be kidding me."

Digging in his jeans pocket, he pulled out keys. "I'll drive you home."

"No," I rushed. "My mom thinks I'm staying at Tate's tonight."

His eyes narrowed on me, and I felt judged. Yeah, I was lying to my mother to spend the night with my boyfriend. And, yes, I was eighteen years old and still not allowed the freedom of an adult. *Stop looking at me like that.*

"Don't move," he ordered, and then turned around, walking back to his house.

After less than a minute he walked back out and started across the lawn to Tate's, jerking his chin at me to follow. I assumed he had a key, so I jogged up to his side as he climbed the porch steps.

"What about Liam?" I couldn't leave my boyfriend sleeping in his car all night. What if something happened to him? Or he got sick? And Tate's dad would have a fit if I tried to bring him inside.

He unlocked the front door—I wasn't sure if he had Tate's or Jared's keys—and stepped inside the darkened foyer. Turning to me, he waved his hand in a big show, inviting me in.

"I'll get Jared to follow me in his car while I drive Dick-wad home in his, okay?" He hooded his eyes, looking bored.

"Don't hurt him," I warned, crossing the threshold and walking past him.

"I won't, but he deserves it."

I swung back around to face him, arching an eyebrow. "Oh, you think you're so much better, Jax?" I smiled. "Do you even know those skanks' names in there?"

His mouth instantly tightened. "They're not skanks, K.C. They're friends. And I'd make damn sure any girlfriend of mine knew how to drive a manual, and I wouldn't have gotten so drunk that I couldn't keep her safe."

His quick temper threw me, and I immediately dropped my eyes, hating the rush of guilt that prickled my skin.

Why was I trying to cut him up? Jax definitely got under my skin, but he wasn't a bad guy. His behavior at school was certainly better than his brother's had been in the past. And Jax was respectful to teachers and friendly to everyone.

Almost everyone.

I took a deep breath and straightened my shoulders, ready to swallow a mouthful of pride. "Thank you. Thank you for driving Liam home," I offered, handing him the keys. "But what about your . . ." I gestured with my hand, trying to find the right word. "Your . . . dates?"

"They'll wait." He smirked.

I rolled my eyes. *Oooookay.*

Reaching up, I worked my messy bun loose, pulling my mahogany hair down around my shoulders. But then I shot my eyes back up when I noticed Jax approaching me.

His voice was low and strong, without even a hint of humor. "Unless you want me to send them home, K.C.," he suggested, stepping closer, his chest nearly brushing mine.

Send them home?

I shook my head, blowing off his flirtation. It was the same way I'd reacted last fall the first time I met him, and every time after that when he made a suggestive remark. It was my safe, patented response, because I couldn't allow myself to react any other way.

But this time he wasn't smiling or being cocky. He might've been serious. If I told him to send the girls away, would he?

And as he reached out with a slow, soft finger and grazed my collarbone, I let time stop as I entertained the idea.

Jax's hot breath on my neck, my hair a tangled mess around my body, my clothes ripped apart on the floor as he bit my lips and made me sweat.

Oh, Jesus. I sucked in a breath and looked away, narrowing my eyes to get my damn head under control. *What the hell?*

But then Jax laughed.

Not a sympathetic laugh. Not a laugh that said he was just kidding. No, it was a laugh that told me I was the joke.

"Don't worry, K.C." He smiled, looking down on me as if I was pathetic. "I'm well aware your pussy is too precious for me, okay?"

Excuse me?

I knocked his hand away from my collarbone. "You know what?" I shot out, my fingers fisting. "I can't believe I'm saying this, but you actually make Jared look like a gentleman."

And the little shit grinned. "I love my brother, but get one thing straight." He leaned in. "He and I are nothing alike."

Yeah. My heart didn't pound around Jared. The hair on my arms didn't stand on end around him, either. I wasn't conscious of where he was and what he was doing every second that we were in the same room together. Jax and Jared were very different.

"Tattoos," I muttered.

"What?"

Shit! Did I just say that out loud?

"Um . . . ," I choked out, staring wide-eyed in front of me, which just happened to be at his bare chest. "Tattoos. Jared has them. You don't. How come?" I asked, finally looking up.

His eyebrows inched together, but he didn't look angry. It was more . . . befuddled.

Jared's back, shoulder, arm, and part of his torso were covered with tattoos. Even Jared and Jax's best friend, Madoc Caruthers, had one. You would think with those influences, Jax would've gotten at least one by now. But he hadn't. His long torso and arms were unmarked.

I waited as he stared at me and then licked his lips. "I have tattoos," he whispered, looking lost in thought. "Too many."

I didn't know what I saw in his eyes at that moment, but I knew I'd never seen it before.

Backing away, he wouldn't meet my gaze as he turned and left the house. He closed the door, locked it, and walked down the porch steps quietly.

Moments later, I heard Jared's Boss and Liam's Camaro fire up and speed down the dark street.

And an hour later, I was still lying awake in Tate's bed, running my finger over the spot he'd touched on my collarbone and wondering about the Jaxon Trent I never got to know.